# THE MESSAGE

'You have one new message.' With one misplaced voicemail, Jen discovers that her marriage is a sham. Numb with shock, she's hiding from the future when she's stunned by a face from the past. Kit was Jen's first love, the one she hoped would never leave. What began as a glorious summer, though, could not last forever. Now, years later, Jen and Kit meet again, both troubled, and forced to confront what happened. Together, can they make sense of it all?

# THE MESSAGE

# THE MESSAGE

*by*

Julie Highmore

**Magna Large Print Books**
Long Preston, North Yorkshire,
BD23 4ND, England.

British Library Cataloguing in Publication Data.

Highmore, Julie
    The message.

    A catalogue record of this book is
    available from the British Library

    ISBN   978-0-7505-3256-3


First published in Great Britain in 2009 by
Headline Publishing Group Ltd.

Cover illustration © Mark Owen by arrangement with
Arcangel Images

Published in Large Print 2010 by arrangement with
Headline Publishing Group Ltd.

Magna Large Print is an imprint of Library Magna Books Ltd.

Printed and bound in Great Britain by
T.J. (International) Ltd., Cornwall, PL28 8RW

For Vera, greatly missed

# ONE

**London, February 2003**

*You have one new message.*

Robert? Jen dropped her bags and pressed the key to listen.

'Hi, John,' said her husband. 'I'm on my way. But, listen, don't cook for me...'

Did he say Jen or John?

'...Jen's class has been cancelled and she's doing one of her bloody Thai things. I promised I'd be home at eight, so we'll only have an hour. Sorry. I might be a bit peckish, though. But, er, no doubt you'll have something long and tasty for me.' Robert groaned and signed off with, 'Can't wait.'

*To listen to the message again, press one.*

'Hi, John, I'm on my way–'

She saved and switched off. She could hear it a hundred times and he wouldn't say 'Jen'.

In the kitchen, on a chair, she stared at her mobile, as though it might offer some sort of explanation. Then hated it, because it had made her cold inside and sick, and had drained all strength from her limbs, and made her hands shake and her heart race and had ended her life, or so it felt. She should unpack the bags, put stuff in the freezer, but she couldn't move.

Had she misunderstood? Misconstrued? The

idea that Robert might have a son he'd kept quiet about suddenly struck her, but then it was gone ... *something long and tasty*... A sweet shop? Sticks of rock, lollipops...? She was clutching at straws – very slippery, fragile ones. Robert didn't have a sweet tooth. He ate desserts out of politeness.

The ice cream, she remembered, managing to get up, legs shaky, everything shaky. After ramming the carton in the freezer, phone still in hand, like vital evidence she couldn't let go of, Jen unpacked the rest. Cereal, tea went in the cupboard; a raw pink free-range chicken, bought at the butcher's, in the fridge. Lemongrass, a carton of yogurt ... she began to taste bile, swallowed hard and ran to the cloakroom.

Afterwards, she splashed cold water on her face and reached for the towel, then rubbed and rubbed at cheeks, forehead, eyes, as though trying to erase everything: images of Robert – her still-attractive husband – naked with a man; the way he'd talked about her. She stopped rubbing and looked in the mirror. Even in its current raw state, it wasn't a bad face. Her father's deep brown eyes and what someone had called an intelligent mouth. She still had no idea what he'd meant. There were one or two stray greys in her dark, shoulder-length hair, but for forty-eight she was doing OK. Not OK enough for Robert, though.

John couldn't be a woman's name, she wondered, lowering the loo seat and sitting down. Short for ... or maybe he'd said Joanne? If it were a woman, at least he'd still be Robert, not someone she'd never known. She picked up the phone from the floor and listened again, and then again.

John, he was saying. Definitely John. *Can't wait.*

She sat rigid, the tap dripping beside her. If only her French class hadn't been cancelled. Celia's daughter had phoned them all. Tonsillitis. Jen would have gone to the pub afterwards, got home around ten, ten thirty. Robert would have made them a nightcap, whisky for him, hot chocolate for her. They'd have read in bed and rolled over and gone to sleep, Robert first. And she'd never have known. Now, ridiculously, she felt she'd made this happen.

She was losing her mind, clearly. And not one part of her body felt the way it had twenty minutes ago, when she'd walked through the door with the shopping, wondering who'd been phoning her in the car, and looking forward to cooking. Now her mouth was dry, her knees ached. Everything ached. She was sweating. Her heart was abnormally loud and she wasn't breathing right. Oh God, she thought, AIDS. When did they last...? Months and months ago... November, perhaps. After the boozy meal and the taxi ride home. His birthday treat. No, once since then. Christmas? Hard to remember something so unmemorable.

Jen clutched the towel and rocked back and forth. Then the phone rang in her hand. In shock, or revulsion, she let it fall on the floor. Robert realising his error? How horrible it would be to hear his voice. No, she didn't want to hear him. Not yet. Or see him. Was he outside the house, too nervous to come in? She reached to the cloakroom door and bolted it.

The phone stopped but the tap continued to drip. Turning it off, Jen found herself staring at

13

the soap dish Robert had excitedly bid for at an auction, insisting it would match the floor tiles perfectly, which it had. She picked it up and tipped out the Pears, then rotated the pretty antique blue-and-white latticed dish just inches from her nose, examining it now in a whole new light. Had she spent their entire marriage missing all the signs? She tried to think of other clues, but everything had become a blur, all hazy and jumbled, along with her emotions.

Jen stayed in the cloakroom, her head racing through flashes of their life: holidays, watching TV with meals on their laps, walks on the heath, having people over. Normal married life, only it wasn't, hadn't been normal at all. Her husband was attracted to men, she thought, staring at her thin gold wedding ring, twisting it back and forth. In all their time together he'd never talked dirty with her, not like that. Romantic sometimes, but not dirty. His computer, she thought. If she had the strength... Another call came, and again she left it. All that life they'd had, such a waste. No children, even, and now no future. Their plan to sell the properties and move abroad, like everything else, was gone. She looked at the ring again, and twisted it up and off her finger.

She wondered about phoning Sarah, but dreaded an awkward silence, then, 'Actually, Jen...' and there'd be a story of him making a pass at some guy at a party; Sarah blurting out stuff she'd been wanting to say for months, years. Jen had told her about Robert's lack of interest in bed – hers too – and how dismal it was when they did get round to it. Dutiful, robotic. How she

14

needed a toyboy, ha-ha. That was before Christmas some time. Sarah had looked uncomfortable and busied herself with a salad. And she hadn't commented, which was very unSarah like. Stupidly – well, now it seemed stupid – Jen had wondered about Sarah and Robert. Just fleetingly, though. The idea of Robert screwing around had been too ridiculous. He'd never been lecherous, or even flirtatious with other women.

Of course he hadn't.

She slid the soap up and put it back in the fussy little dish she'd never seen the point of, then yanked tissue from the roll and blew her nose. 'Shit,' she said, 'I bet they all knew.' She got up, dropped her ring in the bowl of potpourri and unbolted the door.

A glass of wine might lead to another, then another, and her thoughts were muddled enough already. She'd have tea, she decided, and eat. Something simple. Bread went in the toaster and she filled a pan with water. When it was halfway to boiling, she lowered an egg in on a shaky spoon. After buttering the toast, she stood motionless, counting four minutes on the wall clock.

With her meal on the table in front of her, Jen continued to watch the time. Seven twenty-five, thirty. Thirty-five. No longer crying, she still shook, only now it was with dread as the minutes worked their way, too quickly, towards eight o'clock. She needed to calm down, think of something to say. Seven forty-one. She pictured him in his car, either aware of his blunder and chewing a thumbnail, or oblivious and singing along to something. Six minutes to, five to, four.

When the time finally came for Robert to walk through the door, drop his briefcase and kiss, or not kiss, her cheek, Jen stared and stared at the cold congealed egg she hadn't touched. Unable to move. Unable to make the tea she'd forgotten.

# TWO

## Germany, July 1969

'This beats life in the UK,' Kit's mother said, the first time they met. 'Like a Dubonnet, Jennifer?'

Mrs Avery was on the kitchen worktop, filing her nails, and beside her stood a glass of, presumably, Dubonnet. Her long legs were crossed and tanned and she wore strappy gold sandals. Her skirt was short and tight, her hair was shoulder-length, blond and backcombed. She wore thick mascara around her huge blue eyes, and her mouth was full and pouty and covered in apricot lipstick. She was glamorous, posh, tarty and a bit dated, all in one.

Paralysed with indecision, or just ignorance, Jen couldn't answer the question. Did officers' children drink alcohol with their parents? At four in the afternoon? She looked to Kit for help and saw he was pulling Tizer from the fridge. 'No, thanks, Mrs Avery. Just some pop, if that's all right.'

'Oh, please. Do call me Eleanor.' She smiled and revealed disappointingly crooked teeth, then

16

lifted a glass clinking with ice to her pale orange lips. 'And where do you board, Jennifer?'

'I don't,' Jen said. 'I'm a day pupil in Hostert. The comprehensive.'

Kit's mother looked at her blankly, as though she'd never met a child who didn't board. Jen and her friends got bussed to the huge secondary, ten miles from them and even further from other camps. 'Really,' said Mrs Avery. It didn't sound like a question, so Jen didn't answer.

Mrs Avery went back to her nails and Jen turned to Kit, filling two tumblers. Behind them, his mum started singing a Dionne Warwick song: 'I Say a Little Prayer'. She had a nice voice; soft and a bit gravelly, like Dionne's. Jen thought she'd love to be just like Mrs Avery at thirty-eight, or whatever she was.

When a big woman in an apron came and asked Kit's mum to move so she could do 'ze cleaning', Mrs Avery slid from the worktop, swayed slightly on landing, and stood taller than Jen, and almost as tall as her son. Now they were side by side, the resemblance was amazing. Same deep blue eyes, same small nose and face shape. Kit's hair was blond too, but wavier. Like Kit, his mother had a big full-lipped smile, which she now aimed at the cleaner.

'Elke,' she said, 'my treasure of a batwoman.' She swung round to Jen and quickly lost the smile. 'Perhaps we should vacate. Do you play tennis? Kit's got a shocking backhand and I'm desperate to find an equal.'

'Jen played for her county when she was thirteen,' said Kit. 'I bet she'd thrash you, Mummy.'

17

Jen laughed, more at the 'Mummy' than the idea of beating this perfect, apart from the teeth, woman in front of her. 'Two summers ago,' she told them. 'I haven't played much since.' That wasn't exactly true, although there'd been no more tournaments.

'Super!' said Mrs Avery, who didn't seem to be listening. 'I'll book us a court.' She wandered off with her glass, like a tall, graceful model at a cocktail party.

Jen wondered if Mrs Avery knew she was a sergeant's daughter, and if she'd still want to play tennis if she did. What a whole other world it was in the officers' patch. Dubonnet in the afternoon, a batwoman.

'Want to listen to records?' Kit asked quietly. 'In my room?'

'Oh,' Jen said, not expecting that. 'OK.'

Because his dad was a wing commander their house was huge. They passed a dining room, a lounge with French windows, a cloakroom, then went up a wide staircase and along a landing. Paintings and sketches and family photos hung everywhere, and Jen wanted to stop and look closely, especially at the old photos. But Kit was in a hurry. She counted four bedrooms, wondering if his brother was in one, before being led up another staircase to an attic room.

It was nothing like the lofts Jen had peered into with her dad; dark and dusty, and somewhere you shoved old stuff. Here, there were windows and carpet. The walls were covered in posters – something she wasn't allowed because Sellotape pulled the paint off and you had to pay for damage when you moved. Maybe officers didn't get fined, or didn't mind paying.

'Welcome to my humble pad,' Kit said. 'What shall we listen to?'

'I don't mind.'

'Hendrix?' He slipped a record out of its sleeve and held it between palms, then blew dust off, put it on the turntable, lined up the needle and lifted a lever. When the music struck up, he played an invisible guitar for a while, before coming and putting his arms around her. 'Did you see him at the Monterey Pop Festival?'

'No, I've been in Germ–'

'It's a film, silly. Jimi was mind-blowing.'

'Oh.' How stupid she must seem, but he kissed her anyway, all through 'Foxy Lady'. Then he lowered her to the carpet, where they continued through song after song until side one finished.

'More Tizer?' he asked in the silence.

'If you're having some.'

While he was gone, Jen inspected herself in an orangey-wood air-force mirror, the only thing their bedrooms had in common. Her mouth was swollen and she prayed it would go down before she got home. Lifting her long brown hair, she saw the first signs of a love bite. Toothpaste would help, according to Christine. The expert.

All the while, she heard distant voices. Kit and his mother? Was she telling him off for taking a girl to his room? But Mrs Avery – Eleanor – seemed such an easy-going parent. Offering her alcohol. Maybe Kit would come back with a bottle of something, get her tiddly and try and

19

take advantage. Hopefully not.

Jen settled on the carpet again, head propped on one hand. She'd only known Kit six days and wanted to look her best and capture his heart before he met the camp's sexpot, Sonia Durrell, currently on holiday. Kit and his friend Lawrence had wandered into the youth club last week, making all the girls stop what they'd been doing and stare like idiots. Jen and Christine, anyway. The new boys were tall, skinny and equally gorgeous: one quite blond, the other much darker. The blond was in velvety flares and a faded collarless shirt, while the dark one wore beads and, on his feet, beneath the frayed jeans, Jesus sandals. For a while they leaned against a wall and looked around, their hands squeezed into the pockets of their tight, tight trousers.

'Quick, let's dance,' Christine had said, and when the next record started, the boys strolled over and joined them without saying anything, the fair-haired one opposite Jen. Christine's couldn't dance, but Jen's did amazing intricate arm weaving and seemed to go into a trance. She couldn't take her eyes off him, and neither could the boys playing billiards, all smirking like the yobs they were. By the end of the song, she was in love.

'Perhaps I should introduce myself,' her partner said, while they stood there, Jen not sure what to do. 'Kit Avery.'

'Jen,' she said. He was gazing into her eyes and she liked it and didn't like it at the same time.

'Would you do me the honour of another?'

She laughed and wondered why he was talking

like Mr Knightley from *Emma*, which they'd done last term. She expected him to bow and kiss her hand, but then The Doors came on and he turned back into a hippie.

Kit was taking so long that her arm began to ache, so she sat up, reached for an LP and read about Buffalo Springfield. When he finally returned, he didn't sit down beside her, but on a nearby chair, and he didn't put another record on.

'The Tizer's all gone,' he said, his voice quiet and flat. 'Sorry.' Kit checked his watch, as though he'd been given so long to get her out of the house.

'Is your mum cross that you brought a girl to your room?'

He shook his head. 'No, it's ... not that.'

'Oh,' Jen said, guessing what had happened but not daring to ask. She suddenly felt quite terrible, and also silly, sitting on the floor, while he was on a chair. 'I should go, or I'll be late for tea,' she said, standing and realising her error. She should have said 'dinner' or 'supper'.

'I'll walk you home.'

Jen told him not to bother but he insisted. At the bottom of the stairs, he steered her through the front door.

On the way, she was miserable and quiet, while Kit rattled on about his school friends, Magnus and Rick – more people who'd disapprove of her – and about his younger brother, Pip, who got 'tremendously homesick' boarding. When they'd gone through the officers' married quarters,

21

along the road that divided the officers' and airmen's patches, then across the playing field, and were as close to her house as she'd allow, Kit asked when he'd see her again.

'But I thought—'

'Look...' He stepped forward and pulled her towards him. 'I really like you, and I don't think we should let this ridiculous, antiquated hierarchy force us apart. I'm a Marxist myself. Did I tell you?'

'I don't think so.' She had no idea what he was talking about.

'I love my ma, but she does rather speak her mind, especially when she's blotto. She had Susie, the CO's daughter, lined up for me, you see. Anyway, Daddy's not like her. He's egalitarian and I know he'll adore you.'

'Oh?' Jen felt warm and unsettled at the same time. She'd never seen or heard of Susie, but she hated her. There was only one commanding officer, or group captain or station commander, as he was also known. The boss of the camp. Up one rank from Kit's father and a million miles from Jen's.

'Tomorrow?' asked Kit. 'Outside the youth club at two? We could go for a walk, exploring.'

Jen wondered what there was to find, apart from acres and acres of airfield. Unless he meant exploring off camp. 'All right,' she said, and then he leaned them both against a lamppost and gave her a long last kiss.

They were watching telly, boiled eggs on laps. The two blonds – her mum and little Paul – were

22

on the settee. Her much darker and much fatter father was in his chair, wearing a string vest and smoking while he ate. How small the room looked after Kit's house.

'Yours is in the pan, love,' said her mum. 'You'll need to cut your soldiers.'

'Thanks.'

Jen went straight to the sideboard and rummaged through the compendiums of games and Spirograph and Operation for the dictionary. Things were never allowed to be left lying around, not even books. Not that there were many of those. Her mum ordered the *People's Friend* from the Naafi and her dad didn't read.

In Kit's house there were packed bookshelves everywhere, even on the landing. In fact, there'd been loads of stuff just left here and there: racquets and balls, golf clubs, shoes, bags, clothes. Maybe the batwoman dealt with it all. Jen would never find out, not now she'd been barred.

It took a while to find 'hierarchy' because of the spelling. Yes, that was what she thought it meant. Best to be sure, and not start using words wrongly when she was with Kit. 'Here, Kitty, Kitty,' kept running through her head and Jen wondered why the Averys had given him a cat's name. Strangely, though, it suited him. Lovely Kit. She remembered their kissing and got butterflies, then saw Mrs Avery with her crooked teeth and her stomach lurched in a different way.

Jen flicked through to M, but didn't find 'marksist', and she couldn't remember the other word he'd used about his dad. Elegant? Gallant? She sighed and put the book back. The worst thing about going out with Kit would be feeling dim.

'Fetch your egg,' said her mum, 'or it'll be like concrete.'

In the kitchen, Jen tried to imagine Kit's mother boiling an egg or making toast soldiers for him and his brother. But all she could see was Mrs Avery pouring them cheap Dubonnet. Cheap, because all alcohol was cheap on camp. Cigarettes were cheap too, which might be why her dad was a walking chimney. Not that he walked much.

Jen carried her tea through and told Paul to budge up, then squeezed in between him and her mother. The toast was cold and hard, and yes, the egg, when she sliced the top off, was like concrete. But she didn't care, didn't think she could eat anyway. Love did that to you.

Another mad Dutch game show was on, fuzzy and flickering because the aerial wasn't right. RAF Weisfelt was near the border, so they picked up both Dutch and German stations. In Holland they showed English-speaking programmes, like *Coronation Street*, with Dutch subtitles. They also went in for slapstick, which Paul, being eight, loved.

Jen wondered if they were allowed to watch telly at Kit's school, or if they had to do Latin and stuff instead. Kit detested Latin. She told him she hated domestic science, and he said he'd swap any time. She leaned back and closed her eyes and thought about the kissing again. Real kissing, not like when she'd gone out with Dean, and he hadn't moved, so she hadn't either.

'What's that on your neck?' her dad was asking, and Jen jolted forwards. He dropped the stub in his ashtray on a stand, pushed the knob that made it disappear and leaned across Paul for a better look.

Jen let her hair fall forward and gave her neck a scratch. 'Just a gnat bite.'

'You want a dab of Germolene on it,' said her mum, reaching for the knitting she always had on the go.

'Gnat bite, eh?' said her father. He always sounded more Scottish when he was cross. 'More like a toffee-nosed, public-schoolboy, Winco's son bite, if you ask me.' He broke into his horrible cough, then stopped and took in some air, his tummy stretching the string when he breathed out again. 'Don't think you haven't been seen, young lady. Of all the officers, you had to pick the one commanding Supply Squadron. In other words, ma bleedin' boss.'

'Do you *mind?*' Paul was moaning. 'I'm trying to watch this.'

'Less of your lip,' said her dad, rearing back and slapping his bare leg.

Poor Paul. You never knew, with their father, whether he'd laugh or fly off the handle. All eyes turned to the telly, where a blindfolded man balanced a bucket on his head. A woman was shouting in Dutch and the audience was hysterical. Beside Jen, the needles began clicking a little too furiously, and her brother was quietly sniffing, a hand on his red thigh. Her dad took another Senior Service from the packet and tapped it on his wooden armrest.

'What's for pud, then?' he asked.

'Bird's Angel Delight,' said her mum, her voice

with that wobble. 'Jen'll fetch it when she's finished. Won't you, love?'

'Yeah,' she said, staring miserably at the bucket man. She and Kit were doomed. She wasn't good enough for his house and he was too good for hers. She looked down at her lumpy egg and felt both sick and in love. But maybe they always went together.

## THREE

At eight thirty, when Robert still wasn't home, Jen tipped the uneaten egg in the bin. Her teeth chattered and she realised the heating wasn't on. She changed the thermostat, then fetched her mobile from the cloakroom to see who'd called. Robert, twice, but no message. The landline had rung too. This time there was a message. Her fingers trembled in the icy hall as she pressed the key to listen. 'I'm so sorry, Jen,' was all he said. Sorry he was late, or sorry he was gay?

It was so cold, she went upstairs and got into bed, still in her business outfit: skirt, silk shirt, eye-wateringly expensive boots. Smart without being severe. Jen liked her tenants to take her seriously, but not be scared by her. She closed her eyes in the dark room, listening to February weather outside. It was wet, windy and totally appropriate. Slowly, and with a heavy, dizzy, sick feeling that seemed to pin her to the bed, she began fitting things together. A few weeks back,

Robert had been surprised to hear her voice on the phone. 'Oh,' he'd said. 'Sorry, Jen. Must have hit the wrong name in my mobile.' She'd laughed and told him not to be so vain and use his reading glasses. 'Jen' was probably next to 'John', or more likely 'Jon'.

She pictured the scene: Robert perplexed: *But I left you a message saying I couldn't stay and eat.* John/Jon: *No you didn't.* The realisation that he'd done it again. The colour draining from his face, as he tried to remember what he'd said.

And there was something else ... the way, recently, Robert would often, too often, cut a phone conversation short when she appeared. *OK I'll get that into the post first thing. Bye.* Or he'd stop tapping out a number on seeing her. She must have registered these things at the time, to be remembering them now. She just hadn't twigged.

When Jen woke she felt fine. Then it came back and stabbed her under the ribs. She rolled over and switched the lamp on. It was just after one and she knew she wouldn't sleep again. Curled up in a ball, she tried hugging herself better. Why so much pain? Her marriage had ended with shocking abruptness, that was why. She was on her own, partnerless, just like that. Unless ... she stretched her legs, threw back the duvet and got up. Her feet were hot now, uncomfortably so. She wanted to take the boots off but first she had to know if Robert had come home and slept in the guest room. He'd do that when he was late.

Passing the bathroom, she tugged on the light

to help see. She didn't know if she wanted to find him or not. A large part of her still needed a marriage, needed to know he still liked her, if only for a while longer. She pushed at the door and saw his shoes, side by side on the floorboards. Always so neat, Robert. Jen had quite liked those shoes, but now felt loathing for them. She loathed the folded clothes on the chair and she loathed Robert. He'd done this terrible thing to their marriage. Why on earth would she care if he liked her?

How often he'd slept in this room lately. 'The meeting just went on and on,' he'd say over breakfast. Or, 'The train was delayed in Birmingham. Didn't want to disturb you.' There'd been more and more overnight trips too. All lies. He'd been having it off with John/Jon. Oral sex and who knew what else.

In a way, what he was doing, had done, was a double deception. He was neither loyal nor straight. How she'd been duped, she thought, and suddenly she was furious with him, which was easier, she found, than utter distress. More familiar. Like the anger she felt over child abusers, risk-taking drivers... She couldn't be quiet on the wooden floor, so was quick instead. Picking up a shoe, she went to where Robert was beginning to stir and crashed it down on him, once, twice.

His arms flew up, and his eyes, now open, were wild and terrified. 'For fuck's sake!' he said, trying but failing to grab her arm.

She pulled the duvet back and aimed the final blow at where it would hurt most, then, dropping the shoe, left him groaning in the horribly hot bedroom. She'd never hit Robert before, only playfully, and hurrying down the stairs, she felt repulsed by what she'd just done. Assaulting him like that. But then there were different forms of assault, she thought, her hands shaking as she turned off the heating, gathered bag, cardigan, phone and keys and, at the last minute, her laptop. Robert had battered her far more than she had him.

Where to? she wondered, once the engine was idling and the wipers, back and front, were swishing at freezing mist. Not to Sarah's. Not at this hour. Paul's, perhaps, but she'd hate to disturb the children. And it was such a long way. Mum and Dad's? Too far again, and anyway, a bad idea. How sad, she thought. All these years on the planet, and she had no one to go to in the middle of the night. She shivered uncontrollably. She'd forgotten her coat but wasn't going back.

Over her shoulder, she saw Robert in the doorway of their lovely Edwardian north London home, silhouetted against the hall light, knees together, hands cupping his stomach. Her aim hadn't been good, after all. He probably wanted to talk, and for a while, she hesitated. She should go back in and let him explain. Perhaps Jon *was* a woman, after all. An abbreviation of some foreign name ... oriental or Brazilian. But then she thought: man, woman – really, what difference did it make? Her husband had been cheating on her, and the way he'd talked about her had made her feel small and unloved and an encumbrance. No, no explanation. Not tonight, when she was feeling so raw. She put her foot on the accelerator and revved down the street in first gear, remembering, too late, the neighbours she might be waking.

## FOUR

The next time she saw Kit's mother was a week and a half later, in the thrift shop. She'd been sent there with Paul to find him some clothes, and Mrs Avery was one of the volunteer officers' wives that day.

Jen was inspecting a pair of boy's shorts, when she spotted Kit's mum in the corner, folding women's things at arm's length, as though she'd rather not be touching them. She wore a cream-coloured dress and thick gold bangles. A pair of sunglasses sat on top of her head, holding the blond hair off her tanned face. She looked more lovely, even, than the first time they'd met. A lot like Grace Kelly, who her mum called the most beautiful woman in the world.

Jen wanted to die, and she wanted to leave, quickly. But her stupid brother had shot over to the toy table, which was next to the women's clothes. She couldn't shout to Paul and draw attention to herself, and if she went and got him, she'd have to speak to Mrs Avery.

Dipping her head over the faded T-shirts and shorts and tucked-together socks, Jen prayed hard. If Mrs Avery saw her, recognised her, she

30

might tell Kit and he'd think she bought clothes in the thrift shop. Jen hated her mother for sending her here, and she hated her father for spending his money on fags and beer and nights up the Sergeants' Mess, instead of nice new clothes for his children. There were only two of them, after all. It wasn't like they were the Malones, who had to have two adjoining quarters.

Jen refused to wear anything her mum got from the thrift shop: skirts down to her knees, hand-knitted cardigans. Even when she found something half decent, Jen would say it was horrible. The stuff was donated by people on camp, so she'd be bound to come across the owner, maybe at the youth club. Of course, Paul didn't care.

'Look, Jen!' he was shouting, heading her way with a weapon. 'It's only fifty pfennigs! Can I have it? *Please.*' He aimed the thing at her head and made machine-gun noise, so loudly she wanted to slap him. Only her father did enough slapping, so she told her brother to *shush*, and said yes.

'Excuse me, little boy!' came Mrs Avery's officer's-wife voice. 'But have you paid for that?'

Jen felt the room spin, and with her hair still hiding her face, dug into a pocket and pulled out some coins. 'Here,' she said. 'I'll see you outside.'

They were in the hut that Kit had found them. It was beside the golf course and on the far side of the wood, in a spot that no one came to and hardly anyone knew about. During a break from the kissing, she said, 'I thought I saw your mum coming out the thrift shop today. Does she buy stuff there?' It was a test, to see if Mrs Avery had said anything.

Kit rolled towards her on the scratchy air-force blanket Jen had taken from her bed. '*Hardly*,' he said. 'She helps out. Doing her bit for the riffraff.'

'Charming.'

'Oh, sorry, Jen. I keep forgetting you're...'

'Other ranks? Anyway, I thought you were a Marxist?' She'd looked it up in the library.

'Hey, I'm only quoting my ma.'

'Sorry,' she said, not entirely believing him.

Kit flopped an arm over her. 'I long for the day the proletariat rise up and overthrow the capitalist pigs and the aristocracy, and schools like mine will become part of our barbaric and divisive history.'

Jen sighed. It all sounded a bit scary, but that was what the crates and boxes surrounding them were for. Kit had asked his dad about the group of huts. Emergency equipment, he'd been told, in case of a USSR attack. Everything that might be needed for a field hospital: ration packs and special protective suits and mattresses and loads of other stuff. Last time, Kit had opened one of the boxes and found gas masks. 'Far out,' he'd said, putting it on and looking monstrous. That night, in bed, she'd lain awake worrying about the Russians sending bombs over. About one of them landing on their quarter, or on Paul's little school by the Naafi.

Jen wished they could move to a hut with mattresses in because it wasn't all that comfortable on the wooden floor, even with her blanket. Although, sometimes, when they got carried away kissing and Kit's hand started wandering, Jen was quite pleased they weren't on a mattress.

All the huts were locked, but theirs had an unfastened window that sat slightly open all the time. They had to clamber through it, then Kit would prop the window open for air, even though the hut was shaded by trees on one side. Jen liked it best when the evening sun shone through the mucky glass on the other side. Something about the crates and the gas masks and the planes roaring overhead made it dead romantic, like something out of a wartime film. Kit called it their clandestine hideaway.

'Come the revolution,' he was saying now, his face above hers, 'we'll all be equal. Queens, business magnates, paupers. It's going to be an amazing trip.' He kissed her more passionately than ever, as though it was really exciting having a pauper for a girlfriend.

Jen's mother grew up in Essex, her father in the Scottish Borders. While her mum talked a lot, her dad was a man of many cigarettes but few words. This meant that when they quizzed her about Kit they did it in different ways. With her father it was more jibes – 'Off to meet his lordship, then?' Her mum, on the other hand, asked what Kit was like, what his family and school were like, and when she was going to bring him home because she was dying to meet him. Sunday tea was suggested and Jen said she'd ask Kit, but that he might not be able to come, since he was so busy.

'Busy with what?' her mum asked, and Jen had

been stuck for an answer. Listening to records and playing pretend guitar?

'Cricket,' she'd said, because Kit seemed the cricket type. 'He's the chief batter.'

'Batsman,' her dad had piped up. 'Poncy bloody game.'

No, Kit couldn't come for tea. There'd be sardines with bones, all mashed up in a glass bowl. The smell of cabbage from their Sunday roast. Her mum producing school photos. Paul would set Jen up with his whoopee cushion, and her dad would insist on his dripping sandwich. It was a nightmare she couldn't let happen. Not when she was competing with the group captain's daughter.

Once, in their hut, Jen had dropped Susie into the conversation, in a kind of so-what's-she-like? way. Kit had described her as, 'Sixteen. Vaguely horsy. Great fun,' and Jen had wished she hadn't asked. Would she ever be fun enough for Kit? Was horsy good or bad? Barbra Streisand was horsy and men were mad about her. Jen had had no idea it was so hard having a boyfriend.

# FIVE

## Norfolk, February 2003

Kit picked up the slime-covered stick and threw it out to sea. Bunk, dripping and panting, swung himself round and bounded back into the icy waves, like the boisterous, stupid, lovable three year old he was. Pip's boisterous, stupid, lovable three year old.

When the dog returned, dropped the stick at his feet and panted for more, Kit hurled it again with another, 'Fetch!' The repetition was calming, while the cold wind was bracing. It was a good combination and just what he needed. Focusing on the dog, the cold, the waves, the picking up of the stick and the throwing of the stick had relegated Pip to a distant corner of his mind.

'Drop!' he told Bunk unnecessarily, but it was a vital part of the repetition. 'Fetch!'

Bunk was the first to grow tired of the game, distracted by a new arrival: a hairy mix of a dog, although not as hairy as himself. They did a dance-cum-wrestle greeting, while Kit and the owner complained about the weather, but agreed it was, after all, February.

'Just visiting, are you?' The man had a soft Norfolk accent, not as broad as some. He looked elderly, but probably wasn't much older than Kit

35

himself. Late fifties. Sixty, perhaps.

'For a while,' Kit said. He wished Bunk could be less exuberant on meeting other dogs. A little more dignified. 'I'm taking a sabbatical,' he added, then wondered if he should explain what it meant.

'Stop, Sheba!' said the man, although Sheba didn't seem to be doing anything. He yanked his dog by the collar and sat her down. 'From what?' he asked Kit.

'Oh, er ... journalism. Mainly. Freelance.'

'Can you take a sabbatical when you're freelance?'

Kit laughed. 'I think so. A break from work, then.' And to take care of my brother's house, dog and son, he could have added. 'Do you live nearby?' he asked, making an effort.

'Cromer,' said the man, pronouncing it 'Croomer'.

'Ah. Nice.'

'Until the summer, yes. Then thass a bit crowded for my liking.' He was pulling Sheba away from Bunk and reattaching her lead. Kit realised he should intervene.

'Here, Bunk!' he said, slapping his thigh and getting no result. 'Not mine,' he explained.

'No, I know.' He nodded towards the dogs. 'These two are good friends.'

'Really?'

'Been driving the old girl back to this beach for years. We used to live in the village, till I took early retirement.'

'I see,' Kit said, although it didn't make much sense. Cromer had a perfectly good beach.

'His owner...' said the man, gesturing to Bunk.

36

'Bit of a strange one. Any sign of him yet? Philip, isn't it? It was in the local paper.'

Kit had seen the fairly low-level appeal, initiated by the police when Pip had been gone a week. Two paragraphs on page six, and the photo Kit had taken at Christmas; cropped to cut out the party hat. He'd driven up to Norfolk for the Christmas dinner, where the three of them had attempted jolliness. Pulling crackers and reading out the riddles. Wearing the hats. By nine in the evening, Kit had been back in London, relieved it was over. 'No,' he told the man. 'No sign, unfortunately. I'm his brother, Kit.'

'Oh, sorry. Didn't mean to... Only, there's not much resemblance.'

'That's OK.'

'Eddie,' said the man. He held out a gloved hand, which Kit shook with his ungloved, frozen and slimy one. 'He seems like a nice chap, though. Very polite, just a bit on the quiet side. A touch nervy, if you know what I mean?'

'Yes,' Kit said, but he didn't particularly want to analyse his brother, here on the beach, with a stranger. He nodded in the direction of the village. 'Well, better be getting back.'

'See you again, no doubt.'

Kit caught Bunk by the collar and clipped the lead on. He gave Eddie and Sheba a wave good-bye, and as they headed to the water, rather hoped he wouldn't see them again. The small talk, the effort of keeping the dogs apart. What would be the point? He was turning into an old grump, he knew, but wasn't that one of the perks of ageing?

37

'I hope you have good news soon!' Eddie called out from the waves.

'Thanks!' Kit shouted. Then, once more, as he followed the path to the village, his head was filled with Pip, and where the hell he was, and how the hell could he have done this, with Adam's A levels coming up, and after all Adam had been through. No note, just Pip and his old VW gone. Because his father often went off to the odd course or workshop, Adam had left it a night and a day before phoning first his uncle Kit, and then the police.

'Pip's a bit spacey sometimes,' he'd told Kit, 'but he usually tells me when he's going away, and he always phones two or three times over a weekend, more if it's longer.' As a toddler, Adam had, rather cutely, called his parents by their first names, and it had stuck. Kit's guess was that Pip went along with it because, to him, there'd only ever be one 'Daddy'.

'We did have a row the evening before,' Adam had added, 'but still, it's a bit unusual, not phoning at all. Really not like him.' He'd been vague about the row, when Kit enquired. 'Oh, I don't know.. Something trivial.' Before Adam knew it, the local press had got the story from the police and it had become the talk of both the village and his school in Sheringham.

Kit could really have done without this. There were things he could be getting on with in London; his life, for example. But he was stuck here for the time being, miles from anything remotely interesting and in a house that made him want to weep. He was worried about his

38

brother, but he was also furious.

At the village shop he tied Bunk to a post and went in, hoping to pick up something good for lunch, but coming out with tomato soup and finger rolls. He'd take Adam to a supermarket after school, stock up on treats. For his nephew, anything he wanted. For himself, plenty of wine.

The gate had a rusty 'Beware of Dog' sign on it – a dog many generations before Bunk by the state of it – that really ought to go. Someone had scratched 'Psycho', with an insert mark, before 'Dog'. Kit pictured an ugly pit bull raging at passersby and put the sign on his list of things to do, although the screws looked pretty buggered. Top of the list was to try, again, to track down their holidaying, mobile-phoneless mother. No one had told her yet that her second-favourite son had disappeared.

Pip's part-brick, part-rendered house wasn't unattractive. The council had recently given it a coat of paint, and with its unusual shape – the red-tiled roof extending down one side – the place looked almost cottagey. A pretty decent house, Kit thought. A mere stroll from the sea, huge garden. And all for a low rent, or in Pip's case, no rent, what with the housing benefit. Before widowhood had hit him, suddenly and ferociously, like a high-speed train, Pip had worked in local government, in an admin job that hadn't been badly paid. Afterwards, extended sick leave had left him underconfident and fearful of going back, and so he hadn't. He'd tried the odd lowly job since then, but they

39

hadn't worked out. Kit wasn't sure why, but guessed receptionist at an MOT garage, and similar, must have been tough for someone of Pip's age and education. Then there'd have been his inability to fit in, of course. Something his brother, poor bugger, had suffered with since boarding school.

The front garden was a longish path with gravel either side. There were no flowerbeds, but one or two shrubs sprouted from the stones, along with a few dead weeds from last summer. It wasn't beautiful, but compared to the rest in the cul-de-sac, ranging from painfully neat to a scrap-metal yard, it was OK.

Indoors, though, was a whole other story. Once again, on stepping into the only home Adam had ever known, Kit braced himself for the shabby gloominess.

Adam coming home woke him up: the crash of the door, the thump of the school bag, Bunk barking with glee. Was it being away from a full and throbbing urban life that made him nap this way, or simply being fifty? While Bunk went berserk, Kit sat himself up on the flimsy, foam-cushioned sofa. Whoever had thought cottage suites a good idea had never tried one out. 'Good day?' he asked, rubbing his sore arm.

'Pretty foul, actually.' Adam had shot up in the past year and was now almost as tall as Kit. He wore his hair long and his clothes loose, but carried the grungy look well. 'People are either ignoring me because they don't know what to say, or they're being overly friendly.'

40

'Yes,' said Kit, following his nephew to the kitchen. 'I remember that.'

Adam opened the fridge and said, 'Oh.'

'I thought we could go and get food, wherever you normally shop.'

'OK, only I've got masses of homework. Any news?'

'Nope.'

'How about Grandma?'

'Uh-uh. The police are hoping she'll use a bank card soon.'

Adam laughed; something Kit hadn't seen much of. 'Personally, I wouldn't even *take* a card if I were driving around Italy with a multi-millionaire.'

Kit tutted. 'Talk about a crap son. I don't even know this guy's surname and I've let my mother go off with him.'

'Yeah, right. Like anyone can stop Grandma doing as she pleases.'

'True.' Kit went and splashed his face in the bathroom, changed out of his beach clothes, then, back downstairs, found his car keys and jangled them. 'Shall we go?'

Bunk stepped off his doggie bed at these words and followed them to Kit's car. 'He usually comes,' Adam said, horrifying Kit by opening the back door for the dog. It was too late to cover the seat, so he had to take a deep breath and give his upholstery the place it deserved in the current circumstances.

'What do we know about Grandma's bloke?' Adam asked as he buckled up.

'Raymond? Oh, filthy rich from property.'

41

'Jesus, I hate property speculators. And all those buy-to-let bastards. Bumping up prices at the bottom of the market. If it wasn't for them my dad might have bought a house.'

First, he'd had to have had a job, thought Kit. 'I believe Raymond buys offices. Commercial property.'

'Yeah, well.'

'What else do I know about him, let me think. He's based in Hampshire and he's widowed. That's about it. Not even his surname. Grandma could be travelling with a madman.'

'Who bumped off his wealthy first wife, so he could start his business empire?'

'Cheers, Adam.'

After a half-hearted laugh, because death was uppermost in their minds right now, they fell silent for the rest of the journey. Adam fiddled with his mobile, while Kit couldn't help checking each oncoming car for his brother's big round face. Apart from the odd five minutes when he forgot, Pip's disappearance was constantly with him, permeating everything, even a drive to the supermarket.

Kit had thought Emily leaving him last summer was the worst he'd ever go through. Considering her tender age, it shouldn't have come as the devastating kick-in-the-stomach shock that it had. Kit had been with her three years – something of a record – and had even agreed to try for a baby. He'd seen them as pretty settled, but then came the bombshell. Sebastian. Younger, even, than Emily. Disgustingly handsome. Kit talked himself into believing it was the baby deficiency that had sent her into the soap actor's arms, and not, as she'd yelled on leaving, his 'fucking self-absorption'. A trait many would have levelled at Emily herself.

He'd missed her dreadfully, painfully, for the first few weeks, but then found old friends drifting back into his life. Friends who'd owned up to finding Emily difficult, hostile, infantile ... things he'd been aware of, but had overlooked on account of her extreme beauty – those legs – and her love of sex. An enthusiasm that outstripped his, the longer they went on.

'Next left for the car park,' said Adam. 'It's appallingly signposted.'

'OK.' Kit heard so much of his brother in Adam; not surprisingly, since it had just been the two of them for seven years. Adam didn't look anything like Pip, though. More like his late mother, and even more like his Grandma Avery. 'Remember, anything you fancy, apart from alcohol.'

'Cool,' Adam said, sounding seventeen again. 'Pip only buys special offers. Three for twos, or worse, four for threes. He saves like twenty pee and we end up with loads of gone-off sausages we forgot to freeze.'

Kit pulled into a space. He flashed back to shopping with Emily, and how she'd always bump into a friend and talk for ages, while he went off and got all the wrong things.

'And we don't even like sausages,' said Adam, unbuckling himself.

'Tell me about my grandfather,' he said on the

43

way home, when the car smelled of lilies; one of their luxury buys. He put away the phone he constantly played with.

'What do you want to know?'

'Everything. Pip won't talk about him, about ... well, *it*. Every year, though, you know what he does?'

'What?'

'Buys him a birthday card.'

'Grandpa? Seriously?'

'Yep. Every single year. May the seventeenth. "To dearest Daddy, stroke, Grandpa." He signs it, "With all our love, Pip and Adam," puts it on the mantelpiece for a few days, then it disappears.'

'Hmm,' said Kit, not sure what to make of that, and not particularly wanting to talk about *it*, either. Not in a car, that was for sure. And not one smelling of white lilies.

'I've no idea where the cards go. But then we do live in a mess.'

'Yes,' said Kit. 'You certainly do.' Were birthday cards to a dead person an unhinged thing to do? People would go to a grave on a birthday, after all. 'Look, a kestrel,' he said, pointing at the sky, at a welcome distraction. He'd been browsing through his brother's bird books, trying to learn what was what; north Norfolk being a bird-watchers' paradise. 'Well, maybe it is. What do you think?'

But Adam wasn't looking. 'He probably recycles them,' he said, back on his mobile, fiddling away. Texting, game-playing. Whatever it was he did to block out real life.

# SIX

The day after the thrift-shop close shave, Jen was cornering an aisle in the Naafi and heading for bread, when she and Mrs Avery bumped into each other, literally. Jen dropped her basket in shock, just missing Mrs Avery's painted toes. She apologised and bent to pick up the scattered goods, then hoisted the basket of embarrassment – instant soup, instant potato, instant pudding – hoping she'd be gone. But there she still was, all done up in lemon and tapping her chin with her one item, a packet of 'Nearly Black' tights.

'It's Jennifer, isn't it?' she said, with an unexpected smile. 'When are we going to have that game of tennis?'

'Well,' Jen said, trying to look casual, face blazing, 'I'm free most days.'

'How about today, then? Shall we say half-past four?'

'Um...' The thought of a match made her cold, but having said she was available, she couldn't back out. 'OK.'

'Let's play on the courts by the Malcolm Club. They look much shadier.'

'All right.' Jen didn't know there were any others. Perhaps officers had courts tucked away for their exclusive use, which didn't seem fair. At weekends, she and Christine had to queue for theirs.

'See you there,' said Mrs Avery. She strolled off in a way she must have practised, then, just down the aisle, stopped beside a small pram. She leaned over it and put her hand in. Jen saw her say something, but was too far away to hear what. Mrs Avery then straightened up and carried on, past the proud-looking mother.

Jen went that way too, glancing into the pushchair at a quite ugly baby. Odd, she thought, as she headed for tinned vegetables and began fretting about what to wear for tennis. The usual, probably: denim shorts and one of her sporty T-shirts. The light blue one. White plimsolls, white socks. What if Kit came and watched? He'd make her nervous, that was for sure, and she'd play badly and lose.

Jen stood in the queue, three behind Mrs Avery, who was tapping her tights impatiently against her brown arm. What if Kit's mum was hopeless at tennis? That would be embarrassing, because after years of knocking a ball against walls, then a summer tennis camp, then tournaments, Jen was actually quite good. The afternoon's match would probably be a once-only thing, so she might pretend to be rubbish too. Something told her that beating Mrs Avery at tennis might not be a good idea.

By the time they met at the courts, Jen wasn't sure she could overcome her competitiveness and let her win. Then, as an unsmiling and business-like Mrs Avery thwacked practice shots over the net with a force that didn't go with her outfit – short tennis skirt, white halter neck, jewellery,

46

pink Alice band – Jen had a definite change of heart. Suddenly, she saw beating Kit's mother as her only chance of being accepted.

'Best of three sets?' asked Mrs Avery, and when the match started, she turned out to be quite good; better than Christine, anyway. But she wasn't as good as Jen, who won the first set 6–2. By playing half-heartedly, she then let Mrs Avery take the second. They were the only ones on the courts and it was a strangely quiet game. Quiet, that was, apart from the jets taking off and landing. Jen barely heard plane noise any more, but when she did notice the high-pitched roar, she found it quite exciting. Sometimes, in the hut with Kit, it felt as though a plane might slice the roof off.

'*Aagh*, double fault,' Jen heard. She hadn't imagined Mrs Avery to be so serious about the game. She sensed, also, in that final set, as the game became more and more one-sided, that Kit's mother didn't take well to losing.

It went 6–1 to Jen, who braced herself for an unfriendly parting. But, as an out-of-breath Mrs Avery congratulated her and zipped her racquet into its cover, she said, 'Same time next week?' and even smiled.

Gradually, Jen was learning not to be surprised. 'Yes, all right.'

'Or, better still, this Thursday?'

Jen considered playing hard to get, but then she had just beaten her. Thursday, she agreed.

'You're terribly good,' Mrs Avery said at the corner, where she was to go one way and Jen the other. 'Excellent net play.'

'Thank you.' Jen set off before she could colour up and destroy her confident-winner status. As they parted, someone wolf-whistled and she turned, only to see two blokes in uniform leering at her opponent.

You can't win them all, she thought, and floated home. Mrs Avery would tell Kit what a brilliant tennis player Jen was, and he'd like her even more. She pictured herself welcome at the house again, being offered Dubonnet, spending hours on Kit's bedroom carpet. Perhaps Eleanor Avery wasn't so bad.

## SEVEN

Paul and Bev lived in a small terraced house they'd bought at auction, with a view to doing it up in a month, flipping it over and moving on to the next project. Three years and two babies later, they'd got past the wallpaper-stripping phase, but only just.

Their house was in Brighton and had soared in value, even in its sorry state, but their earnings had more than halved since the babies arrived. Bev had taught science at secondary school, and chose not to go back after maternity leave. Meanwhile, Paul carried on earning next to nothing as a youth worker. What puzzled Jen most about her brother and his partner – taking into account the half-installed heating, the broken nights and the ongoing overdraft – was how they could be so bloody happy.

Lying on their lumpy sofa, she listened to them in the kitchen, talking non-stop, laughing, cheering, making baby noises for Frank, singing 'Wind the Bobbin Up' with Phoebe. Cupboard doors slammed, crockery clinked, a blender whizzed, a cat meowed for food... 'Pull! Pull! Clap, clap, clap! Look Phoebe, Frank's clapping! Hooray!' Jen lifted her quilt to see the time, trying not to expose her arm to the fridge-like room. It was twenty past six. In the morning.

She had to work out what to say. When she'd arrived, Paul and Bev had been uncharacteristically silent. Bedding was found and the sofa was cleared. 'Good night,' they'd whispered, and were gone. Used to short bursts of wakefulness in the night, they'd probably trained themselves not to come far out of sleep for someone in need. Jen was thankful for this, since they'd never have swallowed her running-out-of-petrol story.

Regardless of Paul and Bev being the least judgemental people she knew, and the fact that they lived in the gay capital of Britain, she still didn't feel she could tell them about Robert. Jen was the big, financially successful, Highgate-residing sister, who'd married her estate-agent boss, then built up her own portfolio of properties. Seven now, all bar one being let and bringing in more than enough rent to cover the mortgages, and all rampantly increasing in value. Although Paul had often turned to her for advice, or a moan, Jen had never felt the need to confide in her brother. Sarah, occasionally, but never her brother.

She'd tell them she got locked out ... no, she was on her way to ... somewhere. An overnight drive, and the car started making funny noises, and since she was near Brighton... But where could she have been on her way to that was near Brighton, tucked away as it was in the Southeast? She was driving from Portsmouth to Kent, for an early morning train to France. Yes, that would do.

She must have dropped off again because the next thing she knew her brother was sitting cross-legged against a floor cushion and holding Frank, a mini version of himself. Both were pale, blue-eyed and sandy-haired, and a lot like Paul and Jen's mother.

'We brought you tea,' Paul said, pointing. 'Are you OK?'

'Mm, fine thanks.' Jen sat up, wearing the suit she'd now slept in twice, and reached for a mug on the floor. The sun was pouring through thin curtains and had warmed the room a little. The makeshift bed, the tea, the kind look on Paul's face, the sweet baby, the sun ... it was all a bit much and Jen could feel her heart growing heavy, her throat thickening.

To avoid humiliation, she cooed at Frank and took in all the photos and toys and piles of books and games. There were shrivelled balloons, paintings by Phoebe and the oldest TV in town, all on a floor that needed resanding. Food lay everywhere – crusts, bits of rice cake, half-eaten apples and half-drunk beakers. The place was cluttered and grubby and would drive her potty, but it was strangely cosy.

'Sure you're all right?' asked Paul.

'Yes, yes. It's just that...' Jen stared into the mug and replayed the past twelve hours. Robert's message, her horror, the tears, the anger. Then, right there in the warm brown liquid, she saw her husband kissing a man. Real, passionate kissing. It was worse than any image of sex she'd pictured yesterday. The intimacy of it shocked her horribly. 'I think Robert's got a boyfriend,' she said, looking up at Paul.

'You think...?'

It was typical of him to give such a measured response, but then she wondered, from his calm-even-for-Paul manner, if he too had known, or guessed. She reached for her bag and found her mobile. 'Here,' she said, getting to Robert's message. 'Press one.'

Paul's eyes gave nothing away as he listened, then he put the baby down and came over on his knees and gave her a hug. He'd always been the demonstrative member of the family, and although she'd mostly felt uncomfortable with this, right now she welcomed it, clinging on until he gently pulled away to save Frank from the cat, or the other way round.

'Would you like me to call him?' he asked, settling back with the baby and some dubious-looking rusk. 'Tell him you're safe and with us?'

She wanted to say no, but knew it was the adult thing to do. She sat up straighter, as though suddenly feeling supported. 'Would you mind? And if you could find out a bit more about...'

'I'll try.'

When Paul reached for his phone, Jen threw off the bedding and made for the bathroom in a

51

sleep-deprived haze. Any minute, she'd surely wake up from this bad dream and be in her own home. Robert meticulously ironing a shirt, some politician on the radio, toast popping up. She wanted to be home. She didn't make a good house guest these days; missing her own things, finding fault with her hosts' bed/shower/choice of coffee. A sign of age, no doubt, and so un-grateful of her. She was as quick as she could be in a very cold bathroom, before wandering down to the kitchen, where they were gathered again. It was a heat thing, Jen realised. All the gas rings were on.

'No answer,' Paul said. 'I left a message.'

'Thanks.'

Phoebe greeted her like the long-lost aunt she'd become, and Jen felt bad for not visiting more often. Lovely wild-haired Bev – overweight since having Frank, but not caring – made her a full English breakfast, vegetarian style, which Phoebe helped her eat, one arm linked with hers.

When Frank was placed on her lap, while Paul and Bev washed up, Jen realised how deprived of human touch her life had become. The children were warm and soft and fragrant, and she just wanted to sit like that, with them, until she felt better. She should have tried harder to have children, or rather they should have. Looked into the problem, had tests, like other couples do. But life had rattled on. Work and the gym for Robert, while Jen had tennis and her properties. Perhaps they were baby substitutes, the flats and houses.

Jen gave Frank a squeeze and stroked Phoebe's hair again. At home, the touching had wound down to the odd kiss on the cheek. She could have said something. 'I need more hugs, Robert.' But perhaps she hadn't asked because once you get out of the habit, that kind of easy intimacy becomes awkward, almost alien. Robert, she knew now, had his own reasons for not being tactile.

Jen watched her brother and his partner move around the kitchen as they cleared things away. A hand on the other's shoulder, a rub of the other's back ... remarks that made the other giggle. Her brother might have been a softie but he was, without doubt, heterosexual. Although, only a day ago, she'd have said that about her husband.

'Do your duck noise?' Phoebe was asking, and Jen did, over and over, with Phoebe trying to copy, until the landline rang and she knew it was Robert.

'I'll go,' said Paul.

Bev put a CD of nursery rhymes on, perhaps to drown out what Paul was saying, but his voice, if not the words, still came through the wall. It was a long conversation and as Jen sang along she began to wonder if it wasn't Robert at all. But then Paul appeared at the door and said, 'Jen, he'd like a word.'

Bev clicked the player off and Jen shook her head so violently it bumped against Phoebe's. Paul disappeared and her niece howled. Jen did everything to console, and was on the verge of offering a Disney trip, when Bev scooped her child up and pointed to a robin in the garden. And she stopped, just like that. You either have it, or you don't, thought Jen.

Later, wearing Bev's jeans, jumper and coat, she booked herself into a hotel in Brighton. She had no charger for her phone and Paul had sworn not to tell anyone where she was. This made her feel safe, and also in control. Mostly though, she began to feel nothing very much.

With no unpacking to do, Jen lay on the bed, knackered, wondering if this was a brief spell of numbness, owing to lack of sleep, before the insecurity and depression set in. Years of it, perhaps.

When she came to, her immediate thought was of the bins, and whether they'd been put out. They most likely had. Her leaving him wouldn't stop Robert remembering it was Tuesday. She thought about the pricey chicken in the fridge, and imagined him taking it to Jon's, where they'd do something exciting with it. Not Thai, of course. She wondered where he lived. Not too far away, presumably, if Robert could go there, have sex, and get home by eight, for a dinner he didn't like with a wife he didn't want. Jen saw them pulling the wishbone, as she and Robert would have done. What would Robert wish for? Two days ago, back when she knew him, she could have guessed: his father's surgery to be over and successful; exchange of contract on a multimillion-pound property. Now, it might be a non-acrimonious divorce ... half his wife's property assets.

Jen forced herself out of the hotel and to the shops. She bought jeans, tops, underwear and flannel pyjamas, toiletries, slippers and sturdy beach shoes. Bev had said she could hang on to her coat, which wasn't chic but was warm and waterproof and would do. After staggering back to her hotel, she put everything away, and went out again for tea, coffee, milk, cakes and a screw-top bottle of wine. On the way back, she picked up a Chinese take-away, which she ate on the bed with her fingers, having not thought to buy cutlery.

There was a small TV with satellite channels, on which the news was too depressing. Saddam Hussein, WMDs, the UN, Bush, Blair, WMDs, Saddam Hussein... It should have put her own drama into perspective, but instead it made her think of discussions with Robert on the subject. She flicked to a soap, which managed to absorb her in a kind of oblivious way, and relaxed again. It was a very strange place she was in, both physically and mentally, but, for the time being, it didn't feel too bad.

Around nine thirty, sated with Chinese food, wine, cake and TV, she padded to the bathroom and cleaned her teeth. When she'd finished, ready now for sleep, she stared at her toothbrush, standing upright, but very much alone, in its unfamiliar glass. Like me, she thought, and tried to imagine where her husband was. If he was alone or at Jon's; whether he kept a toothbrush there.

'He feels wretched,' Paul had told her earlier. 'Said he's been trying to end it for a long time.'

'A *long* time?' she'd almost screeched, but remembered the children. 'And end what? The marriage?'

55

'No, no, the affair.' Paul had obviously got his brother-in-law to open up, used his youth-worker skills on him. Robert had been seeing Jonathan for three months, apparently. 'Very casually,' Robert said.' And there'd been one other briefer relationship, again with a man. Jen was stunned, sitting there in the messy front room, while Paul filled her in on her life. Two relationships, however casual, she hadn't known or guessed about.

'How thick and unobservant of me,' she said, the queasiness of yesterday coming back. There must have been one-off encounters too. She saw Robert in public toilets, parks, large cupboards. Wasn't that what they did? Promiscuity? Oh God, must stop, she told herself. She, they, had lovely gay acquaintances of both sexes. There was Aaron, and Steph and Jojo. One thing she'd loved about Brighton was seeing guys holding hands. On the other hand, this was her husband.

'Perhaps,' Paul said, 'it's easier hiding adultery of the gay kind. A wife finds a man's name and number on a scrap of paper and thinks nothing of it. Some business contact, a plumber.' Her brother excelled at making a person not feel foolish, and she loved him for it. But she'd still felt foolish. And hurt. And alone.

Jen took the toothbrush out of the glass and put it in her washbag. She got into bed, switched off the light and tossed around for a while, trying not to think, not to cry. Several times she pinched her eyes to stem the tears. Safe, she kept telling herself. You're safe here. There won't be any more shocks.

She was in no doubt that people were trying to

get hold of her – her builder, for one – but the part of her brain that dealt with downlights and floor tiles had switched off. There were bigger things to ponder, like how to survive this.

## EIGHT

On the Saturday after her triumphant second match with Mrs Avery, Kit sneaked Jen into his house while his parents were at an Officers' Mess do. He said they wouldn't be home till the early hours, so she felt quite relaxed. Well, as relaxed as she ever was with Kit, with his handsome face and clever words.

She met his fourteen-year-old brother, Pip, who was dark-haired, brown-eyed, plump and not very talkative. Another family-pet name, she noted. 'Here, Pip!' Or maybe it was after Pip in *Great Expectations*. While she tried to recall a 'Kit' in Dickens, the boys raided cupboards and fridge for Twiglets and German crisps and bottles of Orangina. You'd never know they were brothers, Jen thought, as they filled two wooden air-force trays and Kit held up a bottle of sherry to see how much was left.

From around nine, the three of them sat in Kit's room, eating, drinking and listening to music. Jen drank one small glass of sherry and declined a second, then told them about the camp and what there was to do: the outdoor pool, the youth club, cinema, the Malcolm Club.

Although she'd never seen officers' kids in the Malcolm Club, not in the evening, anyway.

The boys talked about their school. Pip hated it even more than Kit. 'Full of bullies,' he said. 'The teachers, the prefects, all of them.'

'Does your big brother protect you?' Jen asked.

'Absolutely,' Kit said, leaning over and kissing her, but not for long because of Pip.

Jen listed all her postings, but none coincided with theirs. It was odd, they agreed. You moved every two years, but you never came across the same person twice. All those friends just gone. Into the big air-force melting pot.

Somehow, Kit got on to their rich grandfather on their mother's side, who came from 'aristocratic stock' and thought marrying a flying officer, as their father had been then, was beneath their daughter. She also learned that Kit was really Christopher and Pip, Philip.

Pip was shy and hadn't made any friends in the two weeks he'd been at Weisfelt. Although Jen liked him and felt sorry for him, she really wanted him to leave, and she could tell Kit did too. She didn't know if it was the sweet sherry stirring things up, but she'd never longed so much to be held and caressed and kissed. Finally, Kit said, 'Hey, Pip, why don't I take you to Lawrence's house? His brother's fanatical about table football and you're such a whiz at it.'

'Isn't he ten?'

'But a terribly mature ten.'

Kit was on his feet, promising Jen he'd only be a tick. Then Pip heaved himself up and said, 'You know you're just like Ma, Kit. She never wants me around, either.'

'Now you know that's not true, you twit. Come along, it'll be fun.'

Pip, looking as though he had no choice in the matter, followed his brother down the stairs, but with a much heavier step and without once glancing back at Jen. She felt terrible, really terrible. But at the same time, couldn't wait for Kit to get back. She hadn't known that love made people so selfish.

There she was, alone in Kit's room again, only this time she took advantage and had a poke around. Just a quick one. Lawrence lived over the road, in another huge house, so Kit wouldn't be long. Jen didn't know what she was looking for: love letters from some girl, Jen's name in a heart in his diary... Just something that would tell her more about him. Apart from the records – had he carried them all the way from England, or bought them here? – there were quite a few books. One called *On the Road* lay opened on his bedside cabinet, next to some sweet wrappers.

Jen noted what chocolate bars he liked and eased the top drawer open. It had two biros in it. She shut it and opened the bottom one, then wished she hadn't. In it was a dirty magazine, a German one. A quick flick through told her it was quite disgusting. What's more, the women were Germanic and shapely, nearly all blonde, and nothing like her. Jen was stunned, but mostly she felt jealous. These were the kind of girls he liked. So far, Kit hadn't tried anything on – nothing serious, anyway – but why would he when he had this...?

She heard voices, raised voices, and quickly closed the drawer, then went back to where she'd been.

'Shut! Up!' she heard Mrs Avery say. Luckily, a record had just finished. 'I have *really* had enough.' She seemed to be getting closer. Jen wondered if it was Kit she was talking to, but then she heard a male voice that was too deep for Kit or his brother. Just a sort of mumble.

'You are *such* a bore, Roger. All I was doing was dancing with him, not fucking fucking him. You humiliated me, and made yourself look ridiculous too. Now go to hell!'

The man, Wing Commander Avery, Jen guessed, said, 'Ellie, darling–' then a door slammed. She thought someone went downstairs, but it was hard to tell because of the carpeting.

Jen was in shock, not only on account of their sudden arrival, but also the language. She'd never known a mum use that word. On top of that was what she'd found in the drawer. Suddenly, Kit's house had a whole different feel. And it was so quiet that she heard kitchen-type noises. Cupboards, glasses. She didn't dare move, in case Mrs Avery was directly below her. She might have thought she was Kit and come up for a chat. Jen even tried to breathe quietly. Or perhaps Mr Avery was below her and Kit's mum was in the kitchen. An even worse prospect.

She was imprisoned. There was no way she could slip out without danger, and she wanted Kit to come back and work something out. She knew Mrs Avery hadn't mentioned their tennis matches to her son, which pretty much said how she felt about her. He, of course, couldn't bring them up because he wasn't supposed to be seeing her. It was all a mess, and Kit was going to be in trouble. Jen felt uneasy, to say the least, and she desperately wanted to be at home, watching Dutch telly, her brother annoying her.

It was ten minutes or more before she heard voices in the kitchen, then Kit bounded up the stairs and apologised. 'Susie was there,' he said, 'and she's such a talker. Terribly funny. I think Lawrence is sweet on her. Anyway, come and meet Daddy. Apparently, Mummy's under the weather, so they're home early.' He stuck out a hand and helped her up.

'Are you sure?' Jen asked, bothered by lots of things – Susie, now, as well.

'Oh, Pa's insisting. I've told him about you, you see. We're co-conspirators.'

On the first-floor landing, Kit put his finger to his lips and tiptoed. Then, down in the relative safety of the lounge – or sitting room, as Kit called it – Jen saw a small thin man with a grey and black moustache and just a bit of hair each side of his bald head. His face was round, his cheeks pink, and he wore a comical bow tie. She thought he couldn't possibly be Mrs Avery's husband, but then he stood up from the armchair, shook her hand, introduced himself as Roger Avery and said how absolutely delighted he was to meet her. He was hardly any taller than her, Jen noticed. 'I know your father,' he said. 'Splendid chap.'

Jen took up the offer of the settee, and when Kit disappeared for drinks, Mr Avery asked how she

61

liked life at the station and if she'd picked up much German. 'I'm a complete dunderhead at languages,' he admitted. *'Was kosten?* That's about it.' He burst into a genuine and friendly laugh that was nothing like his wife's smile. 'Oh, and, *Noch ein bier, bitte.'*

Jen told him she was doing German at school. 'But you can get by without it, when all you need is on camp.' She wondered if she should have said 'station' but it was too late. So long as she didn't say Raf as one word. Kit always called it the RAF.

'Too true,' said Wing Commander Avery, and Jen couldn't believe she was having a friendly conversation with her dad's very top boss, not counting the CO.

Kit appeared with her lemonade. One taste told her he'd put wine in, but she wasn't about to complain. If Mrs Avery 'recovered' and came down, Jen wanted to be unconscious. While Mr Avery told a story about when he was in Cyprus, she knocked back her drink and quietly asked Kit for more.

'Thirsty, eh?' He grinned and got up.

'It turned out,' said his dad, 'the Cypriot chappie thought I'd asked for hair-removing cream!' He chuckled again. 'I've tended not to try the local lingo since then.'

'Right,' she said, giggling along with him and thinking about the row she'd heard on the landing. How could he be so jolly?

The second lemonade and wine calmed her enough to feel safe in the event of Eleanor Avery appearing. It also loosened her tongue and, while they were on languages, she found herself telling Kit and his father about the time a motorcyclist drove into their car in Surrey. 'The man couldn't understand what my livid father was saying because of his Scottish accent. He asked if he was Swedish.'

Mr Avery found this funny, perhaps because he knew her dad and had heard him angry. Jen wanted to ask him not to mention the story to her father, but Kit's mum was in the doorway and the room went quiet.

Eleanor Avery just looked at them, one at a time, her gaze lingering longest on her husband. Her floor-length pale blue dress was low cut and sleeveless. Her hair was pinned up, but with lots of loose tendrils. Over one arm was a shawl, and she clutched the tiniest of handbags. Jen had never seen anyone as beautiful – not in real life.

'I'm going out, darling,' she said. 'Do enjoy yourself with the children.'

In an instant, Mr Avery's face lost its colour and completely crumbled. It was horrible to watch, and when his wife disappeared from view, Jen wondered if he might go after her. But all he did was stare at the door. She knew from Kit that Wing Commander Avery was seven years older than his wife, but now, sitting in the big armchair, his face pale and sagging, he reminded Jen of her Scottish grampie.

Embarrassed, Jen started surveying the classy ornaments. At home there were one or two souvenirs, a Spanish doll on the sideboard and a collection of glass animals, some of which Jen had bought as presents. Her mum didn't go in for plants because of the watering, but there was one ugly cactus on the telly. Kit's mum, on the other hand, had big plants in big pots, and everywhere there were antiques. Real antiques, probably. Lovely big vases and shiny brass things. A statue of a half-naked woman, like a goddess. A chaise longue in a pale green silky material, and a Persian rug that almost filled the big room.

Jen loved it, all of it. One day she'd have a home like this, but, hopefully, with a nicer atmosphere. No one said a word, while a pretty gold carriage clock quietly ticked. Eventually, Kit took her free hand and stood them both up. He nodded towards the door and led her across the room.

'Daddy's best left, when he's like this,' he whispered out in the hall. He pulled her towards him, buried his face in her neck and sighed. 'We've been rather thwarted this evening, haven't we?'

'Mm.'

Kit stroked her hair. 'Back to my room?'

'I should go,' she said, wanting to and not wanting to. His house was scary but the alcohol had made her want to snog all night.

'If that's what you'd prefer.'

Jen was torn. The combination of sherry and wine and Kit could be dangerous. Yvonne's older sister had got pregnant and it was all hushed up. She'd been sent back to England to live with her grannie and not even Yvonne talked about it. Jen couldn't let that happen to her, because, one, her dad would kill her, and two, she was only fifteen so they might put Kit in prison. And three, she didn't want to.

'Yeah,' she said, decision made. 'I'd better go.'
Kit released her quite suddenly. 'What a drag.'

'Sorry,' she whispered, wishing she'd said yes,
wondering if she still could. But before she knew
it, he was holding the front door open. All the
way home and for half the night, until she finally
fell asleep, Jen felt sure he'd chuck her.

## NINE

It was ex-local authority and had needed work.
Most of the non-privately owned flats appeared
unloved and down at heel, as did their occupants.
Jen tended to hurry up the grey concrete stair-
well, keys poking weapon-like between fingers,
before falling through the door and slamming it
behind her. This she did again today, two hours
after leaving Brighton.

She'd hoped Lionel, plus a tiler and a car-
penter, would be there, finishing off the kitchen.
But Lionel was a busy man with other buy-to-let
investors to finish kitchens for. It seemed Jen's
plan to move into flat 42 would have to be
shelved – for lack of shelves, among other things.

As she checked out the freshly painted walls
and the bathroom suite, she wondered if she
could really live here, in a place far removed from
her Highgate home. There were the rough
neighbours, the busy road. On the other hand,
around half the flats were owner-occupied, and
where in London wasn't near a busy road?

The intention had been to let, perhaps to a young professional couple wanting to be where things were happening, wanting more space than a modern flat offered. Being ex-council, it certainly had space. Other plus factors were its location – a two-minute walk from Tower Bridge – and, more tenuously, the view. With a bit of effort and perhaps a chair, from this top-floor flat of a four-storey block, you could see the new City Hall and one edge of the Gherkin.

Standing there, in the middle of the cold and soulless room, Jen felt ready to make contact with the world, and in particular, Lionel. In Brighton, she'd bought a new phone. She'd been meaning to upgrade for a while, and now that she couldn't look at her mobile without thinking of Robert's message, she switched the SIM card, plugged the charger in and threw the old phone in a bag of empty drinks cans.

Jen wandered around, trying to work out if the two bedrooms and sitting room could be jiggled to make three bedrooms and a sitting room. She'd get more for three bedrooms, rent-wise and when it came to selling. But then again, the beauty of the flat was its spaciousness. She made her way to the half-done kitchen. Base units without doors, no wall cupboards, and a third of the floor tiled. She needed to get hold of Lionel, crack the whip.

A dog barked and someone yelled. It barked again, they yelled again. They could have been right beneath her, it was hard to tell. Things quietened down, but not the traffic roar. Double glazing, she decided. She went over to the big sitting-room window and discovered it was double-glazed. Had she known that before? Before Robert's message. In that other life. The window would have to be replaced. She'd mention it to Lionel, once she could call him.

Jen gave the charger fifteen minutes, then sat on the lino floor – wood or carpet, what had they decided? – and with an intake of breath switched on her phone for the first time in a week. There were missed calls from her mother, Robert, Lionel and others, texts from Lionel and from Sarah, who now knew, it seemed. And seven new voicemail messages. Leaning against the wall in the increasingly cold room, she wrapped Bev's coat around her, for protection as much as warmth, and pressed the key to listen. The first two weren't from Robert, but then she heard his voice.

'Hi, Jen. Let's talk. Please. Phone me back at home? Bye.'

She deleted, but the next was Robert again: 'Look, Jen. Where are you? Paul won't say. Still in Brighton? Hope you're OK, my love. Please phone me. I, uh ... look, I really need to talk to you.'

My love? That was a low blow, and it actually hurt. How dare he 'my love' her, after what he'd done? This person she'd trusted, damn him. 'I'm at home,' he went on, 'worried sick about you. And about us. Can't face the office. Listen, it's over with ... not that there was ever anything ... not really. Christ, I'm so sorry. Sorry for my stupidity.' His voice was cracking and she willed the message to end. 'I don't want to lose you, Jen.

67

Please phone.'

She deleted again, then, heart pounding, moved on to the next. It was her mother. Would she and Robert be staying over, the night of the golden wedding party? For some reason, it was this, her mother's perfectly normal question, aimed at a perfectly normal couple, that got to her. All through Robert's next message, left only yesterday, Jen found herself crying at the unfairness of it all. She'd been so secure and happy, arriving home with the chicken, relieved that the class was cancelled, excited at the prospect of a night in. Cooking, opening a bottle, chatting with Robert about her day. Disloyal, deceiving Robert. *One of her bloody Thai things...* He loved her Thai things, she knew he did.

'Come home,' he was saying. 'Please come back. Or at least phone and tell me you're all right. I can't sleep.'

He sounded as though he hadn't slept, his voice thick with tiredness, and booze, maybe. She wasn't sleeping well either, but had resisted the bottle-of-wine cure. She drank camomile tea, but it didn't seem to help. Robert had never been the best of sleepers, getting up at four sometimes. Things on his mind, he'd said. Now she knew what, of course. It must have been hard... No, *don't* feel sorry for him, she told herself. And she didn't want to hear him missing her, pleading with her to go back. There was nothing to go back to.

She closed her eyes but the tears didn't stop. She wanted to hate him, did hate him. He was an adulterer. Even if he sought something she couldn't give, it was still adultery. He'd cheated. She hadn't known. She felt tricked, stupid, angry, everything negative. The opposite of her real self. Maybe that was why she was so upset. Robert had robbed her of herself.

And this was how Lionel and a young Asian man found her, slumped against the wall and sobbing. What with the traffic, she'd barely heard the key, and there they were, Lionel stopping short when he saw her and lowering a box of tiles to the floor.

'Come on, Jen,' he said, straightening up. 'We're a bit behind, but it ain't that bad.'

The younger guy looked worried and hurried to the kitchen with a second box. 'Ravi,' said Lionel. 'Top man. He'll have your floor done before you can stand up and walk there. Wanna hankie?'

'My bag,' she said, pointing. For some reason, she couldn't get up, or didn't want to. Too weary. How lovely it would be to go to sleep, right there. Wake up and find it all done, furniture, broadband... She closed her eyes and heard Lionel plod off, in that bear-like way he had. Then she heard him plod back. He held out her bag and a can of something.

'Want one of these?' She shook her head, and while she blew her nose, he opened the can and took a swig. 'Trust me,' he said, 'it won't take no more than a coupla days. I'll get Jake the chippy back, a.s.a.p.'

Lionel took out his phone and scrolled, then wandered to a far corner. Jen heard, '...upset ... quick as you can ... no, not frigging farmhouse.

Shaker. Got it?' Various measurements were gone through, and Jen gathered Jake would be with them in two hours.

She'd never tried tears with builders before. Perhaps she would in future.

There was a ticket on her car, which she ripped off with a curse, wondering where she'd have to go to get a resident's permit.

There was so much to do when you left your marriage. For a while, she hovered, tempted to get in and drive home. Was that the easy option or the hard one? She imagined finding Robert hard at it with Jon, over the hall table or halfway up the stairs. She'd have to ring the bell first, which would feel odd and depressing. Then, when there was no answer, she'd let herself in and find he'd done something stupid with paracetamol or the Kitchen Devil.

No, she thought. Not today. And how hard could it be to get a parking permit? She re-attached the ticket to the windscreen, assuming they couldn't give her two, and set off on foot towards Tower Bridge, a coffee and a double-glazed hotel.

# TEN

Kit was giving Lee, Dawn and the 'Litlun' a tour of the house: how the central heating worked, how to light the oven with a match, and how to lock the tricky back door. He'd written down washing machine instructions, TV instructions, and the day to put the bins out. They only lived next door but one, with Lee's worn-out parents, but neither Dawn nor Lee, both eighteen, looked as though they'd ever put a bin out. Another set of instructions conveyed what to do should Pip turn up. Who to phone – Kit, then the police – with the numbers written boldly. What to tell Pip: that Adam was in London with his uncle Kit for half term. And what to do: stay with Pip until Kit and Adam arrived.

He told them how often, and where, to walk Bunk, what to feed him, and what not to feed him, and how, on walks, to make him stop greeting everyone like his long-lost mother. 'A sharp tug on the lead and a forceful, "Sit!" Failing that, a ginger snap.'

He gave the couple two sets of keys and, since they were carless, permission to help themselves to the food he'd got in especially. Looking at them now, he regretted the goat's cheese, bilberries and gnocchi, and imagined Bunk dining well all week.

At two thirty, Kit threw the big rucksack Adam had packed into the boot, and then his own small bag. He'd bring more things from home next week, should it turn out he was in for the long haul. Adam wouldn't be finished with exams and school until June. He'd been offered a place at Bristol, but first had to get the grades.

Kit headed towards Sheringham and the school, with his nephew's detailed but clear map on his lap. Adam would be good at whatever he chose to do, Kit felt, having got to know him. Provided fate didn't screw him up the way it had his father. Considering he'd lost his mother at ten and been stuck with an unstable father ever since, Adam appeared pretty grounded, even in the present crisis.

Nevertheless, a spell in London might be good for him; a decision not totally selfless on Kit's part. He needed to touch base, wind up some work-related issues he'd left dangling. As he drove through the flat landscape, he felt mounting excitement at the prospect of going back to civilisation, if only for a week.

Adam was listing the things he'd like to do: Camden Market, the Eye, Science Museum, Aquarium, Tate Modern... He'd like to buy clothes, he said. 'Only, well, you know.'

Kit smiled to himself. 'Would three hundred cover it?'

'I'm sorry?'

'Spending money.' The least he could do to make up for past neglect, or attempt to. It had never occurred to him, over the years, that his nephew might have needed things. Adam's clothes were in a sorry state and his old PC was slow and frustrating. Sadly, Kit had been preoccupied with larger-scale problems: drought, oppression, torture. He'd sent the odd birthday card with cash in, but should have thought about Pip being on benefits so much of the time, and the impact that would have on a growing boy. 'I'll do a same-day transfer, once I access my online banking.'

'Cool,' said Adam. 'Cheers, Uncle Kit.'

He slotted them into the southbound motorway stream. 'It's on one condition, though.'

'Oh?'

'That you drop the "Uncle" from now on, yeah? It makes me feel ancient having an adult call me that.'

'Sure. And cheers again, Unc–'

'You're welcome.'

'Hey, I've had another idea,' said Adam over their ludicrously expensive snack: two dull sandwiches, two teas, nine pounds. 'There's this sort of friend of my dad's. A woman he met at one of his wacky weekends. The mountain-worshipping yoga group, or something. She's called Elaine and she sometimes phones him. Only, thinking about it, she hasn't called since he went missing.'

'Right,' said Kit, calculating that the moderate bite he'd just taken cost a pound. Pip didn't have an address book, just scraps of paper with people's details on. Sometimes, he'd used the wall. He didn't do email either, and refused to have a mobile. Kit used to find that refreshingly

73

quirky, but now saw it for what it was: Pip being deliberately difficult. 'I don't remember seeing her name, but we could get Lee and Dawn to look.'

'Worth a try,' said Adam, 'although it could be anywhere. On a cereal box or something.' He got his phone out and called home. There was no answer, so he left a convoluted message about what to do in the event of an Elaine calling, and where they might look for her number, if they'd be so kind. 'They're probably walking Bunk,' he said, hanging up and turning to Kit. 'If they lose him, I'll have nothing.'

Kit wanted to say, 'You'll have me,' but knew he was a poor substitute for a devoted dog. 'They won't,' he told Adam, not too convinced they wouldn't.

It certainly was good to be home, even with a seventeen-year-old in tow. He led his nephew to the spare room and left him lying on the bed watching TV, while he made real coffee, went through mail, picked up phone messages and switched on his computer. He replied to emails, sometimes mentioning a family crisis, sometimes not. He scanned all the newspaper websites for reports of an unidentified man, alive or otherwise, being found. Then he checked press releases from the Norfolk police. Nothing.

Since mention of this Elaine person, Kit's spirits had lifted somewhat. The one other time his brother had gone walkabout, aged eighteen and clinically depressed, he'd been discovered after two months with a new girlfriend in a Weymouth caravan. The whole miserable episode had almost cost Kit his finals and it had taken him a while to forgive Pip.

He typed 'mountain-worshipping yoga' into Yahoo, then Google, and got nowhere. Adam had made it up, of course. In desperation, he entered 'Elaine yoga' and was confronted with 230,000 entries. Personally, he'd always felt life was too short for yoga.

They went out for dinner at Kit's favourite Italian, where Adam ate everything but the menu and surreptitiously took in the pretty women. They discussed the only other time he'd stayed with Kit, aged twelve. 'You had that girlfriend with a, er, how shall I put it ... large posterior?'

While he laughed, Kit racked his brain. He wasn't, on the whole, drawn to big bottoms. Kit reeled off names but Adam shook his head at each. This was puzzling. 'Not Brandy, the American?'

'Nope. We all went to London Zoo. Don't you remember?' Yes, he did remember them going to the zoo, but who'd been the third member of the party? 'Let me think...'

'Pip always joked about your string of failed relationships. I think he was just glad you weren't brilliant at everything.'

Kit noticed the past tense, and it stopped him feeling too peeved at the 'failed'. 'Surely a bigger failure is never to admit a relationship has run its course?'

Adam pulled a face. 'I'm no expert, but I'd guess some of those women might not have felt it *had* run its course. Like that one ... was her name Sandra? Yeah, Sandra. Kept phoning Pip in tears.'

'She *did?*' He and Sandra had stayed with Pip one night before a weekend on the Broads, and as far as he could recall that was the only time the two had met.

'She couldn't understand what she'd done wrong, apparently. Wanted Pip to talk to you. He said no to that, but listened to her for hours. He's always good with people who've been rejected. He's just a bit crap with everyone else.'

'I did *not* reject her,' said Kit, astonished, but pleased Pip was back in the present tense. 'We parted amicably. I gave her the stereo system I'd paid seven-eighths for.'

Adam laughed. 'You remember those details but not their names.' He must have seen Kit's face because he quickly dropped the smile. 'Sorry. I'm being a bit judgemental for someone eating a free meal and with three hundred pounds in his account.' He leaned back for the waitress to take his plate and said, 'Wasn't it May? At the zoo.'

'No, no, May was my...' Colleague, he was about to say, but then remembered borrowing her in a panic about his nephew's visit. He must have given the impression she was his girlfriend, deliberately or otherwise. She'd stayed in the flat, he remembered now, but had they...? God, ageing did such terrible things to the memory. 'Well done,' he told Adam. '*May* it was.'

'Big bottom?'

'Oh, yes.'

'Nice, though, I remember.'

'Very.'

'So was Sandra.'

'Yes.' So many nice women in the world, was that the problem? If not settling down *was* a problem. His nephew seemed to view it that way. Perhaps Adam's would be a generation that stayed together, worked at relationships, didn't give up at the third or fourth tiff. 'But what about your dad?' Kit asked, shifting the focus. 'Did he—' Past tense, damn. 'Does he go on dates?'

'He's tried, but ... well, no one compared to my mother. And north Norfolk's not exactly densely populated, so, you know, people get snapped up. Pip's a bit slow off the mark. There was someone at his Introduction to Psychology evening class, but then she got sectioned.'

They looked at each other and paused before laughing, then Kit asked the delicious young waitress for the bill. Adam watched her walk all the way to the counter in her tight little skirt, and all the way back. She gave the bill to Kit, but smiled at his nephew. Where once he might have been miffed, Kit found himself rather pleased. Suddenly ... possibly, he was getting the whole proud-parent thing.

# ELEVEN

Jen, to her relief, hadn't been chucked, and on the Tuesday morning following the Avery-household drama, she and Kit caught a bus to the nearest town, which happened to be in Holland. Kit wanted to buy clothes and a guitar. Jen didn't want to buy anything, or rather, couldn't. She was just happy to be with Kit and to have her mind taken off the tennis match with his mother, later that day.

Jen knew Roermond well, and the first thing they did was to get chips and mayonnaise, served in a paper cone and delicious. In the chip shop, Jen said one or two things in Dutch and could see Kit was impressed.

While they ate on a bench, with the sun shining and young people zooming past on mopeds, she told him the main differences between the Dutch and the Germans. How in Monchengladbach and Düsseldorf no one crossed the road till the lights changed, and they were all immaculately dressed. And how she couldn't find clothes because German girls were much bigger. Kit's dirty magazine popped into her head. 'Shops in Holland smell of patchouli,' she said quickly, so he wouldn't think of big German girls too. 'In Germany they just smell clean.'

Kit laughed at that and it felt good, for once, to be the knowledgeable one. 'I'd imagine it's easier to score drugs here,' said Kit, and Jen said she wouldn't know. 'No?' he asked, grinning. Am I to believe you've never indulged?'

'Actually, no.'

'Not even a little pot?'

Jen filled her mouth with chips, so she wouldn't have to answer. She didn't like the fact that he looked so astonished.

'It's absolutely rife in the sixth, thank heaven. Hard to imagine a fascist regime and A levels without a joint to keep us sane. The last day of term, we all got stupendously stoned. Rick told Magnus he loved him, which we'll obviously rib him about for ever. Honestly, Jen, you should try it. You'd find it blissfully far out.' He leaned towards her ear. 'I managed to smuggle a little through customs.'

More and more with Kit, as with his mother, Jen wondered what she'd got herself into.

'We could have a little puff in our hut,' he whispered. 'Next time?'

'No!' she said, then realised she might be coming over as a Goody Two-Shoes, when in fact she was just nervous. She wanted to ask if Susie 'indulged' but preferred not to summon her up. 'Thanks, anyway,' she added.

Kit shrugged and went back to his chips, and Jen thought fondly of her one previous boyfriend, whose dad got posted a month after they started going out. Dean had been sweet. He liked the Beatles and was keen on go-karting. He'd never made her float through a warm rose-scented starlit sky just by kissing her, but he did have a mum who'd liked her. Maybe you couldn't have it all. Lovely kisser or nice mother.

Kit screwed up his empty cone, aimed for a bin and got it in. Then he took a wad of money from his back pocket and started counting.

Jen was amazed. 'How did you...?'

'Hundred and eighty, hundred and ninety... What?'

'Oh, nothing.' Maybe she didn't want to know. She finished her chips and got up. 'There's a music shop around the corner. But first, you'll need to get some guilders. I'll show you where.'

'I prithee now, lead the way.'

'Sorry?'

'*The Tempest*,' he said, standing. 'I played Stefano, the drunken butler, last year. Terrifically, of course.' He did a bit of drunken staggering, right there in the square, spouting more Shakespeare. Jen wanted to disown him, but then he came and put his arms around her and kissed her, and she was up in the rose-scented starlit sky again.

They went to the bank, then wandered the streets hand in hand. Jen thought she'd never been so happy, or felt so grown up. Kit bought an acoustic guitar, jeans, T-shirts, a jacket, sneakers and three LPs. For someone who went on about capitalism and materialism, he heaved a lot of bags on to the bus home.

Kit's mother hadn't spoken to him all day Sunday, but then she hadn't spoken to his father, either. Approaching the court, a rushed fifteen minutes after getting home, Jen half expected Mrs Avery still to be in a mood and not turn up. But there she was with the usual, 'Hello, Jennifer,' and her short sharp smile, already practising her serve. 'Shall we start?' she asked, the moment Jen reached her end.

They were there to play tennis, it seemed, and Jen felt three days' worth of anxiety lift. She was in a compartment of Mrs Avery's life quite disconnected from other compartments. It was very odd and slightly chilling, but Jen was getting used to it. She was also getting lots of practice in, and with a bit of luck would develop a nice honey tan like Mrs Avery's.

She realised, when they were level pegging in the first set, that Eleanor Avery had improved considerably in a week. This was good, in that Jen didn't need to give her the occasional point, but bad, because she didn't want Kit's mum to start winning their matches. Mrs Avery, Jen suspected, wasn't the kind of person who played tennis with losers. Not for long, anyway. The end of the first set was hard fought, but Jen managed the slimmest of wins with two advantage points.

While swapping ends, Mrs Avery said, 'Shall we have refreshments at the Malcolm Club afterwards? I'm always terribly parched, aren't you?'

Jen hesitated. She wondered if having a drink might force them to talk. Would Mrs Avery use the occasion to warn Jen off her son? Was that, in fact, the reason she'd suggested it? 'Yes, I am,' she said. 'OK.'

Worry affected her game, and for the first time she almost lost a set without doing so deliberately.

Kit's mother paid for everything. This was a relief,

since the baby-sitting had gone quiet in the holidays, with Jen's regulars away. Her measly pocket money might just have stretched to the two drinks and two bits of cake they were now carrying to a table. Just. One day, she'd win Wimbledon and get rich, although not if she played the way she had today. She'd won, but only just, and only because her opponent had the sun in her eyes and missed a vital lob.

Walking across the room, Mrs Avery had the air of someone who got stared at – aware, but pretending to ignore the eyes, both male and female, that followed her. What with the tennis outfit, and looking like a film star, she couldn't help but stand out. They found a free table and sat down, and Jen tried not to feel drab and unattractive in all the attention they were getting. She bit into her Victoria sponge and waited, nervously, for Eleanor Avery to say something.

Kit's mother used a fork on hers and Jen blushed. But her companion hadn't noticed, too busy was she inspecting the walls and notices; her gaze occasionally, and very briefly, resting on two men in uniform by the jukebox. One was a corporal, the other an SAC, and both were giving Mrs Avery the eye. Jen recognised them as the wolf-whistlers, and wondered if they'd stare that hard if they knew she was a wing commander's wife.

Men were so obvious. Luckily, Kit wasn't. Not counting the naked Germans, he only had eyes for her. Mind you, she'd never seen him in Susie's company. Just the thought of Susie gave her a jealous pang. For all she knew, the CO's daughter was like the girls in Kit's magazine. Curvaceous and pouty and devil-may-care. With a bit of horse thrown in.

'So, Jennifer,' said Mrs Avery.

Jen, expecting the worst, gave Kit's mother her full attention and wanted to smile. But there were cake crumbs and cream to worry about, and no serviette in sight. 'Yes?' she said from behind a hand.

'Are we on for Thursday again?'

Jen dabbed at her mouth with messy fingers. 'Yes, definitely.' Relief washed through her, especially when Mrs Avery smiled and said, 'Super.'

'It's good practice,' Jen added. 'And, you never know, I might end up with a nice tan.'

Mrs Avery ran her eyes down Jen's slim, pale, lightly freckled arm, resting on the table. 'I think we'd have to play all day every day for that. Don't you?' She stood up, leaving most of the drink she'd so wanted. 'Four thirty again?'

'OK,' Jen said, not knowing if she was to eat and drink up quickly.

'Do finish my cake,' said Mrs Avery. Then, in her very short tennis skirt, she bent over – right over – for the racquet beneath the table. Jen couldn't believe what she was witnessing. Neither, she guessed from the look on their faces, could the men by the jukebox.

# TWELVE

Lionel had the flat finished, furnished and fully equipped in four days. He hadn't replaced the windows – something about planning permission – but had put secondary glazing on top of the double glazing, as a stopgap. There was a television, stereo and phone. She'd have to wait for broadband. The sofa, bed, crockery, tea towels, everything, came from Ikea, which Jen was very happy with, having been married to an Ikea-phobe. Nothing in the flat would remind her of Robert.

She treated Lionel to lunch by the river in Butler's Wharf, where he dug into his steak and Guinness pie and told her his life story. It turned out not to be that interesting, but after ten surreal, hotel-residing days, it was just nice to be with someone.

He was late thirties and, for such an active man, pretty round. He occasionally mentioned a girlfriend who lived in New Zealand. Jen wondered how a relationship with someone in New Zealand worked, and when the chance came up, she'd ask. 'Anyway, after quitting at the shop, I started the old painting and decorating, found out you can charge them big-bonus city nobs a fortune, taught meself a few other skills, on the job like, and hey presto, got meself a nice little gaff in Wembley. It ain't beautiful. Pre-war, pebble-dashed, but it's home, know what I mean?'

'Yes, I do.' Jen had two of those herself and knew how much space and light you got in a thirties house.

'Was you gonna leave that?' Lionel pointed at the elaborate burger she'd barely touched. Non-stop eating out was less fun than she'd imagined.

'Would you like it?' No wonder he was round. Salads, that was what she'd do in her lovely new kitchen. And all those berry superfoods.

'Might as well.' Lionel lifted her plate over their drinks and moved his to an empty table. 'So, Jen, you coming on the march?'

'The march?'

'*The* march. Tomorrow.'

'Oh, right. I don't know ... I, um...'

'You're against an Iraq invasion, right?'

'Of course. It's just that...' What she was trying to say was that she'd planned to shop for the flat. Cushions, one or two mirrors, a rug. But she knew from past conversations – monologues, really – that Lionel took his politics seriously. 'What time?'

'Midday. Only me and me brother and his partner was planning on joining one-ish. These things never get going on time. Here, why don't you come with us? We're grabbing a bite first, somewhere near the Embankment. Could be in for a long afternoon, what with all them speakers once we get to Hyde Park. Tony Benn, George Galloway, wicked. I'll text you, yeah? Let you know where we are?'

'Well...'

'History, that's what it's gonna be. Rallies in hundreds of cities around the world, but London'll be the biggest. We'll show our so-called Labour leader we ain't putting up with his imperialistic and deluded behaviour. You know, I reckon that vain, lying, puppy-dog of Bush's...'

Jen raised a hand and caught the attention of a waiter. If Lionel was off on a diatribe, she'd need a strong coffee.

The door of the flat across the landing opened, just as Jen was letting herself in. 'Hiyalright?' said a petite blonde woman with a naked brown baby in her arms. Another brown child appeared by her leg and said something. 'No, Destiny,' said the woman. 'It's not them.'

Jen put her food down and went over and introduced herself, then made a fuss of the children. They were very beautiful. Destiny looked about two, and had cornrows and huge brown eyes. The baby was another girl, Jen could see.

'I'm Ruth,' the woman said. She was hard to put an age to. Forty, perhaps, but she was wearing young clothes: low-slung baggy trousers and a short T-shirt. Her tummy was very flat for someone who'd had two children, and very white. 'She's waiting for her brothers to come back with the shopping. We thought you might be them. Wanting her sweets, aren't you, princess?' The little girl nodded and smiled cutely.

'What are your brothers' names?' Jen asked, bending down to her height.

'Um. Maffew.'

'Matthew,' repeated Jen.

'An' Tyrone.'

'Right. Matthew and Tyrone. They're your big brothers, are they?'

'An' Jason.'

'*And Jason?* Wow, aren't you lucky having so many brothers?'

'Yeah, right,' Ruth said, laughing.

'Five children?' Jen asked, straightening up and hoping she didn't look as horrified as she felt. That could be a huge amount of noise.

'Lucky me, eh? Jase, the oldest, went to live with his dad, so really, it's four.'

Jen stroked the baby's cheek. "What's her name?'

'Trinity.'

'That's pretty. Hello, Trinity. Anyway, better get on. Lovely meeting you.'

'Yeah, you too. Let me know if you need anything.'

'Thank you. Will do.'

'And Tyrone's a dab hand with a drill.'

'Uh-huh? I'll keep that in mind.' Jen backed off with a wave at Destiny. 'You must come and have a cuppa,' she heard herself saying, 'sometime.'

'Cool.' Ruth smiled prettily and Jen realised she was probably thirty, not forty. 'Thanks.'

Jen took her groceries into the flat and through to the kitchen, where she'd designated three cupboards for food, but managed to fill only half of one. Why had she said that about the cuppa? The last thing she'd want was someone like Ruth and her tribe hanging out in her spotless flat, moaning about the social, or the absent fathers, or whatever. Mind you, people said that kind of thing all the time – 'We must do lunch' – not really meaning it. There'd be no need to follow it up. She'd try to be a bit less friendly in future. Appear ultra-busy. Ruth surely had lots of single-mother friends to visit; people she had something in common with. Jen made tea with the super-fast kettle. It wasn't snobbery, she told herself, just self-protection. Or prioritising. She took her tea on a tour of the lovely new home. All neat and clean and minimalist and trendy. No, she definitely wouldn't let a delinquent with a power tool in.

Later, she ate a solitary salad at her brand-new table, then soaked in the brand-new bath with a crime novel. It was about a young lawyer discovering his wife's affair, then killing both wife and lover in a boating 'accident'. The story didn't put ideas in Jen's head – there was still half a book to go, and Carl Draper was bound to slip up – but it did force her, as much as she resisted, to sympathise with the wayward partner.

After turning a corner down and dropping the book on the floor, Jen lay back and imagined how she'd have responded, while married, to some incredibly attractive man coming on strong. Terence, her Kingston tenant? Over the years, even recently, she'd been flirted with, asked to discuss things over a drink or dinner, but never by anyone she fancied. And anyway, she'd been happily married, uninterested.

But what if, say, there was a problem with Terence's roof? She'd have to go to Kingston and check it out. No, not the roof ... the bedroom ceiling ... a slight bulge. It would have to be re-plastered, she'd tell him, on inspection. An evening inspection. She'd suggest adjusting the rent, for the inconvenience. *Have you eaten?* Terence would ask. *I was just cooking. We could discuss it over dinner?* She'd accept, he'd open a bottle of wine, they'd drink, eat ... talk easily on a variety of subjects, then get back to the ceiling. *Perhaps you'd like to take another look?* Terence would say, after the meal... Pasta, delicious. He'd come over and help her up. *The bulge is much clearer from the bed...*

The water was tepid. Jen hauled herself up and turned the hot tap on full. That was how easily it happened. You came across someone, the right someone, if you were lucky.

How had Robert come across his boyfriends? The gym, possibly. Hampstead Heath. She shuddered in the warming water. Her own husband, lurking in the shadows, picking up strangers, doing those things with them. Against a tree. Her Robert. Popping out for a bottle of whisky or to stretch his legs after an evening at the computer. Nine or ten at night. That hadn't been unusual. He'd be gone an hour sometimes. You could do a lot in an hour. *The off-licence was shut. Never mind, I'll have a decaff!*

Jen's face grew hot with shame. Not so much because she hadn't known, hadn't realised – after all, he'd had a thing about Ulrika Jonsson; loved Goldie Hawn in *Private Benjamin*. In fact, she'd worried that he preferred blondes, not men. No, it was more the idea that he'd turned to men because she wasn't attractive enough, wasn't exciting in bed. If she'd wondered that, others would too.

Or perhaps it was the water, now steaming, making her flush. She turned off the tap and reclined, ready to go back to her fantasy house inspection. But this time it wouldn't work. Maybe it was visions of gay cruising ... but now Terence – had he been wearing those tight white jeans before? – looked far too gorgeous to be straight.

Jen lay in her brand-new bed going over her options. Shopping or anti-war rally? She and Robert had been furious with Tony Blair and would certainly have gone on the march. Robert may have been a former Tory, and an estate agent to boot, but he deplored the idea of bombing Iraq as much as she did – or she had. During her period of isolation and self-pity in her post-traumatic-shock state, Jen had switched off to other people's troubles. These days, the news washed over her instead of enraging her.

She wouldn't go, she decided. With a million expected, she'd hardly be missed. And the flat did need cheering up, as lovely as Lionel had made it.

With the help of camomile tea and a quarter of a tranquilliser her brand-new doctor had prescribed yesterday – a muscle relaxant, he'd called it – Jen drifted towards sleep, telling herself the decision had nothing to do with the fact that Robert might still go on the march, and that he might have made up with Jon, so he could be there too. But maybe it had. Cushions and a rug would feed her soul. Bumping into Robert and his lover would kill her.

# THIRTEEN

Jen, Kit and Pip were sunbathing on the top of the grassy slope surrounding the pool, telling corny elephant jokes, when something cast a shadow over them and said, 'Room for a little one?'

'Hello, Susie,' said Kit.

The group captain's daughter wasn't that little. She went in and out in places Jen didn't. She had an all-over olive complexion, shown off by her yellow bikini, and masses of blonde curly shoulder-length hair. Jen suddenly felt too pale, too freckled, too brunette, and wanted to put her clothes back on, cover her thinness. When Susie got Kit to move over so she could share his towel, Jen propped herself up for a better look.

Kit introduced them. 'This is Susie. Susie, Jen.'

Susie said, 'Hey, at last. Kit talks about you *all* the time. I'm racked with jealousy, but I'm sure I'll get over it.'

'Oh, hilarious,' said Kit. He pinched her under the ribs and she whacked the top of his arm. Kit did a kind of mock-pain noise, then Susie settled down a centimetre from him and closed her eyes.

Jen could see what Kit meant about the horsiness. She had quite a big mouth and a nose that wasn't long, but wasn't short either. Not small and neat like Kit's, anyway. But opposites attract, Jen thought, as she examined their profiles. She couldn't see a single freckle on the CO's daughter. Not one.

'We're telling elephant jokes,' Pip told Susie.

'Golly, haven't done that for yonks. Right ... um ... oh, I know. What do elephants have that nothing else has?'

'*Baby* elephants,' the brothers said, and Pip tutted.

'Well, pardon me for being unoriginal.' Susie spoke in plummy, private-school, officer's daughter way – as, of course, she would. Kit had said she was at Benenden, Princess Anne's old school. She was a bit like Princess Anne, herself.

Susie and Kit talked about where Lawrence might be and if he was coming, then Pip said, 'Have we run out of elephant jokes?'

Aware of having gone quiet, Jen wished she could remember another. Susie's presence had made her clam up, and she knew from experience that if she didn't speak soon, it would get worse and she'd become more paralysed, more tongue-tied.

'How about other animals?' asked Pip, and Jen's heart raced because she knew a few whale jokes. But what if she told one and it fell flat? Five minutes ago, she hadn't felt inhibited, now she had butterflies and her heart was pounding on top of the racing.

'Oh,' Susie was saying, 'let me think...'

Jen breathed in and took the plunge. 'How do you get two whales in a Mini?'

'I don't know,' said Pip, because he was the keenest on all this and liked to do it properly. 'How *do* you get two whales in a Mini?'

'Over the Severn Bridge.'

They all giggled, even Susie. Then they groaned because that was sort of compulsory. 'Good one, Jen,' said Susie. 'Got any more?'

'No,' she lied. It wasn't worth the risk. 'Sorry.' She lay back and closed her eyes and smiled into the intense heat of the three o'clock sun. When Kit's hand moved over and took hold of hers, Jen wondered if she'd ever been so happy in her life.

Kit offered to go for ice creams. He took their orders and slipped a T-shirt over his head, then was gone, leaving Jen alone, not counting Pip, with the CO's daughter.

When Susie sat up, Jen shielded her eyes to see if she was going after Kit. But she seemed to be scanning the crowds surrounding the pool on this scorching day. Summers in Germany were hotter than back home, the winters like Siberia.

'I wonder if Lawrence is here,' Susie sighed. 'Can't see him. Of course, it doesn't help that I'm blind as a bat without my ghastly specs.'

Jen sat up feeling even happier, if that was possible. Not only was Susie keen on Lawrence, but she wore glasses. 'Let me look,' she said.

She started on her left and took in the sun-bathers. It was Sunday, so the place was packed: families, teenagers, couples, groups of young airmen. She went through the people in the water, one by one, but couldn't see Lawrence, then turned to the sunbathers to their right – her eyes immediately falling on Christine and half a dozen others she knew.

Christine was looking her way, but when Jen raised a hand and waved, her best friend for the past two years didn't wave back. Instead, she said something to Yvonne, beside her, and the two of them stared at her. They weren't friendly stares and Jen came over cold, despite the heat, and lowered her eyes.

It was true she hadn't spent much time with Christine lately. In fact, hadn't been to the youth club since meeting Kit. She'd joined Christine at her baby-sit one evening, but was aware she'd talked about Kit a lot, and his mother, the tennis and everything. Christine had been quiet and not quite herself, and Jen put it down to her not getting off with Lawrence that time. If those two had got on, they could have all gone round together, and Jen wouldn't have felt like the only square peg in a round hole. She and Christine could have had a laugh about their posh boyfriends and compared notes.

Raising her head, Jen saw Christine whispering in Yvonne's ear, hand cupped. The two of them smiled, then, both at the same time, pushed their noses up at her.

'Apparently, I'm one mark fifty short,' said Kit, appearing from nowhere, out of breath. 'Never going to get the hang of this German money. Anyone want to cough up some bread? Not you, of course, Jen, my impoverished one.'

Jen sighed. Two humiliations in a row made her wonder how one afternoon could have so many ups and downs in it. After Susie produced some money, Jen got to her feet and said, 'I'll give you a hand.'

When they returned, Christine and the others had gone, and Jen felt relieved. Then she felt guilty. Should she have gone and had a chat? But there was no point in letting it spoil her day. She was in love, after all. When Christine went out with a  German boy for two months, she'd had no time for Jen.

'I think this is yours,' she said to Susie, offering her a 99.

'Actually, that's mine,' said Pip. His hand shot over and grabbed it from Jen, but managed to knock the ice cream and flake out of its cone as he did so. Jen screamed when the coldness hit her chest. Half the ice cream was in her bikini top, half on Susie's head.

'Pip, you prat,' said Kit, then from the distance came laughter. Christine and the others had moved further away – making a point, Jen supposed – but must have seen everything. Yvonne was pointing at her and saying something, then the laughter got louder. Jen quickly sat down, out of view.

'I'm terribly sorry, Jen,' Pip was saying. 'And Susie. Gosh, your hair. Sorry. Sorry.'

'Oh, it's not a problem,' said Susie, dipping her head, so the ice cream fell off. 'I'll go for a swim and wash it out. Let's share my choc ice, Pip.'

Wiping her chest with a hand, Jen wanted the earth to swallow her up. Was Kit going to think less of her, now she was a complete ice-cream-covered mess? Had he seen her friends laughing?

'Here,' he said, 'let me help.' He picked up Pip's T-shirt and dabbed at her chest and bikini top. His eyes were fixed to what was almost a cleavage, but not quite, and Jen wanted him to both stop and carry on for ever.

Susie somehow broke the choc ice in half. 'OK, Pip, he who eats quickest gets to give the other a severe dunking. Or do I mean *she*?'

'You're on.'

'There,' said Kit, raising his eyes to Jen's. 'All cleaned up. I do apologise for my oaf of a brother.' He leaned forward and kissed her, slowly, wonderfully, on the lips. She could taste strawberry Mivvi.

'Hey,' said Pip. 'What did the rabbit say to the carrot?'

'Don't know,' said Susie.

'Nice gnawing you.' He laughed and Jen could feel he was prodding Kit. *'Gnawing*. Get it?'

Kit stopped the kissing and said, 'Bog off, Pip,' and Jen took the opportunity to glance Christine's way. They all had their backs to her now. Turned their backs on her?

Susie got up and said, 'Race you to the water, Pip?'

'Right you are.' He stood too, big tummy above his trunks. 'Last one in's a moron!'

It was nice seeing Pip come out of his shell, although it made him more irritating. He needed friends, but apparently the officers' quarters were short of fourteen-year-old boys. Plenty to pick from on the airmen's patch, but that would never work.

Jen couldn't help but like Susie, even if she didn't totally trust Kit with her. As she watched the group captain's daughter run down to the pool with ice cream and cornet crumbs on her head, Jen wondered if it was rank and Benenden that made someone so confident, or just personality.

When they'd gone, Kit kissed her again, then sat back and ran a finger from her neck to her bikini top. 'What do you say we retire to our hut?'

Jen tried to read the look in his eye, but couldn't. Kit seemed to her a strange mix of child and grown-up. He was clever and political but liked elephant jokes. He smoked pot but drank Tizer.

'Um,' she said, wondering if she'd be safer by the pool. 'All right. But I have to be home by five for tea.' It wouldn't matter if she was late, but he wasn't to know. She could always change her mind if he behaved himself. Stuck to kissing. 'I mean supper.'

Her mum had made spaghetti Bolognese with tinned mince. It was Jen's least favourite because the tiny bits of meat just about slid through her teeth, and the taste reminded her of dog food. Not that she'd ever tasted dog food, or even had a dog. 'I ate a sandwich at the pool,' she exlained, patting her tummy. And an ice cream. Really full.' She'd made a much better Bolognese, herself, in cookery class.

'You'll waste away,' her mother said, not for the first time.

'Nothing but skin and bone,' said Paul, doing an imitation.

Jen laughed, but her dad switched his ciggie to the other hand and clipped Paul's ear. 'Now, apologise to your mother.'

'Sorry, Mum,' he said, but he wasn't holding his ear, so it couldn't have hurt much. Or perhaps, he was becoming immune. 'Can I have yours, then?' Paul asked.

'OK.' Jen scraped her dog food on to his plate; every tiny morsel. 'It was really nice,' she told her mum. 'Sorry.' The family hardly ever got through a meal without someone saying sorry about something. She'd bet a week's pocket money it wasn't like that in Kit's house.

Jen excused herself and went and lay on her bed, where she tried to think dreamy thoughts of Kit – kissing her, rubbing ice cream off her chest. But Christine and Yvonne kept appearing, pushing their noses up. It was really unfair, Jen thought. They were all just people – her, Kit, Christine, Susie. Who decided who it was or wasn't right to be friends with?

## FOURTEEN

When the time came, Jen couldn't put cushions before the Iraqis, and headed by taxi to where Lionel and his brother were to wait for her after their lunch, outside the restaurant.

The taxi was to save her feet, which were prone to aches and blisters, for an afternoon of walking and standing. On arriving back in London, and after a good deal of trying on, she'd bought smart but sensible pavement-pounding, cushion-soled, black lace-ups, but still wasn't at home in them. If only she could go to Highgate and retrieve her comfy walkers, sitting by the front door under the coats. In her small leather rucksack – also new,

98

like her entire wardrobe – were fabric plasters and co-codamol, just in case. Robert always said she was the Princess and the Pea when it came to her feet.

God, Robert. This wasn't going to be easy, she thought, in the back of the black cab. But what was she to do? Never go out in case she bumped into her husband? And today's event, of any, was hardly the one in which she'd spot him, not with the numbers expected. She'd be squashed together with Lionel and his brother, and something like the Corby Peace Group. She'd see only the faces immediately around her and the backs of several rows of heads.

Still, she couldn't help imagining it happening: finding the needle in today's million-plus haystack. *This is Jon, my lover. Jon, this is Jen, my wife.*

There was a diversion, so she was forced to leave the cab and walk, which, because she was now late, turned into a semi-frantic trot. Lionel was checking his watch and pacing when she finally got to him.

'Sorry,' she said, puffing more than she should for someone her age. 'Diversion ... taxi. Sorry...'

'The others have gone on,' said Lionel. 'But we'll catch them if we run.'

'Run?' What a terrible idea this had been, but she couldn't change her mind after he'd waited for her. 'Just give me a–'

He grabbed her free hand, the one that wasn't trying to calm her lungs, and said, 'C'mon, old girl, it's good for ya,' and Jen found herself trotting again, over the road, around a corner and towards a couple that Lionel was shouting, 'Oi!

Francis!' to.

'No need to hurry,' said Lionel's brother, when they reached him. 'It's gridlock down at Embankment.'

'I got a text from my friend,' said the woman by his side. 'She's been there an hour and not moved.'

The man, a better dressed Lionel, introduced himself as Francis. 'And this is Anna.' Anna was very pretty, very blonde and very young. She looked like someone who could run and run and still have her breath.

Lionel introduced Jen as 'one of my clients', which felt a bit odd, but of course she was. 'Nice to meet you,' she managed to say, hand on her chest again. She'd join a gym. On Monday.

'What do you reckon, then?' asked Lionel. 'What's the plan?'

Give up and go home, Jen wanted to hear, but they'd made a banner, so she wasn't hopeful.

'Shall we join the jam?' said Anna, and that was what they did.

It took for ever to reach Piccadilly Circus, where the two arms of the march merged before heading to Hyde Park. The atmosphere was good, even if the cold grey weather wasn't.

Jen had forgotten how surprisingly quiet these protests were. There was an occasional, 'What a turnout,' from Lionel, or the four of them would join in with some local chant, but the act of walking along, peacefully, in huge numbers, said it all; spoke volumes in fact, about the proposed aggression. The whole thing moved Jen, once or twice, to tears. She was taking part in something big, something that might even change minds, change policy. How lucky, not to have gone shopping and missed out.

The downside of feeling so emotional, was, well, feeling so emotional. Her thoughts kept straying away from war and towards her husband. Robert hadn't come on marches with her back then, when she thought they'd be obliterated by cruise missiles. 'It's all about deterrence,' he'd said. 'They won't nuke us because we'd nuke them back.' He was from a stockbroker-belt background and voted for Thatcher, so his views on things military had come as no surprise.

Robert, however, had never been a black-and-white person. Jen learned early on that he could usually be talked round: paint colour, holidays, restaurants, the newspaper they'd have delivered. She'd thought it would be as easy to sway him politically, but that had taken another twelve, fourteen years, and credit really had to go to New Labour. Robert could still kick off about his higher-rate income tax, but he'd mellowed on so much else and was fervently opposed to invading Iraq; ranting, in that quiet way of his, about Blair following an idiot into war. He'd be here, she knew he would.

Past Piccadilly, en route for Hyde Park, Lionel hooked an arm through hers and said, 'You awight, Jen?' She liked her builder/project manager a lot today, as he showed another, more subdued side to him. 'What a turnout, eh?'

'Mm,' she said, enjoying the contact with an adult human, a man. If he'd been ten years older,

101

thinner, taller, and hadn't worn white shoes, who knew what might have happened?

In recent years, Robert had been developing a bald patch on his crown, in the midst of his still sandy, still relatively thick head of hair. What Jen hadn't realised was just how common that combination was for guys in their thirties and forties, before the real baldness or real grey, or both, took over. By the time they approached the park and rally, Jen must have spotted ten men, who on first glance, from behind, could have been her husband. Each time she'd felt a jolt, before realising again, and thank God, that it wasn't him. This was unsettling, and a distraction from the day's purpose, but perhaps a good thing to go through. If she spotted lots of Robert look-alikes today, then she might become used to bald patches on sandy-haired men.

'Anna needs the loo,' Francis was saying. 'We might nip up to M&S on Oxford Street. How about you, Bruv? Jen?'

'I'm OK,' Lionel told him.

'Me too,' said Jen, although surely there'd be loos in the park.

'Catch you later, then. We'll text, OK?'

'Tea and cake and a sit-down,' Lionel muttered, once his brother had been swallowed up by the crowd. 'That's what they've gone for.'

'Really?'

'Heard Anna say.'

It was a plan with some appeal to Jen. She'd had nothing since breakfast and one toe was sore. But they were almost there; it would be silly not to catch a speaker or two.

The crowd was having to narrow for the park gates and they'd come to a bit of a standstill. Lionel, however, continued to walk on the spot, his excitement mounting. 'Come on, come on,' he kept saying. 'Gotta catch Tony Benn.'

Once they were finally through, walking on increasingly muddy grass, Jen began missing the huddle of the march. There were still hordes of people, but they'd thinned out and she was much more exposed, as was everyone. If she was going to catch sight of her husband, it would be here, in the park.

Lionel speeded up, and so did Jen, eyes blinkered and focused on the distant stage. He's here, I know he is, she thought. With Jon. Please don't let me see them. If only Francis and Anna hadn't buggered off, she could have made her excuses at this point. Gone for tea and cake. Gone home.

'Come to think of it,' said Lionel, slowing down, 'I might need a pee.'

'Me too,' she said. Somewhere to hide for a while.

'Now where are the–'

'There.' She pointed to a row of Portaloos and they veered left to the usual story: a long snake of women queuing for theirs, but no queue for the men's.

'I'll wait by that tree,' he said. 'Try and be sharpish?'

Jen joined the snake. Taking three steps every three minutes, she allowed herself furtive glances at the people passing by and those beyond.

Again, there were one or two bald patches in sandy-coloured heads. Three steps forward. She saw Lionel already waiting by the tree, checking out his mobile. When he looked up, she pulled a face and shrugged. Who knew why women took so long?

When Jen reached third in line, she was actually quite desperate to go. God, this was ridiculous. The men were still dashing in and out with absolutely no wait. She watched each one ... not Robert, not Robert ... turned and grimaced at Lionel again, and moved into second place.

It was then that she saw him. Kit Avery. Leaving the gents' loos, hands in the pockets of his jeans. Same long blond hair, same face, same skinniness ... same age. Seventeen, eighteen ... Kit? She was clearly hallucinating. So long since she'd eaten.

A woman left the ladies, the person in front of Jen went in. She moved forward but didn't take her eyes off the boy. She hadn't thought about Kit for years, but suddenly she was fifteen again ... it was hot, they were in their hut... He went up to a man, not that far from Lionel. An older man, who wore a woolly hat and a scarf that covered his chin. There was something about the straight back. He handed the boy a rucksack, and the boy, young man, bent down and opened it. He took out a package that could have been their lunch. The older man watched the boy, Jen watched the older man, then someone tapped her shoulder.

'Your turn.'

'Oh, sorry ... it's just that...' Jen kept staring at

the man, trying to get a better look at his face.

'Look, do you want to go or what?'

'Yes,' she said, because she really did. She'd be quick. They'd still be there; they were about to eat their sandwiches. She hurried in and was very quick. Quick as a man. But when she came out she couldn't see the young Kit or the other guy. Only Lionel, waving her over in a rather angry fashion.

She ran to him. 'Lionel, did you see two men? Just over there. One wore a woolly hat, the other was young. About seventeen, eighteen... They had a smallish rucksack...' While she spoke her eyes raced over the dozens and dozens of people trudging past, many in woolly hats, lots with rucksacks. 'They stopped for a while near that bench. There. The older one wore a scarf, sort of brownish, maybe grey. He...'

Lionel frowned at the bench, now seating four adults in browns and greys, then at Jen. 'You 'avin a laugh?'

'No. No, I'm not.' Don't cry, she willed herself. She turned three hundred and sixty degrees, twice. The older man had been Kit, she was so sure of that now. Or was she...? 'I should eat something,' she said. 'There must be a stall.'

Her builder looked more frustrated than pissed off. 'Let's find you some grub, then. Before you start seeing Elvis.'

'Sorry, Lionel.'

'Skates on,' he said, plodding off, while Jen did one last circle.

# FIFTEEN

Jen's matches with Mrs Avery began leaving a bad taste in her mouth. It was a bit creepy, the way they never talked, not properly, not even in the Malcolm Club, where it went without saying they'd go, even though Jen would rather not.

Often, she'd consider letting Mrs Avery beat her, just to see what happened. Kit had said his mother loved a challenge, and if she won the fun might go out of it. That was Jen's thinking too. But then, once out on the court, facing the woman who didn't want her in her house, Jen couldn't help but blast away, shot after shot, as though trying to prove she was good enough for Kit, while Mrs Avery tried to prove she wasn't.

Was this going to go on all summer? Every Tuesday and Thursday. No conversation except the score, or 'Out!' or, 'Just in, wasn't it?' Jen's game was improving, so that was a plus, and she *was* getting a tan, which she hoped Kit's mum had noticed. But neither of these made up for the misery she felt each Tuesday and Thursday, waiting for four thirty to come. And why always four thirty? Because, Jen suspected, by the time their match had ended, the men on camp would be leaving work.

For someone who disapproved of sergeants' daughters, Mrs Avery took quite an interest in corporals; one in particular called Mick, who was twenty-seven, single, came from Derbyshire and drank black coffee. Jen knew all this because Mick, who'd formerly lurked by the jukebox, had twice joined them at their table.

He was dark and sort of good-looking, although Jen couldn't see the appeal of men with such short hair, like something out the fifties. She loved Kit's long curly mop, running her fingers through it when they kissed, and even when they didn't. So, although Mick had a nice face and was tallish and quite muscular, he did nothing for her. Which was lucky, since he paid her no attention.

Following their sixth match, on a scorcher of a day, Mick happened to stroll into the Malcolm Club again, and after buying his black coffee, was beckoned over by Mrs Avery.

'Poor me,' she said, while he sat down, took his beret off and rolled up his shirtsleeves. 'Jennifer thrashed me *again.*'

'Did she now?' said Mick, whose voice was a bit nasally and not to Jen's liking.

He'd been the one to approach them, the previous Tuesday, asking if the spare chair at their table was free, and would they mind if he joined them while he waited for his mate. A mate that never materialised, not in the fifty minutes Jen felt compelled to sit there, watching Eleanor Avery flirting, never being talked to. It had been the same story on Thursday, only shorter, because Mrs Avery had been going to a ladies' guest night at the Mess. It didn't seem to bother Mick that she was who she was.

Today, he was sweating and had a five o'clock

shadow. A short lock of either greasy or Bryl-creemed hair stuck to his forehead, and he gave off a very manly aroma. Her mum would have called him swarthy, one of her favourite words. He was a complete contrast to the immaculate and perspiration-free officer's wife. Unlike Jen, who didn't respond well to heat, Kit's mother looked as good at the end of a match as she had at the start.

Mrs Avery propped her chin on one hand. 'But I'll win one day. I *know* I will.'

'I'm sure you're a very determined girl,' said Mick, and Mrs Avery agreed she was.

She sucked lemonade through a straw, her eyes on his. Then she sat back and stirred her drink. 'I usually get what I set out for,' she said. 'Sooner or later.' She gave a slight start and turned to Jen. 'Don't let me keep you, Jennifer. I'm sure you have masses to do. I'll see you Thursday.'

It felt like an order and Jen's inclination was to say, 'Actually, I'm busy on Thursday.' But Mrs Avery had already considered Jen gone; her back half turned on her, as she wiggled her empty glass in Mick's face. 'Something with a bit of a kick?' Jen heard her order, as she gathered her things and left.

That evening they went to the Astra, where *Bullitt* was showing. Kit was keen to see the car chase everyone was talking about, and Jen was keen to see Steve McQueen, only she'd never have told him that. She didn't want him thinking she was just a girl, so as they queued, she said she couldn't wait to see the car chase too. Also, if she started telling him which actors she had a crush on, he might do the same. Maybe he had a thing for Jacqueline Bisset, Steve's co-star, who'd looked annoyingly pretty in photos. Jen had learned from the dirty magazine encounter, and the way he mucked around with Susie, that she could be eaten up with jealousy when it came to Kit.

The film was popular, but they managed to get seats, although not at the very back where Jen had pictured them. Their first evening at the pictures, and here they were three rows from the front, with all the kids who'd lied about their age and a handful of late-arriving airmen, the first of which looked more and more familiar as he made his way past everyone's knees towards Jen.

When she and Kit half-stood to let him by, Mick the corporal said, 'Ta,' to Jen, then, 'Oh, it's you. Hello, Jennifer.'

'Hello,' she said, amazed he knew her name.

'Packed, eh?'

'Yes, very.'

'See you around,' he said, moving on.

'Probably.'

Mick's friends followed and they filled the seats at the far end of the row. 'And who, may I ask, was that?' asked Kit, his arm working its way around her.

'He's called Mick.'

'Not a rival, I hope?'

'God, no.' Only for his mother's affections.

'Good.' He smiled and squeezed her shoulder and kissed her cheek, then worked his way, very slowly, to her lips.

While Jen was melting, Kit's tongue touching

hers, someone shouted, 'Give her a shag!' behind them. 'Go on, we'll all watch!'

When the laughter died down and Kit's arm was back by his side, Jen resigned herself to two hours of guns and car chases. And Steve, of course. But she spent most of the film wondering why Mick the corporal, despite having changed into civvies, smelled of Mrs Avery's perfume.

'Man, I *really* want to go to San Francisco,' Kit said, when they came out.

'Yeah?'

'I have a feeling it's my spiritual home. Either there or Kathmandu.'

'San Francisco looked nice in the film,' said Jen. She wasn't sure where Kathmandu was.

'It's where it's happening, Jen. We should go, when I leave school next year. You'll be almost seventeen. How about it?'

Jen was thrilled to hear Kit plan that far ahead. 'OK,' she said, laughing. 'I'll wear flowers in my hair, shall I?'

Kit squeezed her waist with his lovely strong arm. 'It's compulsory to take drugs there, you know, Jennifer Juniper.' He'd started calling her that after the Donovan song, and she quite liked it. More than Jennifer Boyde, anyway. 'In fact, they won't let you in till you've shown them your stash.'

'Don't be daft.'

'It's true. And then there's the compulsory free love.' Kit's fingers stroked her side, then moved, gradually, upwards and upwards, over her ribs, until she stopped them with her own hand. 'If

110

you don't make love in public every day, they fine you.'

Now he was being really silly, and Jen was pleased to see Susie and Lawrence approach.

'Terrific film,' Susie said. '*Loved* the chase.'

'Superb,' said Lawrence. He turned an imaginary steering wheel and made screeching noises. 'Susie and I thought we'd go play with my bro's Scalextric. Like to join us, you two?'

Kit said, 'Sure.' When he took his arm from her waist and copied Lawrence, Jen checked no one she knew was watching. 'We don't have any plans, do we, Jen?'

The thought of Scalextric made her want to cry. She was hopeless at that kind of thing, and couldn't see the point. After two hours of sheer boredom in the cinema, all she wanted was to go to the hut and kiss. 'I should get home,' she told them, suddenly upset.

Jen found herself walking off. Would Kit follow her, or choose Susie and Scalextric? She lifted a hand in a wave and told them to have fun, then took more steps backwards, while Kit looked at her, then at Lawrence. Jen could tell he was torn. If he followed her, she'd know he loved her and meant all that about San Francisco. 'Bye!' she called out, before turning round and carrying on at the same pace – not too fast, so that he could easily catch up – her eyes fixed on the people in front, her fingers crossed.

Reaching the corner by the Malcolm Club, where the T-junction took you one way to the airmen's patch, the other way to the officers', Jen felt terrible. Disappointed in Kit, angry with herself. He could have asked her first before saying yes to Scalextric. On the other hand, it wouldn't have hurt her to go along to Lawrence's. They didn't have to go to the hut *every* evening.

Jen turned left and held back tears. Why was it they always did what Kit suggested? Because he was two years older? Well, a year and a half. Because his father was a wing commander? Because he was a boy, and everyone knew men ruled the world? She wondered if she was being unfair on Kit, because, thinking about it, she never really suggested doing things. Worried, perhaps, that he wouldn't enjoy anything she came up with. It had been the same with Dean, she remembered. They'd listened to his Beatles records and she'd watched him go-karting.

As she approached her house, Jen had a horrible sinking feeling. She was going to be just like her mum – always agreeing, never criticising. In other words, a doormat. She didn't just have the sinking feeling, she also had pains, low down. Her period was coming, she realised, and it was then that she let the tears fall. Lots of them. She should have said, 'Walk home with me, Kit, before you go to Lawrence's?' That was how someone confident like Susie would have dealt with it. Not just gone off, rudely, childishly.

Jen let herself into the house and heard her stupid dad laughing at the stupid telly. One thing was for sure. It wouldn't be a programme her mum had chosen.

# SIXTEEN

While Lionel was whooping at Bianca Jagger, Jen had her back to the stage, scanning the hundreds and hundreds of faces for the man she'd convinced herself was Kit. All she'd seen were the eyes, nose and top lip, but the more she went over that image, the more familiar it felt. She was taking the risk of spotting Robert, or he spotting her, but the need to see that face again, double-check it, had overridden everything.

'Going to the loo,' she told Lionel, having established the Kit man wasn't near the stage. Perhaps he and his son, if that was who he was, were still having their late packed lunch, on a bench, by a tree. Or – please God, no – were making their way to a coach that would take them to Penzance or Durham.

'Again?' asked Lionel.

'It's the cold weather. Back soon.' She didn't need the loo, she just needed Kit. She pictured finding him, hugging him, and then maybe just leaning on him. With Kit to stand by, lean on, Robert could walk past holding his boyfriend's hand and she'd feel fine, she knew she would.

Weaving her way through and around people, pushchairs, discarded placards, she scoured the faces. No ... no ... no. Round and round and back and forth, she went, on edge, because she might see Robert, frustrated when she couldn't see

113

young or old Kit. They *had* to be here. Why come to the park, if you weren't intending to listen to the speakers?

After twenty minutes or so, Jen looked back at the stage and had an idea. Could one of the organisers make an announcement for her? An appeal for Kit... No, of course not. What a dreadful idea, on such a serious day. It wasn't as though he were a lost child. *Would Kit Avery make his way to Speaker's Corner, where an old girlfriend wants to check out it's you.* But what if she made up some story? That she had Kit's vital medication on her, or the other way round...

A long-fair-haired teenager crossed her path and Jen gasped before seeing it wasn't the same boy; that it was, in fact, a girl. Stupid. The light was fading, her foot hurt. She should give up.

Her phone vibrated and, seeing it was Lionel, she answered, apologised and told him she was fine, and no she wasn't lost. They arranged where to meet and hung up, then Jen checked an unread text she hadn't heard come through. It was from Robert, sent at 14.57. 'I have a feeling you're here. Been looking out for you. Amazing isn't it? Please please call me back. Rx'.

They had a coffee and wrap each, then Lionel went and got another wrap and a muffin. As she sat in the warmth on a window stool, staring out into the darkness that had come down quickly and ended her search, Jen tried not to berate herself. Then she decided she'd been wrong; it hadn't been him and his son. Lots of fair-haired boys of seventeen looked like Kit at that age. This

114

one had stood out because long hair wasn't that fashionable now. He'd caught her attention, thrown her back to her youth and set her imagination going. In the wrong direction, most probably. But now she'd never know.

And she'd never know what might have happened if she'd found Robert's text earlier, called him back. They might have met, gone for a drink, made up in some way, or at least come to terms with their situation. Was she making things worse for herself by ignoring him?

'Whassa matter, Jen?' Lionel asked, wiping his face with a napkin.

'Well...'

His eyes were warm and focused on hers. 'Only you seem a bit fragile, if you don't mind me saying?'

'Not at all. It's just a bit ... you know, private.'

'Course.'

She looked again into the kind eyes of her project manager; the last person she should open up to, since he also worked for Robert's clients. Something told her he'd be discreet, but she had no idea, really. But then would it matter? Sarah already knew, therefore most of Highgate did.

'You've probably guessed,' Jen said, 'that I've left my husband.'

'Duh, yeah.'

'I found out he was having an affair.'

'Robert?' Lionel shook his head. 'Whassa matter with these middle-aged geezers? That secretary, was it?'

'A man, actually. Someone I don't know ... well, I don't think I do.'

'I see.' Lionel shifted on his stool, and looked over his shoulder. 'Well, you hear of that happening.'

'Yes.'

'Never woulda believed it of him, though. Mind you...'

'What?'

'Nothin'.'

'What were you going to say?'

Lionel pulled a face, perhaps wishing he hadn't started. 'Only that he's always what you might call dapper, know what I mean?'

'Yes.' Robert took great care with his appearance – more so than Jen – saying it was vital in his much-maligned, shiny-suited business.

'Musta been shattering?'

'You could say. If I appeared on edge today, it was because I was pretty sure my husband would be here. I haven't seen him, you see, not since...'

'Right, well, that explains why you kept grabbing me arm. In the park, like. Not that I minded. Poor old you, Jen. What a thing to go through. You think you know someone like the back of your–'

'Yes,' she said sharply. Too much sympathy and she'd cry, and anyway, she wanted to tell him about Kit. 'So, I was sort of watching out for Robert, and possibly Jon.'

'Is that his...?'

'Yes. Maybe. I don't know. The thing is, I didn't see Robert, but I did see, or thought I saw, my very first boyfriend. Proper boyfriend, that is, when I was fifteen. With what could have been his son, who was the image of him at that age.'

116

'The blokes by the bench with the rucksack?'

'Mm. I was so stupid. If only I hadn't gone to the loo.'

'How sure was you? That it was him.'

'Well, he was wearing a woolly hat and a scarf, so I couldn't really–'

'Percentage wise.'

'I don't know...' Trust a man to want to quantify something like this. 'Fifty?'

'I see.' Lionel nodded wisely, as though her random figure had helped. 'Have you tried an internet search for him? I mean, before today.'

'No, why would I? I was happily married, or so I thought.'

'Yeah, you're right. Looking up first loves ain't always a good idea. My mate did that, ended up leaving his beautiful curvaceous missus for this skinny ugly woman he'd gone out with when he was fourteen. Said he still saw the schoolgirl in her. People, eh?'

'Yes.'

'Whassis name, your old boyfriend?'

'Kit Avery. Well, Christopher Avery, but everyone called him Kit back then.'

'Unusual, that's good. If he's still Kit, and he's like done summink. Made a bit of a name for himself... Is that likely?'

'Oh, yes.'

'Then he'll probably come up in an internet search. Your computer working all right?'

'Fine, yes.'

'Come on, then.' Lionel slid off his stool and wound a long scarf round his neck. 'I'll give you a hand.'

Jen felt sure she didn't need help with the internet, but the alternative was returning alone to a cushionless, rugless home and beating herself up some more.

It was all over the news, which Lionel switched on the minute they walked in.

'Brilliant,' he kept saying at the shots of the crowds, aerial and otherwise. 'If that don't get the message across to Blair, I don't know what will. No way can he go ahead now.'

Jen was glued to the images too, an old photo of Kit on her lap, hoping to catch sight of his lookalike. She'd rather not see Robert, who she guessed from his text had been alone, or at least not partnered. Perhaps he really had finished with Jon, not that it mattered. Concentrate on Kit, she told herself. Look for hat, scarf, rucksack, son...

The sheer numbers were incredible, the atmosphere fantastic. Reporters talked to a couple from the Shetlands, and to a policeman who was sympathetic to the rally, without actually saying so. When one channel left the scene for ads, or the day's other items, Lionel flicked to a different rolling-news station.

Jen was happy to watch wall-to-wall demo news, inching her chair closer to the flat screen and digibox Lionel had set her up with, her eyes darting hopefully. But then, one by one, the channels began looping. There again were the couple from Shetland, the chirpy policeman...

'Wanna do that internet search?' Lionel eventually asked, but it was past ten and Jen was knackered, and, anyway, would rather do it alone.

'I think I need my bed,' she told him. 'I'll check it out tomorrow. But thanks.'

'Well, if you're sure.' He called for a taxi to take him all the way to Wembley, and she felt bad that she couldn't put him up somehow. She had the sofa, but no spare duvet. On the other hand, a whole afternoon and evening with Lionel, as wonderful as he'd been, felt like more than enough. Sadly, or luckily, she was getting used to her own company.

## SEVENTEEN

The only way she could get a message to Mrs Avery about the next day's match was via Kit. Unlike in the UK, no one had phones. Not that she'd have had the courage to ring Kit's house.

Dear Mrs Avery, she wrote on a page of her exercise book, because Paul had filled the writing pad with drawings of the moon landing. 'I've sprained my ankle and won't be able to play tennis this week. The doctor said I had to rest it. I'm really sorry. Yours faithfully, Jennifer Boyde.'

She carefully tore the sheet out, neatened its ragged edge with scissors, folded it and put it in a small white envelope. On the front she wrote 'To' and 'Mrs Avery', then she got ready to go and meet Kit on the corner by the Astra. Obviously, it was a lie – her ankle was fine – but the prospect of another silent match, and more cake and lemonade and Mick in the Malcolm Club, was making her ill in another way.

Jen put on the short silky skirt Kit liked, and a sleeveless white T-shirt that showed off her new tan. She felt bad about involving Kit in her lie, but couldn't think of an alternative. And, besides, he was lying to his mother all the time by seeing her. Mascara? Kit had said he liked natural-looking girls, so Jen gave her lashes only a quick flick, top and bottom, then ran some Nivea over her lips. She brushed her hair and packed a few things, including the note, into the cloth shoulder bag she'd made out of an old floral skirt.

As usual, she had butterflies. It was the prospect of seeing Kit, combined with a fear that he might not turn up. So far he'd been totally reliable, but maybe one day he'd crumble under his mother's pressure, or decide she really wasn't for him. After the way she'd behaved after *Bullitt*, she could hardly blame him, but they'd met on the usual corner at the usual time the evening after, like nothing had happened. Kit told her how brilliant Susie was at Scalextric, which made Jen doubly pleased she hadn't gone along. He seemed so laid-back, but according to the letters in her mum's magazine, you never really knew with men. Always having affairs with their secretaries or your best friend. If Kit suddenly saw how beautiful Sonia Durrell was, that could be it. Then where would she be? Heartbroken, and with no friends to turn to. It didn't bear thinking about.

Neither did September, when he'd go back to school. Kit would write to her, though. Letters full of words she'd have to look up. And before she knew it, he'd be back for Christmas. But it wouldn't be the same, and what if he found someone else? He'd talked about the girls' school near his... No, she couldn't think about any of that, not with a lovely romantic evening ahead of her. If he turned up.

Downstairs, the remains of egg and chips hung in the warm evening air. Plates, cups and sauce bottles waited on the coffee table for subtitled *Coronation Street* to finish. Everything was shrouded in cigarette smoke because nobody was allowed to open a window. Her dad couldn't stand the dog next door, barking and barking at the children he didn't like much either.

It was Paul's turn to help wash up, so Jen didn't feel bad about leaving the mess. 'I'm off out now,' she said, just as the front door knocker banged twice. 'I'll go!' said Paul, jumping off the settee.

Jen checked herself once more in the lounge mirror and suddenly wasn't sure about the no-makeup idea. Having a tan meant loads more freckles, which showed up more here than they had upstairs. Kit had probably not meant *that* natural. Better cover them, she thought.

While Jen felt around for her tube of Rimmel, her dad shouted, 'Who is it?' to Paul. She took the cap off and squeezed some onto a finger. Kit wouldn't mind a bit of foundation, in the circumstances.

Her brother came in and flopped on the settee. 'It's Jen's boyfriend.'

'What!' she said, her insides freezing, her fingers

frantically rubbing Rose Ivory over cheeks, forehead, chin.

Her mother jumped up and grabbed the stack of plates. 'Quick, Paul, the sauce bottles. Jim, put your shirt on.'

'Don't tell me what to do, woman.'

Jen rubbed a bit more, then flew out to the front door. 'How did you–'

'Asked Daddy to find your address.' Kit shrugged and smiled. He looked gorgeous in the collarless stripy shirt he'd bought in Roermond, and the tight brushed-velvet trousers she loved the feel of. He was barefoot, as he often was. Jen had sensitive feet and didn't know how he could do that. 'Sorry. Thought I'd surprise you.'

'You must be Kit,' Jen's mother was saying breathlessly.

'How do you do?' Kit said, extending an arm around Jen.

Her mum took her pinny off with one hand and shook Kit's hand with the other. 'Ever so pleased to meet you. Won't you come in?'

'No!' said Jen. 'We're in a bit of a hurry. Aren't we, Kit?'

'That's very kind,' he said, stepping in and surveying the hallway – one air-force table, one glass vase with plastic flowers, one painting. 'What a charming picture.'

'Oh, it's one of Jen's.'

'Really?'

'Painting by numbers, but you'd never know.'

Jen had pleaded with her mum not to put it up again when they moved in. 'I did it when I was ten,' she told him.

'I'd have sworn it was a Constable,' Kit said, and Jen laughed, even though this was the most embarrassing situation of her life so far, and would most likely get worse.

'Come on through, Kit,' said her mum. 'I'll put the kettle on. Or perhaps you'd like a sherry?'

'Thanks, Mrs Boyde. A sherry would be groovy.'

'Sweet or medium dry?'

'Sweet, please. Like your daughter.'

'Oh, I say...' Her mother opened the door on to a smoggy, stuffy lounge. 'Make yourself comfortable, Kit, and I'll fetch the Harvey's Bristol Cream.' She liked to call things by their full name: Robertson's jam, Colman's mustard.

'My favourite,' he said.

'This is Kit,' Jen told her shirtless father.

From his armchair he nodded, looked down at Kit's feet and said, 'Oi!' to Paul. 'Off the couch.'

Paul got up and stomped out the room, while Jen and Kit sat down, side by side, arms touching, in order to leave space for her mum. There used to be another chair, but it got sent back when her father bought a second-hand coffin-sized hi-fi cabinet, so her parents could listen to their terrible fifties stuff. After a while, even they couldn't take more Mario Lanza, and now only Jen used it.

Her father held out his cigarettes. 'Smoke?'

'Thanks,' Kit said, easing an untipped Park Drive from the packet. He did smoke occasionally, although more pot than ciggies, he'd told her.

Kit lit his cigarette, gave the lighter back and said, 'Jen tells me you're a Rangers supporter.'

123

And then they were off. Jen had no idea Kit was so up on the subject; that he could name Rangers' and other teams' players; could quote scores. All she'd known was that he supported Spurs, guessing all boys had to have a football team, even if they were at posh schools.

'Of course, you've got an unfair advantage,' her dad was saying, 'what with having Greaves on your team. Pure genius, that one. But what a cruel blow the World Cup was for him, eh?' It was more than he'd said to Jen in a week.

Kit shook his head. 'The leg injury. Catastrophe.'

'Mind you, he was replaced by Hurst, who, as we know—'

'Scored a hat trick!' Kit punched the air, which looked as though it could be punched.

Aye, what a star. Not that I wanted England to win, ye understand?' He winked at Kit and said, 'Now, can I get yous a beer, son?'

'Actually, I think...'

'Mum's pouring him a sherry,' Jen explained, just as her mother appeared with one of her large sherry glasses, full to the gold brim.

Her father put his cigarette out and got up. 'The boy does nay want a nancy drink like that, even if he is a cricketer. Here, son, gi'it to me.' Jen wished someone would turn the telly off, but now it was Tommy Cooper, her dad's favourite.

'No, honestly, Mr Boyde. Sherry's fine.' Kit tried some. 'Delicious, in fact. Thank you, Mrs Boyde.'

'Well, I'll fetch ye a beer, anyway. Knock that rubbish back quick.'

'Cricketer?' Kit whispered when her father had gone and her mum was looking over her shoulder as she quietly opened a window.

'Tell you later.'

'Silly me,' said her mum, covering her crime with the curtain. 'I almost forgot the drinks mats!' She went to the sideboard for the box of 'British Seaside', then came and gave Kit Blackpool Tower.

'Far out,' he said.

Her dad appeared with two bottles and Jen sank into the settee – pleased, scared, she wasn't sure. She folded her arms and sighed. So much for their evening out, if you could call three hours in the hut an evening out. On the positive side, this wasn't half as bad as she'd imagined.

He'd got the best wife in England, Tommy Cooper was telling them. His other one was in Africa. Jen's father roared a chesty laugh. 'Eh, the old ones are the best.' He handed Kit a bottle of lager. 'Get that down ye neck, son.'

When they finally set off for their hut, Kit, with one large sherry and five lagers in him, was staggering. 'You're the real thing, Jen. I love that, and I love you, you know, old bean. The *reeeal* thing.'

'Uh-huh?' She was trying to keep them on the pavement but he was heavier than he looked.

'Not like those privileged Fionas and Annabels at Hopthorpe School, with their capitalist arms-trading daddies, and their stupid skiing, and their total sallowness.'

'Sallowness?'

'Shallowness, Jen, shallowness. Ask any of them to point to Vietnam on a map...' He started singing a Jefferson Airplane song; one she'd heard loads of times. It was from his favourite film, about the Monterey Festival. He had a nice voice, like his mum.

Oh God, his mother. Jen started worrying about her note and entrusting it to Kit. Maybe she could sneak out and deliver it in the middle of the night. But if she got caught by their front door, his mum would think she was just leaving or, worse, calling on him at that time. *And* she'd have to limp. No, her only route was to help Kit sober up with the flzzy drinks they kept in the hut, then ask him to leave her note on their doormat in the morning.

Kit stopped singing, swayed, turned and kissed her sloppily for a while, then carried on. 'Your pa's a gas, isn't he? What was the record he played us?'

'Mario Lanza.'

'That's where it's at, man. Like *really* where it's at.'

'This way,' she said, their hut now in sight.

Having drunk a bottle of Orangina, Kit lay back, stopped talking and within seconds was asleep.

Propped on one arm, Jen examined a Kit she'd never seen before. Still, quiet; eyelids instead of those deep blue eyes; mouth closed and slightly turned down. How different he looked; so serious and serene. His breathing was deep and long. She watched his chest rise and fall under the thin striped cotton, longing for him to wake up and wrap his arms around her and kiss her until she was giddy from it.

But she'd let him sleep as long as he needed. Sleep off the alcohol her father had more or less forced on him. What had that been about? Some sort of test, perhaps, of Kit's masculinity, or his ability to mix with hoi polloi. Or else her dad had just grabbed the opportunity of a drinking partner. The two of them had covered not just football, but rugby, the space race and, to Jen's horror when they first started talking about it, politics. She thought they'd come to blows, but her dad was surprisingly with Kit on most things.

'Aye,' he'd said, at one point. 'Ask any Scot what they'd like to do to the English upper classes and ye'd have to cover your ears, laddie.'

Jen lay back on the blanket, her head on a pillow Kit had brought from his house. How lucky she was, but at the same time, how unlucky. She'd only have him for a few more weeks, if he didn't chuck her before then, of course, which was more of a possibility now he'd met her family. By the eighth of September he'd be gone, then winter would come and there'd be nothing to do but school and the youth club, and writing letters to Kit in her bedroom, wondering if he was with Fiona or Annabel.

She went over their strange evening. Her dad being unusually talkative, her mum saying, 'Carr's water biscuit with Dairylea spread, Kit?' Her brother re-emerging and asking Kit to mend his Airfix model. Kit had been sloshed by then and put the wing on upside down, which everyone except Paul found funny.

Jen closed her eyes and said a little thank you to whoever was up there looking after her. And please, she tacked on, don't let Kit go out with anyone from Hopthorpe School. It wasn't as though he liked them; calling them shallow... Kit's breathing was hypnotic ... in ... out ... in ... and she began matching her breaths to his ... out ... in...

Then slowly, bit by bit, starting with America and moving eastwards, she conjured up a map of the world ... the Atlantic, Europe ... then Russia, India ... down to Australia and up again to China... She knew roughly where Japan was – an island? – but, as hard as she tried ... out ... she couldn't see Vietnam ... in ... encyclopaedia, she thought ... out...

## EIGHTEEN

'kit avery' Jen typed with one finger. She yawned, drank some coffee and there he was. His name, anyway – Kit Avery, highlighted in bold in a page full of entries. 'My God,' she said, leaning towards the screen.

She clicked on the first – kitavery.com – and up came his website. Kit Avery's website. With a photograph of him. And it really was him.. Her Kit. Older, not so much hair – darker, receding hair – but more or less the same. Like a glamorous Hollywood character, who'd been made to age but in a nice distinguished way ... just a few more lines, a few streaks of grey, a little more jowl. The guy she'd seen in Hyde Park? Possibly.

His mouth wasn't quite smiling but his eyes were. Laughter lines fanned out. He looked happy and confident, just as he had when they were going out; for those first idyllic weeks, anyway. He was wearing what looked like a suit jacket, in darkish grey, over a black T-shirt. An urban look, she thought, and good for his colouring. 'Kit Avery Journalist, Author, Political Activist, Human Rights Campaigner.' Yes, of course that's what he'd be.

She wanted to click on 'Biog' but just couldn't bring herself to.

Not yet.

Jen got up from the table and went to the kitchen, dizzy with shock. She really hadn't prepared herself for this. What a thing to do ... just nonchalantly, half awake, start up the laptop and type his name in. She slowly made herself another coffee. Slowly, because she was nervous of reading more. *Kit Avery has been happily married to childhood sweetheart, Susie, for...*

No. Kit and Susie had never had a thing, as far as she knew. But he was bound to be married or partnered, looking the way he did. Successful, concerned about human rights. A handsome, caring, heterosexual man in his late forties would not be single. Or fifty? She did the sums. Fifty last year. He didn't look it, but the photo could have been old. What Jen couldn't understand was why his marital status mattered to her. Was she really feeling so hurt and insecure that she was clinging to the frankly laughable idea that she might get back together with her first love? Someone she hadn't thought about for years, until yesterday?

Yes, she decided, returning to her study, which would also be a bedroom once it had a bed. She probably was.

It didn't surprise her that he'd gone to Oxford and read Philosophy, Politics and Economics. It did surprise her that he'd then done Law, been called to the Bar and practised as a barrister in a London chambers. She imagined the blond wig on top of his blond hair. But he'd given that up to work for an organisation in Africa ... until 1992. She started to speed read, wanting to reach the personal stuff. Last paragraph: '...Kit Avery has been living and working in London for the past decade ... author of three books ... contributes to ... regular column in...'

No mention of family. But perhaps you wouldn't, not if you were involved in controversial human rights' cases, tricky corrupt-government issues... Funny to think he'd been in London all this time, although not surprising.

Jen went back to his home page and the headings: 'Biog', 'Articles', 'Books', 'Reviews', 'Contact'. 'Contact,' she whispered, clicking on it, her heart speeding up. 'If you'd like to email Kit...'

When her mobile rang in the other room, Jen shot up, relieved, almost, to get away from the computer. She'd discovered too much, too fast, and it wasn't even nine yet. Sunday morning, not yet nine ... it must be her mother. She picked the phone up off her naked sofa. Cushions, she thought again. 'Hello?'

'Oh, *Jen*, Paul's told us. About Robert.'

'Well, he wasn't supposed–'

'Your dad's in a right state. You know how he feels about that sort of thing, and there's the anniversary party in July. What are we going to tell people, he keeps saying. Talking about calling it off. He's gone out for his paper, so I thought I'd give you a quick ring. We definitely think you've done the right thing. How are you, love?'

'I'm–'

'Never in a million years would we have thought Robert was– Oh, he's back. Must have forgotten something. Phone you later, once your dad's decided what– Just a wrong number, Jim! Bye.'

Well, that might have been worse. She could have a mother who thought she should stick by her man. Jen had never understood those devastated women by their philandering MP husbands' sides. Still, she didn't want her parents cancelling their anniversary do, not when it was all her mum had talked about for months, as she would until July. Only her mother could spend so long planning a party for thirty.

What was Paul thinking? She was about to call her brother and blast him, but the mobile rang in her hand, and his name came up. 'Hello,' she said, opening the blinds and checking the weather. Just like yesterday's.

'Hi, Jen. Listen, I–'

'I know. Mum rang.'

'Damn, wanted to warn you. I'm *really* sorry. She was just relentless with her questions earlier.

131

They'd called your house and got Robert, and he'd given them part of the story. Anyway, I'm sorry.'

'It's OK. Really.'

'Yeah? They've taken it all right, then?'

'Dad's on the verge of calling off the anniversary party, owing to the shame. But, hey, you've done me a favour. I didn't have to tell them.'

'True. Are you all right? Otherwise?'

'Yeah, yeah.' She wandered back to her laptop and got Kit's home page up. He looked even better this time, now she'd got used to the older version of him. 'I, er, don't suppose you remember Kit Avery? In Germany?'

'I'm not sure.'

'I went out with him when I was fifteen, so you must have been, what eight? Too young, I expect, although you might have heard–'

'Dolly Parton hair and a chopper bike?'

Jen laughed. 'I suppose so.' She'd forgotten about the bike. Pip's bike, actually.

'What about him?'

'Oh ... nothing. Just wondered.'

'Jen, are you sure you're OK? Only, we could all pop up today, if you want. See your new place.'

'Oh God, no.' All of them? Invading the flat? 'I mean, you don't have to worry about me. Waste a whole day trudging up here.'

'If you're sure.'

'I'm sure.' In the distance, she heard the baby. 'But thanks.'

'You know, I think it was Kit who gave me his Monkees albums.'

'Really?'

'I must have said I was a fan. Anyway, he made me promise not to tell you where they came from. I remember that bit.'

Jen smiled at Kit in his jacket and T-shirt. He could have chucked the records but gave them to Paul. 'Have you still got them?'

'Oh, yeah. Phoebe loves them. Listen, better go. Frank's throwing a wobbly in the kitchen. Speak soon. Bye.'

'Bye.' Jen switched off and within seconds it rang again. She pressed reply, wondering what he'd forgotten. 'Hello?'

There was an intake of breath, then her husband said, 'Hi, Jen. Don't hang up. Please.'

She steadied herself against the door frame she'd been passing and waited for him to say something else. She should have checked the screen.

'Jen?'

'What?' she sighed, hand on her forehead. 'What do you want, Robert?'

'I ... it's just that...'

'See. There's nothing to talk about. Only that I'll be starting divorce proceedings.'

'Could we meet? Before you do anything rash.'

'Oh, I'm the rash one?'

'I'm sorry, I... How about lunch? Today?'

'I'm busy.' His voice wasn't having a good effect on her. She'd always liked the fact that Robert was softly spoken, but now she just heard effeminate. And I've got a busy week coming up.'

'Couldn't–'

'If there's practical stuff, you can email.'

'Just for–'

'Bye, Robert.'

She hung up and switched the mobile off completely. After saving Kit's website in 'Favourites', she shut the laptop down and went back to bed. She'd rest for a while, then get up and start the day again.

In bed, in her head, Jen tried writing a message. Long and chatty, or brief and casual? *Came across your website and thought I'd say 'Hi'. Blah, blah...* *My phone number is...* No, no phone number. 'If you'd like to receive a reply from Kit,' it had said, 'please include your email address.' Just her email address, then.

*Hi Kit, came across your name, then found your website. How's your life been?* No, terrible. *I'm living in London too, so perhaps we could meet?* Too pushy. This was going to be hard. Maybe she'd think about it for a few days. After thirty-odd years, there was no hurry.

*Hi Kit,* she began again, unable to stop herself. *Came across your column in...* She'd have to buy a copy of the magazine, but it might be subscription only. *Hi Kit, thought I saw you at the anti-war rally...* What if it hadn't been him? She'd feel silly.

Later. She'd try again later. Right now she was sleepy. Music had come through the wall until the early hours. Tyrone or Matthew. It had been loud and annoying, but Jen hadn't felt inclined to complain, in case it caused trouble, or the eldest son, Jason, was back. Better to have a quiet word with Ruth, she'd decided. Eventually, she'd taken half one of the sleeping tablets her new GP had prescribed for emergencies. He was Scottish and he'd sounded a bit like her father; more Edinburgh, though. Gentler than her short-fused father. She thought about her dad, threatening to cancel the anniversary party her mum was so looking forward to, but he wasn't. Using Robert as an excuse?

Maybe she and Robert should still go. Parade as a couple for her mother's sake. Her parents' friends, neighbours, Jen's aunts, uncles, cousins – they all liked Robert. Most people liked him. Or, he could be away on business. Jen wondered if her mother, the talker, was capable of pulling that off. God, this was such bad timing.

She got up, put her robe back on, found the phone and dialled. When he answered, she took a deep breath. 'OK, lunch,' she said. 'Where?'

No matter how mature, worldly and confident she grew, Jen still felt uneasy going into a pub alone. Even one like this, with its vast open-plan restaurant-like arrangement. Please be here, she thought, and there he was, at a table by a window you couldn't see through.

She stood and watched him; his eyes darting to the door she might have come in, but hadn't; his too-frequent gulps of beer. Jen knew he'd rather be drinking wine, but his was a generation of men who didn't order wine in pubs; not for themselves.

He looked un-Robert-like for some reason. Not just the nerves, more his appearance, which was a bit frayed at the edges, although she couldn't tell why from this distance. Beside his glass was what looked like a stack of letters. He fiddled with them, straightened them, fiddled again.

How confusing it felt, looking at him. Someone she'd known so well and hadn't known at all. Best friend. Betrayer. A man with tastes and drives she couldn't have imagined, playing the part of her husband. Her old life came flooding back as she stood there. The house and garden they'd put so much effort into, the friends, the neighbourhood shops, the strolls, the meals ... everything. She wanted it back, as it had been.

Robert kept drinking his beer and looking at the wrong door, while Jen found she couldn't move. She was trying to get an objective view of him. Would she have put him down as gay if he'd been a stranger, sitting there in his baby-blue shirt with his slightly-too-long hair? Hard to know. She tried picturing him doing things with a man, but it didn't make sense. He was her Robert. All she'd known for decades. He spotted her, waved, and stood up. When she got to the table he leaned forward to kiss her.

'No,' she said, turning away.

'What can I get you?' he asked, covering his embarrassment with a louder-than-usual voice, rubbing his hands together.

'Just water, please.'

She noted his disappointment and was pleased. They'd always had a drink with their Sunday lunch, whether at home or out.

Jen watched her husband walk to the bar. He didn't mince, but neither was it a blokeish, knees-far-apart swagger. You couldn't tell, she thought, hating herself for this scrutiny; hating him for making her do it. Robert and the young nice-looking barman chatted, then the nice-looking barman smiled at Robert as he handed him change. If she went back to him, thought Jen, her radar would always be picking up things like that, however innocent.

'There you go!' he said, still too jolly, still not Robert.

'Thanks.'

'I brought your mail.'

'Yes.' She pulled the pile towards her and was about to put them in her bag, but instead, because of the awkwardness, began opening one. She'd let him do the talking, while she inspected bills.

Robert rearranged a beer mat. 'I sort of prepared what I was going to say.'

'Oh?'

'But now I'm afraid it'll sound like a speech.'

Jen glanced at him, then opened an envelope.

'The thing is...' he said.

The gardener for the Ealing house wanted £954 for 'fence erection'. She looked up at Robert and tried not to think of erections. His eyes were puffy and, astonishingly, he hadn't ironed his shirt. 'Go on, then,' she told him, but his puffy eyes grew red and watery, and although his mouth made shapes, no words came out. 'Did you use protection?' she asked. 'That's all I want to know.' Her hand was shaking, the invoice too. She put them both in her lap.

Robert nodded.

'Always?'

'Yes,' he said, barely audible. Jen was close to

137

feeling sympathy, but it slipped away. 'Shall I get us both some wine?' she asked, more for her sake than his.

He nodded again.

They parted without touching. The two glasses of wine with lunch had helped Robert open up, just briefly – too briefly – before changing the subject. So, sitting on the bus that would drop her seconds from home, Jen still couldn't grasp why her husband had 'dabbled', as he'd put it. 'Just curious,' he'd claimed, when trying to convince her he hadn't been emotionally involved with 'these two people'. Bi-curious. She'd read about that. But curiosity wouldn't last months, as Robert's two affairs had. A curious person might have had a one-night stand, maybe two, and then come to a decision. Surely?

He had come to one decision, though. He wanted her back. He loved her more than anything. But she didn't want to go back, not to a tainted version of their life. And she didn't want him back. Having the dreaded face-to-face had been good, after all. Robert, with his perfectly ironed shirts, his secret desires and his covert liaisons, had no appeal to her now. Although, strangely, she still liked his company. A lot. Maybe that was what it had been all along; liking rather than loving.

Having read every word on the website, she sat back with her glass of wine and stared at his face; her head and senses playing a disjointed film. She heard The Doors. She tasted Dutch chips and

138

bierwurst. There was the feel of velvet. The clean, plastic-like smell of German department stores. Dust in their hut, floating in the sunlight, Kit dancing, the smell of the pool. And then there was Monterey and Jimi's flaming guitar.

Monterey, flames ... military policemen. Jen shuddered and sat up. It was almost midnight. Too late to write a cohesive email. 'Night, Kit,' she whispered. 'Wherever you are.' She shut down the computer, drained her glass, switched off lights, went to the bathroom, then got into bed.

For all she knew, she thought, lying there half an hour later, listening to the roar of traffic, he could be just down the street.

## NINETEEN

The past two days had been spent moving personal items into the lockable third bedroom, a boxroom that had been Kit's study before claustrophobia set in.

Having reluctantly, and somewhat miserably, made the decision to decamp to north Norfolk until Adam's exams were over – whether his brother returned or not, he'd be needed – Kit had contacted an agency specialising in short-term lets. They'd inspected, presented forms to sign, and assured him they had clients frantic for such a lovely place in such a desirable area. Clapham? How it had gone up in the world since he'd bought the flat for a song in the early eighties. Not that a thirty-thousand mortgage had felt that way at the time, when there'd been a young barrister lifestyle to keep up. All that boozing and partying. Theatre, holidays, weekends in Gloucestershire or on boats, often with people he didn't care for. What a relief it had been to board a plane for Africa.

He'd hung on to the flat, though, then retarted it up ten years ago. It had been the only constant in his life, and one that might bring welcome income during his enforced break. Five hundred a week, they'd said. The world had clearly gone mad.

'Ready?' he asked Adam. It was Saturday, late morning, and his nephew appeared anything but ready to go home; lying in his room, texting. They'd had the busiest of weeks, hitting the ground running with the anti-war rally, then packing in the culture, shopping and more culture on a daily basis. New clothes, new up-to-date hair, which Kit had talked him into... Adam had enjoyed the buzz, and Kit had enjoyed Adam enjoying the buzz. It was hardly surprising the kid didn't feel like heading home. 'We'll stop somewhere nice for lunch,' Kit added, to no effect. There hadn't been any news of Pip and the outlook was growing bleaker by the day. If he could have kept Adam in London to do his As, he would have. But it was too late for that. 'And you must be looking forward to seeing Bunk?'

'Sure.'

'And Sasha?' A tall blonde girl who'd twice turned up in a brand-new Mini to see Adam.

140

Friend or girlfriend, he wasn't sure, and he hadn't pried.

Adam grinned, got off the bed, threw his new clothes into his new suitcase, zipped it up, checked his drastically altered hair in a mirror and followed Kit to the car.

Dawn and Lee had managed to further trash a house that always had a trashed air anyway. The Litlun had drawn on the walls already covered in Pip's scribbled phone numbers. Past-their-best saucepans were now burned beyond use, and the mildly worrying drip from the cistern had formed a small lake in the bathroom. Kit couldn't blame them for the toilet, but they might have mopped up. Witnessing the mess, he was tempted to call his London agents and tell them not to let.

Having, ridiculously, thanked Dawn for looking after the house, Kit unpacked his case, again feeling intrusive in his brother's bedroom. Next door, Adam was on the phone and Kit caught little bits, mostly about what they'd done in London. He might have been calling Sasha, or maybe his maternal grandparents, who'd left a message on the landline. They'd retired to the south coast after their daughter died, and were constantly in and out of hospital. Had they been up to it, they could have stepped into the crisis instead of Kit. Their other daughter, Adam's aunt Janice, had been another candidate, but according to Adam she was 'rather sullen' – which sounded, again, like his father talking.

But now he was actually here, properly, Kit didn't really mind. The idea of not railing against the world's injustices for a while was kind of appealing. Instead, he'd devote his time to keeping his nephew's spirits and grades up, and to keeping house. He'd brought reading material, mainly biographies. Encouraged by Adam, he'd also picked up several science books. Aside from experiments with mind-altering chemicals, science was an unexplored area for Kit. At fourteen, and with the enthusiastic support of all three masters, he'd dropped Physics, Chemistry and Biology. At the time it was a huge relief, but when faced with his first Law essay at Oxford, he did rather regret letting the left side of his brain wind down.

Carl Sagan, Hawking, *The Blind Watchmaker...* Kit would ask Adam which to read first. He put a couple of the books on the bedside table, next to a lamp with a dust-covered shade that he might just replace. He yearned to paint and refurnish the entire house, but feared his brother returning when no one was in, freaking out and disappearing again. No, he'd have to endure the wooden-armed, thin-cushioned cottage suite, the rag rugs, the offensive wallpaper. Even taking into account the poverty aspect, Pip definitely lacked his mother's interior-design gene.

Kit hadn't brought his laptop, determined as he was not to write, not to work. And besides, Pip had dial-up, pay-as-you-go internet, so hours of online research would have been out of the question. How he'd fill his days, apart from the reading and the dog walking, was something he'd have to discover as he went along. It couldn't be that hard. Plenty of people did nothing. Pip, for one. And, of course, he'd be there for Adam. Shopping, cooking, washing his clothes ... and if he picked up science quickly, helping him revise. Kit chuckled at the thought, then remembered, with some horror, revising for his own A levels. Or trying to. The Easter holidays, that dim back bedroom in Chesterfield. A room shared with Pip, who lay staring at the ceiling, unspeaking, for most of the fortnight Kit was there. Please, he thought, don't let this be history repeating itself.

Kit shook off the unwelcome memory, but it left him more determined than ever to make things easier for his nephew. And in the longer term, for himself. If Adam failed to get into Bristol, or his other choices, this time, he'd be more than happy to crash with his uncle in London while doing resits, even if his father did reappear. Kit knew this because Adam had said so. 'If that would be cool with you?' he'd added with that broad smile he'd inherited from his grandma, and perhaps his uncle Kit too. 'I'd work in a bar or something. Pay you rent.' While Kit paid tutorial fees, exam fees, and the rest? No way. Adam had to go to uni. And he had to stay sane through this horrible ordeal, or he too could be vanishing in his late forties. Kit had said he could maybe stay during the summer holidays, depending on what happened.

Having never had to look after another person, this was going to test Kit's mettle more than anything ever had. Part of him welcomed the challenge; part of him wanted to go home and continue to write about suffering, rather than deal with it.

143

In the evening, Sasha called in, and she and Adam disappeared upstairs. The first time they'd done this, shortly after Kit's arrival, he'd strained to hear creaking bedsprings, sniffed on the landing for drugs, and at ten thirty, tapped loudly on Adam's door to say he was locking up. What a tense business it was, parenting, although this evening he was more relaxed.

In fact, he left them to it and took Bunk for a walk in the dark. Past the long row of council houses, through the cul-de-sac of seventies chalet bungalows, along a short street of Victorian cottages, and into the heart of the village, where the only sign of life was The Bell. He slowed down outside the pub, dithered for a while, then went in.

Activity didn't quite grind to a halt, but many heads turned and Kit detected a lowering of volume. He tied Bunk to a table leg and went to the bar, where, to his amazement, a voice further along said, 'Evening, Kit.'

He stepped back and saw Eddie from the beach, sitting on a stool with Sheba at his feet. How he must miss the old place, thought Kit. A lesson in not moving later in life. 'Evening,' he replied. 'Can I get you a drink?'

'Ah, let me think. Driving, you see. A pint of lemonade, if you'd be so kind.' He slid off his stool and took the one next to Kit, leaving behind the sleeping Sheba. Any news?' he asked.

Kit shook his head. 'Not as far as I know.' He ordered their drinks, wondering how in the world you'd get through a pint of lemonade. 'I took my

144

nephew to London for the week.'

'How's the lad taking it?'

'Pretty badly, although he's trying not to let it show.'

'That's boys for you,' said Eddie. 'Got two myself, and you never know what's going on with them. Avril, the girl, though, you can't shut her up.'

Eddie introduced Kit to Dave, Ken, Pete and Mac, then proceeded to tell them who Kit was, at which most of them found something fascinating in their drinks. When Bunk spotted a waking Sheba and began barking furiously, Kit left the guys with their hung heads and went over to quieten his dog. Once again, the biscuit worked. By the time Kit was back with his drink, the talk had turned, or returned, to football.

He didn't stay for a second pint, despite several offers. They were a decent bunch, he decided, but he'd vacate and let them chew over his family drama. The landlord told him to come back any time, and Kit thought he most likely would. On the way home, Sandra drifted into his head. He couldn't believe he'd hurt her so badly that she'd turned to Pip, of all people, for comfort and help. He tried to recall why they'd parted, and had a vague recollection of a letter she'd intercepted. But what letter? He couldn't remember, and decided it was all water under the bridge. By the time he and Bunk reached their gate, with the notice he still hadn't removed, Kit's mind was back on Adam. No sign of Sasha's car. Good.

In the sitting room, the antique answerphone

was bleeping. Let it be Pip, he hoped, but when he pressed the play button, he heard his mother's distant voice. 'Pip, it's Mummy, calling from Palermo. I'm trying to get hold of Kit, but think I must be a digit out on his mobile. Perhaps you'd call me back at the hotel?' She gave her number, slowly and clearly, and Kit wrote it down. 'Speak soon. Bye.'

Kit slumped into an uncomfortable chair, his heart flooding with sympathy for his brother. There'd been no 'How are you?' No warmth. She was only phoning Pip to get hold of Kit. He fetched one of the cigarettes he kept for emergencies, found an ashtray, lit up, inhaled deep and dizzyingly, sat down again and dialled.

'Kit, darling!' she said, on hearing his voice. 'Thank heaven! How are you, sweetie? Did Pip tell you we're in Palermo? It's teeming with Mafioso and terribly exciting.'

He forced Bunk out for a final pee and lit a second cigarette, this time in the garden. God, his mother could be so hard. 'Oh, he'll turn up,' she said of Pip, then moved on to Sicilian weather and cuisine. Still, thought Kit, at least she wasn't ailing and needy in a home somewhere, demanding visits and claiming the nurses were poisoning her. She was in good health and being supported by Raymond Somebody. Yet again, he'd forgotten to ask his name. Perhaps he should call her back now, before she became elusive again.

But it had been a long day, what with the drive, and he wanted his bed. 'Come on, Bunk,' he said, slapping a thigh and opening the door. The dog shot in, Kit locked back and front doors, and hauled himself up the maroon-carpeted stairs. The worst of all colours for showing bits, and it went all the way along the landing too. He'd vacuum tomorrow, or get Adam to do it.

Passing his nephew's door, Kit heard a noise. Was Sasha still here, after all? He slowed right down and stopped breathing for a while. Sobbing. Quiet sobbing. Should he go in? Knock first, of course... Or leave Adam to his mourning? It occurred to Kit that Sasha might have finished with him. But that was ridiculous. Who'd chuck Adam?

Now almost weepy himself, Kit crept to his room and had a think. This was tricky. He'd comforted the odd crying woman – many, in fact – and had never felt a natural at it. There was always that horrible feeling in the pit of his stomach, which he guessed went back to what had happened: his dad. *Stop*, he willed Adam. *Please*. He'd announce his presence, Kit decided. That might stop him. He coughed, opened and closed drawers, and hummed all the way back to the bathroom. When he passed Adam's door again, he thought all was quiet, but then he heard more sniffs, another quiet sob. This time he knocked.

'Can I come in?' he asked.

It was almost one and they were still going through photographs. Both on the sitting-room floor. Between them lay dozens of photos and the stack of albums that his sister-in-law, Pat, had filled and detailed. *Holcombe, July 1991.* Adam all blond and bonnie with sand on his cheek, his parents on a rug behind him. Kit wondered who'd taken that one. Pat had been blonde too, and cuddly. Not quite pretty; a very round face and eyebrows that were too low. Africa had got in the way of him ever really knowing her, but Kit's memory was of a pleasant, jolly woman with an endearing Norfolk accent. The last person he'd have imagined collapsing and dying from a heart condition. A condition no one had known about, not even Pat. How Pip had held it together, having been through so much already, Kit would never know.

He put the seaside photo to one side and picked up another. Just Pat and Pip this time, pre-Adam, by the look of it. The two had met when Pip finally got round to university, aged twenty-three or -four. *Pip and Pat,* they'd written, rather unnecessarily, on the back. Kit had always liked that, thinking he too should marry someone with a similar name. *To Pip and Pat, Merry Christmas, Kit and Kim.*

'Look at this,' Adam was saying. He'd begun yawning a lot, and Kit, now bone tired, was hoping they'd wind up soon. Adam twisted the album round and pointed at a faded picture of his father astride a motorbike. *His new pride and joy!* 'It was in the garden for years, under plastic. I think someone came and took it.'

'I never saw him on it.'

'Me neither.' Adam yawned again, long and loud. He placed the album on his legs and turned the page. '*Another* one of them in front of the

148

Eiffel Tower on their anniversary. They must have done that every year.'

Kit was surprised. He hadn't imagined his brother going abroad again, after Germany. 'Did they still go when you came along?'

'I'm not sure. As far as I know I've never been to Paris. I can't get Pip to talk about Pat, or their life before me.' He stared at the photo album but his eyelids were drooping.

'Shall we call it a day?' Kit asked, yawning too, patting his mouth, stretching both arms. 'We could leave these. Carry on in the morning.'

'Bunk might wreck them.' Over on his bed, the dog thumped his tail at the mention of his name.

'Good point,' said Kit. He started picking up the loose photos. How attractively simple his brother's life had been, compared to his. How happy, though, was hard to tell. If pressed, Kit would have said his brother looked genuinely happy in the pre-widowhood photos, and making a valiant effort in the later ones.

'Night,' they both said on the landing.

'Sleep well,' Kit added.

'You too.'

It was the perfect moment for an uncle-and-nephew hug, but Adam fell into his room, and Kit into his.

# TWENTY

Jen sometimes forgot she was in Germany. It was easy to do that, especially in the holidays when you weren't seeing the country every day from a horrible hard seat on a military bus. Just about everything you needed was on camp, especially if, like her, you had barely any money.

There was German and Dutch food in the Naafi, although hardly any, and Germans working on camp, but on the whole you felt you were still in England. Jen's parents knew about six German words between them. Her mum cooked the same things she had at home, her dad smoked the same cigarettes, and they listened to British forces' radio. Life on the station was very British and very safe, and you could buy more or less anything but nice clothes. The downside for Jen was seeing the same places, the same people, day after day, and everyone knowing everyone else's business. It was like living in a village, she imagined, only with lots of aircraft noise and half the villagers in uniform.

So when Kit turned up and said, 'Let's go to Düsseldorf,' she was a bit taken aback.

'It's a long way,' she told him. 'Two buses.' It was early. She wished she'd brushed her hair, wondered if he wanted to come in. 'But if you really—'

'Mönchengladbach, then?' He smiled at her,

but strangely, quickly.

'OK.' Mönchengladbach was halfway to Düsseldorf and only one bus ride.

'Shall I walk around the block while you get ready?'

She nodded and watched him go down the path, shoulders hunched. Something had happened, and she had a horrible feeling it was to do with her note to his mum. She should have realised Kit had been too out of it to follow her instructions last night. Trust her dad to get him drunk and mess things up.

She ran upstairs and had a quick wash, her stomach fluttering, but not in the usual nice way. How stupid, giving Kit the note. Now his mother must know he was seeing her secretly, and she'd probably told him it had to end, or stopped his pocket money or something. No, Kit didn't get pocket money. His allowance. She went to the bedroom and threw on all the things he liked, including the silky skirt again. She didn't bother with makeup because there wasn't time. On the bus, perhaps, but should you do that in front of your boyfriend? Not that he'd be her boyfriend much longer. She should *never* have given him that note. She could have taken it herself, with a pretend limp. Or got someone else to deliver it. If she'd had any friends left, they might have helped.

Jen told her mum she was going out with Kit but didn't mention Mönchengladbach. She and Christine had gone there once on their own and got back so late, because of bus mix-ups, that Christine's dad had been to the military police.

'Pop in the Naafi,' said her mother, unclipping her purse, 'and get some Andrex toilet rolls, would you? Oh dear, I haven't got anything smaller.'

'Never mind.' Jen took the note from her mum with a bit of guilt and a lot of relief. If she lost Kit in the city, she'd have money to get home.

They'd reached the guardroom at the entrance to the camp before he said a word, and then it was, 'Don't you just hate it when your folks argue?'

Jen, who'd been close to tears for the length of the past tree-lined road, wasn't sure what to make of that. Either Kit's mood was nothing to do with her note, or it was everything to do with it and his parents had been arguing about her, Jen. 'Yes,' she lied. Since her dad ruled the roost and her mum went along with it, they never had rows. 'What,' she asked nervously, 'have they been arguing about?'

'Oh ... things.' He went quiet again, and they turned on to the main road that led to the village and the bus stop. It was hot already, and would be even hotter in the city. The big department stores were always cool, but would Kit want to hang around in them? She'd never been to a park in Mönchengladbach, but there had to be one.

It was one kilometre to the bus stop and when they got there and were examining the timetable, Kit put his arm around her. 'It's *sechs*,' he said.

Jen was surprised he knew the German for six, but couldn't see where it featured on the timetable. 'What is?'

'And affairs. It's what their social life revolves

152

around. Ma's, anyway.'

Sex, not *sechs*. Jen couldn't think what to say.

'You must know about all the wife swapping?'

'Well ... not really.' Christine had gossiped about the young couples she and Jen baby-sat for, but that was it. She could have mentioned his parents' row on the landing, but didn't see the point. Then there was Mick.

'One's all for the permissive society,' said Kit, his face next to hers as they continued to stare at the timetable. 'But not when it comes to one's parents.'

'No.' Jen lifted her watch arm. 'There's a bus to Monchengladbach in ten minutes.'

'Couldn't we go further?' he whispered, though there was no one in sight. 'Düsseldorf or Cologne. Berlin, even? We'll find somewhere to stay, or camp, or something. I look older than I am, I've got money...'

'It sounds lovely,' said Jen, 'but my mum thinks I've gone to the Naafi.'

He turned to her and smiled, although his eyes stayed sad. 'You're so sweet,' he said. 'Another time, then.'

It was different from their shopping trip in Roermond, in that Kit was quiet and not on a spending spree, but he did buck up as the day went on. Jen relaxed too, especially when he said he'd left her note on the doormat, where Pip had found it and passed it to his mother. Kit hadn't been around to see his mum's reaction, but Jen imagined her tutting, then tossing it aside for Elke to put away.

The city streets were wide and clean, and the people smartly dressed. Jen and Kit played Spot the Brits. There were lots of army and air-force bases in the area, and in their casual clothes the British stood out. Scruffs, her dad called them, like he was one to talk.

In the restaurant of the Kaufhof, a big department store with big clothes, Kit tried his first sauerkraut. 'An acquired taste,' he decided. He liked the sausage, though. Bierwurst. They went to the beautiful and beautifully cool cathedral, and it was there, when they were sitting side by side in a spot away from the visitors, that Kit talked about his parents.

'They should never have married, that's what my ma keeps saying, and in front of Pa too. I'm certain she'll drive him into someone else's arms, if she hasn't already. The CO's wife, for one, is mad about Daddy.'

'Is she?' Jen saw the bald head, the red cheeks, the funny bow tie.

'Lawrence's father is having a thing with a young flying officer's wife. I don't think Lawrence knows.'

'Crikey.' Jen slipped a hand into his and squeezed it. 'But how do *you* know all this?'

Kit snorted. 'Because Mummy tells me. Usually when she's sloshed, often when she isn't.'

'How awful.'

'I've sort of got used to it, but she will enlighten Pip too, and he's terribly sensitive. Not that she'd notice, or even care. Ma does rather make it obvious I'm her blue-eyed boy. Literally, one could say.'

154

'What do you ... oh, right. Blue eyes.' Jen knew she'd hate it if her mum favoured her or her brother. She was kind to both of them, just as her dad was grumpy with both of them. When Jen was young, he'd slapped her almost as often as he did Paul. She tried to remember when the smacking had stopped. When she was eleven ... twelve?

'Anyway, it's the abundance of cheap alcohol, and the whole ultra-sociable, ex-pat lifestyle. The Officers' Mess is a tawdry, immature den of vice. You should hear some of the stories. Honestly, we're better behaved in our sixth form, and that's saying something. My ma loves it. All those attractive young pilots and navigators.'

Jen wondered how Mrs Avery fitted Mick in. And whether Mick was doing it with loads of other wives. What about her own parents? When they said they were going to the Sergeants' Mess, were they really off to wife-swapping parties? It was hard to imagine her mum swapping anything but knitting patterns, but you never knew. Just the thought made her sick; made her realise what Kit was going through.

He let go of her hand and put an arm around her shoulders. Jen wasn't sure they should be doing that in a cathedral, but still snuggled up. 'You don't think,' she whispered, 'that maybe your mum's making it up?'

'She can exaggerate, it's true. But no, I've seen things, heard things.'

'Oh?'

'Forgive me if I don't go into detail, but–'

'I know.' She rubbed her head against his cheek,

and tried to work out how she felt about this new vulnerable Kit, with this horrible thing going on in his life that he'd only be able to talk to her about. He'd hardly tell Susie her mum wanted to do it with his dad. And he wouldn't tell Lawrence about his dad because, in Jen's experience, boys only talked about sport, bikes and music.

'No doubt they'll divorce.'

'*No,*' said Jen. 'Surely not?'

Kit shrugged. 'It's become quite the trend amongst school parents, so Pip and I would hardly be pariahs.'

Jen was shocked. 'I don't know anyone whose parents are divorced.'

'I'm sure you don't.' Kit kissed her cheek and sniffed. Had he been crying? He seemed so laid-back, so blasé, about it all, but maybe he was really hurting inside. Jen knew she'd have been blubbing like anything, but Kit was a boy, and boys, she was beginning to learn, dealt with things differently. She wouldn't lift her eyes and look, in case he was embarrassed. 'The thing is,' he said, 'with position and privilege comes choice and freedom. And, hence, immorality.'

'I see.' Even when he was upset, he was so clever. The way he summed things up. It could have been a quote, but even finding the right one was a knack.

A large, middle-aged woman in a navy suit appeared at their side. She whispered something forcefully and pointed at the door. Kit moved his arm and they both stood up. '*Entschuldigen Sie, bitte,*' Jen said, as they passed.

Kit said, '*Danke,*' his one German word.

156

They were back on camp around six. Too late for Andrex toilet rolls, and with quite a dent in the money Jen had been given. She went home for tea, having arranged to see Kit later. They thought they might go to the youth club, where Kit could dance and get things out of his system, and Jen could try to make up with Christine and the others. It had been Kit's idea, the making-up. He'd told her it would be the 'big' thing to do, and she thought she could see what he'd meant, but she wasn't exactly looking forward to the evening. Still, there were worse things to go through in life, like your parents having *sechs* with everyone.

'Sorry,' she said, while her mum handed her faggots with Smash and tinned carrots. 'I left the toilet rolls on a bench and when I went back they were gone.'

Her mother counted up the change and frowned, but because her dad was in the room, didn't say anything. Only, 'Well...' and, 'That's a shame,' giving her daughter a look. If there was a prize for not complaining, her mum would be world champion.

Kit wasn't in the mood for the youth club, after all, which was absolutely fine by Jen. They went to the hut, where he wasn't in the mood for kissing, either. But he did cuddle her, tightly and silently, for an hour and forty minutes. Jen knew this because she kept checking her watch over his shoulder.

'To hell with them,' he finally said, making her jump. 'Mummy, anyway.'

This worried Jen. It wasn't the sort of thing you wished on your mum. 'You don't mean that,' she said, stroking his back with the hand that hadn't gone to sleep.

'We used to do things, you know, as a family. Now they're hungover every day. I'm fine, but Pip doesn't have pals, and Ma and Pa could be ... I don't know, showing him Germany.'

'Mm,' Jen said. She and her family only ever went to Roermond to shop, or to a huge German supermarket half an hour away. They'd been told at school about places of interest, locally, but Jen hadn't thought they'd interest her dad. Or her brother. If her mum had passed her driving test, the two of them could have gone together. Castles, medieval places; all the way to Cologne, even. 'Well...' She was about to say *they* could take Pip places, but then changed her mind because he could be really silly and it might spoil things. '...it's just a few weeks till he's back at school.'

It was a stupid thing to say, since Pip hated boarding, and only reminded her that Kit wouldn't be around for ever. *And* it made her sound selfish, and like she didn't care. Susie wouldn't have said it.

'Jen, you're so empathetic,' Kit said, hugging her tight and kissing her forehead.

'Am I?' Did it mean the same as pathetic?

'Always feeling others' pain.'

At last he kissed her properly, and when he'd finished, Jen checked her watch. Two hours till the first kiss. She knew he'd go off her once he met her family.

# TWENTY-ONE

**March 2003**

Jen couldn't believe what she was witnessing, but then again she could. They'd all known this was coming, but for the attack to be broadcast into her home in this manner, as it was so predictably and nauseatingly happening, was obscene.

'Criminals,' Lionel said, beside her.

Their feet were on the coffee table, the remote was in between them. On their laps were bowls of spicy chicken stew. Jen wasn't making much headway with hers, glued as she was to explosion after explosion taking place in Baghdad. She wanted to suggest they turn it off, but the images were depressingly compelling.

'Bastards,' said Lionel, mopping his bowl with a huge chunk of bread and shoving it in his mouth.

Jen watched him for a while, wondering if all men except Robert were inelegant eaters. No, she decided, after going through her father, her brother and various others. And Kit would be an elegant eater, with all that breeding.

Thoughts of Kit bothered her now. That morning, she'd finally, and after several weeks and a hundred drafts, emailed him. But so far she hadn't heard back. It could be, she kept telling herself, that going via a person's website involved delays. If Lionel had been less of a builder and more of a techie, he might have known. The person who would know was Robert, but she could hardly ask him how long her first boyfriend might take to get back to her. Not in his current state: on antidepressants, apparently, and still not going to work much. 'It's hard to give a toss about properties,' he'd said on the phone.

An unfortunate choice of word, Jen had thought, but then she was still seeing sex – and, in particular, male-on-male sex – everywhere. So much so, that she wondered if she'd ever believe a man to be completely heterosexual again. Newscasters, footballers, actors, the man trying to sell her the *Evening Standard*. Lionel, for example. Why would a youngish, good-lookingish, if a bit overweight, guy hang out with a woman in her late forties he had no romantic or sexual interest in? Could it be that the rarely mentioned girlfriend in New Zealand was a smokescreen? Not that it would bother Jen if she were some kind of mummy substitute for Lionel. She liked his company, and it wasn't just because he was there and her old friends weren't.

She'd missed Sarah, but not the rest of them: the dinner-party people she and Robert had gathered, many as a result of Robert selling them a house in the area; arty types, academics, freelancers making websites or jewellery; interesting, opinionated people, most of whom would claim, whilst sitting on goldmines and schooling their children privately, to be left-leaning. Lionel, on the other hand, was the real thing.

'Bastards,' he said again.

'Yes,' she agreed.

'Ain't you eatin' yours, Jen?'

'Not really.' She passed her bowl over. They were always doing this. 'I'm finding it hard to watch murder and destruction *and* eat.'

'Me too,' he said, digging in. 'Don't seem right.'

After an hour, she'd really had enough. 'I think I'll check my emails,' she said.

'Again? You joined some dating thing, Jen?'

'No, no.' *Worse,* she should have said. *I'm waiting to hear from someone I no longer know, and feel my world will collapse if I don't.* Why was that? 'I'm just expecting an important message. To do with work.'

Lionel cocked an eyebrow. 'Yeah, right. Anyway, none of my business.'

No, she agreed, but didn't say. She and Lionel had a hard-to-define friendship, in which no one quite knew the rules. They went out, once or twice a week. The cinema, the odd gig in a pub a friend of his was doing. Lionel had lots of friends and acquaintances, which made it all the more puzzling that he hung out with her.

She got up and gathered the bowls and forks. 'Would you like cheesecake, Lionel?'

'Is Bush a redneck?' he asked.

Nothing. Not unless she counted Robert's latest, telling her his father had gone in for his by-pass operation, saying how worried he was, naming the hospital, then ending with a 'Miss you'. Jen felt sorry for Robert, which was the aim of his email, but mainly she felt disappointed; then as she shut the laptop down, stupid. She'd read many of Kit's articles now and it was clear where he stood politically: not that far from his stance at seventeen. He'd almost certainly be watching the TV transmission, perhaps penning something as he did so. Should he be emailing anyone at this historic time, it would hardly be her.

Jen went back in the sitting room and asked Lionel if he fancied going for a drink.

'Yeah, all right,' he said, as usual. He was the most easygoing man she'd ever come across, until it came to politics. They put on coats and scarves and ventured upriver on foot: Lionel going on about Bush, Blair and Saddam; Jen trying, but failing, to change the subject. At London Bridge, they took the Tube for the West End. A drink and a good film was the plan. Jen's plan. It would take their minds off the real world.

Over a drink, they went through the cinema listings. *The Pianist* was showing at a couple of places. Jen had read dazzling reviews, and although Lionel said he was happy with anything, he did ask twice if *The Lord of the Rings: The Two Towers* was still on.

'*The Pianist* it is then,' said Jen emphatically. 'Fancy another drink?'

'Is George Michael gay? Oh. Fuck. Sorry, Jen.'

She left the cinema emotionally drained. To go home and watch a little bombing would be light relief after *The Pianist*.

'Talk about harrowing,' said Lionel, who'd jumped and gone 'Aargh!' when the German officer had appeared and surprised the hiding Jew.

Jen had too, but not as loudly. 'Did you cry when he played for the Nazi geezer?' Lionel asked. 'I did.'

This Jen knew, because Lionel tended not to do things quietly, even sniffing. As with most loud people, he had no idea he was loud. 'Listen,' she said, 'it's pointless you coming all the way back to Southwark.'

'Don't be daft, me van's there.'

The truth was, she wanted to go home alone and have the freedom to check her emails hourly, if the urge took her. 'I know, but–'

'Come on, old girl.' Lionel hooked an arm through hers. 'I'll get me head down in your study and let meself out first thing. Big job on tomorrow. You won't know I'm there.'

'Well, OK,' she said. And maybe it would be nice to have a human in the flat after all she'd been through: the bombing of Baghdad, the Holocaust.

Switching the light on, she saw it was just after two. She'd woken in a panic, realising she should never have put 'Remember Germany?' in the subject line of her email. It would just bring back that terrible night. She could almost cry. After all the time she'd put into drafting a message, she'd gone and trashed it with that. How stupid. How really, really stupid. No wonder he hadn't replied.

After trying in vain to get back to sleep, she finally gave up. Half a tablet, maybe? She sat up, put the light back on and opened her drawer. And warm milk too. That should do the trick.

In the kitchen she filled a mug, put it in the microwave and gave it forty seconds. After the ping, she carried it through the sitting room and along the corridor, turning off lights as she went. Then, in bed, she slowly sipped and waited for drowsiness to return. When it didn't, she went over *The Pianist* and counted her blessings for having been born when and where she had. Others, such as those poor souls in Iraq, were nowhere near as lucky. Thoughts of the bombing led to thoughts of Kit, and thoughts of Kit led to thoughts of her foolish email and his lack of response to it.

She'd checked on coming home, then shut the computer down for the night. But now it occurred to her that world events could be keeping Kit awake, and that he might not have been offended by her email heading at all. That he might have been busily dealing with correspondence since midnight. Or perhaps he was a regular night owl. Jen knew a few people who emailed in the early hours, or at dawn. Would it be possible, she wondered, to just creep into her study and go online without waking Lionel? She'd be really quiet. Rotund people always slept deeply, didn't they?

It was the little ditty that made her guest stir, the one it played on firing up. Lionel made a low noise on the sofabed, while Jen bent down and peered at the black keyboard. She had to type her password in, and by feeling her way around, got it at the second attempt.

She was clicking on her email icon, when some-

164

thing touched her ankle. It not only touched her ankle, but caressed it. 'Jen,' it said, in a strange rasping kind of way. 'Jen.'

'Sorry to wake you, Lionel,' she whispered. 'I was just checking my emails.' She wanted to move the ankle but actually couldn't. What was he doing? Dreaming about her?

'There are therapists for that sort of thing,' he said, sounding more himself. 'Email addiction. c'mere.' His hand made its way up her calf and squeezed, leading Jen to lose her balance in the eerily lit room and topple on to the sofabed. She quickly sat up, but Lionel's large arms came and encircled her.

'Listen, Lionel,' she began, only the warm milk was taking effect, and perhaps the tablet too, and he was rubbing her arm in such a comforting way.

'Shhh,' he told her. 'I ain't after your body, Jen.'

'No?'

'Not unless you're offering, like.'

Jen found herself leaning into her former builder's embrace. 'I'm not.'

'It's good that's sorted, then.'

'Yes.'

'It's just nice to have a bit of a cuddle in this fucked-up world, don't you think?'

Jen was sort of touched by Lionel's affection, or need, or whatever it was. And as she lay down properly beside him and he pulled the duvet over them both, she felt tears well up. And then, before she knew it, they were pouring down her face, and she was sniffing as loudly as Lionel in the cinema.

'There, there,' he said.

Jen lay with her back to him, his arms around her waist, his hand still stroking one arm, and she cried and cried on the new-smelling pillowcase. She cried for the loss of her husband, her marriage, her proper life. And for the people of Iraq, and how men could resort to violence, with no regard for children and the elderly, or pets or wildlife... Mostly, though, she cried for the fact that just as her ankle was grabbed, she'd read 'No new messages' on her laptop screen. Or perhaps that had been the trigger.

'That's right, old girl,' said Lionel. 'Let it all out. If I had neighbours as noisy as yours, I'd be crying too.'

'Sorry,' she said, tuning in to the *thud-thud, thud-thud,* which had become like a heartbeat she no longer heard.

## TWENTY-TWO

**April 2003**

Kit found it both puzzling and liberating that the things he'd believed about himself were proving not to be true at all. For one, he didn't need to be continually productive. In fact, he was barely driven at all, given the right circumstances. And he didn't need his space, as he'd informed many a woman. He and Adam were living cheek by jowl and he'd never felt so domestically comfortable. Having another person around could feel like a bonus, rather than an intrusion. Who'd have believed it?

Adam's explanation involved cortisol. 'When the day-to-day stress goes, your cortisol levels drop and you gradually chill.' They were on the beach with Bunk, stick-throwing. Adam was off school on the pretext of stomach ache. It was a Friday, which somehow made skiving more acceptable. 'That must be what's happened.'

'I'm stressed about your father.'

'I know, but that's different. Finding Pip isn't your responsibility, you see. Especially now you've done all you can.'

Had he? 'You're my responsibility. Wouldn't that make my cortisol levels rise?'

'You'd have thought,' said Adam. 'Anyway, that's not entirely true. You know you could walk away tomorrow and someone else would step in. Like Aunt Janice, God forbid.'

Kit had never thought himself stressed. Just busy, like most people he knew. Life was full of goals. Articles he had to write, places he had to see, plays he had to catch, women he had to have. And deadlines too. Weren't goals and deadlines the whole point? Of existence? Hadn't he rather enjoyed all that?

'Drop!' he told the dog, then realised Bunk already had. He picked up the stick and threw it with a, 'Fetch!' which amused Adam for some reason.

'You don't have to tell him, you know. He could no more not fetch, than he could *not* eat every ginger snap you give him.'

'Less of your cheek,' said Kit, 'or I'll be summoning your aunt.' Bunk had actually tired of ginger snaps and moved on to bourbons, Kit's favourite.

At home, before they'd left, on the radio and TV, Saddam Hussein's statue had been about to topple. Only weeks before, Kit would have been gripped, calling friends and jotting down notes. But both he and Adam had found the scenes depressing, possibly for different reasons. Adam's mind could have been on his disappearing father, rather than the might of the US military. So, rather than go back to the house, they decided to extend their walk to one that would take them off the beach and in a five- or six-mile circle. Kit trusted Adam to know where they were going. The weather had bucked up and spring was everywhere. Adam looked almost happy, and Kit definitely was.

The angst and fear over Pip had numbed down to an ongoing, almost background, worry. The police weren't doing anything. People disappeared all the time, and when they took their car, there was no reason to suspect foul play. Suicide, perhaps, but that just meant waiting for a body to turn up. Kit was both hopeful and resigned to the worst having happened.

Meanwhile, he was being a surrogate in all manner of things: student loan application, student accommodation. Whenever a next of kin was required, Kit put his own name and contact details. Now that life revolved around his nephew, and he was enjoying the fact that it did, Kit believed he might even resent his brother's reappearance. Upsetting the applecart twice, as it were.

He'd never have shared that with Adam, though, who still rushed to check the post. 'Pip would probably write, not phone,' he'd said. 'And he wouldn't know where to begin with email.'

Pip's approach to communication, which had, not that long ago, seemed dinosaurial and perverse, was now making sense to Kit. Their costly and insanely slow internet made going online an expensive chore, and not the cheap fix it had become in London, where it had come to dominate his home life. Kit had pondered upgrading it all, particularly for Adam's sake, but then discovered that life in a low-tech house had its advantages. For one, he spent more time outdoors. But also, having been forced off the internet drug, he'd managed to expand, or rather reinflate, his attention span. When, before coming to Norfolk, had he last read an entire book? He couldn't remember. In the excitement of searching the great database of the internet, with all the distractions that involved – a paragraph or two here, then a link to somewhere else – Kit had lost, he realised, the ability to concentrate, or to read deeply.

But it hadn't gone for ever. Once more, he was immersing himself in books, reaching the end of long articles, even going back over paragraphs to make sure he'd grasped things. How much more satisfying it was than all that skimming, all that jumping around. At present, he was working his way, deliciously, through a book on Mendel, the father of genetics. A man who might not have spent seven years watching peas, if he'd had the internet.

They stopped around four, at a pub called The Crane, whose walls were adorned with drawings of cranes. 'There's a flock on the Broads,' Adam explained, while Kit ordered the drinks. 'Bit of a tourist pull.' Kit knew this, since he'd been genning up on local birdlife, but didn't say.

In the garden, in the sun, Bunk worked his way through a bowl of water, Adam through a fruit drink, and Kit through a pint. The beer was welcome and refreshing at the time, but ten minutes later, when the walk resumed, Kit regretted ordering it. His legs were heavy and his eyes wanted a nap. He'd know next time.

Back at the house, Adam offered to cook, while Kit made his way upstairs, feeling every bit his age. So much for healthy country air. He flopped on his brother's bed, stared at his brother's ceiling cracks, and thought about his brother. Every now and then it hit him that he ought to be doing more to trace Pip. Appeals in newspapers and shop windows, on local radio – something like that. And had he gone through Pip's scribbled numbers thoroughly enough?

Kit's eyelids grew heavy and the ceiling cracks disappeared, and then someone was calling him. Adam. 'Coming!' he replied, dragging himself into wakefulness. He'd go online later, he decided, sitting himself up and rubbing life back into his face. There must be missing persons' websites. Perhaps he'd post something.

Since Pip would never email, and since his mother had made him cross with her lack of concern about Pip, Kit hadn't bothered picking up messages. Luckily, his wasn't a profession that others relied upon too much. The magazine had announced his sabbatical, he had no books in the pipeline, and there was no need, financially, for freelance articles, now the flat was being let.

He'd looked at his emails a week ago, mainly to see if Emily had been in touch. There'd been lots of junk mail, one or two messages he'd replied to out of politeness, and several emails that had been redirected from his website. Having lost interest in work, he hadn't looked at those.

Again, the old computer cranked itself into action. No wonder Adam used Sasha's PC, two villages away. A quick check of emails, he decided. Quick? After typing in the account name and password, Kit drummed his fingers, said, 'Come on, come on,' and felt his cortisol levels rise. Meanwhile, the tower by his leg croaked and groaned and tried to remember what to do. Just as he thought of getting himself a drink, there was his inbox.

A lot of junk, as usual. He deleted those. There was one from his mother, with a photo of herself and Raymond in Florence and details of their travels. Any news of Pip?' she asked, finally. 'I'm sure he's hiding away Piplike in a monastery or something. Do keep me posted? Oodles of love, Mummy xxxx' Monastery? So much for the Swiss finishing school.

He wrote a curt reply and moved on to the next,

a message redirected from his website, praising a piece he'd done on Zimbabwe. Reading it gave him a bit of a boost and he found himself scrolling down to the previous website messages for more positive feedback. He'd forgotten how good that felt. 'Check your facts!' was the subject of one. He gave that a miss. The next said, 'Remember Germany? Hi from Jennifer Juniper.' Immediately, a song filled his head... 'Wild Thing' ... Hendrix. 'Jen?' he whispered, opening the email. 'Bloody hell.'

## TWENTY-THREE

She and Christine were in the youth club, nattering. They'd made up when Jen went round to Christine's with a magazine she'd borrowed ages before. It was a pathetic pretext, so pathetic that Christine had laughed, invited her in and made them both a strawberry milkshake. She'd been full of the gossip. Mainly, it was about who people had got off with; a subject Jen never used to enjoy that much because she never got off with anyone. Too shy? Too skinny? She wasn't sure what it was that put most boys off her, but hadn't put Kit off.

Christine, on the other hand, got through lots of 'lads', as she called them, but then she always made it obvious who she fancied. For one thing, Jen could never do that, and for another, she didn't often fancy anyone. Perhaps she'd been too picky or Christine wasn't picky enough.

'Why don't you come to the Airmen's Club, Saturday?' Christine said. 'Bring KitKat.'

'Maybe.' Jen had avoided the dances because of Christine and Yvonne. Kit would love to go, she knew. He always said dancing made him high. 'But if you call him that, I'll kill you.'

It was nice being back in the fold, in the youth club. And on top of that boys kept coming over and chatting her up. Like Martin and Steve, who were a year above her at school and had never paid her any attention. Steve wondered where she'd been, even though the entire youth club knew about Kit. Martin asked if he could get her another drink, and how about going to the flicks some time? Christine just sniggered beside her, which was odd because normally she'd have wanted the limelight herself.

Jen let Martin down gently, despite the fact he'd been rude to her in the past and didn't deserve it. She did dance with him, though, and also with Steve and a new boy called Ricky, who she might have got a crush on, if it hadn't been for Kit.

It was all a bit odd. Either boys' interest in you grew once you'd got a boyfriend, or something in her had changed. Maybe being in love made you prettier. Maybe it was her tennis tan.

Everyone got kicked out at ten, and she and Christine walked back through the camp.

'1 could see you liked the new lad,' Christine said, as they dawdled behind the others. 'The way you was flirting with him.'

'I was not!'

'Flippin' 'eck, Jen, you was flirting with all the lads tonight.'

'Was I?'

'*Yeah.* I don't know what's got into you. Or maybe it's KitKat who's got into you?' She squeezed Jen's arm and gave a dirty laugh. 'If you know what I mean.'

'No,' said Jen, 'he hasn't. And don't go telling people that because it wouldn't be true.' Not that that would stop her.

According to rumour, Christine had gone all the way with more than one boy, but she'd never talked about it, at least not to Jen. Sometimes, she had no idea why they went round together, except Christine could be good fun. But when you moved a lot, you made friends quickly and became sort of stuck with them until your dad got posted again. In her experience, anyway. One of the good things about air-force life was that you could get away from anyone who might be bullying you, or who you just didn't like, but they thought you did. It worked the other way too, and Jen had cried buckets with a best friend once, when best friend's dad got posted. At the time, it had felt like the end of the world, but after a couple of letters the contact had fizzled out. New friends had come along, new best friends. Jen wasn't sure how she'd feel if Christine moved, but it wouldn't ruin her life.

They were just passing the tennis courts, about to turn towards the airmen's quarters, when Jen spotted Kit in the distance and her heart flipped, because he was with Susie. He was also with Lawrence, but it was Susie who registered – probably because she had her arm through Kit's. Susie also had her arm through Lawrence's, but still, a huge jealous jolt brought Jen to a stop.

'What?' asked Christine. She looked the same way as Jen and said, 'Uh-oh.'

'Here,' whispered Jen, tugging Christine towards a bush by the Malcolm Club. Kit hadn't seen her and she didn't want him to, and she really didn't want to get into conversation, not with Christine and her big mouth there. Who knew what she might come out with about Jen and Kit, or about Jen and the youth club boys. 'Quick.'

The three of them were laughing a lot as they approached. Susie was such good fun, no wonder Kit was spending his evening off with her. Jen hoped they weren't talking and laughing about her, though. How embarrassing that would be, with Christine listening too.

Her heart began pounding as the two of them lurked behind the bush, Christine shaking with the giggles. She was terrified of what she might hear, like Kit being flirty with Susie. They all chuckled again as they walked, painfully slowly, towards the junction, and more and more Jen wished she hadn't hidden. If Kit had seen her, he wouldn't say or do the wrong thing. 'Oh God,' she whispered.

'What?' said Christine.

'Shh.'

'And why are you hiding from your boyfriend?'

'*Shh.*'

175

'Hey, chaps, they're all coming back to me,' Susie was saying in her posh voice. Jen willed Christine not to say anything. Even a whisper would be heard now. 'OK, what do you *get* if you cross an elephant with a biscuit?'

'It's not swimming trunks?' asked Lawrence.

'That's an elephant and a swimming pool, you ninny.'

'OK,' said Kit, and Jen felt wobbly at the sound of his voice. 'What *do* you get if you cross an elephant with a biscuit?'

'Crumbs!'

'Ha, ha!' said Lawrence. 'Superb!'

'For real,' said Kit. 'Your turn, Lawrence.'

'OK...'

When they'd passed and it was safe to come out, Christine stood and stared in the direction they'd gone. 'Flippin' 'eck,' she said, hands on her hips. 'What upper-class twits.'

How Jen could have shocked and impressed Christine by filling her in on the officers and their wives. But watching him disappear into the distant blur of the officers' patch, Jen was feeling extra loyal to Kit. He hadn't spent their evening apart chasing girls, getting drunk and taking drugs, as she'd feared. Just telling stupid jokes. In fact, her behaviour had been far worse.

'I don't know what you see in him,' said Christine. She had her compact open and was dabbing powder on in the dark. She stopped and peered over the top. 'Unless it's his great big...' Jen tutted and walked off, while Christine giggled, snapped her compact shut and caught up. 'Bank balance, I was going to say. Honestly, Jen, your mind.'

They'd left the hall light on, as usual, and Jen crept to the kitchen for a glass of milk. She was still buzzing from all the interest the boys had shown, and didn't feel much like sleeping. If she put the telly on, her dad would wake up and yell, and anyway, there'd be rubbish on. So she sat in the silent lounge for a while, thinking about Kit, and about the new boy, Ricky, and about how nice it was to be friends with Christine again. Yvonne had even come over and talked to her.

There were one or two creaks on the stairs, then her mum appeared in her big frilly cotton nightie and sheepskin slippers. Her hair was in rollers, her face glistened with cold cream. 'Hello, love,' she whispered. 'Kit called round about, ooh, three-quarters of an hour ago.'

'Did he?' Jen couldn't help smiling. Was one evening apart too much for him?

'He brought a note. Here.'

Jen took it, her good mood fading. 'Thanks.'

'Oh, love, I do hope it's not...'

Me too, she thought. She read 'Jennifer' – how formal – and went cold.

'He had some friends with him. A nice-looking girl with big teeth. I invited them in, only they could see we were...' She gestured to her nightie. 'Aren't you going to open it?'

Jen's heart had turned into a lump of concrete. Kit knew she'd be at the youth club, that she wouldn't be home. 'Of course,' she told her mother. She got up and took the envelope out of the dark room, with a 'Night.'

'Oh... Night-night, then, love.'

But in the light of the hall, the handwriting looked different and not at all like Kit's. She took the stairs two at a time and closed her bedroom door quietly. Her dad did *not* like being woken before he was ready.

Switching the lamp on, she flopped on her bed and slowly ripped the envelope open. One sheet. She unfolded it and took a deep breath. 'Jennifer,' it said, 'Kit tells me your ankle is fully healed, so perhaps we could re-commence the tennis. Two o'clock tomorrow? Eleanor Avery. PS. I'll assume this suits you unless I hear otherwise.'

Jen's entire body relaxed, and she just lay there grinning. Mrs Avery had actually discussed her with Kit and given him a note to deliver. Amazing. After a while, she got up, changed into her T-shirt nightie, tiptoed to the bathroom and back, and quietly closed her door. After reading the note again, she crept downstairs, put the light on and went to the sideboard. From it she took the dictionary she'd used more in the past few weeks than in the whole of her life. 'Recommence', she found in the list of 're-'words. She smiled, put the book away, and went to bed both happy and unhappy. Tennis again.

# TWENTY-FOUR

Jen tidied borders and swept the patio. Having skimmed the Kingston property pages, she was hoping for a valuation of around two hundred and forty or fifty. After expenses, she'd see a profit of a hundred thousand, which wasn't bad for a lick of paint, two boiler services and a rotary washing line; all she'd done in two years. The garden took her ten minutes. 'Compact', 'easily managed', she thought, ready for the man from Powell and Powell.

From one end of the open-plan downstairs, Jen watched Terence straightening pictures. He wore a shirt as black as his hair and slightly crumpled grey cotton trousers. He was quite gorgeous, but he was also thirty-two. And the photo he was straightening now was of his stunning girlfriend, Alexa, the reason he was moving to Cornwall.

'There,' he said, head cocked at Alexa. 'Would you rather I went out, Jen? Might make the place look bigger.'

'No, no.' If anything, Terence would add value. 'Unless you'd prefer to go?'

He stayed, the man from Powell and Powell came, and Jen's tiny, one-and-a-half-bedroomed house-stroke-cottage was valued at a staggering two nine nine, nine fifty. 'Couldn't we say three hundred?' she'd asked, but apparently it would have put people off.

The plan was to sell one of the properties in order to see herself through the divorce. And since Terence was moving out, and since the valuation had been so astonishingly high, it would, she decided there and then, be the Kingston house. Properties were flying off the shelf, so by the summer, she'd have a nice wad in the bank, and eventually an even bigger pile coming her way from either Robert or the sale of their home. Their once-lovely home, now blighted by deceit. Robert had yet to decide what to do with the house, still hoping she'd come back, no doubt.

Recently, he'd met her in a car park with a boot full of the things she'd requested by email: clothes, books, CDs, gifts and so on. But sifting through, back at the flat, she'd felt a gloomy reminiscent mood descend. Soon, she was shoving it all in the large hall cupboard: the dress she'd worn to Robert's brother's wedding; the Nanci Griffith she and Robert had played and played; presents he'd given her and a handful of painful photographs. They were mainly from way back, when Robert would pose with an arm around her: the two of them in Marrakesh, looking radiant, Robert planting a kiss on her one Christmas. She hadn't asked for photos, but could hardly blame him for trying.

She'd request nothing else from home, not even the jewellery he'd deliberately forgotten. 'Oh, sorry, shall I bring that another time? Tomorrow?' And everything he'd brought her – minus the photos, which her parents could have – would go to charity shops. Even her clothes. A fresh start all round was essential, but for that she needed money. Hence, the sale of a property.

Driving home, after a few days in Brighton and the Kingston detour, with the sun out and the streets of London beginning to blossom, Jen experienced something close to happiness. It wasn't the real thing, because she'd known how that felt – passing her driving test, becoming an aunt, hearing the agent's valuation on completing her first gruelling project. She'd had help with that one from Robert, who'd come up with the deposit. From property number two, a tired flat in Ealing, she'd been on her own.

No, it wasn't exactly happiness. Optimism, perhaps, and the realisation that she had so much going for her. She was financially secure, in good health and not that old. If they got cracking on this gene therapy business, she might only be a third of the way through her life, or so she'd read at the dentist's.

Back home, Jen listened to a message from a distraught Robert, arranged two more valuations on the Kingston house, unpacked her case, and watered her one very thirsty plant. The flat was feeling more like home now, what with the things she'd picked up over the weeks. Not too many things. She was going for uncluttered; all the more so after staying with Paul and co.

A real bed tonight, she thought, almost ready for it now. She'd trusted Lionel to get it and he'd chosen well. 'Pocket sprung with hand-stitched sides,' he'd told her. 'The dog's bollocks of mattresses.'

She'd begun to sleep well again, immune now to the low-level rap, slammed doors, voices on the stairs. She'd wake at the sound of little Trinity, but perhaps no woman, not even a childless one, could zone out a baby crying. But that had become less frequent. She was sleeping through, most nights, Ruth had said, last time they'd chatted on the stairs. She'd looked exhausted, with dark rings under her eyes. Her hair had been clean but lank, as though it needed a good cut. One of her sons had been helping her haul the buggy up, Trinity still in it, bags of food dangling from the handles. The building had an ancient lift, but no one seemed to use it, especially not Jen. Neither she nor Ruth had mentioned the 'cuppa' again. Both realising, perhaps, how their lives were worlds apart.

Opening a window, Jen took in the rooftops for a while, thinking about Robert and how she was the last person he should be calling in a state. As much as she liked him and felt sorry for him, Jen was having trouble feeling her husband's pain – really feeling it. She had no desire to go back to him and wondered why he'd want her to. She wouldn't return his call, she decided. Robert had friends he could talk to, and he could afford counselling, if it came to it. Someone like Lionel, that was what Robert needed.

She wondered where her builder was and if he fancied doing something. She tried his home and mobile numbers with no luck, which was annoying. Perhaps it was time to find new friends and acquaintances. Join a group or class or get a part-time job.

After filling the washing machine, Jen flicked through the TV channels, found nothing, put the radio on instead, and made herself a coffee. Three hundred thousand! She still couldn't believe it. Was the market peaking? Should she gradually sell all her places, as the tenants' leases expired? She'd have a look on the internet, she decided, wandering through to the study with her mug. See what the experts were forecasting. First, though, since she'd been away three days, she'd check her email.

Later, much later, Jen lay on the sofa going over his message, going over her reply, going over his reply to her reply. Norfolk. Pip missing. Nephew. A levels. Spare bedroom. Why didn't she come up?

Had Kit emailed when she'd first got in touch, her reaction would have been elation. But in the couple of weeks it had taken him to discover her message, Jen had put all, or almost all, thoughts of him aside. Now, lying there, listening to dogs and traffic through the open window, she wasn't fantasising madly; her heart wasn't beating wildly. She felt a little trepidation, but mostly she was concerned. Poor Kit. Poor Pip. Poor ... had he said his nephew's name?

She wouldn't give her old clothes to charity just yet. Some of the outdoorsy things might come in handy, and there would be changeable weather to cater for. She had two days to sort out work-related matters and get her hair done. Train or car? If she drove she could take her wellies. In spite of all its RAF bases, Jen had never been to that part of the world. She pictured miles of sea-drenched mud. Hadn't the land been reclaimed? Or was that Cambridgeshire? 'It's beautiful,' he'd said in his email. Neither had suggested they talk on the phone before Wednesday. Trepidation, perhaps.

She woke in the night with butterflies. She was going to see Kit! And he was single, which was amazing. Hard to believe, really. Said he'd never married. From the tone of his email, Jen had the feeling they'd get on as well as they once had. She rolled over, smiling to herself, then rolled back. It was no good, she couldn't sleep. So much for pocket springs. Perhaps half of one of those tablets? They were meant to be for emergencies, but this could be considered one. She sat up and put the bedside lamp on.

Odd, she thought, that he was still single. Theirs was a generation that tended to marry, despite all the free-love talk and seventies feminism. She reached into the drawer for the box and found half a tablet, which she managed without liquid. Pip had married, apparently, but his wife had died. Kit hadn't said how. She remembered Pip as someone who'd struggled socially, hadn't been happy at his school. Shy and overweight and uncoordinated. But at least he'd found a wife, unlike his brother. Jen had a few female friends who hadn't married or lived long term with someone, but couldn't think of a male friend, her age, who hadn't. There was Aaron, of course, but he was gay...

Staring at a spot on the far wall, waiting for the

sedative to kick in, Jen felt the butterflies turn from pleasant to unpleasant. 'Please, *no*,' she whispered, competing with a siren. There was always a siren in this part of town. 'Not Kit.'

## TWENTY-FIVE

**August 1969**

'Long time no see,' said Mrs Avery. Her hair was in a very high ponytail, like a blonde fountain on her head. She wore a proper tennis T-shirt, but with tiny pink shorts that matched her button earrings. 'How have you been, Jennifer?'

'Er, fine ... thanks.'

'And your ankle?'

'Much better ... thank you.'

'Jolly good. I've missed our matches. Now, which end would you like?'

'I don't mind,' Jen said, wondering if Mrs Avery had been at the Dubonnet.

They had a warm-up, then began a game; Mrs Avery insisting Jen serve first. There was a slight breeze but it was still baking hot. Sweat began pouring down Jen's face early on, but not, as usual, her opponent's. However, being cool as a cucumber didn't help Mrs Avery's game, which had gone a bit rusty through lack of playing. Either that or she'd had a late night swapping husbands.

Her tennis might not have been good, but her mood was, and when they reached the end of the two-set match – a walkover for Jen – Mrs Avery laughed breathlessly at the net. 'Congratulations *again!*'she said. She was redoing the ponytail that made her look eighteen – from a distance. 'Would you like to come back for refreshments?'

'To yours?'

'Uh-huh.' Mrs Avery wound a band round her hair, then took the racquet from between her knees. 'I have a jug of lemonade, apple, orange and mint in the fridge.' She bobbed her eyebrows and smiled. 'We'll have it with ice and pretend it's Pimm's.'

'OK,' said Jen, trying not to look or sound suspicious. Or worried. Would Kit be there? Would it be uncomfortable? Embarrassing? She had no idea what Pimm's was, but the lemonade sounded lovely. She could always drink up quickly and make her excuses; baby-sitting, or a doctor's appointment. No, not the doctor. Kit's mum might think she was going for the pill. 'Sounds nice.'

On the way, Mrs Avery talked about Wimbledon; mostly the male players. She thought John Newcombe was an absolute dish, and to a lesser extent, Tony Roche. 'Those Australians,' she said with a sigh.

'Yes,' said Jen, although she hadn't seen Wimbledon for ages. When they showed bits on Dutch news, her dad always turned over. 'Have you been playing tennis long?' she asked.

'Rather. Nanny had me on our courts aged five.'

A really long time, then, Jen almost said. Kit's mother was hard to talk to, but Jen couldn't work

186

out why. She was scary, that was part of it. 'Did you have your own courts?'

'Oh, everybody did then.'

She wished Mrs Avery would ask *her* something, but at the same time she didn't, because the answer might remind her that Jen was from a different class. Like, 'Actually, my mum's never played tennis in her life.'

It seemed to take an age to reach their house, with Mrs Avery humming, in the end, when conversation dried up. Finally, they were walking through the side door into the kitchen, where it was beautifully cool. Jen asked if she could use the toilet, not knowing if she should have said bathroom or powder room or something. Walking along the hall, she checked the dining room and lounge for Kit, but there were no signs of anyone. It seemed she was alone with Mrs Avery and it didn't feel that good.

The house smelled nice, though. Spices and lemons and the batwoman's polish. And flowers. There were even flowers in the cloakroom. *Cloakroom*, she thought, not toilet.

Back in the kitchen, her face now splashed with water, her hands soft with almond hand cream, Jen took the fancy drink with its curly straw from Mrs Avery and followed her out to a patio. Was Kit in the attic? She thought about saying something loudly, so he'd come and save her. But loud could be seen as common, so she said, 'Lovely garden, Mrs Avery.'

'Oh, Jennifer, please. I think we know each other well enough for "Eleanor".'

Jen wondered if she'd ever known anyone less,

187

but smiled and nodded and sucked on her ice-cold fruity minty lemonade.

Kit's mother arranged herself on a lounger, which she manoeuvred to more of a recline before slipping on a pair of sunglasses. 'Tell me, Jennifer,' she said, now facing the sky with her arms by her sides, one hand still holding the glass. Her drink was a different colour from Jen's. More reddish. 'How are you finding Kit at the moment?'

Jen had no idea what to say. He'd been a bit quiet, a bit down, ever since their day in Mönchengladbach. Recently, in the hut, he'd told her that being with her was like having a joint after an arduous day in class. That she made him feel relaxed and happy. 'Fine,' she told Mrs Avery.

'Really? I'm awfully worried about him.'

'Oh?' Jen tensed up. Was there something she didn't know about … a serious illness?

'He's become monosyllabic. Barely speaks to me, in fact.'

Jen relaxed. Kit's mum was just worried about herself, or *for* herself. Jen closed her eyes, smiled and raised her face to the mid-afternoon sun. She might be a lowly sergeant's daughter but she was Kit's relaxing joint. Mrs Avery, on the other hand, had been sent to Coventry by her son, was average at tennis and couldn't spell.

The sunbed creaked as Mrs Avery sat up. Jen opened her eyes and watched her lift the sunglasses and turn to her. 'I thought perhaps with you around, Jennifer, he might come out of his shell.'

'Oh, right.'

'Teenage boys are famously grumpy and rebellious and detest their parents, but it's terribly out of character for Kit to be this way.'

'Yes.' It was hard to know what to do. Should she say, or at least hint at why Kit was angry with his mum? If she said the right thing, nice and tactfully, Mrs Avery might mend her ways and not get divorced.

'Excuse me.' Mrs Avery swung her bronzed legs round, got up and went indoors. 'Kit, darling!' she called in the distance. 'Jennifer's here!'

Jen's insides began spinning. Kit's mother expected her to smooth things over, which was a big expectation. She reached for Mrs Avery's glass and took a gulp. The drink burned as it went down. It tasted foul, but she took another gulp and put it back

Mrs Avery returned, followed by Kit, who appeared to take the fact that Jen was sitting in his garden in his stride. 'Hello,' he said, leaning against the French window frame, looking lovely and as though he'd just woken up. He wore shorts and his legs were as tanned as his mother's. He scratched his head and gave her a beautiful smile. 'Want to come up?'

Jen shot Mrs Avery a look and said, 'Your mum and I were just chatting.' *Mother*, she thought. Aargh.

'Darling, why don't you join us?'

Kit pulled a face, then stepped down and hopped on bare feet over the hot paving slabs. 'Shit,' he said, falling into the chair.

His mother said, 'I'll get your shoes, darling,' and disappeared again.

'What's going on?' Kit asked Jen.

'We played tennis,' she whispered, leaning forward. 'I got invited back.'

'Jen, have you been drinking?'

Mrs Avery appeared with Kit's lovely scruffy sneakers, then she fetched a drink for him, and a big brolly, which she slotted into a nearby table. The chairs got moved into the shade, and glasses got put on the table.

'Now, tell me,' she said, sitting down, 'what have you two been up to lately?'

Kit shrugged. 'Nothing as exciting as you've been up to, Ma.'

Mrs Avery beamed at her son. 'Don't be silly, Kit. You know my life's as dull as mud. I mean ... have you seen any good films, for example?'

'Oh,' said Kit, scratching again, 'let me think. There was *The Graduate*, wasn't there, Jen?' He was smirking in a way Jen had never seen. She'd never seen *The Graduate*, either. 'You know, about the sex-mad older woman?'

'Oh, for goodness' sake, Kit.' Mrs Avery drank from her topped-up glass, then put it down on the table, a quarter full. Jen imagined her throat burning.

'What?' said Kit.

'I do wish you'd grow up.'

'I will, if you will.'

Mrs Avery tutted and shook her head, then looked at Jen, as though it was her turn to say something to him. Only what on earth could she say? She looked into her drink and stayed quiet.

'How's the guitar coming along?' Mrs Avery said, after a brief silence. 'Does he play to you,

Jennifer? Kit will never play for me.'

Kit had learned a few chords, and was always trying to impress Jen with new songs, 'House of the Rising Sun' being the latest. 'Not that much,' she told his mum, not wanting her to feel even worse, and not wanting to make Kit look bad.

But now he was shaking his head at her. 'Jennifer Juniper,' he said disappointedly, and she felt she couldn't win with either of them. She needed something urgent to do, but just had to decide what it was. Dust her room? She'd been promising her mum for days. 'Oh dear,' she said, looking at her watch. 'I'm going to be late.' She stood up, drained her glass and put it on the table. 'Sorry. Lovely drink, thank you, Mrs Avery.'

'*Eleanor.*'

'Late for what?' asked Kit.

'Um.' Jen tried to think what to say and where she'd left her racquet. She felt light-headed. From the sun, perhaps, or the tension, or Mrs Avery's drink. 'The doctor's,' she told them.

'Which one?' asked Kit's mum.

'Oh, er...' She'd been once, about a corn on her little toe. Who had she seen? Dr Evans? 'I think it's Dr Evans.'

'Aah, the gorgeous Nigel,' said Mrs Avery. She smiled at no one in particular and swung her sunglasses. '*Wonderful* bedside manner.'

Kit said, 'Christ, Ma,' scraped his chair back and slouched back to the house.

Jen gave his mother a little wave, even though she seemed miles away, and followed him in, then, by the front door, he pulled her towards him. 'Are you all right?' he asked. 'Nothing terminal?'

'No, no. Just...' Now she'd started, she'd have to come up with something. And she wished she hadn't lied to Mrs Avery, who obviously knew Dr Evans well, and might find out she didn't have an appointment. 'A corn,' she said, pulling a face on his shoulder, and wondering if she could have made things worse if she'd tried. Still, at least she was welcome at the house. Until she wasn't again.

## TWENTY-SIX

Jen had booked herself into The Bell for two nights. This saved Kit from having to clear out the guest room. Somewhere in there was a bed, but he'd never seen it. An old friend, he'd told Adam, from Germany. Enough information for now, he'd felt, and if Jen turned out to be a horror, he'd leave it at that. She'd be arriving at four, at the train station. It was approaching one thirty and Kit was experiencing some anxiety. He'd been in war-torn countries, had near air misses, been on hundreds of potentially scary dates... Things didn't tend to unnerve him. A walk, he decided. Bunk, reading his mind, reached the lead before he did.

In a box, in London, tucked away in the locked room, was a photo of Jen. He hadn't looked at it for years, perhaps decades. As he and Bunk hit the beach, Kit recalled what he could of the image. Long dark hair, parted in the middle. A pair of curtains covering half her cheeks and the edges of her eyes. The fashion, but it had also helped her hide from the world. An ankle-length skirt, as a change from the minis. Floral, or paisley, something like that. Sleeveless white top, the trace of a smile. Skinny, shy, sensitive, eager-to-please Jen. Kit smiled to himself and threw the stick he'd found for Bunk. She'd been a great kisser too. Luckily – because that was all they'd done for hours on end, in that stifling storage hut, or in his room. Nice, he remembered, if a tad frustrating at seventeen, or any age.

Kit eked out the dog walk, returning to the house just before three. He took a quick kneeling-down shower with the grubby plastic hose attached to the bath taps, dressed, then changed what he was wearing, changed again, and set off.

She said she'd recognise him from his website and she did, walking straight up and offering a hand, then changing her mind and kissing his cheek.

'Jen?' he asked stupidly. Of course it was her. He'd been looking out for stick-thin, but she'd put on weight, as people do. Which was good, as it suited her. Same eyes, but with faint lines here and there. Same pretty features, shorter hair, although almost at her shoulders. Darker than before. Coloured, perhaps. She wore black trousers and a grey polo-neck jumper, in lambswool or cashmere or something soft. She was trailing a case that would do for a fortnight. 'How lovely to see you,' he said, and it really was.

'You too. Any news of Pip?'

He was slightly thrown by her question. It was one people had stopped asking. But to Jen, Pip was a new story, a fresh emergency. 'Unfortunately not,' he said. She'd soon realise how they'd all given up. 'Here, let me take that.'

'I can manage.'

He smiled at her. Actually, he couldn't stop smiling. 'You wouldn't have said that at fifteen.'

'I know,' she said, and laughed, exactly as she used to.

In the car, when Kit was creeping out of Norwich in rush-hour traffic, boring Jen with Adam's A levels because it was a nice neutral subject, her phone rang.

'Hi, Paul,' she said warmly.

Paul?

'What!' she said, then, 'Why...? Oh, no... Oh, dear. Really...? Oh *God*, I'm so sorry, Paul... No, but... No, he can't drive home, not if he's been drinking. There's that hotel I stayed in...? I can't... Norfolk, visiting an old friend. Yeah ... yeah ... all right ... all right ... OK ... I'll call you in a little while... And thanks, Paul... Bye.' She held the phone and jiggled it for a while, then put it away and leaned back in her seat. 'Interesting A level combination,' she said, 'Biology, Chemistry and English.'

OK, thought Kit. 'Adam can't decide if he wants to be a scientist or a poet.'

'Perhaps he could do both?'

'Maybe. A science degree would be a good start, though.' They ground to a halt at more traffic

194

lights. 'Is, er, everything OK?' He nodded towards the bag on her lap.

'Yeah, yeah.' She snorted prettily. 'My ex-husband's pitched up at my brother's. Robert's taken it all rather badly, you see.' She shrugged prettily again. 'But then perhaps he should suffer.'

'Oh?' said Kit, but she turned to her window and stared at a wall.

'Your accent's changed,' Jen told him.

They were in the country at last and, thank God, heading for the coast. 'Oh?'

'Not quite so top drawer.'

'That's Clapham for you. Yours has changed too.'

'Posher?'

'Yep.'

'Well,' she said, 'that's Highgate for you.' She attempted a laugh. 'Funny, isn't it?'

'What?'

'You know, life. Where we start, what we become.'

'Mm,' he said. He wanted to hear about the marriage, but they had time for that. 'It is.'

'And, er, how's your mother?'

'She's good. Still very active.'

'Great!' Jen said, but then she sighed, giving away her true feelings. 'And does she live...?' She did a whirly thing with a finger.

'Around here? No. Hampshire. But she's been in Italy since Christmas.'

'Living there?'

'No. She's on a sort of ever-extending holiday

with her partner.'

'But surely she came back when Pip–'

'No. We didn't see the need.' He flashed her a smile in case he'd been sharp. Too much to explain. 'She still plays tennis, you know.'

'Wow.'

'And you?'

'I did before...Yes, yes I do.' She'd told him very little in her emails. Divorcing, no children, owned a few properties.

'How about your parents?' he asked. 'Are they both still...?'

'Alive? Yes, they are. They haven't changed much, either. Actually, Dad's more mellow. They moved to Essex when he retired from the air force. He made chief tech in the end.'

'That's great. I liked your parents.'

'Yeah. They liked you too. Not just because you were the only officer's child ever to visit them.'

'Pretty radical, eh?'

She laughed. 'Well, you were a radical. And very anti the military, I remember.'

'Not now,' he said, grinning. 'So long as they behave themselves. I was a bit of an idiot, wasn't I? I'd read *Das Kapital* and wanted to change the world, but I didn't know anything.'

'*You* didn't know anything? I can't believe how uninformed I was at fifteen. I thought you were a genius.'

'So did I. God, I must have been unbearable. Anyway. I've seen enough now to know how necessary the military is, so long as it doesn't get into the wrong hands. The Americans', for example.' They both laughed, and she started to say something, but he got there first. 'And you live in Highgate?'

'Oh, er, no. Not any more.' She turned her head away again and looked through her window.

'Ah,' Kit said, wishing they could get to The Bell, get her booked in, get a drink inside them. 'Not far now.'

'So,' she said, as they entered the village. 'How's your love life up here?'

Young Jen would never have been so bold. 'Quiet,' Kit told her. 'As you'd imagine.'

And is there a woman pining for you in London?'

'A woman?' he said, chuckling. 'No, no.' He turned and smiled but she was gazing at him, wide-eyed, scarily.

'A man?'

'I'm sorry?'

'I suppose I'm asking if you're gay.'

'Jesus, no.' He flashed her a look. What was going on? 'Do I seem gay to you?'

'Oh God, Kit. I'm sorry.' She touched his shoulder briefly. 'It's just that...'

'What?'

'Oh ... long story.'

Bunk and Adam chose different ways to greet their guest. Bunk bounded, jumped and licked. Adam sloped into the room, hands in pockets, and almost nodded. Kit introduced his nephew to Jen.

'Ah, yes!' she said, with an unexpected clap. 'It *was* you at the Stop the War rally. Although your hair was longer?'

Kit and Adam could only stand and stare, then Adam said, 'How come? I mean, all those people, and, like, you hadn't even met me?'

She took an envelope from her shoulder bag, and from the envelope, a photo. 'Here.' She handed it to Adam.

'What?' he said, head jerking back as though someone had hit him. 'Is that...?' He passed it on.

Kit looked at the photo, looked at his nephew, back at the photo, back to his nephew. 'Was this taken in Germany?'

'Don't you remember?' Jen looked slightly hurt. 'Anyway, I thought it was *you* at the rally, still aged seventeen. Thought I was going mad. And then I saw you, Kit, only I wasn't sure and then I was stuck in ... well, another long story.'

Adam took the photo and shook his head. 'It could be me, couldn't it? He held it at arm's-length. 'Except I'd never wear a tablecloth with a hole in it.'

Kit rolled his eyes. 'Poncho, Adam.'

They ate at The Bell, where Jen's portfolio came up.

'How many properties?' Adam asked.

'Seven. Although I'm about to sell one.'

'For a nice little profit, no doubt?'

'Adam,' Kit said quietly. He didn't like his tone. Jen smiled, hopefully oblivious. 'Actually, yes.'

Adam sighed, long and deliberately. 'And you do this ... why?'

'Top up, Jen?' asked Kit.

'Mm, yes, please.' She held the stem of her

198

glass, while Kit poured. 'I suppose,' she said, returning Adam's stare, 'I do it, or *did* it, because it was enjoyable. You know, tarting the places up. Some only needed a coat of paint, others were completely transformed. That can be very satisfying.'

'Charging top-whack rents must be satisfying too?'

'I'm not sure I do,' Jen said, with a disarming smile.

Adam went back to his food, disarmed, perhaps, and Kit quickly filled the silence. 'Remember those cold and draughty married quarters, Jen? No central heating and ice on the inside of the windows?'

'Officers had that too?' she asked, laughing. 'Those metal windows that never quite closed?'

'Sounds like our place,' said Adam, 'before the council got its act together.'

'It's very nice now,' said Jen.

'Yeah, right. I'm sure you think it's a palace.'

'Adam,' Kit said again, more forcefully.

Adam put his knife and fork down. 'Sorry,' he said, looking at his half-eaten plate. He took the napkin from his lap and put it on the table. 'I should go.'

'No, don't,' Jen said, she went to put out a hand, then withdrew it.

'Come on,' said Kit. 'Eat up.'

'No, really.' Adam pushed his chair back. 'I've got work I should be getting on with. Revision. Sorry. Have a nice...' He stood and nodded at the contents of the table. 'See you later.'

'OK,' Kit said, embarrassed by his nephew's

behaviour, and hoping Jen would realise it was nothing she'd said. Once his nephew had left the room, he turned to Jen. 'I'm sorry. He's just very–'

'I know,' she said, putting a hand on his arm to stop him. 'I know.'

Jen appeared relaxed after that, helped perhaps by the, 'Mm, yes, please,' every time Kit waved the bottle over her glass. She'd made a valiant effort with Adam and appeared to be a lovely woman, just as she'd been a lovely girl. Nice to look at and good company, she would, he hoped, become a bit of a prop. Until her arrival and the surprisingly enjoyable pub meal, Kit hadn't even known he wanted a prop.

'Adam *hates* the fact that I buy houses,' Jen said, once they'd finished dessert. Her cheeks were flushed and he remembered how easily she'd blushed.

'Oh, not really. I expect his father's got a hang-up, that's all. Kids these days aren't left-leaning, anti-materialistic rebels. Not in my experience.' Kit wondered what experience he'd actually had, outside of young people emailing him. Just Adam, really, who veered towards the environmental, rather than socialist.

'Anyway, I'm thinking of selling up. Everything.'

'Really? You could miss out on millions, if the market keeps rising.'

'And if it doesn't? Remember the early nineties? Also, I feel like doing something different. Property reminds me of my marriage.'

There was an uncomfortable silence, when Kit should have asked what happened, but Jen had been so upbeat, he didn't want to spoil things. Let her tell you, he thought. But she didn't, and the silence grew longer, and then they both went to say something at the same time.

'After you,' said Kit.

'I was going to say ... well, I've often wondered what happened, you know, after Germany. After we lost touch. I wrote to you, often. I don't know if you...'

'Yes, I think I did get them. But you know what boys are like. Not the best communicators in the world. Not when it comes to letters, anyway.'

'No,' she said. She looked hurt again, frowning at her drink. 'I suppose not.'

Kit guessed he must have been inadvertently cruel to her too. He said, 'Sorry,' and pictured young Jen, left behind in Germany, waiting and waiting for a letter. Why hadn't he written? It would have been so easy. Most teens were thoughtless, though. Boys the more so, perhaps. 'But what with everything that had happened...'

'That's OK,' she said. She offered him more wine, but he shook his head. 'Was it–'

'Pretty bloody awful? Yes. Far worse for poor Pip, though. I carried on boarding, as I only had a year left, but Pip had to go to a secondary modern in Chesterfield.'

'He hadn't passed his eleven-plus?'

'No. Private schools overlooked that, if you were willing to pay their fees. Or the RAF was, at any rate.'

'But wouldn't the Air Force have carried on

paying? Considering everything.'

'I don't know. I mean, it was all rather complicated. And, besides, Pip loathed boarding. He was desperate to leave that school. Don't you remember?'

'Yes. Yes, I do. Listen, shall we order another bottle?'

'Er, yeah.' He couldn't believe they'd got through the first. Adam had drunk fizzy apple, and Kit, preferring red, had probably had only one glass of wine. He waved at the waitress, who was there in a minute with another bottle. A Pinot Grigio. Jen had said it was her favourite and now she was proving it.

'Thanks,' she said. 'Sorry. I interrupted you. How did you both cope?'

'Well, the school holidays weren't exactly fun, but for Pip it was all-year-round hell. He became more and more withdrawn, and then actually disappeared for a while, when he was eighteen.' Kit told her the story of the girl and the Weymouth caravan.

'Aha! So he's done this before?'

'Yes.' Was Jen getting louder, or was it his imagination? He watched her take another sip of wine and then another. Meanwhile, he toyed with his own glass. He fancied a beer but that would be rude. 'There's no girlfriend now, according to Adam. Hasn't been since Pat died.'

'How did she—'

'Heart. Very sudden. Nobody had known there was a problem.'

'God, how tragic. Pip must have been devastated?'

'Yes,' said Kit, 'we all were.' He'd flown back for the funeral, but he ought really to have stayed longer. Lots of Pat's relatives, Kit remembered, spilling out of the house. He must have thought Pip and Adam would be all right. 'Anyway, Adam says his father was never able to form a relationship after that, always comparing women with Pat.'

Jen was peering into her glass. She drank more and peered again. 'I wonder if I'll do that. That is, if anyone happens along. Compare everyone to Robert.'

'What's he like?'

'Oh ... nice. Friendly. Warm. Always on the go, always doing things. A bit on the conventional side, but then maybe I am too. Not sure I know who I am at the moment. Anyway, everybody *loves* Robert. My friends, my family, the bloody window cleaner. Robert's clients end up being his friends. Do you know the type?' She laughed and poured herself more wine. 'Aren't you drinking? Here. Top up?'

'Just a little,' he said, holding the base while she added a dribble to his full glass.

'And Robert loves everyone too. And when I say everyone, I mean everybloodyone.'

'Right.' He was getting the picture. Adulterer.

Jen snorted. Not quite so prettily this time. 'Although some more than others. Especially ones with...' She put the glass against her cheek and peered at Kit's shirt pocket. Or else she was miles away.

'With...?'

'Cocks,' she said. Too late, she looked around to

203

see who'd heard. But it was past ten and there was only the distant table-wiping waitress. Jen leaned across the table. 'My husband fucked men.'

'Oh?' he said. Not that her words needed explaining. 'I mean, I'm so sorry to hear that.' So that was why she'd asked those questions in the car, about his sexuality. Kit had once been with a woman – Frankie, not her real name – who'd just left a woman. He and Frankie had been together a month or so, before she announced they weren't really gelling, physically. This was something that hadn't gone unnoticed by Kit, or so he convinced himself. The experience had left him wondering, for a while at least, about any woman he met. 'Do you want to talk about it?'

'Yes and no.' Jen knocked back her wine and semi-slammed her glass on the table. 'In fact, no,' she said. 'Not now.'

'OK.' He held up the remains of their second bottle, wondering if she had a drink problem. 'Would you like to finish this?' he asked, testing her, perhaps.

Jen lifted her glass and wobbled it. 'Is George Michael gay?' She fell about in a kind of swaying, head-hung manner, but when she looked up she seemed to be crying. Crying with laughter, or crying? 'I'm so sorry,' she said, reaching for her crumpled napkin, or perhaps it was his. Dabbing at her nose. 'It's just such a relief, being here. Feeling – I don't know – safe and supported, I suppose, after the past ghastly couple of months.' Her mascara had smudged. She sniffed and gave him a trembling smile.

'And it's lovely having you,' said Kit, gesturing for the bill. Supported? Suddenly the whole world needed his support. As fascinating as the my-husband-was-gay story sounded, he'd get her to her room, go home, crank up the computer and look up tomorrow's trains.

'I ought to phone my brother back,' she was saying, 'but I can't face it. I'll end up feeling guilty, even though Robert's the one who fucked around.'

Kit smiled apologetically at the waitress and scribbled his name on the debit card slip. 'Do you remember your room number?'

Jen squinted at him for quite a while, frowning, eyes still smudged, as though he'd asked her something really hard. 'Thirty-two?'

He laughed. 'I'm not sure The Bell's that big. Got your key?'

'Ah.' She veered towards her bag on the floor, steadied herself on a nearby chair, rummaged, and pulled out first her own keys, and then the room key. 'Three,' she said.

'That's more like it. Ready?'

She stood up and wobbled, and before leaving the table, blew her nose into the napkin.

Marriage, Kit decided, guiding her through the dining room and the bar, past Eddie and the others on their stools, had a lot to answer for.

# TWENTY-SEVEN

The first person she saw was Sonia Durrell, back from her holiday, all made up and in the shortest of skirts. She was with Yvonne, who leaned over and whispered something in her ear. Or more likely shouted. You had to shout over The Flying Colours, playing on stage. Jen had seen them before. Five airmen. They were quite good, but no matter how many beads they wore, they still looked like airmen. They were doing 'Young Girl', one of Jen's favourites. She was keen to dance but they were going for drinks first.

'What a blast!' shouted Kit.

Jen squeezed his hand and hoped he hadn't spotted Sonia. Sonia had definitely spotted Kit. She and Yvonne, and now Christine, were gawping rudely. Or perhaps it was Susie they were staring at, because you never saw officers' kids at an Airmen's Mess dance, let alone the group captain's daughter. Lawrence, tall and dark and curly-haired, followed at the rear, as Jen led everyone to the bar, taking a convoluted route to avoid her friends.

Kit and Lawrence ordered beers, and Susie a vodka and lime. Jen wanted lemon barley, but chickened out and asked for cider. Kit paid, as usual, and they made their way back to the dance floor, where Sonia, Yvonne and Christine were being chatted up by airmen. After finding a table

206

for their drinks, the four of them joined the dancers. Young married couples with their funny jerky movements. Older couples jiving. Everyone Jen knew was doing the latest, where you just moved your feet and wrists a bit, nothing else. Then there was Lawrence not dancing in time, and Kit in his psychedelic, wavy-arm trance. Susie was wiggling her bum energetically, arms held high, head nodding, hair flying, like a go-go dancer in a cage. Jen watched Susie with admiration and horror, while she, herself, just moved her feet and wrists a bit.

They alternated drinking with dancing, and then Lawrence decided to do only the drinking part. The Flying Colours took a break too, but Jen, Kit and Susie carried on dancing to the records being played, mostly Motown.

It was then that Christine and the others, without the airmen, came and danced right next to them. Jen couldn't make out if they were being friendly or confrontational. She tried smiling at Christine but didn't get one back. It had been Christine's idea that Jen brought Kit here, but she probably hadn't meant half the officers' kids too. Having friends was hard work. Maybe Pip was better off without them.

Sonia, the show-off, swayed her hips almost as much as Susie, only more tartily, in her turquoise halter neck and tiny skirt. Occasionally, she shot Kit a look and Jen wanted to kill her, but Kit was miles away. Probably San Francisco.

Steve, Martin and a couple of others from school appeared, and just hung around watching. It was a bit off-putting, but Jen focused on Kit and soon forgot they were there.

For a while it went quiet. The records had stopped and the group were picking up their guitars. Jen and Kit were about to join Lawrence, when Martin swaggered over and said, 'Aren't you going to introduce me to your friend, Jen?'

'This is Kit,' she said. She didn't like the look on Martin's face, or the way he was sticking his chest out. 'This is Martin,' she told Kit.

'Hi,' said Kit, smiling and holding up the palm of his hand.

Martin sniggered and Jen, suddenly on edge, said, 'Actually, we were just going to...' She nodded towards Lawrence, sitting at a table on his fourth or fifth beer.

'What's the matter?' Martin asked. 'Too stuck up to speak to your old mates, eh?'

'Of course not. It's just that–'

'Only the hofficer's lot good enough for you now?' He got hold of her arm. 'Stay and have a dance.' Jen tried pulling away, but he wasn't letting go. 'I know you've always fancied me, Jen. Forget this stupid toff in his girlie shirt, and let's have a nice slow dance, yeah?'

'Let go of her!' Kit said forcefully. 'Or I'll bop you one!'

'Oh, you'll bop me one, will you? Here, Steve, come and listen to this.'

'It's OK, Kit,' Jen said. Martin was always getting into fights at school and he usually won. Kit might have been a bit taller but Martin was all muscle, and now he was getting Steve in.

'Let go of her!' Kit yelled again.

A group was forming and Jen felt her stomach

knotting up. Once again, she tried yanking her arm away, and Martin tightened his grip. *'Ow!'* she cried out, and before she knew it Kit had walloped Martin in the face, and then her arm *was* let go of because Martin was on the floor.

'You can't say I didn't warn you!' said Kit, putting an arm around Jen's waist and pulling her towards him. Steve helped Martin up and then the two of them charged at Kit and began laying into him. Jen screamed, and when one of the blows almost landed on her, she stepped back.

'Stop it!' she shouted, but others were egging them on, Christine included. Then Lawrence was suddenly there and thumping Steve, over and over, which surprised Jen because he was normally such a gentleman. Now he was like a savage. 'Stop!' she shouted. 'Stop it!' She looked around for someone in authority, like the men on the door. But then, as quickly as it had started, it was over. Martin and Steve were walking away and Lawrence was helping Kit up.

'Did I miss the fun?' Susie asked over her shoulder. 'I was in the bogs.'

Jen pointed at Martin, tucking his shirt in. 'He picked a fight with Kit.'

'Oh, did he?'

Jen went over to Kit, who immediately apologised. He had blood around his mouth and was holding his middle.

'Don't be daft,' she told him.

'Just defending your honour, and all that.'

'Thanks,' she said tearfully, wishing he hadn't done it because he looked such a mess, but glad in a way that he had. She tried hugging him but he winced, then from behind came the loudest cheer. Jen swung round to see Martin on the floor again, and over him, Susie, shaking the hand she'd just punched him with. People were clapping and whistling but the group struck up and drowned it all out.

'Come along,' said Lawrence, propping up Kit with his shoulder. 'Time to retreat, guys.'

His dad was so sweet. He dabbed at Kit's face with warm water, then with antiseptic, while Jen warmed milk for three cocoas. 'I remember my first fight,' Wing Commander Avery was saying. 'It was with Harry Parsons, the school bully.'

'This wasn't my first fight, Pa.'

'I'm sure it wasn't.'

'Although, obviously, I'm a pacifist.'

'Of course you are, Kit. Anyway, I was no match for Hairy Harry, as we secretly called him, on account of the moustache he grew at fourteen.'

'He sounds awful,' said Jen.

'Oh, he was. I couldn't walk for two days but became something of a hero for taking him on.'

Jen divided the saucepan of milk between the mugs, stirring each as she went. 'Martin's our school bully.'

'Now you tell me!' said Kit. He laughed and went, *'Ouch.'*

'You may have a broken rib or two,' said his dad.

'It feels awfully like it.'

'Shall I get Nigel Evans to come and have a prod?'

'I don't know ... if you think it's best.'

'Not that one can do anything for broken ribs, of course. But Nigel may have something for the pain.'

'Where's Mummy?' asked Kit.

'I'm not sure. Having a chinwag with Margaret, I expect.' Both Kit's and his father's eyes went to the wall clock, then Jen's followed. It was ten past eleven.

'Let's not bother the doc,' said Kit. 'I'll grab some sleep. See him tomorrow.' He heaved himself upright. 'Help me to my room, Jen?'

His dad smiled and nodded at her. 'I'll drive you home once he's in bed. Twenty minutes?'

'Thank you,' she said, picking up their cocoas and wondering if all officers were as nice as him.

Kit went straight to his wardrobe and rummaged around at the back. He produced a battered holdall, unzipped it and pulled out a tobacco tin. Then he came and eased himself down on the floor beside her and leaned against the bed. 'The only thing for it,' he said. 'Johnny Joint.'

She watched him take a small brown lump from the tin, then a lighter and some cigarette papers. He flicked the lighter on and waved it over the edge of the lump, then took a paper out and crumbled some of the lump into it. He took a pinch of tobacco from the tin and added that, then rolled the paper and licked it. 'I hope I didn't embarrass you,' he said. His voice was a bit raspy, and she wondered if his lungs and ribs were horribly damaged, all because of her.

'No, silly. You were great.' She watched him

211

light the joint then suck on it. He sucked again, deeply and quite noisily. He didn't breathe out for a while and when he did the smell of pot gradually wafted her way. She'd never smelled it before, and it wasn't unpleasant. Kit offered her the joint but she declined.

'Take lots of deep breaths, then,' he said, kissing the end of her nose.

Jen kept an eye on the time, and after a quarter of an hour, thought she shouldn't keep Kit's dad waiting. It was lovely, lying against the pillows, against the bed, cuddling Kit better and listening to him. He was talking about what he was going to do with his life, which was to save the world, basically. His words were soft and blurry, and if she hadn't had Mr Avery on her mind, Jen could easily have fallen asleep.

But then the peace was broken by voices downstairs. Mr and Mrs Avery ... then just Mrs Avery. growing louder and closer. When it was clear that Kit's mum was mounting the stairs to the attic, she and Kit sat themselves more upright. Or at least Jen did.

She stepped into the attic, all dressed up in peach. Peach dress, peach hairband, peach shoes. The only thing missing was peach lipstick. Rubbed off by Mick, no doubt. Or someone. Mrs Avery stood still, her hands on her hips. 'Well, Kit,' she said, 'not exactly a pretty picture. But if you will mix with people like that, what do you expect?'

'Fuck off, Ma.'

Jen couldn't believe her ears, or the fact that

Kit was laughing. 'It was all my fault,' she said.

'We know *that*, Jennifer. What were you thinking, taking my son to that place?'

Jen couldn't answer. People like that, she thought. That's how she sees me.

'I wanted to go,' said Kit. He ran a reassuring hand over Jen's hair, then her shoulder, but it didn't help.

'Do you have *any* respect for your father?'

'Ha!' said Kit. '*Ouch.*'

'What's that smell?' asked Mrs Avery. 'Kit, have you been...?'

'Yep.'

Jen braced herself for an explosion. Her dad would have gone berserk, not that he'd have recognised the smell. She pictured Mr Avery, pacing around downstairs, and tried to work out how to get past his wife, but then Mrs Avery kicked her shoes off and padded over the carpet towards them. She sat down on the floor elegantly, legs tucked to one side.

'Any left, darling?' she asked. 'I've had one hell of an evening.'

'Sure,' said Kit. He reached for his tin and Jen watched him start the whole procedure again, convinced she was in a dream.

'I should go,' she told Kit, but was rooted to the spot, wanting to see what happened. Kit warmed the lump, he crumbled, he rolled, he licked, and he handed the end result to his mother.

'It's jolly good stuff,' he told her.

'Super, darling. Thank you.'

'Ready to go, Jen?' came his father's voice. 'Don't want your parents worrying!'

213

'Coming!' she called back. She stood up on weak legs and stepped over Kit and around his mother.

'Bye, Kit,' she said at the top of the stairs. 'Hope you feel better tomorrow.'

'Night, my lovely.'

'Bye,' she said to his mother, with a quick wave.

'Good night, Jennifer.' Mrs Avery spoke in a strange wheezy voice, her face surrounded by the smoke she'd blown out. She took another puff and handed the joint to Kit. 'Now,' Jen heard as she went down, 'tell Mummy about your silly heroics.'

## TWENTY-EIGHT

She couldn't face breakfast, and she couldn't face moving, so she carried on lying in bed, going over her evening. Their evening. The end of it, at any rate. She'd been drunk, but she could remember it all. The worst combination. On the chair was her suitcase, and in the suitcase were the painkillers she took everywhere for her feet. This time her head needed two tablets, but her body wouldn't go and get them.

She sat up slowly. How embarrassing, she thought, how excruciatingly embarrassing. She imagined Kit telling Adam all about it, or maybe not all. The two of them having a laugh. God. It had been going so well too. Seeing Kit after all this time had been great, and she hadn't fallen back on old habits and been tongue-tied with him. As it turned out, tongue-tied would have been good. Why had she drunk so much? Adam? Kit hadn't made her nervous but his nephew had.

Pushing the duvet off, Jen hauled herself round and up and over to the suitcase. From downstairs came kitchen sounds but no kitchen smells. She could well have missed breakfast. In the en suite, she washed the pills down with a handful of tap water, then splashed her face and patted it dry on a towel. She tried cleaning her teeth but it made her retch.

Back in bed, waiting for relief, she remembered more. Doing that classic thing of not quite finding the lock with her key. She felt dreadful, humiliated, now, thinking about it. About Kit saying, 'Here, let me.' The worst thing was he hadn't been laughing, or even smiling. A drunk man was hilarious, a drunk woman sad and disgusting. One thing that will never change.

If she phoned down, would they bring her coffee? No, she thought, better not. The room might reek of alcohol fumes and that would get around this small community. She'd go down. Eventually. Shower, dress, have coffee, take it from there.

Jen came out of the bathroom to the sound of her mobile. 'I'll call you in the morning,' Kit had promised, before the kiss on the cheek and the swift turning of his back on her. Here goes, she thought, running for the phone and checking the caller. Her brother.

'Hi, Paul,' she said, relieved, sitting on the bed, then falling back on the pillows. 'I'm *really* sorry for not getting back to you yesterday, only–'

'Listen, Bev and I think you should come down.'

'Now?' It didn't seem such a bad idea, solving, as it would, the embarrassment issue. She'd leave Kit a message – *Husband crisis. Had to take off.*

'I know, and I'm sorry. I expect you're having a lovely time seeing your friend, but ... it's just that Robert's talking Beachy Head.'

'What? Not seriously?'

'It's hard to tell. He hasn't mentioned suicide to you, then?'

'Not in so many words. Oh God, I'm *so* sorry about this, Paul.' Robert had two brothers of his own – why pick on hers? It was just a ploy to get her there. A pretty childish and inconsiderate one. 'I know he's been depressed and taking something for it, but maybe he needs more than that. Therapy of some kind.' Her head felt better. The shower had bucked her up. 'Shall I speak to him?' she asked, and within seconds Robert was on.

'I know this is out of order, Jen.'

'Totally.'

'I can't bear to be in that house, you see. Without you. Without there being an *us*. It's just awful.'

'Sell it, then.' How hard she sounded. 'If you don't like being there. You'll have to sell or buy me out, so why not sell?'

'But that seems so ... final. And that makes me want to kill myself.'

'For God's sake, Robert. Phoebe isn't listening, is she?'

'Bev took the kids out. I need to talk to you, Jen.'

'We are talking.'

'See you and talk to you. Tell me where you're living, and I'll–'

'No. And besides, I'm away at the moment.'

'Yeah, Paul said. Visiting someone.'

'Yes.'

'Male or female?'

She sighed. 'An old friend.'

'Male, then. Christ, I've made such a mess of my life. I've lost you, now the business is suffering because I can't put the work in ... next the house. My whole fucking life's just disappeared.'

'Mine too, Robert. I've lost my home through no fault of my own, and I'm supposed to feel sorry for *you*?'

'Why are you being so rigid, Jen? It's not like you.' He was about to cry again, she could tell. Robert hadn't been a crier in the past. Only when his mother died. 'I can't go on,' he said.

'Yes, you can.' She needed to change tack. Being firm, hard even, was never going to get him out of Paul's house. She sighed and rubbed at her hair through the towel. 'How about meeting up, once I'm back in London?'

'Come to the house, Jen. Come home and talk to me. Please. I sit and watch the front door, you know. Waiting for you to walk through it. Willing you to.'

'Oh, Robert.'

'Ridiculous, but I just can't bear the thought of

you never being there again. It makes me want to end–'

'I know, I know.' Would it be so bad, she wondered, going to the house? Perhaps there'd been a long enough gap now. Just being in Norfolk and seeing Kit had added distance to her old life, however disastrously last night had gone. She could pick up the things Robert had forgotten to bring her, maybe even lay a ghost to rest. 'OK,' she said, 'I'll come and see you in a few days. At the house.'

Robert sniffed. 'Thank you.'

'But promise me you'll leave Brighton today and go straight home?'

'Yeah, I will. Promise.'

'Call me once you're in Highgate, so I know.'

'OK.'

'And drive safely.' It was something she'd always said, but also a way of winding down the conversation. Jen was keen to get off the phone, or at least back to Paul.

'This friend,' Robert said, 'is it an old flame?'

'Put Paul on,' she told him, because she wasn't going to lie. He'd done enough of that for both of them.

It was a sweet village, and Jen could smell, if not see, the sea. A short stroll away, Kit had said, which they'd leave for today. If he decided to avoid her this morning – feign illness or something – she'd go on her own. Walking past the cottages, and then into a street of newer homes and around the corner to the council houses, Jen became increasingly wobbly. Perhaps breakfast would have been wise, even a snack from the village shop she'd passed. But it was too late now, since she was opening the gate and walking up the cracked garden path.

'I'm mortified,' she said, when Kit opened it with a coolish, 'Hi.' She shook her head and attempted a grin, but was so lightheaded she probably looked drunk again. 'And *so*, so sorry. I barely drink these days and I just can't hold it.'

'You did try and hold rather a lot.' His eyes smiled but not his mouth. 'Come in. Had breakfast?'

'I missed it.'

'I'll make you something, then. What do you fancy? Fry-up, cereal, continental?' He grinned at her and she relaxed. 'Can't face anything?'

'Um,' she said, now suddenly hungry, as opposed to lacking food. Perhaps relief did that. 'The fry-up sounds good.' He wasn't pissed off with her, or wasn't showing it. She followed him through the dull-coloured sitting room, to the dull-coloured kitchen. Even in its current state, her head was tearing out the fireplace, knocking down walls, laying wood floors. 'I think I must have, I don't know, just relaxed a bit too much.' She wouldn't mention Adam, not yet.

'I expect you needed to, after all you've been through.'

'Still, it was no excuse, and I'm *really* sorry, Kit.'

'Stop apologising, will you?' He took things from the fridge, while Jen peered through the net curtain.

'Nice garden,' she said.

219

'It could be.'

'Huge, anyway.'

'I've barely been out there.' He joined her at the window, pulled back the net and peered too. The grass was scrappy and long. There were one or two shrubs in need of pruning and what might once have been a pond.

'No?' she said, breathing in his nice soapy smell. 'I'm actually quite missing mine, now I'm in a flat.'

'I've never had one to miss.'

She'd heard, yesterday, how he'd lived in the same flat, on and off, for decades. Jen had noticed that people brought up in the Forces either couldn't move, or couldn't stop moving, as adults. Jen would have been in the latter camp, if it hadn't been for Robert's reluctance ever to leave his home. Something he still had, it seemed. Jen often thought the whole property thing had been a way of curing her itchy feet.

'Tea or coffee?' asked Kit, moving away and towards the cooker.

'Oh, coffee, please. With a drop of brandy ... ideally.'

'Or would that be brandy with a drop of coffee?'

Jen laughed but started to feel unsettled, or perhaps too settled. Kit was easy to talk to. If she'd asked Robert for brandy, he'd have taken her seriously. She'd bantered with her builders and plumbers, but never her husband. Why was that?

While Kit cooked, Jen wandered into the front room, followed by Bunk, and took in the ghastly

220

three-piece suite, carpets, rugs and wallpaper. There was an attractive old sideboard, though, almost the length of one wall, on which were propped three photographs in frames. In the middle was Wing Commander Avery, smiling at the camera in full uniform; his cheeks as rosy as Jen remembered them. That lovely man, she thought, picking it up and looking closer. It wasn't an official photo. In the background was a vase of fresh flowers, beside a large fireplace. Not their German quarter, she could tell that. Also, he looked younger than he had in Germany; a little more hair, a slightly thinner face.

She put the photo back, and picked up the one to the left. Pip with his wife and a young, very blond Adam, aged around six or seven. They were in the garden – the same garden she'd just seen, only in the picture it was full of colour and the lawn was neatly mown. Pip was an older version of the boy Jen had known, with a slimmed-down body, but the same large face. Pat's fair hair had been whipped up on one side by a breeze, and her eyes and smile were bright and playful. Husband and wife had arms around each other, and Pip held his son's shoulder. A happy little family, unaware of the faulty heart beating away under Pat's gingham top.

The third photograph was of Kit and Pip, aged around twelve and nine. They were standing in front of a plane on an airfield. Taken by their father, perhaps. Kit had cropped hair and a cheeky face, almost as round as his brother's. He wore a white short-sleeved shirt and grey school-type trousers. It was the most conventional Jen had ever seen him. She looked around for more pictures, but those three were it. None of Pat's relatives, none of Mrs Avery.

It was a run-down, uncared-for room, with scribbles on the wall by the phone. Kit had told her it couldn't be more different from his own place, but that he wasn't inclined to touch anything, in case it upset Pip. Someone had been round with lavender polish, though, or air freshener. Whatever it was, it hadn't quite masked the smell of dog.

Back in the kitchen, Kit gestured towards a tiny table, set for one, by the back door. Jen went and sat down and watched him move around the room in black cotton trousers and a mucky-green top. Casual but expensive. He was as straight-backed as he'd been as a boy, although taller now. Six foot or more. His hair was cut well. A London cut, she guessed. He had the kind of features – small nose, full lips, high cheekbones – that aged slowly, and Jen could see he'd have no trouble pulling younger women.

Nice to look at. Comfortable in his own skin too. Robert, as charming and friendly as he could be, always had an edginess to him. But then living with a secret would make a person uncomfortable. As she watched Kit cracking eggs, slicing mushrooms, Jen felt her stomach flutter. She hoped it was just hunger, and when he put a mouth-watering plate in front of her, she dug in. He'd sprinkled herbs on the tomato, added Tabasco to the mushrooms. Nice touches, she thought, feeling calm and cared for, as Kit washed the pan at the sink, talking about The

Bell and someone called Eddie.

He kept flashing her smiles, as though genuinely pleased she was there. Smiles she couldn't have imagined an hour ago. Pleased, perhaps, to have another adult around in this out-of-the-way spot. Adam was at school all day, and a dog was only so much company.

'That was delicious,' she said, when she'd finished. 'Thank you.'

'My pleasure.'

'What do you do here?' she asked, taking her plate to the sink, then sitting down again. 'If you're no longer writing.'

'Well, I've rediscovered reading.'

'Yeah?'

'And keeping house takes up a good portion of the day. As does Bunk.' The dog opened an eye at the mention of his name. 'What's that saying about work expanding to fill the time available?' He smiled and slowly wiped the pan with a tea towel, then put it in a cupboard. 'Heaven knows how I used to write, travel, give talks *and* do the dishes.'

He took her on a tour of the north Norfolk coast, past Sheringham and along to Blakeney and Holkham. They stopped several times to get out and walk along the coastal path and back, or stand and look at the salt marshes, or tramp in the dunes. The day was sunny and overcast in turn; one minute like summer, then cold enough for a coat. 'Wow,' Jen kept saying. She tried to imagine setting up home in one of the villages, in a pretty red-brick cottage, close to a marsh.

'Could you live here?' she asked Kit at one point.

'Not twenty-four seven,' he'd said. 'Could you?'

'Maybe.'

The area had a quite different feel to other seaside spots – wilder, flatter, marshier; a haven for birds and boaters. Much of it had been reclaimed, and Cley-next-the-Sea, with its lovely big windmill, now lay a mile inland. They ate a late lunch there, in a pub, then went over cobbles to the enormous, raised church, which felt more like a cathedral.

Yes, Jen thought, perhaps she could live here. It was undeniably beautiful. A mix of wild and serene. And it was a long way from Robert.

'I think Pip chose Norfolk,' Kit said in the car, 'because it was here that we were last happy, as a family. Before Pa's posting to Germany. Pip applied to UFA in his twenties, met a local girl there, married her and settled. It just doesn't make sense, why Pip and I are so different. Why we took such different routes. And this ... his buggering off after all the years he's devoted to Adam. That makes no sense, either.'

'Unless...' Jen began, then stopped.

'Unless he's had an accident? Died?'

'Mm.'

'Well, yes. I suppose there is that.'

Jen watched the countryside go by. The view inland wasn't as interesting as the coastal one, but she couldn't stare through Kit's window, because that would mean staring at him.

'Do you know Kierkegaard?' he asked.

224

'Just the name.' She smiled to herself, remembering how ignorant he'd made her feel. Never deliberately.

'He said, "Life can only be understood backwards; but it must be lived forwards".'

'Ah, yeah, I've heard that. So, when I'm ninety, I'll understand why I married a gay man?'

'Maybe. And I'll understand why marriage never appealed.' Kit drummed on the steering wheel for a while. 'Actually, that's easy to work out.'

When they reached Wells-next-the-Sea and a cream tea, Robert phoned to say he was home. Jen resented the intrusion into her unusual, slightly ethereal day trip, but she had asked him to call.

'When are you coming?' he wanted to know.

'What? Oh, um, at the weekend, I expect.' She was booked into The Bell for one more night, but was considering staying another day and night, or at least waiting for Kit to suggest it. She'd definitely be gone by Saturday, though, because his nephew would be home during the day. Jen wasn't sure if it had been her drinking, or the fact that she owned several properties that had made him so hostile over dinner. Or perhaps he was always like that. 'Saturday?' she asked Robert.

'What time?'

'Oh, I don't know.' She hated herself for sounding impatient. 'Can't we discuss this...? Three o'clock?' Too late for lunch, too early for dinner.

'OK. Thanks, Jen. Thanks for agreeing to come. I–'

'Speak to you later,' she said. 'Bye, Robert.'

She switched off the phone completely, and raised her eyebrows at Kit. 'Now that I *won't* be looking forward to. Going home for the first time in months.'

'Do you have to?'

'Yeah,' she said. 'I think I do.'

Kit asked how she and Robert had met, and Jen started at the beginning, with her father's posting back to the UK, and how that had messed up her A levels. She'd done a secretarial course, worked in an office on camp for a couple of years, then left home and gone to London in search of excitement and an amazing career. 'Instead, I got a lonely bedsit and a job at a small estate agents. For some reason I got stuck there, then when Robert joined as a partner, we started going out and ... sort of fell in love.'

'Sort of?'

She tried to think back to how she'd felt in 1975–76, during the engagement that her mother, convinced Jen was marrying into money, had been so thrilled about. Secure was how she'd felt, primarily. After all the years of moving house, moving school, making friends, losing friends, making new friends – she'd found herself in one place with one constant companion. In 1977 she'd got married, bought a house and found herself pleasantly rooted. She shrugged at Kit over the teapot and jam and scones. 'It wasn't a grand passion.'

'Ah,' he said. 'Shame. But then, grand passions tend to burn themselves out quite rapidly.'

'Are you speaking from experience?'

226

'Absolutely.'

Jen laughed, but for the first time in decades she felt the old painful jolt.

# TWENTY-NINE

'The world's changed so much in ten years,' he said. They were on the grassy slope by the pool, lying side by side in sunglasses and swimwear. Jen was covered in sun cream, Kit wasn't. He had an olive complexion, like his mother. They didn't burn, they just went straight to golden brown. 'No more military service, thank heaven. Can you imagine trying to get guys like me bowing and scraping and polishing our boots all night? Half my pals are anarchists, the rest are drug addicts. We'd either refuse to salute, or be incapable of it.'

Jen thought saluting was just a way of showing respect. Also, she secretly liked the idea of her dad having to salute people younger than himself – especially the women, the WRAF officers. Kit, though, had a thing about it. Wherever you went on camp, men and women were saluting. When in uniform, airmen had to salute any officers they came across, and junior officers saluted senior officers. The senior person would then salute back; always in that order. Kit called it 'positively feudal', comparing it to peasants touching their forelocks at the squire. Sometimes he'd salute young SACs or corporals when they passed, to even things up, but they'd just call him an effing hippie and tell him where to go.

'Muhammad Ali. Now he's my hero.'

'You like boxing?' Jen hated it, herself.

Kit laughed. 'No, you nincompoop. Muhammad Ali refused to be drafted and fight in Vietnam.'

'Oh, that.' Jen blushed, but he couldn't see.

'Marcus and I went on an anti-Vietnam rally last year. Bunked off school for three days and hitched to London. Did I tell you?'

'No. Did you get found out?'

'Of course. The school contacted Daddy and he gave me a gentle bollocking over the phone, and the headmaster stopped our privileges for a while, but it was entirely worth it. Such a barbaric war and so pointless, don't you think?'

'Yes,' she said. She'd seen footage of bombing and poor Vietnamese peasants on Dutch telly, but didn't really know what it was about or why the Americans were there. She'd have quite liked Kit to explain, but he'd gone quiet. Thinking about the rally, most likely. Maybe he and Marcus had met some girls there. She said, 'My dad would kill me if I went on an anti-war rally. Him being in the Raf. I mean RAF.' She'd never do it, that was for sure. What if it got her father into trouble? Kicked out the air force, or something?

'My pa just said he was hugely disappointed in me, that I'd let the side down. I'm not sure Daddy knows which side I'm on, or most likely doesn't want to know. Anyway, he was pretty laid-back, compared to how someone like Lawrence's pa would react.'

'Yeah?' Jen had seen Lawrence's dad only once washing his car on the drive. He was tall and handsome, like Lawrence, and it had been easy to see why that young officer's wife fell for him.

Kit's finger stroked hers. It was too hot for anything more, and besides, he was still sore in places. Jen prayed Martin wouldn't walk past and have a good laugh, but the pool was fairly empty. Some inter-station match was going on and she could hear the distant cheering. The place would fill up when it was over.

'Hey,' said Kit, 'almost forgot to tell you.'

'What?' He was going back to school early? On holiday? His parents were getting divorced?

'The Monterey film's coming to the Astra. They showed a trailer last night.'

'You went to the pictures last night?' He was going to rest his pummelled body, he'd told her.

'Lawrence and Susie dragged me along. *Planet of the Apes.*'

'Oh.' Why hadn't he called round for her? Not that she'd want to see *Planet of the Apes.*

'Didn't think it would be your cup of tea.'

'Yes, it would.'

'You hated *Bullitt.*'

'No, I didn't.' How did he know that?

'And, anyway, it was all terribly last minute. In fact, we missed the beginning.'

Good, she thought.

Kit rolled on to his front, groaning on account of his ribs, took his sunglasses off and lay with his head facing her. 'Monterey. What a blast. You'll love it, Jennifer Juniper.' She felt his eyes on her and wanted to cover her face with her hair, which wasn't possible, lying on her back. 'I adore your freckles,' he said.

'I hate them.'

'Freckles can be very sexy.'

'They can?'

'Mm,' he said. 'Look at Jacqueline Bisset.'

Jen knew he was paying her a compliment but all she could think was that Kit fancied Jacqueline Bisset, found her sexy. More sexy and attractive than he found her. He must have spent the whole of *Bullitt* drooling over her. She almost felt tearful, which was stupid. If he'd only tell her she was more attractive than Jacqueline Bisset, she wouldn't feel so terrible. But what were the chances of that?

Kit was humming a Canned Heat song. Then he started singing it, just quietly. Jen had heard it so often, she could have joined in. Not that she would have, in case her voice wasn't good. It was hard to tell, yourself. Kit stopped and said, 'Hey, you'll get to see Hendrix setting his guitar on fire, then smashing and smashing it to pieces. Man, that is *such* a gas.'

Jen turned and looked at his yellowy-green bruised cheek, and at the sheer joy in his face. How weird it must be, she thought, being a boy.

Pip loomed up and made her jump. 'Thought I'd find you two here. Anyone for ice cream?'

'No, thanks,' said Jen. Not after her last experience.

Kit said, 'Maybe a Tizer?' and when Pip was gone, he and Jen sighed at the same time.

An hour later, the place was packed and unpleasant. At that point, Kit and Jen would have gone to their hut, but with Pip in tow they stayed. He was quiet and no bother, but it was hard just to talk about stuff with him there. Kit went through *Planet of the Apes* in detail, which actually made Jen sorry she'd missed it.

'I wish I'd been there,' Pip said. He was sitting up, still in all his clothes and tugging at grass. 'Instead of listening to Mummy and Daddy fighting.'

'What about?' asked Kit.

'The usual. Then Daddy went out and Mummy came to my room and...'

'What?'

'I was rather upset because of all the shouting ... and, anyway, she got horrendously cross and told me not to be a baby. That everybody's parents have their little squabbles. I expect yours do, don't they, Jen?'

'All the time.' She tried a laugh but it came out oddly.

'Then, after about an hour, Daddy came home and found Mummy had gone out and then when I talked to him about my brilliant school marks, just to take his mind off Mummy, he was ... well, awfully quiet. Just sitting in the armchair, staring into space. You know how he does, Kit. Drinking whisky.'

'Yes.'

'Mummy came back at half eleven, then you were home about midnight, and I felt better. Because we were all there then, like a family.'

'Midnight?' asked Jen. She sat herself up and looked down on Kit.

231

'We played table football.'

'You and Susie?'

He chuckled and stroked her arm. '*And* Lawrence.'

'I wish I'd been *there* too,' said Pip.

'Didn't your ribs hurt?' Jen asked.

'I'll say. Played like a total prat.' Kit sat up slowly and with a grimace. 'Listen Pip, it'll be OK. Lawrence says his parents bicker and have affairs too. It's all to do with being here, and being sort of stuck on the station, and all the practically free booze flowing around.'

'I know, but we've only just arrived. I can't bear this every school vac for two or three years.'

'No, I know. But I'd imagine the novelty will wear off. Next time we're here it'll be winter, and they'll all be too cold to … you know.'

'Christmas means parties,' said Pip miserably.

'Well, yes.'

Jen wished she could say something to help, but theirs was an alien world to her, still. 'I think I'll have an ice cream now,' she said. 'Come with me, Pip?'

'All right,' he said, chucking grass into the breeze and hauling his big body up. 'I'm famished.'

'Are you playing tennis later,' asked Kit, 'with my ma?'

'Unfortunately, yes.'

'If you don't want to play, don't.'

Jen pulled a face. 'It's not that easy. Your mother's so…'

'Christ, Jen,' he snapped, 'why are you such a doormat?'

232

It was like a slap in the face, one of those unexpected ones women were always giving men in films. 'I don't know,' she said quietly.

'One can be peace loving and laid-back and all that, but sometimes one simply has to speak one's mind. And you never do, do you?'

She didn't know what had got into Kit, but he was scaring her with his sharp words and the cross expression. Thank goodness Pip was having a swim and hadn't heard. Jen knew she should say something tough back, to prove Kit wrong, but inside she was crying and soon she'd be really crying, and then he'd realise what a complete drip she was and chuck her. 'You've reminded me,' she said shakily, looking at the watch she'd left on so she could tell how tanned she was getting. 'I should get ready for the match.'

'Just don't go,' he said. 'Stand her up, then she won't bully you into playing again.'

'Listen, I was joking just now. I like playing your mum at tennis. It's good practice and I always win.' She leaned over and kissed his forehead, then got up off her towel. Kit didn't move, or say anything, although he might have tutted. A lump formed in Jen's throat as she folded her towel. For the first time ever, she wanted to be with Mrs Avery, more than her son. 'See you later in the hut?'

He may have nodded, she wasn't sure.

'Say bye to Pip for me?' she asked, and he didn't answer. Or perhaps he hadn't heard, since her voice had shrunk to a wobbly whisper.

Mrs Avery sauntered up to the courts in a bright

floral dress and silver slingbacks. Jen got the short sharp smile. 'I'm afraid I can't play today, Jennifer.'

'Oh. Are you all right?'

'Yes, yes. Something's come up. Terribly sorry. I, um...' She unzipped her shoulder bag and dipped a hand in. Was she going to pay her, or something? But out of the bag came a bottle of perfume, which she tugged the top off. 'Simply must dash.'

'I see.' Jen felt stupid in her shorts and white plimsolls, and annoyed that she'd have to go home and change before she could do anything else. Not that she had anything to do now Kit was in a mood. Maybe he wouldn't even go to the hut later.

'Let's play tomorrow, instead. Say three o'clock?' Mrs Avery gave her ears and wrists a spray and put the top on. 'You could come back for tea. That'll entice Kit down from his room. The child spends too much time up there. Dreadfully unhealthy.'

'No,' said Jen. 'I can't play tomorrow.' She imagined Kit watching and stopped herself adding, 'Sorry.'

'Friday, then.'

'I think I've had enough tennis. For a while.' She put her racquet back in its case and picked up her tube of balls. 'It's been great, though. Thanks.'

Mrs Avery looked flummoxed. 'I see,' she said. 'But *do* call round?' It was almost a plea. 'Or better still, come and have lunch tomorrow? I'll do a vichyssoise. Kit's favourite.'

Kit floated into Jen's head. *Say no.* 'I can't

tomorrow, but thanks anyway.'

Mrs Avery breathed in, deeply and loudly. 'Well, perhaps another time?'

'Yes,' Jen said, and not wanting to appear rude, added, 'That would be nice.'

They said goodbye and went in different directions. Jen towards the airmen's quarters, and Kit's mum to the officers'. How easy that had been, *and* Mrs Avery had asked her to lunch. What was it ... 'fishy sois' – something like that. English dictionary, or her little red French one? She wasn't, actually, that keen on fish. Obviously, it wasn't Jen's scintillating company Mrs Avery wanted, just her son's. But still.

Near the bend that would take her past the playground, Jen spun round and walked backwards for a while. Kit's mother, she saw, was no longer on her way home, but had doubled back and was rounding the corner by the Malcolm Club. She disappeared from view and then a door slammed and an engine revved up. A small open-top sports car shot over the junction, heading towards the guardroom and the outside world. Kit's mother, tying a headscarf over her windswept hair, glanced Jen's way, then back to the road ahead. Mick the corporal was driving.

Long after they'd gone, Jen stared at the trail of smoke. She thought about Mrs Avery and her silver slingbacks and her squirts of perfume. She imagined Mr Avery, later, in his chair with a drink and Pip alone in his room. And Kit, smoking pot to cheer himself up. And nobody there to make them fishy ... whatever it was.

Back home again, having changed ready to go and meet Kit, Jen made an effort to talk to her family. How she loved her mum, bringing them plates of corned beef, tinned potatoes and half a tomato. A whole one for her dad. Jen asked her what she'd been doing all day and her mum said, 'Oh, a woman's work is never done!' and laughed.

Then Jen asked Paul the same thing and he said, 'Playing Batman and Robin with Neil. He made me be Robin all the time.'

'Aah,' she said, 'never mind.'

'Then we trapped insects and burned them with a magnifying glass.'

'Paul, that's horrible!'

'You'll end up a bloody hooligan,' said her dad. His mouth was full of food and they all waited while he chewed and swallowed. 'No exams to your name and a criminal record by the time you're eighteen. Mark my words.'

'Poor little insects,' said her mum.

Paul burst into tears. 'It was Neil's idea. He *made* me.'

'Oh, love, I'm sorry.'

Jen sighed. Another meal, another sorry. And this time it was her fault.

'You want to get yourself some decent pals,' said her dad. 'That Neil's an evil wee bully, just like his father.'

'He is *not*,' said Paul.

Jen wished he'd just stay quiet. She waited for the slap that didn't come, only because her dad was lighting a cigarette and eating at the same time. He had one eye on his plate and the other

236

on a game show. He puffed, he coughed, he ate, then he puffed again. He had a tummy that made him look pregnant, a five o'clock shadow and ash on his vest.

How nice it would be, Jen thought, to live with *her* mum and Kit's *dad*. There'd be lots of laughs and jolliness, and maybe they'd all play Monopoly on Sunday afternoons; Mr Avery patiently helping Paul. Monopoly was Jen's favourite. She loved accumulating houses and hotels, charging people rent when they landed on her squares. At the last camp, she'd played a lot with her friends, but she'd never suggest it to Christine. Kit, perhaps? Or Susie? Jen had tried playing with her mum but it was too easy bankrupting her. And her dad never joined in anything like that. He always called them *'bored* games' and did an exaggerated yawn.

'Are you seeing Kit later?' Jen's mum asked her.

'I'm not sure. He's a bit...' She was about to say bruised, but her parents didn't know about the fight. '...tired.'

'Oh, right. All that cricket, I expect.' Her mum sliced at her corned beef. She always had smaller portions than the rest of them, even Paul.

# THIRTY

Jen booked a third night in The Bell and spent the day wandering around Norwich with Kit. It took her back to Roermond and Mönchengladbach, only they weren't entwined in the way they had been then, and Kit wasn't spending as much money.

They did the castle and the market, but mostly they walked aimlessly and talked, stopping occasionally for a coffee and a bite. Jen was learning more about Kit's life: Africa, articles and books he'd written, women he'd lived with. And she was slowly, bit by bit, filling him in on her marriage and the Robert business. Slowly and bit by bit, because she had a lot less to tell Kit than he had to tell her.

Jen couldn't make out quite where Kit was going wrong with women, or even if he thought he *was* going wrong. Whether, for him, the perfect relationship was short and sweet. His explanation, in most instances, for why he and Brandy, or Di, or Sandra, etc., had split up was that they'd grown apart. He said nothing derogatory about any of them, only good things. Except for selfish, unfaithful Emily, that was.

'I'd been very lucky up until Emily,' he said over a coffee. 'Or rather, unaffected. Unlike my brother, poor bastard. Losing his one big love.' Kit talked again about Pip comparing every

238

woman unfavourably with Pat. 'Surely you'd stop doing that after a while?' he asked Jen, as though she would have the answer.

Late afternoon, they found themselves in Norwich Cathedral. 'Remember Mönchengladbach?' she asked, as they took a seat in the longest nave Jen had ever seen. 'The cathedral?'

'Didn't some Gestapo woman kick us out?'

'Oh, yeah. So she did.' Over the two days, they'd reminded each other of things the other had forgotten. It was fun, but all the reminiscing did bring back the pain of Kit leaving and the agony of not hearing from him. He'd doubtless tell people they'd 'grown apart' – countries apart, in their case. Jen began to see herself as the first of Kit's short-and-sweet girlfriends.

'Have you seen the ceiling?' he asked.

'Wow,' she said, looking up. 'It's amazing.'

'See the carvings in the stone? They're called bosses.'

'Uh-huh.' There were dozens of different-sized clusters at the joins of all the ribs. Elaborate stone carvings.

'Apparently, there are over a thousand, and each one tells a different story.'

'Incredible.'

'Isn't it?'

As she strained to look at them, Jen was aware of Kit's arm landing on the back of her seat. He was most likely supporting himself for a good view, but she nevertheless leaned back, gradually, until she could feel him with the top of her back, the base of her neck. They took their time inspecting the ceiling bosses, and he didn't move his arm until someone behind coughed.

Jen sat up straight and looked over her shoulder. It wasn't a large German woman, just an elderly man clearing his throat, on his knees and about to talk to God. She and Kit smiled, got up and walked back down the nave. It was tempting to reach for his hand, but obviously she didn't.

They took a long and winding route back, via the east coast, which had a very different feel. In places, there was quite a drop to the sea, and there weren't the marshes or pine trees of the north. It was nice, and invigorating, but by the time they'd reached the promenade at Overstrand, Jen felt she might have seen enough water for a while.

'Are you missing London?' she asked, when they were back in the car for the final leg home.

'Only the coffees. They try at The Bell, but...'

'Yeah, I've had one.'

'Besides that, no. This feels like a holiday, although with quite a bit of angst thrown in. Bloody Pip.' He turned and smiled at her. 'If he turns up, I'll kill him.'

Jen imagined she'd feel the same if her brother buggered off with no word, leaving a bewildered family. Paul would be the one person in the world never to do that, of course. She'd bet all her properties on it, if she hadn't sold them first. Dipping into the simple life of Pip and Adam, and now Kit, had got her thinking about downshifting. Just her and a small house, somewhere cheaper than London. Somewhere pretty and friendly. North Norfolk? Maybe a dog, maybe a cat. Both. She'd have to work, because the money wouldn't last for ever. But that would be fun, finding something different to do. Train to be a teacher, learn a craft. Anything but houses.

Kit put the radio on and they listened to the news, then *The Archers* and around half of *Front Row* before reaching the village. 'The Bell or my house?' asked Kit. He tutted. 'My house. Listen to me.'

'Yours,' she said. 'If that's OK?'

'Of course it is.'

They passed The Bell and the closed village shop, went past the green and a group of teenagers on a corner, then turned into the council houses.

'What's this?' said Kit, as they pulled up. 'A visitor?'

Jen didn't know about cars, but whatever it was parked by the gate looked expensive and incongruous. They got out and Kit strolled over to the flashy silver-grey job.

'Ma?' Jen heard him say.

A woman clicked down the path, arms open. Her hair was blondish white, her heels red. 'Darling, darling Kit,' she said. She kissed both of Kit's cheeks and hugged him with her head on his chest. 'What a glorious surprise.' She ushered her son towards the house. 'Come and meet Raymond. You'll adore him.'

Kit looked over his shoulder at Jen, who'd remained by the car in a state of mild panic. He gestured for her to come and then he winked. She had no idea what he meant by that. 'Don't

241

worry, I'll take care of you,' hopefully. But all the old feelings were back, and she felt small and insignificant, and, once again, snubbed. Had Mrs Avery not spotted her, or deliberately not spotted her?

She wavered for a while, wondering whether to slip away, back to The Bell. Kit's mother may be an elderly woman now, but they could be the worst. She'd leave for London first thing in the morning. Get to Norwich by taxi; give Kit a call when she was on her way...

No, she wouldn't. That would be cowardly and ridiculous. She clutched her bag and jacket, took a deep breath and went through the gate. 'Beware of Dog' it said, but it was Bunk she was least afraid of.

## THIRTY-ONE

He was there, in the hut, waiting for her. 'Sorry, Jen,' he said, from where he lay on his back, hands buried in his blond locks. 'These ribs are making me a tad grumpy.'

She lowered herself beside him carefully, without touching him. 'But you were right, I am a doormat.'

He lifted his head and eased his arms out, turned on his side with a wince and lay an arm across her. 'But that's what's so adorable about you, Jennifer Juniper. You're a natural-born flower child. The genuine article. Full of goodwill

242

and selflessness and compassion, and all those lovely traits most of us don't have, but pretend we do. You never want to hurt anyone's feelings, do you?'

She could smell something spicy on his breath. How exciting it must be, she thought, eating at the Averys' every day. 'No,' she told him, 'I don't like hurting people's feelings.' But wasn't that because she didn't want them angry with her? Didn't want to lose their love or friendship? Wouldn't that make her selfish, not all the things Kit just said? Maybe everybody was selfish; they just showed it differently. 'But I did speak up for myself with your mum today.'

'You did?'

She told him what had happened: telling his mother she didn't want to play any more, turning down her lunch invitation. She didn't tell him they hadn't actually played, or about Mrs Avery doubling back to Mick's car and zooming towards the guardroom. If ever the moment was right, she'd mention the corporal. Not now, though, while Kit was being complimentary and in pain too.

'Good for you,' he said. 'But it's vichyssoise, not *fishy*ssoise.' While Jen coloured up, Kit kissed the end of her nose and laughed, then he groaned and lay back, staring at the ceiling. 'Nice of Ma to offer *you* lunch, when she didn't turn up to feed her own family this evening. Luckily, Pa enjoys messing about in the kitchen. He made a vicious curry that had the three of us in tears.'

'Wow,' Jen said, half listening. She saw his mum in a seedy basement club, drinking schnapps and

243

trying different drugs. Then in a plush hotel room, with a bottle of champagne in a bucket of ice. 'My dad never cooks,' she said. 'Well, toast.'

Kit slept for a while and Jen tried to, but couldn't. When he woke, she told him she wanted to go home because she needed to sleep. Which was true. Having to keep secrets was making her really tired.

They were all asleep when the knock on the door came. At first, it was part of Jen's dream, then she opened her eyes and heard it again. Immediately, she thought of Kit. Leaping from her bed, she grabbed the frilly dressing gown her mum had got from a catalogue, then decided against it. If it was Kit at the door, he'd go right off her. After quickly brushing her hair, she headed for the landing before anyone else woke up. Anyone else being her dad. She tripped down the stairs as lightly as possible, and when the knocking started again she ran at the door, opened it, and found not Kit standing there in the streetlight, but Wing Commander Avery.

'I'm dreadfully sorry,' he whispered. There was a smell of alcohol, like whisky. He put his hands in the pockets of a tweedy jacket and hunched his shoulders, as though cold on this really hot night.

'Are you all right?' she asked.

'What's going on?' her mother called out. 'Who is it?'

'No one,' Jen said, trying not to shout, but she heard her dad mumbling and extra footsteps on the landing, then the stairs.

When her parents joined her at the door, Kit's

dad said, 'Oh, goodness. I'm so terribly sorry to wake you all, only...'

Kit! It was bound to be about Kit. Something had happened, that was why Mr Avery was looking so tense. He had bad news, and Jen was about to faint before he even told them. 'What is it?' she asked him, her voice trembling. 'What's happened to Kit?'

'Kit? Oh, no, no.'

'Pip, then?'

'No. Look, would you mind terribly if I came in?'

'Of course you can, sir,' said Jen's dad, who was never civil when woken up, but managed it for his boss. 'Come into the lounge and the wife'll get yous a drink.'

'Thank you.' Wing Commander Avery stepped into the hall and smiled weakly at them all. 'I'm probably making a mountain out of a molehill.'

'Excuse the mess,' said Jen's mum, pushing open the door to the ultra-tidy lounge and switching on the top light. 'What can I get you, er ... I'm sorry, I don't know–'

'This is Kit's dad,' explained Jen.

'Oh, I say! Goodness me.' She put one hand on her chest, while the other started tugging curlers out. 'Shall I put the kettle on for tea, or perhaps you'd like Horlicks, or something cold? Robinson's barley water? Jim, have you still got those Watney's–'

'Please. I really don't want to put you to any trouble.'

'It's no trouble at all. I often make myself a cuppa in the night. You know, when I can't sleep

245

because of the heat or because Jen's not home yet.'

He smiled at her, which made his mouth disappear into his moustache. 'Well in that case, tea would be splendid. Thank you, Mrs Boyde.'

'Right you are.' She did a sort of dip. Not quite bow, not quite curtsy.

'Take a seat, sir,' said Jen's dad, going over to his own chair and picking up his cigarettes. 'Smoke?'

'That's very kind, thank you.' He sat on the settee under the harsh light, and looked small and sad and quite old.

If it wasn't his sons, it must be his wife, thought Jen. Suddenly embarrassed about the short nightie, she excused herself and ran upstairs for her frilly dressing gown. In her room, she looked at her watch. Twenty past two. Suddenly, she wasn't just groggy, she was worried too. But also excited. The only drama the Boydes had ever had was the washing machine catching fire and her dad spraying it with an extinguisher that he'd, luckily, brought home from work. Whether he was supposed to bring things home was doubtful. One of the perks of Supply Squadron, he'd tell them. Maybe Kit's dad did it too.

A mountain out of a molehill, he'd said just now. Intrigued, Jen hurried downstairs before her mum got out the photos, or Wing Commander Avery told them Kit didn't play cricket.

# THIRTY-TWO

Jen dropped her things on the bottom stair, then walked down the hall and through the door. On seeing her enter, a white-haired man got out of his chair. Kit and Mrs Avery were standing in the middle of the sitting room, and both turned to look at her.

'Do you remember Jen?' Kit asked his mother. 'Jennifer. From when we were at Weisfelt?'

While Jen approached her with an outstretched hand, Mrs Avery's lined and faintly leathery face turned pale. Her eyes, still huge but less blue, flickered, just briefly. 'Yes, of course,' she said. 'Your father was a sergeant. We played tennis.'

'Yes.' Jen was fifteen and a lowly airman's daughter again. She smiled, in spite of herself, but didn't get one back. Mrs Avery was clearly stunned, or perhaps reeling from the reminder of Germany. 'Do you still play?'

'A little.'

'Me too.'

'And this is Raymond,' said Kit.

Jen shook his substantial hand. He was tall and, like his girlfriend, beautifully turned out. They were very Milan couture – she in a pale cream dress that could only be Italian, accessorised with bits of gold jewellery and a gold watch. Her hair, still thick, was carefully layered for added volume. Raymond wore a light crease-free summer suit, tan loafers, no socks. He could have passed for a suave Italian, but Jen knew he was from Andover. 'Charmed,' he said, holding her hand too long.

'Is the house often left unlocked?' Mrs Avery asked Kit.

'Not usually, but it has been known. Isn't Adam here?'

'No,' said Raymond. 'No sign of any of them, in fact. We were about to find the local hostelry, weren't we, darling? Rather peckish.'

'Ravenous, you mean. And I'm not sure I've ever seen such a dismally empty fridge. Goodness. But that's Pip for you. Anyway, it's thrilling that you're still here, Kit. I wasn't expecting that bonus.'

Was Mrs Avery losing it, wondered Jen, or had Kit not given his mother the full picture? Thinking about it, he had been curt on the subject of her not returning from Italy when Pip disappeared. Maybe she didn't know. Jen felt a horribly awkward moment coming up. One she'd rather miss. Perhaps she could slip out to the loo, or back to The Bell.

'What do you mean, Raymond?' Kit was saying. 'No sign of any of *them*.'

'Well, your brother, his son and little ... er. What have they called it, darling?'

Mrs Avery took a deep breath. 'Roger,' she said and breathed out again.

'I'm sorry?' said Kit, running fingers through his hair. He sat down in one of the armchairs and gestured for everyone to sit too. They did. Jen sat in the other chair and Raymond and Mrs Avery on the sofa. Jen wondered if she was still called Mrs Avery. There would be no way now of not calling her Eleanor. 'I'm a bit confused here,' Kit went on. 'The only Roger I know is ... *was* ... Daddy.'

'Ah!' said his mother. She clapped a little clap. 'Thank *heaven* they changed their minds! Who'd do that to a child, with all those super names around now? Archie, Hugo ... George.'

'Look,' said Kit, 'perhaps we should get some food in you, Ma. You're making no sense. I'll ring The Bell and book a table.'

'Excellent!' Raymond rubbed his big hands together. 'Can't wait to get stuck into some decent English nosh after months of bloody pasta. I hope they do a first-class steak?'

'Yes, they do.' Kit got up and went to the phone, booked a table for fifteen minutes' time and sat back down. 'Now,' he said, 'would you two mind starting from the beginning. Why exactly are you here?'

'We've come to see the baby,' said his mother. 'Shot straight up from Heathrow, assuming it, and they, would be here.'

'What baby?'

'Oh, Kit. My grandson, of course.'

'What grandson?' came Adam's voice. 'Isn't that me?' He was leaning against the doorframe; beside him was Bunk.

'Hello, Adam,' said Mrs Avery. Suddenly she was all smiles. 'What a handsome young man you are now. Come and give Grandma a lovely big hug.'

Adam did as he was told, if self-consciously,

then sat himself cross-legged on the floor with a panting and very wet Bunk. 'I don't understand,' he said, turning to his uncle. 'What's going on, Kit?'

Kit shrugged. 'Search me. Please, Ma ... Raymond?'

'Your mother received an email,' Raymond said crisply but with an exasperated sigh. 'From Pip.'

'Are you sure?' Jen asked. 'I thought Pip didn't do email?'

'Of *course* I'm sure,' snapped Mrs Avery. 'And, clearly, he does.' Still hostile, thought Jen, taking in the narrowed eyes. Still hadn't forgiven her – if she'd ever known, that was. Jen would stay quiet; leave Kit to do the talking.

'Saying?' he asked them.

'Oh,' said his mother, 'I couldn't tell you verbatim. He thought I'd like to know I had another grandson ... that they were calling it Roger, after Daddy. Born April first. Eight pounds something.'

'There you go,' said Adam. 'It was obviously an April Fools' thing. Some twisted bastard. Pip doesn't do email, and why wouldn't he tell *me* something like that? I bet it didn't mention who the mother was supposed to be. Jesus, talk about sick.'

'Actually, there was a woman's name,' said Raymond. 'Wasn't there, darling? At the bottom.'

'Yes,' said Mrs Avery. 'Now let me think ... Pip and...'

'Wasn't it Elaine?'

'Elaine?' asked Kit. He shot Adam a look. 'Did you say Elaine?'

'Pip and Elaine...' Mrs Avery's brow creased, then uncreased. 'How terribly clever of you, darling. Elaine it was. Now, do we know who–'

'*Fuck*,' said Adam. He jumped to his feet – quick and agile – making Bunk bark. 'Fucking Pip.' He stormed out of the room, followed by the dog, and after a while, a less agile Kit.

Eleanor Avery shook her blond-grey head at a bewildered Raymond. 'If there's trouble to be made, one can always rely on my younger son.' She stood up and smoothed her dress. 'Let's make our way to the restaurant, shall we, dear?'

'Good plan,' Raymond said, getting to his feet. 'We'll leave it to them sort out their little drama. Perhaps Kit might give us directions.'

To The Bell? Jen could have told them, but she remained where she was and quiet, like someone who wasn't even in the room.

## THIRTY-THREE

Wing Commander Avery wasn't far into his tea and biscuit before he said, 'I wonder ... would it be possible to have a word with Jen? It's rather, um, delicate.'

'As you wish, sir,' said her father, glancing at her in a 'you'd better not be in trouble' way. He put his cigarette out in the whirly ashtray, stood up, and with a sharp jerk of his head, told his wife to leave too.

'Is there anything else I can get you?' she asked

251

as he ushered her out.

'No, thank you. You've been most hospitable.'

'Good night, sir,' said Jen's dad.

'Good night,' said her mum. 'Ever so nice to meet you.'

'You too, Mrs Boyde.'

Don't curtsy, Jen willed her, and then they were gone and she began to feel sick.

'I really am awfully sorry about this,' said Wing Commander Avery. He'd lowered his voice, as though ears might be pressed to the door.

'That's OK.'

'It's just that my wife ... Eleanor, hasn't come home, and I wondered if you'd have any idea where she may be?'

'Me?' Jen saw the sports car, the trail of smoke.

'Pip said you left the swimming pool to play tennis with Eleanor. Is that right?'

'Yes.' Jen felt a blush coming on, which would make her look guilty, when she had nothing to look guilty about.

'Only you didn't play tennis, did you?'

'No. But how do you—'

'Pip went home shortly after you left the pool. When his mother went out she, well, she wasn't exactly dressed for tennis. Left her racquet behind too.'

'Oh.' Jen took a deep breath. 'Well, I went to the court but when Mrs Avery came she said she couldn't play today and she left.'

'Did she say why she couldn't?'

'No.'

'Did you see which way she went?'

Jen was blushing horribly, she knew. 'I ... we

252

walked to the corner, by the Malcolm Club, and she went one way and I went the other. She was heading home, I thought.'

'But she didn't go home, not according to Pip, who didn't leave the house again.'

This was awful. Should she tell him or not? What if it all came out later, from Kit's mum herself, that she'd watched them drive off? Jen was certain Mrs Avery had seen her.

'Could you guess, perhaps, as to where she may have gone?' Kit's father ran a hand over the bald part of his head, back and forth. 'I'm frightfully worried. I need to know who she's with, whether there's been some ghastly accident. I thought, perhaps, since you meet up so regularly for tennis, that you might have an inkling. Before I inform the MPs.'

The military police? Jen stared at her lap, afraid to tell him, afraid not to. If they interrogated her, she'd have to tell the truth. 'Mick,' she whispered.

'I'm sorry?'

She cleared her throat and looked up. 'He's called Mick and he sometimes comes and talks to us at the Malcolm Club, after tennis. He's a corporal. I saw her go off in a car with him. A sports car. It was open top, so I saw her clearly. They were heading towards the guardroom, so I expect they were going off the camp. I mean station.'

'A corporal?' Mr Avery slouched back in the settee, looking defeated, as if he'd just received a knockout blow. 'You wouldn't happen to know his surname?'

'No, sorry.' Kit would kill her for not telling him about Mick, and especially about what she'd seen that afternoon. How stupid she'd been. She could feel herself getting tearful. 'He comes from Derbyshire, and I think he works on planes. A mechanic, or something.'

Wing Commander Avery sat himself upright again and smiled at her. 'That's very helpful, Jen. Thank you. I'll leave you to sleep now. Once again, I'm so sorry to have involved you in all this.'

'That's all right.'

'Also, I do hope this won't put the dampers on your tennis practice. I've heard how good you are, and how keen.'

'Actually, I've—'

'Five or six matches a week, isn't it? She's rarely there when I come home for lunch. Just a note to say she's playing tennis. Evenings too. You'll both be Wimbledon standard soon!' He chuckled, but then he must have seen the look on her face. 'How often?' he asked quietly.

'Twice, most weeks. Sometimes not that.' She knew she was making things worse, but couldn't stop. 'For a couple of weeks we didn't play at all because I'd hurt my ankle.'

He nodded slowly, and clasped his hands in his lap. 'I see. Listen, Jen, you don't have to worry about me repeating any of this. Strictly confidential, eh?'

'Thank you.'

'Not even Kit will know. Unless you want to tell him.'

'Maybe. Anyway, I'm sure Mrs Avery will turn

up. She might even be there when you get back.'

'Let's hope so,' he said, but his face had a different look now. Not desperate, any more. Just upset, and maybe a bit angry. What had she done, Jen wondered, as he got up and made his way to the hall, then thanked her again and headed into the night.

Jen stood in the hallway, staring at her Constable, her head buzzing with tiredness and with Wing Commander Avery's words. From upstairs came the sound of feet on the landing and the gentle closing of a door.

## THIRTY-FOUR

Kit had ushered his mother and Raymond back into the sitting room, then phoned The Bell and delayed the meal by half an hour. Raymond looked distressed about it but Kit didn't care.

'One really wants to give up on Pip,' his mother was saying, and Kit had to bite his tongue. The things he could have said. Not that he had much sympathy for Pip, himself. In fact, he might just kill his brother when he saw him, if Adam hadn't got to him first.

Jen was making tea and Adam wouldn't come out of his room, so the three of them sat in the sitting room, pondering the situation and what should be done about it, and managing to get nowhere.

'A jolly good sirloin,' said the steak-obsessed

Raymond. 'That'll get the grey matter working. Ah, tea. Marvellous. Thank you, my dear.' He took a mug from the tray with a wink at Jen, and Kit hoped he'd never become that kind of elderly man.

'Here you are...' Jen said to his mother, as though about to use her name, then changing her mind. 'Milk. Sugar?'

'Goodness, no.'

When Jen handed Kit his mug, he smiled and gave an exaggerated 'Thank you' to make up for his mother's rudeness.

'I think I'll get back to The Bell,' Jen said. 'Have a little rest. It's been a busy day.'

'Yes,' he agreed, and the image of resting with her, and how nice that might be, filled his head. 'But you will join us for dinner there?'

'Dessert, perhaps. I'm not that hungry.'

She said her goodbyes, even calling up the stairs to Adam, and left. Then, after biscuits were dunked and teas were drunk, Kit and his mother went on the internet, signed into her email account and copied down Pip's email address. It began with a 'el', so was presumably Elaine's. And it was with BT, so probably traceable. His mother made no mention of Jen, as they sat there, and so Kit didn't either.

He called the police and gave them all the details, then he, his mother and a very quiet Adam were driven by Raymond to the pub. There, a room was booked for the night and three G and Ts and a cola were ordered and taken to their table in the window.

Following more pointless speculation about Pip, the conversation moved on to Italian travels. Raymond got his camera out for a mini slide show and the atmosphere lightened considerably. As did Adam, who was laughing at his grandma's anecdotes. He may have been pissed off with his dad, but Kit knew Adam well enough now to sense his relief.

His grandma was telling him about a 'scrumptious young Adonis' who'd tried to pick her up in Milan station. 'I must say, I found Italian men exceptionally attentive, whatever their age.'

'It's true,' Raymond said proudly cupping her hand. 'Your grandmother still has what it takes.'

Kit decided Raymond was all right, and obviously fond of his mother. He even knew his surname now, from when they'd booked the room. 'Bowen,' he'd announced at the desk. Kit watched them, touching and smiling and happy, and wondered if they'd marry. Eleanor Avery-Bowen had a certain ring, he thought.

The desserts arrived, but Jen didn't. 'Excuse me,' Kit said, and he left them to their ice creams and sorbets and went through to the hotel area and up the stairs.

She came to the door all made up and lovely. 'I was just coming down,' she told him. 'How's it going?'

'Fine. Ma's on good form, telling Italian-men stories. Shallow as a puddle, but she's managed to buck Adam up.'

'Good.' Jen grabbed her key and bag and then stopped and took a deep breath. 'Here goes.'

He thought about slipping a reassuring hand in hers, but didn't. 'It'll be fine,' he said. 'They really like you.'

'Very funny. Well, Raymond, maybe.'

'So, tell me,' said his mother, when she'd run out of things to say about herself. 'Are you two an...' she did inverted commas with her fingers, '...item?'

'Er, no,' Kit said, and he told her about Jen spotting them at the rally, then looking him up on the internet. 'Until two days ago, we hadn't seen each other for thirty-odd years.'

'Not since Germany,' said Jen.

'It's been great catching up,' he said, turning to her. 'Hasn't it?'

'Yes,' she said, 'it has.'

A chair scraped back on the flagstone floor and Adam stood up. 'Sorry,' he said, 'but I have to go. Homework. Revision.'

'I'll be back soon,' Kit told him.

'No need.'

'See you tomorrow,' said Raymond.

'Yeah. Night, Grandma. Night, Raymond.'

Kit watched his nephew leave the room. He didn't like the hunched shoulders, the abrupt departure, the way he hadn't wished Jen good night. His father might have come back from the dead, but something was still very wrong. 'Listen, do you mind if I bow out too?' he asked. He sensed Jen stiffen beside him. 'If *we* bow out,' he added. 'It's been a long day, and, to be honest, I'm worried about Adam. Another big shock for him. Perhaps we should check on him, Jen?'

'Yes,' she said. 'Yes, let's.' She was up before he was. 'It's been lovely seeing you again, and meeting you, Raymond. See you before I go, hopefully.'

'No doubt,' said his mother, while Raymond stood and bowed his head and might have kissed Jen's cheeks, if she hadn't been halfway across the room.

'I'll settle up,' Kit told them, taking his wallet from his back pocket.

'No, no.' Raymond held up a hand. 'This is on me.'

In the bar, Jen said, 'Look, I won't come. Adam's being a bit odd with me. It'll be better if you go and talk to him on your own.'

Kit couldn't disagree, but at the same time he wanted to hang out with her; tell her how he felt about Pip and Adam and the baby, if it existed. Talk to her the way he had back then, when his and Pip's lives had somersaulted out of control. 'Could you stay another day?' he asked.

'I'd better not. There are things I have to do for the rentals. And there's Robert.'

'Ah. You're going to the house, then?'

Jen nodded. 'Demons to face, ghosts to lay. You know.'

'Is that why you came here?' How cocky, he thought, and wished he hadn't said it.

'Don't be silly. How was I to know your mother would roll up?'

He laughed. 'Don't go first thing, though. Let's have coffee or something?'

'OK.' She leaned forward and upward and

kissed his cheek. 'Good night, Kit. And good luck with Adam.'

'Thanks,' he said, not wanting to move, wishing he had slipped his hand in hers earlier.

Adam was in his room, but came down when he heard noises. 'You all right?' Kit asked.

'I dunno.'

'You must be relieved? I know I am.'

'Yeah, yeah, of course. Well, if it's true. Oh, there's a message from some policeman, asking you to call back.'

'Right.' Kit went to the phone and dialled the number in the message. The sergeant gave him an address in Norwich. Norwich. So close all this time. Kit said no to the offer of sending a couple of PCs round. 'We'll go,' he said. 'But thanks.'

He hung up and went back to the kitchen. 'Fifty-three Wellington Street, Norwich.'

'Norwich,' said Adam, the same way Kit had. 'Fucking hell.'

'I know. Jen and I could have been yards from him today. The police sergeant gave me a phone number. Shall we...?'

'No way. I don't want to talk to him. Nor Elaine.'

'Let's go and sit down. Come on.'

Adam gave him a yeah-whatever shrug and slouched through to the sitting room. As usual, he sat on the floor, and, as usual, Bunk came to join him.

'I'll call the number, but you don't have to talk, OK?'

Kit was surprised to see his hand shake as he

picked up the phone and tapped in the number. What if Adam was right, and it had been some practical joke, played by Elaine, or some other Elaine who had nothing to do with Pip? Then they'd all come crashing down again; Adam the hardest.

'Hello?' said a woman.

'Oh, hello. I'm sorry to bother you, but I'm trying to get hold of Philip Avery.'

'Ahh,' she said. It was almost a sigh. 'Are you his brother?'

'Yes. Is he with you?'

A baby was crying in the background. A very young baby. 'Yeah, he is. But...'

'What?'

'I don't think he'll come to the phone,' she whispered. 'He hasn't been good, you see. I've wanted to ring you but he wouldn't let me. Threatened to disappear. I didn't think he would, what with the baby, but I wasn't sure. Bit of a breakdown, you might say. Anyway, I found his mum's email address on a postcard in his pocket. When I got home from the hospital, I wrote her an email, pretending it was from him. Seemed like the decent thing to do, tell her she had a grandchild.'

'Why didn't you ring his home?' Kit whispered back, not sure why he was whispering.

'Well, there wouldn't have been anyone there, so no point. He said his lodger had moved out.'

'His lodger?'

'The one who used to answer the phone some-times.' Kit took his time to respond. Pip hadn't told Elaine he had a son, or Adam he had a

261

pregnant girlfriend, or even a girlfriend. Adam was in the room, watching, listening, and still looking fragile. 'Would it be best if I came to you? I've got the address.' He repeated it, just to be sure.

'Why don't you phone? Say, tomorrow evening. Give me time to prepare him. We're always here in the evenings, because of Roger.'

'Roger?' His father's face flashed past. 'Oh, right. How is he?'

'Fine. Growing. Hard work. What with your brother and having a Caesarean, it hasn't been easy.'

'No,' said Kit. 'I can imagine.'

'Although Pip's been a big help, practically. I, er ... I'd better...'

Kit got the impression Pip was approaching, as Elaine's voice changed. 'Thanks for calling. Speak to you soon. Bye.'

'Tomorrow,' Kit said, but the line was dead.

'Well?' asked Adam.

Kit sat on the sofa and took a deep breath. He needed to do this sensitively. 'Your dad's there, Adam,' he said. There was no response, so he carried on. 'And there is a baby. Roger. Your half-brother. Elaine said that–'

'*Elaine*,' Adam said, staring at the floor. 'Jesus.'

Kit paused. In fairness to Elaine, should he tell Adam his father had kept him a secret? Perhaps not yet. 'She said that the baby is fine, and that Pip is too. She sounds like a really lovely woman.'

Adam snorted. 'Yeah,' he said, shooting up. 'But she's not my mother. She's not Pat.' He looked down at his uncle and glared. '*Is* she?'

And suddenly, Kit understood. 'Wait,' he called to his nephew. 'Adam, please. Come back.'

Adam stopped in the doorway and visibly drooped. 'How could he?' he said, his voice choking.

'Come and sit down.'

Adam went back to the same spot and Bunk rejoined him. He didn't look up while Kit spoke.

'It wasn't true, was it, Adam? That your dad compared all women with your mother?'

Adam didn't respond.

'But you did?'

Again, he said nothing.

'Didn't you?'

His nephew finally nodded.

'And is that, in a roundabout way, why you've been a bit funny with Jen?'

'No, I haven't.'

'I sort of became a father to you, and so you saw Jen... Well, never mind that. It's all going to be OK, Adam. Your dad's alive, that's the important thing. No, he hasn't been very honest—'

'To say the least.'

'But then I'm sure you didn't make it easy for him.'

'Christ, why would I? My mum was really special, the three of us were special and things were just perfect ... you know?'

'Yeah.'

'You knew her. She was... I loved her so much and then she was gone. There in the morning, gone when I got home from school. Just gone, like that, when there were so many hideous people in the world who could have died instead.'

'I know, Adam. It's not fair. Life isn't fair.' Oh God, what was he saying? Clichés. Platitudes. Someone should have taken more care of Adam, in those early days, weeks, months, when Pip would have been bound up in his own grief. Found him a therapist, or something.

'I couldn't bear the thought of anyone else being here, doing the things she used to do. Do you understand?'

'Yes,' said Kit. 'I understand. But it was a long time ago. And now you're almost eighteen and about to leave home, so perhaps you could be a bit more...'

'Grown up about it? I have tried, believe it or not.'

'Well, these childhood traumas can mess you up for years.'

'If you let them, you're going to say.'

'No, I'm not. I have had some experience, you know.'

'At least you and Pip were a bit older.'

'That's true, but it's bloody painful at any age.'

'Is it?'

'Absolutely.'

Adam nodded to himself and stroked the dog. 'I suppose I have been pretty selfish. And I do feel really bad about...'

'What?'

'Oh, this row we had.'

'Just before Pip disappeared?'

'Yeah, the evening before. He started talking about how he thought he might like to get married again and I sort of exploded and called him disloyal, and didn't give him a chance to tell me about Elaine. I suppose that was what he was trying to do. You know, leading up to. At the time I thought he was talking generally. Told him to at least have the decency to wait till I'd left home, then stormed out.'

'I see. But, still, you weren't to know—'

'He actually had a girlfriend, plus a baby on the way?' Adam shook his head and laughed. 'God, what a complete prick I was.'

'Well ...' Kit laughed too and felt himself relax for the first time in hours. Since he'd pulled up outside with Jen, in fact. Feeling it was time to change the subject, he said, 'It was nice seeing Grandma, wasn't it? The bombshell aside.'

'Yeah, yeah. Good fun. Only...'

'What?'

'It's a bit odd, don't you think? That someone like Grandma, who takes, like, no interest in other people, should rush up here to see a baby.'

'Oh, she's *always* loved babies,' said Kit. 'Grandma's never passed one she didn't coo at. She did a stint of nannying, when she ran away from home. Perhaps it goes back to that.'

'I didn't know she'd run away from home. Is that where my father gets it from?'

'Maybe. She went back again, apparently, when her father threatened to disinherit her.'

'As you would.'

'She wasn't to know he'd eventually lose his fortune through bad investments.'

'Yeah, Pip told me about that. Often. The family fortune being squandered.'

Kit said, 'You all right now?'

'Yeah, I think so.'

'Need anything? A drink? A stroll round the village with Bunk?'

Adam looked him in the eye, at last. 'Actually, I'd love a spliff.'

Kit laughed. Should he tell Adam his grandma might too? 'How about a game of chess?'

'I'll win, you know?'

'I know you will.'

'OK, then.'

## THIRTY-FIVE

She parked where she always had, got out, locked the car, mentally crossed herself, and walked up the black and white tiled path she used to call hers. He'd cut back the rosemary bush, she noticed. It had been planted too close to the path, that was the problem. They'd brush past it and smell the pungent herb for hours. The paint on the front door looked tired and dull. The brass letter box too. No doubt they had when she'd lived there, but in Southwark she'd got used to brand new. There was no time to decide between knocking and letting herself in, because the door opened itself. Or, rather, Robert opened it.

'Hi,' he said, smiling crookedly. His eyes were wide and fish-like. Nerves, perhaps. 'Welcome home.'

There was no point in correcting him; Robert knew she wasn't coming home. 'Hi,' she said, stepping in. Same slight chill in the north-facing

266

hall, her comfy shoes beneath the hooks. Her black winter coat, two of her jackets. Almost, but not quite, the same smell to the place. People add their own aromas to a home, she guessed, then took them away. 'How are you?'

'All the better for...' His voice cracked and he smiled, not so crookedly. His face seemed fuller, a bit doughy. 'I can't believe you're here, Jen.'

'No. Me neither.' After her initial bravado, she was suddenly tense and tingly, standing there in all the familiarity, waiting for him to lead her somewhere. She couldn't wander around, since it was no longer her home. Robert was the host but he just stood there too. 'Shall we go in the kitchen?' she asked.

'Yes,' he said, jumping slightly. 'Good idea. I'll put the kettle on. Oh, and I bought cakes.'

'I'm dieting,' she told him.

Nothing was different but everything was different. There was the note to herself on the kitchen board: 'Send cheque window cleaner.' He must still be waiting for it. And all the same plants on the windowsill, watered and doing well without her. She wasn't sure what she'd expected. Perhaps for Robert to have let things slide. *Look. See. Everything's gone to pieces without you.* The only thing different was Robert himself. He'd put on weight, she saw now, in just a few weeks. Some drugs could do that. She took a seat at the table, remembering the last time she'd sat there. Gazing at an egg, waiting.

'Has Jon been here?' she asked, surprising both of them with her question.

He hesitated. A bad sign, she thought, counting the seconds.

'I told you that's over. Was over immediately. The moment you left. What would you like to drink?'

'Just water, please.' She didn't want to watch him make tea in their old pot, hand her the mug she'd liked best. 'I can't stay long, sorry. I'm meeting someone later.' She'd arranged a get together with Lionel, as an escape route.

Robert looked hurt, as she'd known he would. He took a tumbler from the glasses cupboard and a bottle of water from the fridge. 'Oh,' he said, 'still or sparkling?'

Had he forgotten already? 'Still, please.'

'Of course. Stupid. These tablets I'm on make me dozy.' He put the glass on the table and his hand shook as he poured.

'What's happening with the house?' she asked. 'Have you had it valued? Decided what to do?'

'Please, Jen,' he said. 'I know you're bitter, and you have every right to be, but have a little compassion. I'm very fragile, at the moment. I'm sure I'll get better, stronger. The psychiatrist said months, rather than weeks, if I take the tablets, keep up the counselling. I'm not gay, Jen, I'm really not. I don't know what came over me.'

'Don't you mean who?' she said, with a short Mrs-Avery-type smile. She used to have compassion – Kit told her she had, many years back. Not now, it seemed. 'How's the garden?' she asked. If she couldn't say anything nice, she'd try boring.

'Lovely. Everything in the garden's lovely,' he

said, and he began to cry.

It was easier, being outside. The house had felt
claustrophobic with all its things, all its mem-
ories. Robert had stopped crying and got the
deck chairs out, and now they faced the spring
sunshine and the beginning of colours that would
peak in June. They'd both put so much work into
the garden; planned with drawings, got excited
when things bloomed. She wondered if Robert
saw it the way she did now, as something of a
white elephant. An embarrassing reminder of
what they'd had and lost. But it did look lovely:
lush and colourful.

Robert was chatty, thank God. Telling her his
father was recovering, and that 'Young Simon'
was managing the office well. That Sarah had
been something of a rock for him. 'I'm sure she'd
like to see you,' he'd said, but Jen hadn't responded. Let Sarah be Robert's friend now, she'd
thought, glad he had someone to talk to. He also
had his new shrink, apparently, an American
called Walter.

'He says that sexuality can be highly mutable,'
Robert was telling her, 'for some.'

'Really?' Jen said, but she didn't want to hear
about that, not from her husband, however
helpful it might have been for him to offload. 'I'm
just going to...' She pointed back at the house
and heaved herself from the deck chair. Could
she face the cloakroom and the soap dish? Maybe
not.

'Are you sure you wouldn't like tea?' Robert
asked. He looked up at her with his watery eyes

and his puffy jowls and cheeks. He'd always had a flat stomach, but not now. Her husband had gone, she realised. Mostly his doing, but it was partly hers. 'And an éclair? I got two especially, from–'

'OK.' How dreadful she'd feel if he did take his life. She shivered at the thought, or because it had clouded over and she was cold. She'd eat his cake, if it would make him happy, then go. 'Thanks.'

Robert had kept her stuff out: shampoo, conditioner, face cream, deodorant. All where she'd left them that terrible day. Her towelling robe still hung on the back of the door and her shower cap on its hook. The things she'd used that morning before going off to do an inventory in Woolwich.

She washed her hands, then sat on the edge of the bath, taking in the creepiness of it all, trying to conjure up her old happy settled self. Not that she was unhappy now, but she wasn't that calm and contented Jen; the one who'd last hooked the robe on the door. Through the floor she heard Robert pottering, as she had a million times. Rustling up something, while she was in the bath. 'Ready!' he'd call out. Sometimes she'd fallen asleep and he'd knocked on the door. 'Wakey, wakey, Jen.' He could have come in, but he never had, not in recent years. Now it made sense: he hadn't wanted to see her naked.

Jen got up and went to close the toilet lid – an old feng shui habit – but then she spotted, there in the loo... why hadn't she seen them before? Two swollen cigarette butts; fat and brown, with tendrils of tobacco floating out of them. Had Robert taken up smoking? No. Impossible. He'd always hated the idea, the smell, everything about it. He was one of the few people Jen knew who'd never smoked, not even in his teens. She'd given up, herself, when she met him, because he was repulsed by it.

She tried picturing him puffing away in the bath, or in bed. But it was too ludicrous, considering his aversion. On the other hand, he wasn't really himself at the moment. Perhaps the drugs had changed his tastes, and combined with the stress and depression... Still, it was unlikely, she thought, trying but failing to flush the things away.

Downstairs, having passed the sitting-room door, Jen stopped, reversed and popped her head in. She'd loved that room. They'd knocked the middle wall down on moving in, making a gorgeous long and wide space, with the original fireplaces, ceiling roses, floorboards, doors, door furniture, picture rails, everything. Not long ago they'd removed the bookshelves and cut ornaments to a minimum. They'd replaced the three-piece suite with modern cream sofas and gone for a sleek dark dining table. The room was as she'd left it, if not a little neater. The large mirror gleamed, the peace lily thrived. Had Robert lavished attention on the room for her, or for the smoker? She still loved it, she realised, whoever he'd done it for. It was the one thing she'd like to pick up and transfer to Southwark.

As expected, he'd made tea in the old pot and

was now filling 'her' mug. But she'd got used to being there now, amongst all their possessions, and it didn't bother her. The glazing on the teapot was covered in fine cracks, and the mug he handed her wasn't as nice as the new ones at the flat. Silly that she'd got herself wound up earlier, about things, just things. 'Are the anti-depressants helping?' she asked.

Robert gave a little start, as though taken aback by her sudden interest in him. 'I'm not sure. I sleep better, but still feel as miserable as fuck when I wake up. Walter said it could take time to find the right medication.'

'And tell me to mind my own business, but are you drinking a lot? Paul said... I mean, I know you're not supposed to with some tablets.' She bit into the éclair and went to cake heaven. Perhaps it was cakes, not medication, making Robert chubby.

'Yeah, I can with these. I'm not *over*-drinking, despite what Paul may have thought. God, I must phone him. I was in bad shape and they were so kind.'

'Well, it is Paul's forte.' She got up and walked over to the kitchen-roll holder, pulled off two squares and handed him one. Look at me, she thought, no longer the guest. 'So,' she said, 'got any new vices?'

'Pardon?'

Jen laughed at his expression. 'Sorry, that came out wrongly. It's just that people sometimes do things like, oh, take up smoking. You know, during a crisis?'

'Me? Smoke? Are you kidding?' He grimaced at

272

the very idea and bit into his éclair. 'I've definitely got a sweeter tooth, though. You were always trying to get me into desserts, weren't you?'

'Yes, I was.' They were quiet while they ate, then she said, 'So, you're definitely not smoking?'

'No, Jen. What is this?' But almost before he'd finished speaking, his expression changed. Somewhere, as he wiped his mouth with the tissue, a penny had dropped. 'But a friend ... more of a colleague, who called by the other day, was smoking. If you can smell cigarettes.'

'Ah.' But why carry the ashtray all the way upstairs to empty it? If they had to be flushed away, there was the cloakroom.

'Tell me about your flat,' Robert said quickly.

'I already have.'

'Er, yeah ... only...' He was floundering, but luckily for him, her mobile rang.

Jen dipped into her bag and saw it was Lionel. 'Hi,' she said. She stood and took the phone to the back door with a 'sorry' gesture to Robert. The door was open and she stood half in, half out, ready to dash into the garden, should Lionel get loud.

'Hiya, Jen,' he said. 'I'm afraid I ain't gonna make our meeting. The clutch on me van's gone, and I've got a mate here putting a new one in.'

'Oh.' This didn't sound good, but she loved hearing Lionel's voice in this surreal situation.

'Thought he might be done by now, but he says it's a bit of a bugger.'

'Ah.'

Anyway, I'm gonna need me van tomorrow, and as much as I'd love to jump on the Tube and come and see you, I think my mate would be mighty pissed off if I left him, know what I mean?'

'Right,' said Jen, trying to think quickly. 'I'll come and pick you up, then.'

'Nah, no need. It's gonna take a while.'

'You'll be there in ten minutes, you say?'

'You what?'

'OK. No. No trouble. See you then. Bye.' She hung up and switched the phone off completely. 'My friend caught an earlier train,' she told Robert. 'I'm going to have to–'

'The friend from Norfolk?'

'What?' she said. 'Oh, no. Not him. Another one.' But then she had images of Robert being jealous and distraught after she'd gone. Suicidal. 'It's a woman. A new friend. Lillian.'

'She has a very deep voice,' said Robert, 'this Lillian.'

'Yes, she has.' Jen picked up both mugs and both plates and took them to the sink. 'But I'd like to come and see you again,' she said, needing Robert stable, while they sorted things out.

'When?'

'I'm not sure.'

'Tomorrow? I hate Sundays.'

'No, not tomorrow, Robert. I'll call you.' She said it in a don't-call-me way, sounding harsher than she'd intended. 'Thank you for the tea and cake.'

His eyes were fixed on the teapot, and she realised he wasn't going to get up.

'I'll see myself out,' she said, and she did, turning at the kitchen door to see if he'd follow, then walking down the hall, scooping her walking shoes up on the way. 'Bye!' she called out from the front door, not expecting a response and not getting one. Should she go back, or leave him to sulk? Kit's father flashed into her head. In a chair, whisky in his hand, staring and staring. She hovered, listening to her own breathing, unable to shut the door. 'Bye!' she tried again.

Jen closed her eyes and quietly swore, frustrated at the spot she'd been put in. Robert had stirred up trouble in the first place, and was now heaping this on her. Then again, she had to remind herself, he was ill. Just as she'd been ill a couple of years back, with a bad case of shingles. He'd helped her then, for weeks, while she was knocked out. More than helped ... done everything. His job, her job, all the shopping, cooking, cleaning. He'd always been there for her, in fact. Confidant, friend, investor and workman on her first property. It was possible, on balance, that she owed Robert more than he owed her.

She stood on the top step, listening to the silence. He hadn't moved. It could be he'd sit like that for hours. Or perhaps he'd get up the moment she slammed the door and call the person who smoked, invite them over for a bite and a DVD. It was possible but unlikely, she thought, stepping back into the house. She put the shoes back in their spot and hung her handbag in its old place, on the newel post. The stair carpet needed replacing, and had for a while. Strange how she'd jump on something like that in her rental properties but hadn't in her own. They'd focused on the main room, she guessed, and would have got round to the stairs at some point. The green had been Robert's choice, but she'd thought it too dark for a narrow Victorian house. It needed coir or seagrass matting; good against the white.

'Jen?' said Robert. 'Are you still here?'

'Yes, I am.' She took her phone from the bag and made her way to the kitchen. 'Lillian had to turn back,' she told him, pretending to read a text. 'Thinks she left the iron on.'

## THIRTY-SIX

She'd been about to write, 'Nine days till Kit leaves,' but put the top back on her pen. She wouldn't keep a diary any more. Too depressing. She wasn't sure if it was just the next day being the first of September, or what, but the air felt different; everything felt different. Chillier, somehow, even though it was still baking hot. Kit hadn't been himself for the past week, and as much as she liked to think it was because he was leaving her soon, Jen guessed it was his parents bringing him down. Or, put another way, his mum.

The day after Wing Commander Avery dropped in on the Boydes, she'd bravely gone round to Kit's to see how he was, and how his dad was, and above all, to see if Mrs Avery had come home. She had. In fact, she'd answered the door and said, 'Yes?' – like she was talking to a door-to-door

276

salesman. She'd looked tired and rubbed at her temple, as she let Jen in and shouted, 'Kit!' then said, 'Oh, you may as well go up.'

Jen hadn't told Kit about his father's visit, and guessed he would have mentioned it, if he'd known. Generally, what he talked about was music. He'd been to Roermond and bought more LPs and seemed to spend most of his time, when he wasn't with her, in his room, listening to them. 'My sanctuary,' he'd called his attic. Away from the insanity.' He wasn't seeing much of Lawrence and Susie, either, which Jen was secretly pleased about.

She put her diary in the bedside drawer and pulled the sheet and one remaining blanket back over her. She'd never written much in it anyway, and a lot was in code, and sometimes, when she'd looked back, even she couldn't read it. Yes, diaries were depressing. Especially this one. A month ago, she'd been so happy and in love. Now she was unhappy and in love.

She put her hands together on the scratchy blanket and prayed for her dad to be posted back to England, somewhere near Worcester. *Please, God, about five miles, or less, from Kit's school, if that's possible, if there's a camp near there. And soon. Before Christmas?* He could sneak out of school and meet her. They'd find another hut, or something ... somewhere. The trouble was, Kit would come home for Christmas. Then she'd be stuck in England and he'd be in Germany. With Susie. Having fun, because Susie was so good at that. There'd be parties, and then New Year's Eve, when he'd be bound to kiss someone at midnight. Kiss Susie, maybe, and realise he'd loved her all along. No, that would never do. *Please, God, don't let my dad be posted just yet, but make this term go quickly and please don't let Kit go out with anyone from Hopthorpe School, or even like anyone from there, and please make him write to me. Once a week would be OK.*

On the other hand, she thought, while she was dressing and the smell of Sunday bacon was filling her room, term time was long and the holidays were short. Just two or three weeks at Christmas. She prayed again for a UK posting. Even if it wasn't to a place near his boarding school, they could meet up often. Go to London or the seaside. And, anyway, just being in the same country as Kit would feel better.

He'd be leaving school in less than a year and maybe he'd get a summer job before going to university and not come back to Germany at all. Then he'd be bound to meet someone else. If her dad didn't get posted home, it would be hopeless, she realised, just hopeless. Worse still would be a posting to Singapore or Cyprus or some place a million miles away. It was horrible, being fifteen and not having any power. All you could do was run away from home, but that wasn't an option with no money. Unless she and Kit...

'Breakfast, Jen!' called her mum.

'Coming.'

'It's on the table!' Breakfast and dinner, or lunch as Kit would call it, were always at the table behind the settee. Tea tended to be on their laps, watching telly, unless it was something Paul might spill. Jen much preferred laps and telly, especially when her dad was home.

Heading for the stairs, she prayed again, coming up with a better idea than all the posting business. *Please, God, make me go off him.* It was the only solution and she should start working on it right away. Like picturing him in that poncho he wore when the evenings got cold. Since Christine had called it Kit's giant bib, that was all she could see.

'There's been an almighty rumpus,' Kit told her. 'Or should I say another one.' They were by the pool with a million other people, grabbing the last bit of summer. He was wearing cut-off jeans – short, tight and frayed against his gorgeous legs. How hard it was going to be to go off him. 'Over Christmas, this time.'

'Why?'

'Pip's insisting on going to our grandparents in Kent. Pa's folks. Says he doesn't want to come back here for the hols.' Kit rolled on to his front and rested his head on his folded arms. He closed one eye and looked at Jen with the other. 'When Daddy said what a splendid idea it was, and that we should all go, because it's years since we spent Christmas with them ... well, Mummy freaked out.'

'Oh dear.' Jen wasn't surprised by Mrs Avery's reaction. From what Kit had told her, his dad's parents weren't exactly well off. His granddad had been a train driver and they lived in a bunga-low. Imagining Mrs Avery in a bungalow, missing all the Officers' Mess seasonal fun, was impossible. 'So you're not going?' she asked, crossing fingers.

'Nothing's been decided.'

'I hope you don't.'

'Why? I never get to see Nanny and Granddad Avery. They're terribly nice and they vote Labour, which, obviously, I admire them for.'

What did he mean, *why?* 'It means I won't get to see you for ages, if you don't come back for Christmas.' Jen couldn't believe she was having to say this.

'Aah.' Kit pulled an arm from beneath his head and put it around her waist, while she sat very straight and unmoving – rigid, now, with disappointment. 'That's so sweet,' he said. 'And, of course, I'll miss you too.' He lifted his head and kissed her shoulder, then withdrew his arm, put it back under his head and closed his eyes. 'You'll get to see me at Easter.'

This couldn't be happening. He didn't love her, after all. Not the way she loved him. How stupid she'd been. How really stupid. Or was it just that boys were like that? Didn't feel things as much. Her eyes filled with tears, but she didn't mind if he saw them. Maybe it would make him care about her if he did. Her cheeks were wet and she didn't bother wiping them. Let him see how cruel he'd been.

'But don't worry too much,' he said, with a chuckle. How could he be laughing, when she wanted to die? 'My ma usually gets her own way.'

'That's what she told Mick,' Jen said, her voice all thick. It just came out.

'Who?'

'Mick, the corporal.' She shouldn't be telling him this but she'd got the devil in her, as her mum would say. If he could be cruel, so could she. She used her arms to wipe her cheeks, one at a time, then reached for her skirt and dabbed with that. Kit still had his eyes closed and hadn't even noticed she'd been crying. 'Your mum's boyfriend,' she said, and that made him look at her. She dipped her head and let her hair flop.

'What?'

'You mean you haven't heard?' *You'll get to see me at Easter* – why was he so unbothered about such a long gap? Was God answering her prayer and making him too horrible to love?

He rolled over and sat up. 'Mummy's having a fling with a *corporal?*'

Jen nodded, wishing now she'd said nothing, but it was too late.

'Huh,' he said, shaking his head, smiling. 'Man, that's so far out.'

Jen was confused. She'd been hoping to shock him, not please him.

'How do you know?' he asked.

'Well, I don't for sure, but...' She took a deep breath and told him about the Malcolm Club, and Pip seeing his mother all dressed up, and the sports car and his dad coming round at two in the morning.

'He *what?* God, poor Daddy. You've been a tad secretive, Jennifer Juniper. You and my pa.' Kit put an arm around her, while his other hand wiped her cheek. 'But, hey, no need to be so distraught. They are *my* parents.'

281

'It's not–'

'Personally, I'm bloody happy.'

'You are?'

'If you knew my ma and her prejudices, you'd know how utterly cosmic this is.'

'I think I do–'

'A *corporal*. Far fucking out.'

'Yeah,' Jen agreed, although she hated him using the f-word.

'So, what's he like?' Kit asked, after sleeping for a while, or pretending to. 'Mick.'

'What do you want to know?'

'Age? Looks? Is he a prat or an OK sort?'

'You saw him,' said Jen, 'in the cinema.' She explained about Mick passing them at *Bullitt*.

'Jesus. Much younger than Mummy.'

'Yeah. He's all right, actually. Just a bit...'

'What?'

'Full of himself, I suppose.'

'Cocky? I think that's her type. Someone who'll answer back. Unlike my father.'

'Doesn't it bother you?' asked Jen. 'That your mum's, you know...'

'Of course. But one's become accustomed to all this crap. All I see is divorce, so why get wound up about things? A corporal is rather cool. Almost anarchic, don't you think?'

'I don't know. If it was my mum having an affair, I'd want to kill her.'

'*Your* mother?' Kit laughed loudly, and Jen felt insulted on her mum's behalf. She could look really pretty sometimes, all dressed up for the Sergeants' Mess. Natural blond hair and big blue eyes, all of which Paul had inherited and Jen hadn't. 'Your ma's far too sweet,' he added. 'You should count your blessings, Jennifer Juniper. Appreciate your parents.'

'I do!' Suddenly, she didn't like him calling her that. And she didn't like being told what she *should* do – as though he were much older, or her teacher, or parent. Kit was really annoying today, first with his attitude to their being apart, now this. If she had the courage, she'd tell him not to be so unfeeling, or so bossy. Did she have the courage? She took a deep breath and turned to him, but what she saw stopped her saying anything. He just looked so sad. Lying on his front, staring into space – well, at her elbow. He was frowning, his mouth was down at the corners, and he could easily have been about to cry.

'I wish I had your parents,' he said, and he pulled an arm out from beneath his head again, and put it around her middle and pulled her towards him. 'Of course I want to see you at Christmas, Jennifer Juniper. If we're not here, you should come and join us in Kent.'

He was doing it again, but now she didn't mind the 'you should'. He was inviting her to spend Christmas with him. No matter how impossible that would be, for several reasons – Mrs Avery being the major one – it was a nice gesture that made her feel wanted again.

'It's a blast staying there. Granddad plays steam train recordings and they've got garden gnomes with fishing rods, and psychedelic carpets that bring on Mummy's migraine. In the evenings, Pip and I play card games with them and laugh a lot. It's so terribly normal, Jen. Do you know what I mean?'

'Mm,' she said. She was about to say they sounded like her grandparents, but Pip arrived with a, 'What ho, chaps!'

Immediately, Kit said, 'Why didn't you tell me Pa was frantic with worry about Ma the other night? I'm guessing you knew?'

Pip got a towel out of his duffel bag and spread it on the grass. 'If you weren't in the attic listening to loud music all the time, *you* might know what's going on in your own family.'

'Hey, cool it.' Kit rolled over and sat up. 'It's a bad enough scene without you getting heavy too.'

'I know.' Pip stripped down to his swimming trunks and flopped on the towel. 'That's why I'm going straight to Nanny and Granddad's at the end of term, no matter what.'

While the brothers discussed Christmas, which seemed light years away to her, Jen tried to work out where Kit was on her likeability scale. Half an hour ago, he'd have been around four out of ten, but now, with his air of sadness and his invitation to Kent, he was up at eight or nine.

'Well,' he was saying, 'at least there's one good thing happening in my life.'

Jen waited for the compliment; for a hand to come and touch hers.

'*Monterey Pop*. This Friday, at the Astra.'

Her smile drooped; probably became a pout. Not that anyone was looking. Kit was back at four.

'Lawrence, Susie and I thought we'd have a record session first, get us in the mood.'

So he *was* seeing Susie and Lawrence, and, what's more, had arranged all this with them.

'Want to join us, Jennifer Juniper?'

'Maybe.' He was down to three, now, even two. Did loving a person always include hating them too? Feeling hurt and excluded half the time? If so, it just wasn't worth it. She'd rather just do things with Christine.

Kit lay back and sang 'Jennifer Juniper'. Usually, she loved his voice but now it irritated her. Yes, she was ultra-sensitive, but how could he be so oblivious to her up and down emotions, to how his words and actions affected her? He traced her five fingers with the tips of his, then, mid-song, picked up her hand, guided it to his mouth and kissed it. Kit was in control, she realised, as her heart filled up with love for him. Completely in control.


## THIRTY-SEVEN

Jen woke up in her old bed, and beside her was her old husband. Robert had kicked off his half of the duvet and she took in his foetal position: facing her, fingers splayed as though reaching for her. This had been his idea, but it was on her terms.

She couldn't hear him breathing, but saw that he was. The tablets, he'd said, knocked him out each night. Gently, quietly, she got out of bed and went to the bathroom. There, she unhooked her old robe and headed downstairs. The Sunday paper had been delivered – so huge, it had to come through in four parts. She gathered them up, as she'd done a thousand times, and took them to the kitchen. A Sunday breakfast, she thought, would be nice. It was all there, in the fridge – eggs, bacon, mushrooms – as though he'd known, or hoped, she'd stay.

She made coffee, poured two mugs, put them on a tray and went back to the bedroom, the newspaper wedged under one arm. 'Robert,' she said, placing a mug on his bedside table. 'Coffee.'

Her husband stirred and took deep noisy breaths. 'Thanks,' he whispered, eyes closed.

'It's still all Iraq,' she said, getting back into bed and dividing the paper up into sections they'd read and those they wouldn't. 'Blair looking smug.' She dropped the discarded ones on the floor, then piled 'Culture', 'Business' and a magazine on top of Robert. It was as though the past three months hadn't happened. Almost.

'Mm,' he said, eyes still firmly shut, his head tilted away.

If she'd cared, Jen might have thought he hadn't wanted to look at her. But she didn't care, which was why she could do this. Robert needed her, emotionally, but she didn't need him. As far as she could tell at this early hour, that felt good. And it felt good to be surrounded by the familiar, in their lovely house in its quiet neighbourhood. She'd missed it, she realised now. Perhaps she could divide her time between two homes? Keep her bolt hole. However, she thought, turning over the page she'd skimmed, there was no need to

286

decide anything yet. 'Robert,' she said, more forcefully this time.

He made waking noises and slowly sat up. 'Sorry,' he said, rubbing at eyes, reaching for his mug. 'Sorry, my love. And thanks.' He still hadn't looked at her but she was looking at him. The puffy face, the stubble, the T-shirt stretched to capacity over his new tummy. How unappealing, she thought, and he turned to her with sleepy-dust eyes. 'It's so lovely having you here, Jen.'

She smiled and nodded and went back to the paper and flicked over another unread page. It wasn't that she disliked him. Robert was hard to dislike. In fact, she'd remembered last night, as they'd chatted about everything except homosexuality, that she liked him a lot. He could be a bit literal, it was true, but he was a good listener, never said anything sharp or hurtful. Even in his depressed state, he'd shown an interest in what she'd been doing, how she'd been.

He'd brought her up to speed on the local gossip, not including his own contribution, surprising her with some of it; making her laugh. All the people they knew, the shared knowledge and history – she'd missed that too. Robert had always loved gossip and she'd liked that about him.

People, married people, came to all kinds of arrangements. And since romantic or sexual jealousy wouldn't be an issue for her, perhaps she could live with him again, in the house she loved, in an area she loved, with their beautiful garden that was about to flourish. And it was so quiet.

She strained to hear something, but no dogs barked, no sirens wailed. The Williamsons, next door, weren't Puff Daddying and slamming doors. Had it always been this peaceful?

The stair carpet would have to go, but she knew Robert, in his desperation, would agree to anything. Separate bedrooms, for example. If the third bedroom, a large study-cum-store, were cleared out, they'd each have their own room. A must, she thought, listening to him drink, breathe, clear his throat. They'd live like brother and sister, or housemates, without the minor obligations of a proper marriage – being home for dinner or watching the same TV programmes. She'd buy another set, for her bedroom. This room.

'Finished with that?' he asked.

'Yep.' She folded the news section and handed it over, then took 'Culture' from him and began not reading that too.

It could just work. As nice as Lionel, and she, had made her Southwark flat, this was home. It was where she felt the most comfortable and relaxed. It must happen all the time, she thought. A husband comes out, or gets found out. Emotional readjustments take place, practical ones too, and then normal life, of a sort, goes on.

'I think I'll have a bath,' she said, closing the section, folding it and dropping it on the pile beside the bed.

'I'll start breakfast, shall I? In ten, fifteen minutes?'

'Great.' This was how people were meant to live. In twos. One bathing, while one cooks.

Aloneness was unnatural, unless you were a black widow spider.

He knocked on the bathroom door. 'I'm about to start cooking.'

'OK.'

Jen lay back in the bubbles, grinning, contented. It was fine that he hadn't come in. In fact, it would have been inappropriate. They'd slept side by side but hadn't touched. It was quite clear, quite understood now, that this was a completely platonic relationship, as opposed to the semi-platonic one it had been. With the aid of the Pinot Grigio he'd got in especially, she'd said, 'I'll stay tonight, because I can't drive home. But no sex, Robert, or anything resembling it. There'll never be any more of that.'

'I know,' he'd said, attempting a sad but understanding expression. How relieved he must have felt.

She'd find a lover, she thought, and there, suddenly, was Kit, all tall and manly and urban-looking, cooking her breakfast in his brother's grotty kitchen. But was she his type, any more? It was hard to tell if there was attraction on his part, but then she'd always felt unsure of herself in Kit's presence. Painfully insecure, she recalled, aged fifteen. The best thing about Robert was that she'd always, more or less, been herself with him. It might not have been the most exciting of relationships, but it had a certain peacefulness – the recent crisis excepted.

'Coming!' Jen called back, when he said it was

ready. She dressed hurriedly, rubbed at her hair with a towel, then brushed it, dabbed some face cream on, quickly made the bed and bent to pick up the pile of newspaper sections.

Who read all this stuff? 'Sport', 'Travel', 'Your Money' ... three magazines, one of which had slid under the bed. She lay almost flat to reach it, and caught sight of something by the wall, directly beneath the headboard. The room was filled with light now, and Jen was close enough to see it was a condom packet. Horrified, she retracted her hand, but then stretched out, grimacing, and reached the packet, pulling it out from under the bed. It had been ripped open and was empty. Images filled her head, as she lay there, on her front, on the floor of the bedroom she'd mentally bagged for herself, smelling bacon, hearing *The Archers*. Robert and a man, sweating and grunting. 'Performax' it was called. 'For longer-lasting sex'.

Normal life, of a sort, goes on? No, it doesn't. It can't. She threw the packet back and sat herself up, the reality of having an actively gay husband rapidly sinking in. She went to the bathroom and washed her hands, then washed them again, and while her fingers dripped over the basin, she looked in the mirror at her ridiculous self. Brother and sister? Housemates? Who had she been trying to kid?

It was an effort, but aware that she still had to tread carefully, Jen ate the meal he'd produced. The newspaper, open beside her on the table, allowed her not to say too much. Just the odd,

'Mm,' or, 'Uh-huh?' as his rattled on about the garden, the government, the weather, while she tried, over and over, to take in the thrills of a Reykjavik mini-break. She went back to the beginning, starting the first paragraph again, when Robert said, 'How about a stroll on the heath and then lunch?'

She couldn't answer. All she wanted, after a decent interval, was to tactfully extricate herself from the house, the situation, Robert.

'What?' he said. 'What's the matter, Jen? You've gone really quiet.' A hand came her way and she quickly moved her arm.

'I have to go home.'

'But this is your home.'

'No,' she said, standing. He stood up too and this time his hand landed on her shoulder, as though to prevent her leaving – or that was how it felt.

'Don't go, Jen. Please. I can't be alone.'

She twisted herself away from his grasp and walked across to the counter and her handbag. 'But you're not always alone, are you?' She turned and he was right behind her, much too close.

'What?'

Jen moved and Robert moved with her, like a large and miserable shadow she couldn't shake off. 'Who was it?' she asked, sounding horribly shrill. 'Jon?' She hated the way she sounded, and for someone who no longer cared, she was making too much of this.

'Who was what?'

'There's a condom packet under my ... the bed.'

Robert coloured up and finally backed off. He plonked himself down on the chair he'd left and hung his head. 'No,' he said, a hand over his face. Please don't cry, Jen thought, but guessed he would. 'Not Jon.'

'Some random pick-up, then?' Why did it matter? They'd been separated. He could sleep with any man he pleased. Why didn't she stop haranguing him and just go?

'It was Sarah.'

Jen laughed. '*Sarah?*'

'Yeah.' He lifted his head and looked her in the eye. No tears, after all. 'Sarah.'

'But...' Did she believe him? Sarah smoked. Her husband, Sean, had had a vasectomy.

'We'd become close and, well, anyway, I won't go into detail, but it was a disaster.'

Jen's first reaction was to feel slightly reassured – it wasn't just her. But, then, as she digested the news, came disappointment in Sarah, who had the loveliest husband ever and three beautiful children. 'I see,' she said quite calmly, considering. 'Do you think maybe women don't do it for you any more?' This was unreal, discussing such things with Robert, her husband, in their kitchen, in which they'd normally ask whether to put chilli in, or if all the Brie had gone.

'Christ, Jen, it wasn't that. I've told you, I'm *not* gay. Jesus.' He ran a frustrated hand through his hair, up to the bald patch and back. 'She wasn't *you*, that's why I didn't ... couldn't...'

'Yeah, right.' She took advantage of him sitting and made for the door. This time she wouldn't be manipulated into coming back. 'Either you're lying to me, or you're in denial. I'm sorry but I really do have to go now.'

'Jen, please. I'm so sorry about Sarah. It was just—'

'Bye, Robert.'

On the way, she picked up her comfy shoes, then closed the front door firmly behind her. Beside the car, she phoned Sarah and asked if she could call round. Sarah sounded flummoxed, understandably, and suggested they met at a café.

'Robert told me what happened,' Jen said. 'But don't worry, I'm not angry.'

'Thank fuck for that,' said her old friend, breaking into her throaty laugh. 'See you in twenty.'

Sarah, Jen realised, was another thing she'd missed.

While she waited in the café, she heard a text come through. Robert? She groaned, took the phone out and read it. 'How was yesterday with Robert? Pip coming for lunch with new family. Wish me luck. Wish you were here. (Really) Kit x'

She read it again and was working on a reply, when Sarah fell on the chair opposite, with a new bob in a new colour, and said, 'I have no idea what got into me. Or Robert. Unless it was the vodka. I'm so sorry.' She looked up at the waiter. 'A latte, please.' She half got up, leaned across the table and kissed Jen's cheek. 'If you tell Sean, I'll have to kill you.'

Jen didn't repeat Robert's mobile phone message

word for word, only the gist of it. But even the gist had Sarah's jaw dangling. She said, 'He didn't tell me that bit. Jen, why on earth didn't you call me? I mean, I'd contact you immediately if Sean left me an obscene gay message.'

'Sean?' said Jen, and they both laughed. In spite of being a top surgeon at a top hospital, Sarah's husband was a bit of a lad: supported Arsenal, drank pints, watched *Top Gear* and wouldn't know one end of a soap dish from the other. He was funny and kind too, and Jen had always liked him. 'Why,' she asked Sarah, while Sean was in her head, 'did you do it? With Robert? It wasn't just the booze, surely?'

Sarah checked over each shoulder. '*Try* to do it, you mean.'

'Whatever.'

'I'm full of guilt, don't worry. Do you really want the grisly details?'

While the coffees arrived, they fell silent. Sarah was looking good. Hair all in auburn shades, a lovely bright smile. She'd always known what to wear and today was no exception. A snug, dark-red leather jacket that Jen would have passed as too young on the rail. It wasn't, and suddenly, she wanted one just like it. A chunky orange necklace that should have clashed with the jacket, but didn't. Everything else was black, which you were told not to wear over forty-five, but clearly could. Jen, herself, was in yesterday's drab outfit. The one she'd chosen carefully, so Robert would go off her, agree to the divorce and put the house on the market at once. 'Yes,' she said, when the waiter had gone. 'All the details.'

Sarah took a deep breath and started at the beginning with Jen's departure. Robert had been devastated, anxious. Wasn't sleeping, couldn't go to work. 'Basically, in a terrible way. I made him go to the doctor and there was some improvement, but not much. He went back, was put on different tablets and got referred remarkably quickly, with a word in the right ear by Sean, to a psychiatrist.'

'How often were you seeing Robert?'

'Oh, daily.'

'No!'

'Mm. He usually came round to us. Often at dinner time, and he'd eat. Not that much, but he obviously craved company.'

'God, Sarah, I'm so sorry.' For the first time, Jen saw how immature her initial reaction had been: hitting him, charging off like that in the middle of the night.

'Sean minded, I could tell, even though he didn't say. You know Sean. So ... well, I began calling in on Robert, on my way home from work. That way, we'd avoid the whole awkward dinner business. And then, last Thursday, Sean was playing five-a-side football for the hospital, and the kids were all out doing things, and Robert had actually cooked something for once. He talked me into eating with him, and drinking wine with the meal. And, you know, he can be great company.'

'Yes.'

'Anyway, he produced a bottle of vodka and said had I ever tried it with cranberry, and next thing I knew we were in bed. I still can't believe it. Not that Robert isn't attractive. Like a lot of–' She stopped and stirred her coffee.

Was she going to say gays?

'Well, it was all rather clumsy and we had a fit of the giggles. He, er ... let's just say he let himself down. Or never actually...'

'Got up?'

'Blamed the medication. Combined with the drink. Anyway, afterwards – after nothing, that is – we had a chat about things. He did. About you, mainly, and the fact that you were coming home, and how excited but nervous he was about it. Then I got dressed and left, and when I called him on Friday, he apologised and so did I and it was all forgotten.' She took a sip of her latte, then another. 'So, have you?'

'What?'

'Come home?'

'Oh, I don't know.' Jen thought again of the house, the neighbourhood, having a good friend around the corner to natter to. Perhaps she could stay, have that buddy relationship with her husband and no more. On waking that morning, she'd been quite happy. Back amongst their things. Secure, home, safe.

'He really loves you, Jen.'

'I know, but...'

'But what? You'd always wonder what he's up to?'

'No, it's not even that.' Jen finished her latte and sat back in her chair. 'I just think I'd be bored.'

'Ah. Well, in that case forget Robert and tell me

why you were grinning like a lunatic when I arrived.'

'I was?' she asked, doing it again. She'd tell Sarah about Kit later. First, she had to clear something up. 'Do you think Robert's really bisexual? Gay, even?'

'Ah. I thought you might ask that. Sean and I have sort of discussed it, a bit, and what with the little incident the other evening ... well, I'm not sure, but if I had to place a bet, then *yes*, I think he probably is.'

'What do you mean about the little incident? The fact that he couldn't perform?'

Sarah leaned forward. 'No. More than that. He wasn't... Oh, I don't know.'

'What?'

'I suppose I'm just used to a man who loves women's bodies. My body. *All* of it.'

'What are you saying?'

Sarah sighed. 'There were places that Robert... Christ, Jen, am I going to have to draw pictures? You said yourself it was dismal. Remember?'

'Well...'

'Do *you* think he's gay?' Sarah asked. 'By the way, they say there's no such thing as bisexuality when it comes to men. They've done tests.'

'Who have?'

'Americans, I expect. Attached things to their doodahs and shown them porn.'

'Right.' Suddenly, Jen didn't want to hear more. She sat back, indicating, she hoped, that the subject of Robert was drawing to a close. 'I haven't told you I came across an old, er, friend recently.'

Sarah's eyebrows shot up. 'Old love?'

'Of my life.'

Sarah's hand shot up too. When the waiter came, she asked for the lunch menu. 'Change of plan,' she told him.

## THIRTY-EIGHT

Kit had gone and bought four tickets early, and now they were all in his room listening to Jefferson Airplane. Kit and Lawrence were smoking pot, while Jen and Susie weren't.

'It makes me paranoid,' Susie said, right by Jen's ear, on account of the music being loud.

Jen said, 'Yeah, me too,' hoping Kit couldn't hear, and the two of them stuck to Tizer.

When they weren't puffing at the joint, both boys played imaginary guitar. Jen couldn't picture any girl she knew playing an invisible guitar. She had to admit, though, watching Kit with one hand on the neck, the other fiddling with the strings, that it did make him look sexy.

The room had filled with pot smoke, despite the open window, and when Wing Commander Avery's half-bald head appeared through the stair railings, Jen panicked a bit, although nobody else seemed to. He had a cigar in one hand, which might have masked the pot smell, and in the other was a glass of something like whisky.

Kit moved at a snail's pace and turned the volume down. He smiled at his father and said, 'Hi.'

'I was just wondering if you've seen Mummy?'

'Er, no. Not since we ate lunch in the garden. Around one.'

Mr Avery frowned and took a swig of the golden liquid. 'Pip tells me it was her thrift shop day. That she went out around two.'

'Yeah, I think that was what she was doing.' Kit sounded as though he was talking in slow motion, and he kept grinning, which didn't seem right, considering his dad looked concerned and was drinking whisky at half-past six.

'Ah, well,' said Wing Commander Avery. 'Probably chinwagging somewhere. Women, eh? Ha-ha.' He started to disappear, then came back. 'A little less volume, perhaps, Kit?'

'Sure.' Kit held his hand up and made a V. 'Peace and love, Pa.'

Again, Kit's father began to disappear, and again he reappeared. 'Could I tempt you chaps with dinner? I'm having leftover rabbit, fried up with potatoes and artichokes. Pip isn't hungry, for once, so there'll be mounds.'

'Actually, we're off to the flicks soon,' said Susie. 'But thanks, awfully.'

'Yes, thanks,' said Jen, who'd had her tea at five. She'd never eaten rabbit or seen an artichoke, but she knew what a potato was. She felt sorry for Kit's dad, having to make his own tea, and no one to share it with – praying his wife wasn't in bed with a corporal somewhere, and that she'd come back and make him a nice pudding. Something French, maybe.

"What's the film?' he asked.

'*Monterey Pop*,' Kit told him.

'A comedy, is it? I love a good comedy.' He chuckled, as though remembering one he'd seen. 'Have a jolly time.' And then he was gone; the cigar smoke mingling with the pot; the music suddenly loud again.

Jen thought Kit might say something about his mum, or about his parents' fights, but perhaps he didn't because the others were there, or perhaps he didn't because he was stoned. It worried her, a bit, that she was going to the pictures with someone high on drugs. What if a suspicious person told the military police? Then they'd all get arrested and she'd end up with a criminal record for the rest of her life, even though she'd only had Tizer. It might be in all the papers, like Mick Jagger and Marianne Faithfull. *Officer's son and girlfriend caught with drugs!* Only Kit wouldn't have any pot on him ... or would he?

She could pretend she was ill and not go. But then Kit would be so disappointed, since he'd told her so much about this flaming film and how she *had* to see this band and hear that song. She wasn't even sure she liked a lot of the stuff Kit played her; some of it had guitar solos that went on and on until you were desperate to hear the singer again. She and Christine had always loved Motown.

It was Susie who said, 'Time to go, chaps.' She helped Lawrence up and then Jen did the same for Kit. He was floppy and giggly, and again, Jen thought of getting a headache or faking flu. This was going to be so embarrassing, on top of dangerous. Her one hope was that, as with alcohol,

300

people sobered up from pot in the fresh air.

They got to the Astra without being arrested and walked past the ticket queue and straight in. Once they were settled in their seats, at the halfway point Kit and Lawrence had chosen, Jen relaxed, at last. Kit took her hand and gazed at it and told her how truly beautiful it was, and Jen thanked him and watched everyone pile in. She was hoping to spot Mick, because that would mean he wasn't with Mrs Avery, and that Mrs Avery might be back home doing pudding. A couple of times she turned to look at the rows behind, but she didn't see him, and she couldn't keep turning and staring, so she eventually gave up and concentrated on what Kit was saying about her 'exquisitely tapered fingers'. It was nice having the attention, even if it wasn't the real Kit talking.

There were the usual adverts and some trailers, then the certificate came up saying *Monterey Pop* and Kit immediately dropped her hand and began clapping and cheering. Since it was only a film and not the real thing, he was the only one to do so. He put his fingers in his mouth and did a few loud whistles and someone behind said, '*Sshhh.*' Jen slid down in her seat and took one of the little sweets Lawrence was passing round. At least, she hoped they were little sweets.

While Kit got more and more carried away, grooving away in his seat, Jen was surprised at how good the film was. The gorgeous groups on stage, the hippies in their amazing clothes, with their children and their psychedelic buses. She kept imagining her and Kit there, camping, lying around looking at the sky, dancing. Everyone seemed so happy and relaxed. They were out of their minds on drugs, but still...

Suddenly, The Who were being introduced and Kit was cheering again. He got up and danced, but the people behind complained and swore, so he made his way to the end of the row and did his arm-waving stuff in the aisle by the wall. Lawrence followed and did his funny ploddy head-bobbing thing, and then Susie went too. Jen wanted to watch the film, not dance, so she stayed put. Also, she didn't want to look stupid. Nobody else was dancing, although she could see lots of heads in front, nodding to the music. Jen swayed her head and sang along to 'My Generation', just in case Kit was looking, so he'd know she was enjoying herself.

When the three of them didn't come back to their seats at the end of the song, and just carried on dancing to the next one and then the next, Jen felt a bit uncomfortable. She looked over at Susie doing her go-going, and wondered if Kit would think she, Jen, was really boring. If so, there wasn't much she could do about it. A million Deutschmarks wouldn't make her go and dance in the aisle, not when Christine and the others might be in the audience. They'd probably tease her all next term. Imitate her, even. She knew what they were like. How great it must be, she thought, being Susie. Not caring what others think and leaving in a week.

Being conscious of the empty seats around her

and the way-out dancing of her friends did begin to spoil the evening. And, as much as she liked the film, she wished she hadn't come – just to be abandoned like this. But then Jimi Hendrix came on, playing 'Hey Joe' with his teeth and doing his brilliant 'Wild Thing', and Jen found herself mesmerised. She couldn't believe it when he lit a match and set fire to his guitar, and then squirted it with lighter fuel. First she closed her eyes, thinking the whole stage would go up in flames and people would die, then she opened them to see if Kit was still dancing to this peculiar, violent scene.

But Kit wasn't dancing, he was talking to two military police, both in their uniforms and hats and quite a contrast to Kit and Lawrence and everyone on screen. Kit, now standing still, had one of the MP's hands on his shoulder. Arrested, thought Jen, horrified. The cinema manager must have contacted them because dancing wasn't allowed in the Astra, or because he'd suspected drugs. Had she missed them being frisked? Finding something in a pocket? The other MP rounded them all up with an arm, in a 'come this way' fashion, and before she knew it, Jen's three friends were being walked up the side aisle. Kit didn't beckon to her, or even look her way, as far as she could tell. Either he was trying to protect her, or he'd forgotten she was there.

With a thumping heart and a sick feeling, she tried to watch the film, but all she could see was Kit in handcuffs, locked up in the guardroom, waiting for his dad to come and pay bail, or talk them into dropping charges. Poor Mr Avery, she thought, maybe a bit disloyally, this was all he needed.

After a while, which could have been two minutes or twenty minutes, Jen got up and passed all the knees and feet and handbags, and walked towards the exit with her head held high. It didn't bother her any more, who was witnessing all this. What she cared about was Kit, not herself. And his dad, of course. Going through the door, then past the kiosk, and out into the light, she wished she hadn't waited; wished she'd followed immediately, because now she'd have no idea where they'd been taken. Should she hurry over to Kit's house and tell his father, or go straight to the guardroom to see if Kit was there? Jen had never known anyone get arrested on a camp before, or anywhere.

She walked down the short path and reached the corner before she saw them: Kit, Susie, Lawrence and the two policemen. Pip was also there, standing between the MPs, one writing on a notepad.

Kit sat on the kerb, head in his hands, and beside him was Susie with an arm around his shoulder. This wasn't right, at all. *She* should be comforting him, not Susie. If Kit asked, she'd say she didn't see them leave with the MPs. No, she wouldn't. He might have seen her watching, out the corner of his eye. Anyway, she was there for him now, and running the last twenty yards to the little group. She had nothing to fear, she kept telling herself. All she'd had was Tizer and a sweet. The sweet! 'What if...? But it was too late, she was there now.

'What's happened?' she asked, slowing down, puffing, as though she'd run further. Kit looked up at her with strangely cold eyes, then hung his head again. Shame, perhaps. Nobody answered. She said, 'Pip?' and when he turned to her, she saw something far worse in his eyes. 'It's Daddy,' he said. 'His car ... it...'

'It what?' Again, nobody answered but she started feeling really cold. 'Wild Thing' was still playing in her head. 'Kit?'

'It hit a tree,' said a policeman, when no one seemed able to speak. 'On the road to Roermond.'

Jen gasped and felt herself jump, as though a tree had hit her too. She saw a horrible mangled car, on fire, like Jimi's guitar. 'Is he...?' she asked, and it was Susie, mouth quivering at the corners, who nodded.

The MP nodded too. 'Fatal, I'm afraid. A tragic accident.'

Jen heard a horrible moaning noise, and realised it was coming from her. She put a hand over her mouth to stop it.

'Or not,' said Pip quietly.

Kit said, 'Shut up, Pip.'

'What do you mean?' asked the MP, while the one with the pad wrote something down.

'He's talking crap,' said Kit. 'Can't you see he's in shock?'

Pip was shaking badly, and Jen wanted to go and hug him but the policemen were in the way, and anyway, she felt so sick she wasn't sure she should hug anyone. 'Have a jolly time,' he'd said. They should have stayed and eaten the leftover

305

rabbit with him. Kept him company.

'I think we should get you lads home,' said the chattier MP. He nodded towards the crowd pouring out of the cinema, then pointed at their car. 'Can only fit three of you in, I'm afraid.'

'Will you come, Jen?' asked Kit.

'Yeah, of course,' she said, even though she wanted to run to her own home and get into bed and have her mum make her something comforting. Ovaltine, Marmite toast, and tell her it wasn't her fault, even though it was.

'And you've no idea where your mother is?' asked the other MP, tucking the notepad inside his jacket and helping Kit up. 'No Tupperware parties this evening?'

Kit shot Pip a look. 'No,' he said. 'Not that we know of.'

Jen wanted to cry but couldn't. She should have been discreet and not mentioned the corporal and the sports car zooming off. But she'd opened her big mouth and now that lovely man was dead and she wanted to be too.

'Let's go,' said one of the policemen.


## THIRTY-NINE

Kit thought one chicken might not suffice, so he was cooking two; one at a time. He'd peeled a ton of potatoes, scraped carrots and washed broccoli, all without the aid of his nephew, who claimed to be studying in his room. His mother and Raymond were at The Bell, and no offer of help had come from them either, thank God. In their individual ways, they'd been driving him nuts, waiting to meet this baby.

As he prepared, he listened to *Desert Island Discs*, which helped dampen his anxiety about the day's big get-together. His idea. Pip had been all for gathering on neutral territory, but when Adam stormed out, which he was bound to do at some point, Kit would rather it occurred at home. He also thought his brother should come to the house, even briefly, for both his own and Adam's sake. Pip had continued to resist, but then Elaine had come on the phone and said not to worry, she'd talk him round on this one. She was dying to meet Adam, she said, now she'd been told of his existence, and Pip's mother too.

How keen they were to meet her was another matter. As much as their mother slagged off Pip, she placed most of the blame on Elaine. 'Colluding with him, honestly. Forgiving him for the deception. Some women have no backbone when it comes to men.'

Pip had said little over the phone, only that he'd been unable to face Adam with news of the baby, or tell Elaine about his son, in case Adam scared her off; that he'd 'sort of shut down with the stress of it all' and was on some kind of horse tranquilliser.

Kit threw the potatoes in with the second chicken and gave the roasting pan a shake. What fun this was going to be.

The sound of a crying baby wafted through the

open window. This wasn't an unusual noise in the cul-de-sac but something made Kit look out, one leg in his trousers. There was his brother, locking up his ancient VW and looking a whole lot better than Kit had expected. Slimmer, perhaps. Beside him was a youngish blonde woman, carrying the baby in a bucket-like seat. They were early. As much as he'd wanted them to come, early wasn't good. It meant more, possibly strained, time to get through before Raymond and their mother – the talkers – arrived.

Kit quickly finished dressing, brushed his teeth, knocked on Adam's door and said, 'Your dad's here,' then made his way downstairs to greet the guests. Or homecomers. Whatever.

Downstairs, Elaine was already on the cottage-suite sofa, baby attached to one breast. 'Hello,' he said, not sure where to look. He settled on her nose, which was pretty and upturned. All in all, she wasn't unlike Pat. 'I'm Kit.'

'Elaine,' she said with a sweet smile. 'Hi.' She eased the baby away from her, twisting him round a little. 'And this is your new nephew, Roger.'

'Hello, Roger,' Kit said, in an appropriate sing-song way, but he couldn't take in the baby's face on account of the very lovely breast beside it.

'Pip's just fetching the paraphernalia.'

'Ah, right. I'll give him a hand.' He stepped back into the hall, where Pip was approaching, laden with bags and blankets and a Moses basket.

'Yo, Bro,' Pip said. 'I'd forgotten how much crap they need.'

Kit took the basket off him. 'Not something

I've experienced. Ma isn't here yet. I think we said twelve thirty.'

'Well, that's a relief. Where's Adam?'

'Hello,' came a voice on the stairs. 'Nice of you to drop in.'

While he was making three coffees, Kit had a quiet word with his brother, to let him know there shouldn't be too much more disruption. 'It's really important that Adam gets the grades in his As. His place at Bristol is reliant upon them.'

'I *know*,' said Pip, in an I-am-his-father way. 'Don't worry, we'll make sure he revises.'

'You're planning on moving back in? I mean, I'm not sure that would be the best thing for Adam right now, and I'd be perfectly happy to stay and–'

'Have you seen the size of Elaine's place? No room to swing a baby.' He laughed at his joke. 'No prob, Bro. Thanks for all you've done and all that. I mean, my behaviour was terribly cowardly, and tough on Adam. Obviously, I feel wretched about it. Anyway, you've been an absolute star, but you may return to London, resume your old life. I'm pretty stable now I'm on this drug, so everything'll be cool. Yeah, Bro?'

This was new, all the 'Bro' and 'cool' business. Nerves, perhaps.

'I'm not sure, Pip. Shouldn't we ask Adam what he wants?'

'It's my house.'

'I know, but–'

'Pip!' cried Elaine. 'He's puked everywhere!'

'Coming!'

All over the suite, Kit hoped.

'It's funny that you've got similar names,' said Adam. 'Eleanor. Elaine.'

His grandmother rolled her eyes. *'Hardly.'*

Adam had been allowed a glass of wine with lunch and had mellowed considerably. Having initially sat on the sitting-room floor glowering at his half-brother, he was now cradling him at the table and helping himself to a second glass. 'And Elaine, you look quite like my mum.'

'That's enough,' Kit said quietly.

Adam pointed at the photo of Pat. 'Look. She does.'

Everyone did look. Kit, his mother, Raymond, Pip and poor Elaine. It was an awkward moment, saved by Raymond. 'Did we tell you about the blighter in Venice, who took a photo of your mother and me, then proceeded to skedaddle with my camera?'

'No?' said Kit, suddenly keen to hear more of Italy.

'It was your mother who gave chase, grabbed the strap and snatched it back.'

'You did?' asked Elaine.

Kit's mother wobbled a proud head. 'I play tennis, you know. Keeps the muscles taut and ready for action.' She lowered her eyes to Elaine's post-natal waist. 'You should try it.'

'Maybe I will.' Elaine gave her a lovely big smile. 'When Roger's a bit older.'

Kit saw his mother jolt at the name again, then Raymond was off on a tennis story, about the

310

time he'd met Jimmy Connors in a restaurant.

When Elaine asked, 'Who?' Kit realised how young she was. Still in her thirties, he'd guess. Throughout the meal she'd been pleasantly chatty, while Pip had been reserved. No mention was made of his disappearance or breakdown, although it had been obvious, at times, that their mother was champing at the bit.

All in all, things weren't going badly.

While Elaine and baby napped upstairs, the rest of them took advantage of the weather and walked Bunk to the beach. With a little manoeuvring, Kit had managed to separate his mother and Raymond from Pip and Adam, who were throwing sticks together and, hopefully, rebonding. They appeared to be talking, but a sea breeze made it hard to listen in.

While his mother compared the beach unfavourably with that of Terracina, and Raymond described their boat ride into Capri's Blue Grotto, Kit wondered if his role in this family drama was coming to a close, and how he felt about it. He'd grown attached to the place. And Adam, of course, and the crowd at The Bell, the dog ... having the beach on the doorstep. Who'd have guessed he'd be so happy in a dreary council house in a cul-de-sac in a village in East Anglia? The idea of returning to an empty flat in Clapham almost unsettled him. What did he use to do there?

'In the evening,' Raymond was saying, 'when the tide was too high for the boats, your mother swam into the grotto, didn't you, darling? Signs everywhere telling you not to, but you know your mother.'

'Oh, yes,' said Kit. Always breaking the rules, he wanted to add, but didn't. She'd been on her best behaviour, give or take a couple of comments to Elaine. Remarks Elaine had either not detected the cattiness in, or deliberately not reacted to. Perhaps Pip had primed her.

Of course, going back to London might have its attractions. Jen, for one. His new friend. New, old friend. How different she was from the sweet and timid young girl he'd known. Not that she wasn't still sweet. She'd been in his thoughts a lot, since leaving, but whether he'd been in hers was uncertain. She hadn't, for example, replied to the text he'd sent that morning. He should never have put that kiss. Too forward, damn it, when it was just meant to be friendly. Every female who texted him put a kiss after her name. Too late to worry about it now, and, anyway, London had other pluses. None of his family was there, for a start.

He wondered how long his mother and Raymond were planning on staying at The Bell, now they'd met Roger. On arriving, his mother had swept the little thing up and held him for a good half-hour, until lunch was dished up. 'Does he have a middle name?' Kit had overheard her ask Elaine, as he was leaving the room. 'Pip,' she was told, and he'd hovered by the door and held his breath, waiting for a response that didn't come. Yes, he was almost proud of his mother today, and might tell her so later.

'How long do you think you'll stay?' he asked

her now.

'Oh, another day or two. Raymond let friends use his house, you see. They'll be out tomorrow, then the cleaners will do their bit. Tuesday, Wednesday, I'd imagine. And you? Are you going to leave your nephew's future in your useless brother's hands?'

Put that way, Kit was suddenly undecided. 'We'll see. Whatever Adam wants is fine by me.'

'One would hate to see the boy go the way of his father. Drop out of school, hole up in his room. Run away. Crack up with monotonous regularity.'

Now it was Kit's turn to practise restraint. 'No,' he agreed, attempting a glare he hoped she could read. 'One wouldn't.'

Back at the house Kit sat down, while Elaine made tea. There'd been a packet of assorted biscuits at the back of the cupboard, which she might not have checked the sell-by date on, but had nevertheless arranged on a plate and handed round. He liked Elaine, he decided. She and Pip were very different, but that often worked in a relationship. Complementary. Yin and yang. When Pip answered a question with a monosyllable, Elaine would coax something longer from him. And Pip, he guessed, stopped Elaine being tiresomely upbeat. For the first time in his life, Kit vaguely envied his brother.

Roger was asleep in his basket, with Bunk on guard beside him. Next to them, Raymond was trying to persuade Adam into a gap year. 'See the

313

world, I say. It'll make a man of you. There'll be time for all that academic nonsense later.' Adam was nodding politely and secretly checking his phone.

Kit, then his mother, took a biscuit from Elaine. Pip, beside his mother, was fidgeting in an armchair, tapping a foot, drumming his fingers. 'Tablet time?' Kit heard Elaine whisper.

Pip looked at his watch, said, 'Half an hour,' and continued to fidget. What would happen, Kit wondered, if he didn't take his medication? Something he should discuss with Elaine before abandoning Adam.

'Now stop that, Raymond,' his mother said sharply. 'Just because nobody went to university when you were young, back in the Dark Ages. One has to have a degree to work in a chip shop these days.'

'Why would he want to work in a chip shop?' Raymond asked with a hearty laugh.

It was approaching five. Kit found himself wishing some sort of satisfactory solution would be reached, and everyone would disperse; that he and Adam could be left to kick back, half-dozing in front of the TV. Some Sunday evening period thing.

'Elaine's brother works in a fish and chip shop,' said Pip. 'Well, owns one. Two, in fact.'

Kit heard his mother sigh before continuing with her biscuit.

'An entrepreneur, eh?' said Raymond. 'Sounds like my kind of fellow, ha-ha.'

The only sound to be heard for a while was Pip tapping his foot on the carpet. People ate their biscuits and drank their teas, and the big hand on Kit's watch moved up to the twelve.

It was Adam who broke the silence, addressing his dad. 'So, are you moving back in, or what?'

'Of course!' Pip's leg jigged a little faster.

'Why so hasty?' asked Raymond.

'What exactly,' asked Pip, 'does it have to do with you?'

'Well!' said his mother. 'I see second-time fatherhood hasn't improved your manners, Pip. We're simply concerned about Adam, as is Kit. You may not have made a success of your life, but I'd like to see my grandson do so. Now, I think you owe Raymond an apology.'

Kit rather wanted to be left out of things, and chose to stay quiet. Pip's eyes were changing, he noticed. Wider, wilder.

'I rather think Raymond should apologise,' Pip said. 'After all, he's not my father.'

'No,' said his mother shakily. 'Raymond's made of far sturdier stuff.'

Pip jumped up, looking completely wired and ready for a brawl. Thinking he might hit their mother, Kit was about to intervene. But then Elaine took his brother's hand in hers and gently eased him back on to the chair. She whispered in his ear and reached for her handbag. A little early, perhaps, she was giving him his pill.

'I'm sorry, Pip,' said Raymond. 'You're right, of course. None of my bloody business. But, you know, I didn't get where I am by not sticking my oar in.' He laughed but no one else did.

Elaine said, 'Pip's sorry, too. Aren't you, Pip?'

Before he could answer, the doorbell rang,

making the dog leap up and bark, and, in turn, the baby cry. 'There, there,' Kit's mother said, getting up and reaching Roger before Elaine could.

'I'll go,' said Adam. 'It's probably Sasha.'

Thank God, thought Kit. Thank God for Sasha. 'I'll walk back to The Bell with you,' he told Raymond and his mother, standing up and stretching his arms. It was a deliberate and transparent attempt to draw things to a close. How desperate he was to leave this gloomy room. Surely the others must be? Perhaps he'd take Bunk for another walk. Blow the cobwebs away.

'Hello,' came a familiar voice, and he swung round, arms still in the air, to see Jen, not Sasha, in the doorway. 'Gosh,' she said. 'Hope I'm not intruding on your nice family gathering?'

'Oh Lord,' Kit heard his mother say. 'This is all we need.'

From the look on her face, Jen must have heard too. If his mother hadn't been seventy-two, and if she hadn't been holding the baby, now calmed and lying on her shoulder, he might well have hit her.

# FORTY

It had all happened so quickly, and now he was gone and she was on the school bus on the first day of term, listening to Christine rabbiting on about *Rosemary's Baby*, which she'd managed to get into last night. Christine could pass for eighteen when she was all dressed up and made up, and with tissue in her bra. And, besides, the people on the door never asked. It didn't sound like Jen's kind of film, but she was happy for Christine to talk her head off because then no one could mention what was still the talk of the camp.

An accident, that had been the unofficial verdict, although there'd be an inquest at some point. Those with enough German had translated an article in a newspaper – one that hadn't held back on the gory details – and word had got around about the alcohol level in Wing Commander Avery's blood, and the witnesses who'd seen him lose control of his car on a bend, career across the road and slam into the trees. Where he'd been going, no one knew. On a pointless search for his wife, Jen guessed, but would never say that. Not even to Kit, who she'd seen only twice since the *Monterey Pop* night: once, the following day in their hut, where she'd held him in her arms and he'd cried, on and off, for an hour or more; and then, again, two days later, when she'd called at his house to find them all packing.

The last time she'd been there Mr Avery was alive, and it was horrible seeing his uniform jacket hanging on a peg with his hat on top. Guilt had flooded through her again and made her stomach knot up, her legs go weak. He was to be buried in Kent. The funeral would be in five days' time. Mrs Avery needed to be there to make arrangements. On hearing all this, Jen thought her life, as well as Mr Avery's, had come to an end.

It had hit her then, standing in Kit's attic room, watching him fold the clothes she'd helped buy, that her boyfriend was never coming back to Germany. Suddenly, she hadn't been able to control her emotions. 'You will write to me,' she said, hearing a stupid wobble in her voice, 'won't you?'

He'd promised he would, and that he'd come and see her, even if he had to hitchhike all the way. But he hadn't come over and given her a cuddle, or kissed her, or anything, and she'd felt increasingly miserable. By the time he'd clicked shut his case and heaved it off the bed and to the top of the stairs, Jen had been sobbing into her hands.

How selfish, she thought now. Kit had lost his dad and she'd been crying for herself. But, then again, she had been crying for Mr Avery too, and Kit and Pip. Not so much for Mrs Avery, who'd given her the filthiest of looks, then dashed around, barking orders at Elke and telling Nigel the doctor what should be treated as fragile by the removers, and not looking as though she needed anyone to cry for her. She must have been upset and guilt-ridden, but she'd hidden it well. Maybe some people were a lot less emotional than others, lucky things.

Christine was telling them all about Rosemary giving birth to the anti-Christ. 'On the sixth of June, nineteen sixty-six. Get it?' When nobody answered, she said, 'Six, six, six, you thickos!' and laughed eerily, as though she might have been affected by the film. 'Personally, I'd have smothered it,' she said. 'Better to be dead than–' Yvonne was nudging her and she stopped. 'Oops. Sorry, Jen.'

## FORTY-ONE

'It was straight back to school,' Kit was telling her, 'following the funeral.' They'd driven to the next village for a drink, avoiding his mother and Raymond at The Bell, and Adam and Sasha at home. Jen was tired from her long drive but Kit looked even more exhausted. 'Just a couple of days at our grandparents', I seem to remember, then we were on the train to Worcester.'

'That must have been tough.'

'In a way. Pip and I were given no time to mourn, just thrown back into the thick of prep and rugger and the rest. All of which my brother loathed. I think it actually helped me, but for Pip it simply piled agony on top of the agony. Ma took him out of school at Christmas, by which time she was shacked up with Mick in a flat in Chesterfield. You remember Mick?'

Had Kit forgotten her part in things? 'Of course.' Jen saw the Malcolm Club, the swarthy looks, the sports car. What she couldn't see was Mrs Avery in a flat in Chesterfield.

'He'd left the RAF and was working as a car mechanic. He used to come home covered in grease and reeking of the stuff, then take his overalls off and hand them to my mother to wash. And she would. Can you imagine?'

'No, I can't.'

'My grandmother, on Ma's side, was in a home and, basically, my mother had nowhere else to go, while the pension or whatever got sorted out. Mick wasn't earning much and she was forced to work for a while. Got a job as a hairdresser's receptionist.'

'I can't imagine that, either.'

'She hated every minute of it. The people, the humiliation. Left the minute she could. Anyway, I think she probably loved Mick, or was in love with him, or infatuated. He's the only person I've ever known who could order her about.'

'Did you get on with him?'

'I suppose so, but it was an effort, and Pip's disapproval permeated the place. Pip wouldn't make an effort, but I pretended to be interested in the motorbike Mick was stripping down, that sort of thing. He took us to football matches at Derby. That was good. But I wasn't there much. Christmas, Easter, a couple of half terms. I spent the summer before Oxford staying with a friend in France. By then, Ma had funds and was moving them all to Hampshire.'

'Mick too?'

'Yes. It lasted about seven years, remarkably. Mick was a decent sort, though. He'd taken my mother and her boys in, which was something. Needless to say, Pip hated him. At first, anyway. He blamed Mick and my mother for everything, but in a silent, locked-in-his-room way. Call me shallow, but I was too busy with A levels and music and girls to dwell on events the way Pip did.'

'Girls?' asked Jen. She was suddenly jealous. How ridiculous. 'That school near yours?'

'Hopthorpe?' Kit grinned and rolled his eyes. 'I became pretty expert at scaling walls at mid-night, I tell you. Oh ... or perhaps I shouldn't be telling you?'

Jen shrugged. All those wasted prayers, pleading with God to make him not go out with anyone. 'Don't worry, I found a new boyfriend after you left.'

'You did?'

He looked almost upset. 'Ricky. You might have met him.' Boyfriend was stretching it. It had all happened the following spring. They'd had a few snogs behind the youth club, then gone to the cinema one time and snogged through a film. 'Dark-haired, good-looking.' Dull, she could have added, and not you. It had soon petered out.

'I'm pleased,' said Kit. 'Since I was such an un-feeling bastard, not replying to your letters. How thoughtless and self-absorbed youth can be. Actually, not just youth.' He stared into his wine for a while.

That last girlfriend, thought Jen, still niggling. 'What happened with Mick, do you know?'

He looked up and blinked. 'Oh, er, he began gambling heavily. Which, on its own, was bad enough, but then he started working his way through Mummy's money. There were terrible scenes, according to Pip, who'd regularly gone back and stayed. Eventually she kicked Mick out. Listen, can I get you another?'

'Better not,' Jen said. 'I should either contact, or go to, The Bell for a room.'

'Don't be silly,' he said, smiling at her.

Jen knocked back the rest of her wine, trying to work out what he meant and how she should respond. Was he suggesting...? Surely not. That would be inappropriate ... wouldn't it?

'There's a bed in the spare room.' Kit was frowning; seemed to be thinking out loud. 'Although it's hard to get to. I could always use the sofa.'

'No, no, I will.' That flimsy thing? She wouldn't sleep a wink. 'Thanks.'

'I'm so pleased you came,' he told her before they got up. 'In fact, I may never have been so pleased to see anyone.'

'Was it that bad?' she asked. He'd been talking more of the distant past than the afternoon's events.

'No, not really.' He reached for her hand on the table and gave it a squeeze. 'I just wanted to see you again.'

'Me too,' she said, although it had been Sarah who'd talked her into dashing home, showering, throwing things in a bag and driving for three hours. On the way, she'd had serious doubts, but Sarah's 'two bites at the cherry', 'God works in mysterious ways' and other clichés, were still fresh in her head and spurring her on.

Back at the house, the sofa was occupied by Kit's mother. Her legs were tucked up elegantly and her arms were partly entwined in a cerise pashmina. 'At *last*,' she said.

'Thought we'd come and have a powwow about Pip,' said Raymond. 'A post-mortem, as it were.'

Kit said, 'Good idea,' although he didn't look that pleased. He went back to the hall and shouted, 'Adam! Could you come down?'

Several feet were heard on the stairs, then Adam and his girlfriend came in. Sasha – slim, blue eyes, long fair hair – was introduced to Jen, and the two of them sat on the floor with Bunk. They'd brought along the distinct odour of dope, and what with the strong uncle/nephew resemblance, Jen was thrown back to Germany: the attic, skinny Kit in his cheesecloth shirts. She may have been horribly unsure of herself then, but she'd never ever, not really, felt that kind of day-after-day buzz since. Of course, thought Jen, having babies might have helped – brought excitement and infatuation into her life. But no, she'd only been in love the once, she realised, looking at Kit. Which was really rather sad.

'Sit beside me, Kit,' said his mother. 'And let's hear your opinion.'

'I'm not sure I have one. Adam, how did you think your dad was?'

'To be honest, much better. A lot more together than the person who disappeared.'

'Maybe you have to be,' said Jen, 'when there's a baby to take care of.'

'Not that you'd know,' said Mrs Avery, and again Jen was back in Germany, but not liking it so much.

'And Elaine's cool,' added Adam. 'I think, you know, if they, like, want to live here it would be OK.'

'Sure?' asked Kit.

'They don't have much room where they are, and Elaine said if the baby cried in the night during my exams, she'd take him out in the car.'

'I see.' Kit seemed slightly miffed. 'You've got it all worked out, then, you and Elaine.'

'Thing is,' said Adam, 'it won't be for long, since I'll be coming to London after my exams.'

'You will?'

'Isn't that what we agreed?'

'Well...' Kit looked to Jen, perhaps for help.

'There's always a room for you in Hampshire,' said Kit's mother. She too glanced Jen's way. 'If your uncle doesn't want to be "crowded", as they say.'

'Darling, don't forget Madeira,' said Raymond.

'Ah. Well, in the other hols, then.'

'Sasha would like to come too, wouldn't you, Sash? If that's all right, Kit?'

'I, er...'

Raymond stood up. 'Talking of Madeira, fancy a snifter, anyone?' He rubbed his hands together.

324

'What have you got, Kit?'

'Nothing, I'm afraid. It all went at lunchtime.'

Raymond was suddenly keen to leave. 'Shattered, aren't we, darling? Early night. Just the job.' He was up and jangling his keys, and Mrs Avery, who appeared very much awake, got off the sofa in a graceful and effortless manner that belied her years.

'We'll see you again, no doubt, Jennifer?' she said, giving her the smile. Jen spotted, for the first time, that the teeth had been fixed. Or were false. 'Before you leave, or we leave.'

'I hope so.'

'At The Bell, no doubt?'

'Actually...'

'Jen's staying here,' said Kit.

Jen tensed up. Was he going to explain the sleeping arrangements? Should she?

'I see,' said Mrs Avery. She glanced around the room, in a rather-you-than-me way. Up at the tiled ceiling, down at the raggedy carpet. 'There was a hotel we simply couldn't stay at in Ragusa. Smelled like a zoo, looked like a squat. I told the hotelier I'd rather sleep in the car, and he overreacted in that way Italians do so well.' She threw her pashmina over a shoulder and followed her partner. At the door, she gave the room a wave and a *'Ciao'*, and disappeared.

'I love your nan,' sighed Sasha. 'She's such a character.'

'Isn't she?' said Jen.

The call came twenty minutes later. Kit covered the mouthpiece and pulled a face at Jen. 'Ma,' he said quietly. 'Wanting to know if you'll play tennis in the morning, on the village courts.' She shook her head but Kit carried on with the face, which was apologetic and pleading at the same time. 'She sounds very keen,' he whispered. 'Hasn't had a game in ages.'

In spite of the instant, Pavlovian butterflies in her stomach, Jen said, 'OK. What time?'

Kit asked his mother and said, 'Eleven?' to Jen, who couldn't hide her resentment as she nodded. The evening had suddenly been ruined.

She and Kit stayed up late, chatting quietly downstairs, not wanting to disturb Adam, whose school bus would come at seven thirty, then wind its way through the villages. They talked till almost one, about places they'd been, plays they'd seen, and people and politics, health and parents. Kit was so much easier to talk to at fifty than he'd been at seventeen. Or perhaps it was just that she'd gained confidence and had less to lose now. She liked him a lot, found him attractive and wanted to keep him in her life. But if he suddenly disappeared, her world wouldn't fall apart, as it once had. How dramatic everything had felt back then, as a teen. A time, she thought now, when we're at our most alive.

First, it was the wall clock ticking away. She got out of bed and removed the batteries, then got back in and waited for sleep to come. She'd always preferred complete darkness, but lamplight was pouring through the thin curtains. After switching the lamp on again, she found a sheet in the laundry pile and tucked it over the curtain rail, doubled up. Back in bed, the light off, the room suitably dark, she may have slept for a while, but then voices woke her. Raised voices, and a baby crying. She couldn't hear words, just volume. Bunk must have heard too because he started barking. Before long, the landing light was seeping through the gap around her door, and then there were feet on the stairs and the bass of a male voice chiding the dog.

By the time Bunk had been calmed and the neighbours had stopped their arguing and fed their baby, Jen found herself tossing and turning, or trying to, in a two-foot-six bed – the kind she'd grown up with. Fine when you're eight, like a strait-jacket when you're forty-eight. She thought about her crazy day. Waking up with Robert. Sarah. Robert and Sarah. Trudging up to Norfolk again. Kit. Lovely Kit. He'd been pleased to see her. His mother less so. Tennis, Jen remembered. In a few hours she'd be playing Mrs Avery again. How bizarre. Well, unless she could get out of it.

## FORTY-TWO

Going to the supermarket with her family had been good, because just about everything on camp reminded her of Kit. Even her own house, in which he'd spent hardly any time. He'd knocked at that door, walked down that path, sat there, used that ashtray. Almost two weeks now and she wasn't able to 'get over him', as Christine kept saying she should. Everywhere, there were reminders, and all Jen wanted was to stay in her room because it was one place he'd never been.

Normally, she'd have helped her mum put the food away, but she was on her bed reading *To Kill a Mockingbird* for school. Or trying to, because even that made her think of Kit. He'd once read this page, these words. It was his second favourite book, after *On the Road*. When Mrs Fairbanks announced it as the set text for the term, Jen had nearly fallen off her chair. She couldn't wait to discuss it with him, when he finally got round to writing. Perhaps he'd help her put something clever in an essay.

Closing the book, she opened her bedside drawer. The piece of paper was becoming worn from the handling, but she couldn't stop double-checking the school address he'd hurriedly scribbled down in the middle of packing. She was sure she hadn't got it wrong on the envelope. And she wouldn't have got it wrong three times. But maybe he wasn't back at school yet. He could still be with his grandparents, she thought, being supportive of his mum. Mrs Avery might have suddenly been hit by it all. Jen had heard that the worst time was after the funeral, when you're no longer busy and the shock's worn off.

She pictured Kit's face on returning to school; discovering not one, but three letters from her. He'd smile that lovely big smile and rush to his room, or dorm, or whatever. In all the letters she'd asked how he was and said she was missing him, then told him about the change in the weather and various bits of news. Not too much about Weisfelt, though, in case it reminded him of the horror. More about school. How everything had got serious because of next summer's O levels. How she liked English best, and what an amazing coincidence it was, being given that set book. There was a good reason for him not replying, there had to be.

Kit's handwriting went back in the drawer with the one picture she had of him. 'Please send me another photo!' she'd asked in her last letter, and she'd put in one of herself that she'd got her mum to take. Actually, her mum had taken four because Jen couldn't decide what to wear and kept changing her clothes. On the last day of the holidays, Jen had taken the film to a shop in Roermond, and after four hours of hanging around, collected them, flicked through and known instantly which she'd send Kit. The one that hid her skinny legs.

After pulling the sheet and blanket right up, Jen closed her eyes and tried to nap, because that would make the day shorter and then Monday, and the possibility of a letter, would come quicker. But she was cold and getting hungry for her tea, although it was only quarter to four. Last night she'd been really cold and had woken up loads of times, wishing she had the blanket back, the one in the hut.

Jen's eyes popped open, and she no longer felt sleepy. If she was really brave, she could go and get it now.

Someone had managed to break the lock, and Jen immediately pictured Kit, kicking at the door in his misery, and maybe even anger, over his dad. But when she walked in through the door – how odd that felt – there were empty beer bottles everywhere, and cigarette ends and empty crisp packets. Kit would never have done all that; left such a mess. He used to burn joss sticks, but now the place reeked of stale wee.

In a way, Jen was pleased not to find it exactly as they'd left it: a can Kit had drunk out of, the blanket still crumpled from their cuddling. In fact, where was the blanket? She looked around, panicky. If she didn't find the thing, her dad would have to pay for it. And she'd freeze all winter. But there it was, bunched up in a corner beside a stack of boxes, as though it had been used as a seat.

She went and grabbed it, shook it, rolled it up and hurried to the door. The place was an eyesore, the smell was foul. Jen had imagined herself sobbing uncontrollably, but she was just glad to get out.

Her feet took over and she found herself entering the officers' patch, walking past the semi-detached junior officers' quarters, then along the tree-lined road towards the bigger detached houses that the wing commanders and the CO lived in. Lawrence's little brother was kicking a ball around with a friend. Jen smiled but he didn't acknowledge her; just whacked the ball into a makeshift net between two trees; shouted and punched the air. How lovely, she thought, to be ten and never to have had your heart broken. Not that hers was broken, not yet. One day next week her dad would come home with a letter from Kit. She'd stopped running to meet him each day. It would come when she was least expecting it. When she was engrossed in something on telly, for example, her father would drop an airmail envelope in her lap. 'From his lordship, no doubt.' He still called him that, but in an affectionate way.

There was a new car on the drive, replacing the one mangled in the trees on the way to Roermond. Everything else looked the same. You'd hardly know, she thought, that a brand-new family was living there. A yellow cuddly toy in one window, that was all. People disappeared, then others came and replaced them. It felt eerie, staring at the house with all its previous life wiped out. And the wind didn't help, swooping up leaves, then swirling them round and dropping them. She'd always liked autumn. The new term, catching up with friends from other camps, the colours of the countryside on the way to school. Now, all she saw was dead leaves, dead people.

She clutched the blanket for warmth and comfort, but it didn't stop her shivering. 'My fault,' she whispered, and turned for home.

# FORTY-THREE

Kit's mother was already there, measuring the height of the net with two racquets. She wore lilac shorts that ended well above her knees, with a sporty white T-shirt and chunky gold earrings. Her headband matched her shorts and her trainers combined both white and lilac. 'A little higher,' she said, 'if you wouldn't mind?'

She still has good legs, thought Jen. But then the legs are the last to go, so they say. She went and turned the handle.

'More. More. Stop!'

Mrs Avery weighed the racquets. She held one out for Jen. 'Here. They're all terribly light these days. Nothing to choose.'

Jen took it and made her way to the other side of the court. She hadn't packed for tennis, and in her black walking shoes, jeans and Jigsaw cardigan felt all wrong. When Mrs Avery lobbed a ball over the net, Jen ran, swung at it and missed, proving, perhaps, how large a role the right clothes played.

The tennis courts badly needed resurfacing, and as they warmed up and she was slowly getting used to the shoe situation, Jen made a note of the potholes to avoid on her side. Her opponent's shots were as you'd expect from a septuagenarian: gentle, a little erratic, unthreatening.

'Shall we start?' said Mrs Avery, and they met

at the net to spin a racquet for first serve.

Jen somehow found herself at the wrong end sun-wise, and serving second. Her head was still fuzzy. More coffee – that might have helped. Or a decent night's sleep. The ball was coming her way again. She ran, swung and hit it into the net.

'Forty love!' shouted Mrs Avery.

How had that happened? Wake up, Jen told herself. Concentrate. She moved across to take the next serve, but when it came, she was too far from the bounce. The ball was just in, where the centre line met the base line, and fast too. Really fast.

'Love game!' Mrs Avery shouted gleefully. 'One, love! Your serve.'

A group of truant teens on the swings app-lauded. Cynically, no doubt, but that didn't stop Kit's mother taking a small bow. 'Go, Grannie!' a boy called out, and Mrs Avery blew him a kiss. They laughed and clapped again, and it was clear whose side they'd be on for the rest of the match.

Jen's head felt better now. Flushed with adren-alin, perhaps, as she realised what was going on. During the warm-up, her opponent had lulled her into thinking she'd grown weak with age. How clever, how manipulative. Jen collected the balls and got ready to serve.

'Good shot! Well done!'

'Thanks,' said Jen. Following the shaky start, the first set was going her way.

'Two four!' she called out to Mrs Avery, having just broken her serve again.

'I *know*,' came the reply.

The kids had stopped cheering since Jen took the lead, but hadn't lost interest. It was a form of intimidation, of course. There were five in all, most of them smoking. It took her back to her teens, hanging around the swings on the nights the youth club wasn't open. She'd smoked too, for a while, in order to fit in. She'd gone back to it at eighteen and got hooked, then given up for Robert.

'Love fifteen,' shouted Mrs Avery. It was more of a wheeze than a shout, though. And she was stooped, a hand on her chest.

'Are you all right?' Jen asked.

'Fine,' she said, straightening up. 'Perfectly fine.'

'Want an ambulance?' someone shouted.

'That won't be necessary,' Mrs Avery told him with a smile. 'At least, not yet, ha-ha.'

Jen won another love game, and began to feel bad. 'Shall we just make it one set?' she asked, as they changed ends.

'Good gracious, no,' puffed Mrs Avery, her face drawn, her eyes somehow saggier. 'That would be most unfair. Best of three, my dear.'

'OK ... but maybe we should rest between sets? I don't know about you but I'm knackered.' Jen chuckled but her opponent didn't. 'I bought water for us, on the way here.'

In spite of the breathlessness, Mrs Avery managed to lift her chin, straighten her back, rally herself. She looked Jen up and down, in the way she'd so often done. 'Well, if *you* feel you need to,' she said, walking off unsteadily. 'My serve.'

'So, do you do anything?' she asked.

Jen told her about the properties. They were on a bench by the swings, not far from Mrs Avery's fan club. At first, they'd been silent, listening in to the youths, and it had reminded Jen of the Malcolm Club. 'But I'm considering gradually selling up, once the leases expire. I'd like to try something else.'

'Talk to Raymond before doing anything rash. It's his area, you know. Mainly commercial, but the market is the market. He left his son in charge for six months, but I can tell he's eager to be back at the helm. I suppose you'll live off the profits?'

'Only for a while. I'd like to start another business, or learn another skill. Or both.'

'Well, you're no spring chicken, so think twice about giving up the properties. Everyone's feverishly speculating that there'll be a bust, but Raymond thinks that's tosh.'

'Really?' How strange this felt, having an almost normal conversation. 'I suppose I could sell some and keep some.' She smiled at Kit's mother. Could they be friends, of a sort, after all? Age had mellowed her, or perhaps she'd given up on Kit ever finding the wife of her dreams. 'Did you work?' Jen asked.

'Of course,' bristled Mrs Avery, finally breathing normally. She screwed the top on her bottle and stood up. 'I was a mother,' she said, 'and an officer's wife. I'd call that two full-time jobs.'

'Absolutely,' said Jen. She hadn't mentioned her stint at the hairdresser's, but that was understandable.

'Ready to play on, or do you need longer?'

'No, no. I'm fine.' Jen finished her water, gathered her things and hobbled across the grass. One foot was suddenly sore. She felt weary and she really didn't like the audience. She wanted to say let's call it a draw, but knew what response she'd get.

'My serve, love three,' said Mrs Avery, now with resignation in her voice. Jen had played three games on automatic pilot, her mind elsewhere. This was pretty much a doddle, now Mrs Avery was tiring. The sunny morning had gradually turned grey, and a large black cloud was threatening rain. Jen's hope now was to get the match finished before a deluge.

'Love fifteen!' one of the kids called out, when the ball hit the net.

Jen considered letting Mrs Avery have a few points, but the rain cloud was inching closer, and more and more, all she wanted was to be doing something nice with Kit. A walk. Shopping. Anything.

'Love thirty!' they shouted in unison.

'Come on, grannie!'

'I'm trying!' Mrs Avery told them. She smiled their way, then did a couple of pre-serve bounces. 'Here goes!'

When the ball arrived and landed with surprising ferocity, Jen made the snap decision to miss it. 'Hey, an ace!' she said, watching it bash the fence behind her. 'Well done!'

Mrs Avery walked towards the net, then steadied herself on it. 'I'd rather,' she said breathlessly, 'you didn't patronise me, Jennifer.'

'Oh, I'm–'

'Considering you wrecked my life with your indiscretion, it's the least you can do.'

'I did what?'

'Less of the naïvety, *please.*'

While Kit's mother walked back to the baseline to serve, Jen stood, stunned and appalled. Something cold ran through her every vein. All these years, Mrs Avery had blamed her for what happened. Just as she'd done, herself, in the beginning. Ridiculously. Until she'd talked it through with Christine, who'd said, 'What were you expected to do, lie to Kit's dad?'

'Ready?' she was asked.

Jen went towards her own baseline, feeling shaky and nauseous. 'Yes,' she said. She'd never have anything with Kit, not even a friendship. Not if this woman was always in the picture, bearing resentment. Last night, before bed, Kit had given her a lovely prolonged hug, then a stroke of her hair and kiss on the cheek. Chaste, yes, but with an undercurrent of ... something. Something she'd like, yes, but not something she desperately needed. Later today, she'd drive back to London. Get away from the whole upsetting and confusing scene.

'Come on, Venus!' shouted one of the girls, and as Mrs Avery whacked at the ball, she even grunted like a Williams sister. The powerful serve looked like another ace, but Jen sprinted as though her life depended on it. After her racquet made a beautiful *thwack*, the ball headed straight back towards her opponent. In fact, it was going directly towards her opponent, who clearly hadn't been expecting the return and seemed not to be moving out of its way. After a last-minute attempt to avoid the ball, followed by a stumble, Mrs Avery was hit on the head and fell to the ground with a terrible cry.

Jen dropped her racquet and ran round to where Kit's mother lay on the tarmac. Her eyes were closed, her cheek was bright red, there was blood under her earring. Please don't be dead, Jen prayed. Not you too.

'Now do you want an ambulance?' shouted a kid. Some of them laughed, others were making their way past the fence and through the gate.

Jen stood up, shaking. 'Give me a phone, one of you. Please. And someone go to The Bell and ask for Raymond. Quick.'

'Is she breathing?' asked the first to arrive – a girl, who looked as sick as Jen felt.

'I don't know,' she said. 'Would you check? I can't...'

A boy handed Jen his phone. 'Got a mirror?' he asked. 'That's what they do on telly.'

'Her chest's moving,' said the girl. 'Look.'

'So she int dead.'

'Kit?' said Jen. 'Come to the courts, could you? Bring a car.'

'*What*–' she heard, before hanging up.

'Could someone get that bottle of water?' she asked, pointing towards the gate.

A boy fetched the half-full bottle and Jen quickly unscrewed it and poured the remains of the water over Mrs Avery's face. There was something quite satisfying in the act, especially when Kit's mother moved her head, spluttered and

338

generally showed signs of life.

'I'm so sorry,' Jen said.

'And so you should be,' rasped Mrs Avery. 'So you should be.'

'Yeah,' said one of the boys. 'Knocking an old lady out like that. You could've killed her.'

Mrs Avery's eyes closed, then opened for a while, then closed again, and it felt like an age before a car door slammed.

'What's happened?' asked Kit, running over and crouching beside Jen.

'Hit by the ball,' his mother told him, her eyes popping open again. 'Ouch, my ankle.'

Above the trainer, her leg was swollen and already colouring up. Beside the swollen leg was a four-by-four-inch pothole, but nobody was making the connection. Jen would have said something, but found she couldn't. Suddenly, she was inhibited. Scared to open her mouth, in case the wrong thing came out and Kit went off her. He looked so good, it was almost unbearable. Kneeling next to him, on the rough tarmac, she was fifteen again. In love with him, terrified of his mother.

This wouldn't do, not so soon after the Robert turbulence. Just when she'd got her emotions under control, she couldn't go falling for a charismatic man with a terrible track record and a vampire mother. She'd never felt like this when married. Always felt in control. She could say anything to Robert, and had. This timid person wasn't her. Or, at least, wasn't a Jen she liked being.

'We should get you to a GP, Ma. Can you

move? Does anything feel broken? Perhaps it's best to keep still and I'll call for an ambulance. What do you think, Jen?'

'Oh, do stop fussing, Kit.' Mrs Avery pulled herself up to a sitting position, her cheek swelling now, as well as her ankle. 'Jennifer didn't quite manage to kill me off. Did you, dear?'

'I'll call you,' she told Kit through her car window.

He was upset, that was clear, but Jen felt she had no choice. Go home, or stay and be drained of all contentment and personality. Not to mention control.

'Promise me you will?' he said, reaching for her hand on the steering wheel.

She squeezed his fingers, then let go and put the car in reverse. 'I promise,' she said, manoeuvring the car in the cul-de-sac, then pulling away with a wave.

But not for a while, she thought, once out on the main road. Not for a while.

A young, possibly teenaged couple with two small children were being let into Ruth's flat by a son. Matthew, presumably. He had fair hair, like his mother, and looked about twelve. Jen had seen Tyrone several times. He was mixed race and around fourteen. Matthew waved at Jen, and she tried to wave back but had her case in both hands, having carried it up the stairs. 'Hi!' she called out, but the door was closing behind the last toddler.

She put the case down and found her keys. If

only she'd come straight home from Highgate yesterday, and stayed home. Not listened to Sarah. It was fate, no doubt, bursting her little Kit bubble.

Inside the door, on the floor, was a bright pink envelope. It must have been hand-delivered because mail came to the boxes in the hall. Jen wheeled her case through to the bedroom and put the kettle on before picking it up. It said 'Jen' in big round joined-up letters. Inside, the big round curly writing continued, inviting her to Trinity's first birthday party, between four and six p.m. She checked the date. It was today. Then she looked at her watch. Twenty to five. That family must have been going to it.

'Bugger,' she said. One more hold-up on the M25 and she'd have missed the event. Obviously, she was too drained to go. The tennis, the trauma, the drive home. And, anyway, she'd hardly fit in. Already she could feel herself disapproving, as the bass of something loud, rappish and inappropriate for a one year old was belting through the wall. It was nice of Ruth to invite her, but if she made a point of not going, she'd be, well, making a point. Tomorrow she'd buy the little girl a present and apologise to Ruth. Explain that she'd been tired from travelling. Her son had seen her with the suitcase.

Jen made herself coffee, picked up emails, then lay for a while on the sofa, trying not to go over it all but hearing that voice and those words, again and again. Did Kit's mother really believe Jen had wrecked her life, or was it some weird throwback thing because she was elderly and getting a bit dotty? Not that it mattered too much. The important thing was to shake off the feeling of inferiority that had begun to seep in the moment Mrs Avery appeared, and had gradually engulfed her over the past twenty-four hours. She was working class, a sergeant's daughter. Uncultured, ignorant, unwelcome. 'People like that,' she heard Mrs Avery say, back then, to Kit. Jen couldn't remember the context, just the words.

Was the music getting louder? She sighed, rolled on her side, then got up and made more coffee. Surely Ruth knew how a baby's birthday party should go? Or perhaps she didn't. A door slammed. More people arriving. Adults, perhaps. Friends of the boys, bringing drugs. If it went on late, she wouldn't get the early night she needed. And what if it turned into an all-nighter, this so-called baby's birthday party? You never knew with … with what? People like that?

She went back to the invitation. 'Hope you can come!' was squeezed in at the bottom, then 'Trinity' and an 'x' and a squiggle the baby herself had done. Yes, Jen thought, of course she could.

After a quick shower, still wrapped in towels, Jen folded a piece of A4 paper into four and drew a picture of a cake with one candle on. She wrote inside, then filled out a cheque for twenty pounds, leaving the payee blank, and slipped that in. She found an envelope, covered it in moons and stars, and wrote 'To Trinity'.

'There,' she said, and made her way to her wardrobe, wondering if she should dress up or down. The family going in had been neat as pins. Up, perhaps.

It was all over by seven, and Jen stayed to help Ruth clear up, while Destiny and Trinity's father – a gentle, good-looking young Kenyan whose names Jen never quite grasped – put his exhausted daughters to bed. He and Ruth seemed to get on well and had done a lot of laughing and joking around. Watching them had made Jen miss Kit. Why, she wondered, had she been so reactive?

'No way,' Ruth told her, when Jen asked why she and the girls' dad didn't live together. 'I already got four kids at home.' She laughed, scraping plates and washing them, while Jen dried. The boys were working on the sitting room, one of them even hoovering. 'He's still my boyfriend, mind. You know, we still...' She moved her slim hips suggestively and laughed again, and Jen wondered where Ruth found the energy for sex as well.

Her neighbour appeared fragile, but she was obviously a strong woman, with pleasant, well-behaved children and warm relationships with boyfriends, current and past. Matthew's dad had turned up at the party and been greeted like a much-loved family member, by Ruth, by everyone. He hadn't stayed long, but nobody had complained. People work things out, Jen realised. Relationships. They come to arrangements. They compromise and respect. She thought of Robert and how she'd judged him, and now she was about to punish Kit for his mother, or for her own timidity.

Jen thanked Ruth for the party, said goodbye

and went back to the flat with a whole new take on herself. Her supposedly dysfunctional neighbour had shown her that if she wanted something with Kit, which she did, absolutely, then she needed to toughen up a bit. Grow up, even.

## FORTY-FOUR

How noisy London had become. Kit got up from his desk and closed the window, then went back to the email. He was reconnecting with an editor, offering to write a piece on Iraq. Since he'd tuned the world out in Norfolk, the article would involve a lot of research, which would be a drag, even with the internet. He yawned as he typed. A day and a half back in his old life, and Kit couldn't remember when he'd last felt this unmotivated and restless. Just the thought of writing – on Iraq, on anything – bored him to death, but the holiday-rental income had ceased and he needed to earn a crust.

Having sent that email, he rattled off a few more. Then, drawn to the beautiful spring day, he switched off the computer and headed for the common. Having got used to regular walks, he couldn't imagine spending hours on end inside, in front of a screen.

It was lovely out, but the traffic was fast and annoying, and the people jostling him on the pavements were rude and annoying. Kit was thankful not to have Bunk with him, but as soon

344

as he hit grass and space, he missed his old walking partner. His exuberance, his interest in everything. Bunk should be here, enjoying this. All the new things to sniff. Pip wouldn't walk him as often as he'd got used to with Kit, what with the baby. And Adam had revision to do and would be gone soon. Hopefully, not to London. Or at least not to Clapham. Kit was almost certain he'd talked his nephew out of that.

Thinking about it, was it wise to have a baby and a dog? The risk of mauling, etc. Perhaps they'd be pleased to get shot of him. Kit watched a woman throwing a ball for her Labrador and felt bereft. The dog hared off, turned and hared back, then stood with its tail wagging, refusing to drop. He'd offer to take Bunk. Give them a call later. It might mean driving all the way back to Norfolk, but that was fine. With Jen not phoning, as she'd promised, and replying only curtly to his texts – 'Rushed off my feet. Will be in touch!' – what else was there to do?

Jen, it seemed, and if she was to be believed, was as busy as everyone else. Last night he'd called several friends to say he was home and see if they'd like to meet up, only to be met with borderline snubs. *Yeah, great, let's arrange something when I'm back from the States/not so snowed under/got the extension finished...* So much activity, such constant activity. Surely that wasn't right? When did people stop and reflect? Or just look? A couple of weeks back, he'd spent almost an hour watching seagulls circling and swooping. It had been quite wonderful, and so calming. On other occasions, with Bunk lying panting and exhausted beside him, he'd simply stared out to sea, looking at nothing; barely thinking. Just experiencing. Or being. People had no time to be, any more. Maybe they never had.

Kit strode on, trying not to look at the dogs in case they made him homesick. No, now he was being silly. This was his home, even if he hadn't had much of a homecoming. He'd lost his column, he'd discovered. Lost it to a whipper-snapper, whose clumsy prose and overly strident views made Kit cringe. Take three months out, he thought, and everyone forgets you. Friends, colleagues; they all move on in your absence.

He'd come back expecting everything to be the same, but London was noisier, the flat was a dull place to hang out and work was uninviting. It had all changed. Even Clapham Common had lost its appeal. No sea to gaze at or breathe in, and he could still hear the traffic. That was new too. Kit had never heard traffic from the common before.

She hadn't been answering her mobile, at least not when he'd called from Pip's phone, or his own mobile. He had no land-line number for her and she didn't have his. But he wanted her to have his, just in case. In case of what, he wasn't sure, but it was an excuse to call again, or at least try to. What had caused this distancing, he didn't know. But he couldn't help thinking he should have insisted on taking the horrible little guest room himself. Or, perhaps Jen had been expecting to share his bed. She had, after all, come rushing up to Norfolk, following his text. But when they'd hugged on the landing, he hadn't picked up any 'let's do it' vibes. Just the opposite. She'd been tense. Not ready for another relationship, he'd guessed. Then there was his mother, of course, being barely civil to Jen. He'd hoped the tennis match would get them bonding, but it had ended in disaster and more sharp words. No wonder Jen had flown. He'd have done the same, himself. 'Good!' was all Jen had texted back, when he'd told her of his mother's rapid recovery,

Perhaps she didn't want to get hurt by him again; that could be it. She may have brushed off his teenage cruelty with some tale of a new boyfriend, but he'd seen through it. He'd behaved so badly after their lovely summer. There'd been no excuse for ignoring her letters, not even bereavement. He'd lived in the moment, aged seventeen, and maybe Jen could sense that he still did. No real ties or responsibilities. Not even Adam, when it came to it.

Kit tried to eat a thrown-together sandwich, but found he wasn't that hungry. Maybe he should leave her be. There were other women to call, although none sprang to mind immediately. And really, what would be the point? It was Jen's company he wanted – craved, even – in this big empty place that used to be home. A braver man would get in a cab and turn up at her flat unannounced. Of course he'd have to know where the flat was.

Kit decided on eight forty-five, thinking she'd probably have had dinner by then. It wasn't too late, either, and it gave him time to down a couple of slugs of the whisky he'd bought for courage.

Not that she'd answer. She never answered. He paced around as he waited, the tedious day nearing its end. Not one of his work-related emails had been replied to. Was he being forced into an early retirement? If so, he absolutely did not want to spend the next unemployed forty years alone. He put his glass down and counted on his fingers. Thirty years. Or, with luck, twenty-five.

Twenty to nine. He'd do it now. He felt nervous, despite the whisky. This was crazy. She was just a woman. A very sweet woman. Picking up the receiver, he quickly tapped out the number he now knew by heart. Beside him, scribbled down, was the message he'd leave, about how he was back in London and how she might like his home phone number because his mobile had been playing up.

To his surprise – perhaps because she didn't recognise the number – she actually answered. 'Hello?' she said, sounding buoyant.

'Hi, it's me.'

There was a pause, then, 'Hey, how are you?'

'I'm good. How are you?'

'Fine. Busy.'

'So you've said, several times.' He hadn't intended to sound resentful. He hadn't intended to sound anything. He'd expected voicemail.

'I've been meaning to call,' she said. 'Sorry.'

'That's OK.'

'So, you're back in London?'

'Yes.' She had checked the number on screen, then. 'It all feels a bit strange.'

'Yeah?'

'Mm. Listen, I know you're busy.'

'Well…'

'But I'd really love to see you.'

Another long pause. An intake of breath. 'Now?'

*That* he hadn't been expecting. 'Now would be great. Where–'

'I'll come to you,' she said.

'Oh, right. Fantastic.' She was being unusually forceful and he liked it. 'Let me give you my address.'

'I've got it.'

'How–'

'See you in an hour.'

Jen entered the flat like a whirlwind. A very pretty one, all done up and wearing heels, earrings, lipstick, perfume, the lot. 'Your bloody mother isn't here, is she?'

Kit shook his head, still stunned by her appearance. 'Hampshire,' he managed.

'Good.' She smiled and walked back to where he'd propped himself against the door. Slowly, as she moved towards him, she let her leather, very un-Jen-like jacket slip off her shoulders, down her arms and on to the floor. The little black dress was strapless and tight, her hair full, her eyes playful. She slid an arm inside the jacket he'd taken ages to decide on, and kissed him. 'I hope your bed isn't two foot six,' she said.

# FORTY-FIVE

## July 2003

She'd asked to be picked up at eleven thirty, and he was there on the dot, in a suit, with his own separate anniversary gift. The event was to take place in the function room of the Prince of Wales, her parents' local. Since looking up old air-force pals online, their guest list had spiralled to around sixty. This was good news. The less intimate the occasion, the less awkward her parents would feel about Robert.

After a quiet, trouble-free journey, they arrived to find the car park almost full. The entrance to the ground-floor function room was festooned with balloons, all with '50 Golden Years' on them. That they'd reached this landmark was astonishing to Jen, who felt her mum deserved her own personal endurance award.

'Ready?' she asked by the door, and he nodded. She took a deep breath, pushed it open and walked in.

'Aunty Jen!' cried Phoebe. She ran over and hugged one leg.

'Hi, Phoebe.' Jen put her present on a table and picked up her niece. 'You look very pretty. Are you having a nice time? Where's your daddy?'

Phoebe pointed across the room to Paul, who'd spotted them and was waving. Jen waved back, and said, 'Coming?' over her shoulder.

'Sure.'

'They've got chocolate fingers,' Phoebe told her. 'And, look, so have I!'

So she had. 'Yuck. Maybe we should go and wash them, after I've said hello to Daddy.' Jen wondered what state her pale green dress was in, but there were so many people it might not matter. As she and her niece wove their way through the bodies and glasses and plates of buffet food, Jen failed to recognise anyone, and her relatively short parents were nowhere to be seen. This was such a relief. Much better than expected and a lot less intense.

'Who's that man?' Phoebe asked in her ear. 'Following us?'

'He's my friend, and a friend of Grandma and Grampie's from a long time ago. His name's Kit.'

'Kit like kitten?'

'Yes.'

'He looks more like a lion.'

Jen laughed and glanced back. 'So he does.' Kit did a roar that made Phoebe squeal. She roared back, then he roared and she roared until they reached Paul, who was beside an inglenook, spooning something into Frank.

'No!' said Paul, when Jen did the introductions, her free arm around Kit. 'God, you're a dark horse, Jen.' He shook Kit's hand. 'You know, I've still got your Monkees records.'

'I had Monkees records?'

'Oh. Well, maybe it was another boyfriend.'

Jen rolled her eyes and left with Phoebe to find soap and water. While her niece stood on tiptoe at

351

the basin, Jen slumped against the wall. So far so good. She'd decided to ask Kit along only two days ago. They were together, her divorce had got going, so why not, she'd thought. And what better way to prevent questions about Robert, than to turn up with a partner? Kit. Partner. It still felt odd, but at the same time completely right. And surprisingly easy, once she'd made the effort to change her mindset. Sarah had helped, phoning to say she'd given up smoking. 'It's willpower,' she'd told Jen. 'Simple as that. I read a book that tells you to visualise, over and over, being the person you want to be. In my case, a non-smoker.'

'Can we go and see the lion again?' Phoebe shouted under the dryer.

Jen laughed. 'OK.' Perhaps she'd start calling him Leo. He looked like a Leo. 'Come on, then.'

After the conversation with Sarah, and with her tennis-court panic still fresh in her mind, Jen had taken every opportunity to visualise. Before sleep each night, on the underground, as she walked, at the sink. Everywhere, when she remembered. 'You have to really believe you *are* that person,' Sarah had said. 'Right now.'

Calm, confident and happy. That had been Jen's list. She'd been tempted to add devastatingly witty, but knew her limitations. After ten days of self-indoctrination, and thinking Kit must have been back in London by then, she'd been about to call him and put the new Jen, or real Jen, to the test. But then he'd called her.

'Do you remember Kit?' she asked them. 'From Germany?'

Her mother's hand flew to her chest. She looked lovely in her lilac suit and pretty necklace. 'Well, I never.'

'Good to see you, laddie,' said her dad, calmly shaking Kit's hand, as though Jen was always turning up with old boyfriends. 'You're wearing shoes these days, then?'

'Jen made me.'

'I can't believe it,' said her mum. 'Jen, you could have warned us. How are you, Kit?'

'Fine. And you? Happy wedding anniversary, by the way.' He leaned across and kissed her, then handed over his present. 'Just a little something for you both.'

'Oh, you shouldn't have, Kit. Honestly...'

'Don't be daft, woman. Think how much we've spent on this bloody bash.'

'Oh, Jim! Ignore him, Kit. We thought we'd open our presents later. Thanks ever so. Now, tell me what you've been up to. How's your ... mum. Is she still...?'

'Around? Yes, very much so, as Jen will confirm. They get on like a house on fire.'

'Literally,' Jen said with a shudder. 'Listen, I've left your present somewhere, I'll just go and–'

'I'd have known you anywhere,' said her mum, hooking her arm through Kit's. 'Tell me, what do you do? Something ever so clever, I expect. Honestly, the words you used to use. Sometimes, they'd go right over our heads, wouldn't they, Jim?'

'Speak for yourself.'

Jen slipped away. She recognised a couple of Scottish aunts she should really talk to, but kept her head down, as she made for the table she'd left the gift on.

'Jennifer?' A man's voice said. It was her cousin, Kevin. Her mother's brother's son. Quite a bit younger than her, but now shockingly middle-aged. 'Long time no see. How are you?'

'Fine, fine. And you?'

'Good, yeah. More weight and less hair than last time I saw you, ha-ha.'

'Yes,' she said rudely, not thinking. He'd been lovely-looking at one time. How differently people age, she thought.

'Where's Robert?'

'He, er, actually, we've split up.'

'No! No one told me. What hap–'

'Listen, desperate for the loo.' She pointed. 'I'd better...'

'I think you're going the wrong way.'

'Ah.'

'You know, I'm sure Mum said you *and* Robert were coming. That Uncle Jim had said that.'

'No, no.' Please God, no. 'Catch you later, Kevin.'

Following her overnight stay in Highgate, Jen had barely spoken to Robert. Not deliberately. She, or perhaps they, just had little to say. Robert had ceased the emotional pressure, and the only thing discussed in emails and his occasional calls had been the house. His plan now was to buy her out, although how he could take on such a huge debt and still sleep, Jen had no idea. Still, he was in the right business for a cheap dodgy mortgage.

The ties with Robert were finally being cut and

life had become less stressful and more fun; quite wonderful, in fact. She and Kit took it in turns to stay over, but also gave each other space. Sometimes they'd go a week without meeting up. And she still had lunches and evenings out with Lionel, which was nice, because Sarah had suddenly become too busy to see her. Jen suspected a lover, maybe even Robert. Perhaps they'd given it another go and it had worked.

Yes, things had calmed right down on the Robert front, and the last thing Jen wanted was for him to turn up at the anniversary party. Cousin Kevin was surely wrong, but she felt she should check.

The gift was where she'd left it, and as Jen made her way back to her parents, she was accosted by a couple who hadn't seen her since she was six, at RAF Benson. 'Your mum pointed you out. Not that you've changed!' Jen rather hoped she had. They told her all about their son, Geoff. She couldn't remember Geoff, but pretended, for as long as she could, to be interested in his rise to head teacher, then excused herself.

Her parents were now talking to a couple their own age, who Jen should probably know, but didn't. She inched up to her dad, and from behind, said, 'Robert isn't coming, is he?'

Her father turned round, took the present Jen was holding out and passed it on to her mother. 'Not as far as I know. He sent us a card and present, and left a message on the phone yesterday.'

'Is that Robert?' asked her mum. 'Our son-in-law,' she explained to her friend.

'What did he say in his message?' Jen asked.

'Well,' said her mum, 'he wished us a happy anniversary and, let me think, oh yes, said how sorry he was about ... um–'

'Not being able to come?' Jen said quickly.

'Busy chap,' explained her dad, and the friends nodded.

'Maybe we should give him a ring?' said her mother. 'To thank him. I mean, it was ever so thoughtful. And the gold pens he sent are beautiful.'

'Aye, maybe we should. I'll fetch ma phone from the car.' Her father picked up his pint. 'Any excuse,' he whispered as he passed Jen, 'to get away from this lot.'

'And have a smoke?' she asked. There were signs everywhere, politely asking people to refrain. 'Mum said you've cut right down now?' They'd all nagged him for years, to no effect.

'Just two of an evening. But I'm breaking me rule today on account of the bloody stress.'

On the far side of the room, Jen saw Kit holding Frank and talking to Bev. He was coping so well with all this, but then she'd expected him to. Rather like her husband, he could slip in anywhere socially. Gold pens, she thought. That was very Robert. 'I'll come with you,' she said to her father's retreating back.

Jen told him about her plan. How she'd already warned three of her tenants that their leases wouldn't be renewed because she'd be selling. One had thrown a fit and threatened to move out as soon as he'd found somewhere, the others said they'd be happy to show buyers around.

'And what are you going to do?' asked her father. 'Once you've sold them all?'

She wouldn't tell him, just yet, that she'd treat them to a holiday out of her profits, and give Paul money to finish his house. 'I'm not sure. Maybe something a bit more worthwhile. I've been helping out at this drop-in centre for single parents. We give advice and support and I really quite enjoy it.'

Ruth had told her about it, and said, as a joke initially, that they needed volunteers, if Jen had time on her hands. She'd gradually got used to hearing two year olds swear, just as she'd got used to her neighbours' music. They were such a nice family, Ruth and her clan. Even the boys, who'd happily come over and help her move or fix things. Tyrone was quite a wit too, and lovely-looking. Far from pitying Ruth, Jen almost envied her.

'It's good to give something back,' she told her father.

'Oh, aye? That Kit hasn't been putting cloud-cuckoo commie ideas in yer head again?'

'No,' she said, laughing. But maybe he had. His accounts of his time in Africa had certainly got her thinking.

Still, there was no need to decide anything yet. Kit was tiring of London and feeling direction-less too, so Jen was biding her time, trying not to fantasise about some shared move or project. It was early days, and maybe at some point Kit would reach his relationship boredom threshold. Although, somehow, Jen doubted that would happen. This felt different, he'd said, and the Norfolk experience had changed him. Jen had no reason not to believe him.

'It's hard for a woman, being left on her own,' her dad was saying, with a shake of his white-grey head. Her parents had the same colouring now, after looking so different for years.

'Oh, I don't know.'

'I canny forgive him for what he did.' Her father ground out a cigarette with his big black shoe. 'That Robert. We had them in the Raf, ye know. Even before it was legal.'

Jen rolled her eyes at him. 'Honestly, Dad.'

'Anyways, no doubt he's seen the error of his ways. I don't suppose there's any chance of you two, you know...?'

'I'm with Kit now, Dad.'

He reached in the car for his mobile, then locked up. 'Now, if ye'd asked me, way back, who'd turn out a pansy, I'd have said that one.'

'Kit?'

'Flowery blouses, hair like Diana Dors. And we know what lads get up to at public school.'

'Yes,' she said laughing. They scale the walls of the nearest girls' school. 'So, are you going to phone Robert?'

'Good God, no. I'll let ye mother do it. They can have a nice wee girlie talk.'

'Dad, will you stop it!'

He laughed in a hearty, throaty way, and got out his cigarettes and lighter again.

'I'll just go and see if Kit's all right,' she said, and left him to his smoke.

Kit had promised not to drink, so that she could. She went and got a glass of white wine from a young girl handing them out at a table, and it occurred to her, not for the first time, that she ought really to have helped her parents organise this party. Perhaps she'd send Kit home and stay overnight, then she could at least lend a hand clearing up. Kit would be fine with it. He was fine with most things.

She took her glass to where he was talking to a young man and an older woman. All in all, he'd mingled much more than she had. Kit introduced them, impressively remembering their names, and told Jen they were from her mother's amateur dramatics group.

'Oh, yes?' she said. Jen had no idea her mum had taken up acting. What a neglectful daughter she'd become.

'Lovely woman, your mother,' said the young man. 'An absolute gem behind the scenes. She only joined a month ago but invited us all to her party!'

'Oh, that's my mum for you.' No wonder the place was packed.

She took Kit to one side and asked would he mind if she stayed. Of course, he didn't. He kissed her. Jen wanted to tell him she loved him, but didn't. Not yet. They'd known each other thirty years – sort of – but it was still early days. Wandering off to find her mother, she felt life couldn't get any better. And if, for some reason, it got worse for a while, then it would surely get better again. Perhaps age made a person more resigned to all the ups and downs.

She did a quick detour to avoid the Scottish aunts – she'd find time for them later – and approached her parents, now sitting on two chairs against the wall and suddenly looking washed out; their faces drained of all colour, rather like their hair. Once again, she felt guilty. It had obviously been too much for them, at their age.

'Guess what?' she said cheerfully. 'I've decided to stay tonight and help clear up. I'll take you both out to dinner, if you like? Or lunch tomorrow, if you prefer. There's that restaurant you love. Oh, what's it called?'

There was no response and their flat expressions didn't change at all. Then her mother lifted the mobile and carefully tapped out a number. 'Did you know?' she asked, handing her the phone.

'Know what?' Jen put it to her ear and listened to ringing, then the click to voicemail.

'Hello,' came her husband's soft voice. 'We're sorry, but neither Robert nor Jonathan is able to take your call right now. Do leave a message, or try our mobiles...'

Jen pressed the end-call button and stared at her parents. 'No, I didn't,' she said, handing the phone back. 'But I'm fine with it. In fact, I'm happy for him.' She automatically looked for Kit's face above the crowd, wondering if he'd left yet. He might still be in the car park, she thought, when she couldn't see him. Maybe if she ran...

'Jen, love?' said her mum. 'Are you really OK?'

'I just have to–' she began, but there he was with the Scottish aunts, bending over to hear them. He said something and they threw their heads back with laughter. Jen felt herself relax, the wobble over. Of course she wouldn't have chased after him. Honestly. Kit looked up, perhaps feeling her gaze, and gave her his big smile. 'Yes,' Jen said, more to herself than her mother. 'I'm really OK.'

## ACKNOWLEDGEMENTS

Enormous thanks to my sister, Carol Pearce, and my parents, Pam and George Highmore, for their invaluable help with the German sections. Special thanks also to Flora Rees for all the patience and support over the past eighteen months, and for being such a brilliant editor.

The publishers hope that this book has given you enjoyable reading. Large Print Books are especially designed to be as easy to see and hold as possible. If you wish a complete list of our books please ask at your local library or write directly to:

**Magna Large Print Books**
Magna House, Long Preston,
Skipton, North Yorkshire.
**BD23 4ND**

This Large Print Book for the partially sighted, who cannot read normal print, is published under the auspices of

## THE ULVERSCROFT FOUNDATION